D0442074

ECHOES BETWEEN US

ALSO BY KATIE McGARRY

Only a Breath Apart

ECHOES BETWEEN US

KATIE McGARRY

TOR TEEN

A TOM DOHERTY ASSOCIATES BOOK

NEW YORK

ECHOES BETWEEN US

Quotes from Evelyn Bellak's diary, *Fond Memories of Ray Brook: A Diary,* January 1, 1918–November 18, 1918, courtesy of the Adirondack Research Room, Saranac Lake Free Library.

A Tor Teen Book
Published by Tom Doherty Associates
120 Broadway
New York, NY 10271

www.tor-forge.com

Tor® is a registered trademark of Macmillan Publishing Group, LLC.

Library of Congress Cataloging-in-Publication Data

Names: McGarry, Katie, author.
Title: Echoes between us / Katie McGarry.
Description: First edition. | New York : Tor Teen, 2020.
Identifiers: LCCN 2019041386 (print) | LCCN 2019041387 (ebook) |
    ISBN 9781250196040 (hardcover) | ISBN 9781250196064 (ebook)
Subjects: CYAC: Ghosts—Fiction. | Brain—Tumors—Fiction. | Compulsive
    behavior—Fiction. | Alcoholism—Fiction. | Dating (Social customs)—
    Fiction. | Family life—Fiction.
Classification: LCC PZ7.M167156 Ec 2020 (print) | LCC PZ7.M167156 (ebook) |
    DDC [Fic]—dc23
LC record available at https://lccn.loc.gov/2019041386
LC ebook record available at https://lccn.loc.gov/2019041387

Our books may be purchased in bulk for promotional, educational, or business use. Please contact your local bookseller or the Macmillan Corporate and Premium Sales Department at 1–800–221–7945, extension 5442, or by email at MacmillanSpecialMarkets@macmillan.com.

First Edition: January 2020

Printed in the United States of America

0 9 8 7 6 5 4 3 2 1

VERONICA

In my early morning stupor, I stumble down the stairs and into the kitchen. I smile at the sight of my mother sitting at the window seat of the circular turret at the far side of the room.

Mom's in her favorite white sundress, the one that has spaghetti straps and lace around the hem. The sunlight hits her straight, long blond hair in a way that makes her glow and she has this soft presence about her that warms my heart. It's my mom, my best friend, and I know everything will be okay as long she's in the world.

"Good morning," I say.

At the sound of my voice, she turns her head in my direction and gives me one of her patented glorious smiles. Maybe she's smiling because my hair is one big rat's nest or because it's August and I'm in winter Minnie Mouse pajamas, rocking them like I'm six instead of seventeen. Regardless, she's happy to see me and that makes me elated.

"Morning." My truck-driver father is elbow-deep in waffle batter and is completely unashamed that his black T-shirt and worn blue jeans have been bombed by flour.

No matter what Dad makes in the kitchen, he'll be covered in it from head to toe. How he manages this, I'll never know. But it's an art form he excels at and I applaud him for the effort.

"How did you sleep?" he asks.

"Good." I shuffle across the room and take a seat next to Mom. Still cuddly, I lean my head against her shoulder and the pillow behind her, and she laces her fingers with mine.

We reside on the second and third floors of this humongous three-story Victorian house my mother purchased with her minimal inheritance years ago. The first floor we rent out for additional income because living there would be creepy. Years ago, people died mysteriously on the first floor, and what eleven-year-old wants to sleep in a room where people died? But the great news is that dead people in houses make them cheap and this place was practically a steal.

With my enthusiastic but non-helpful help, Dad renovated our floors. He turned the third floor into two bedrooms and a bath, and the second floor into our living space and kitchen. Besides the half bath, closets and pantry, the second floor is wide open. Because Mom loved the color of a sky on a cloudless day, the walls are a sunshine blue with white trim.

Dad sings along with an eighties song that's playing from the speakers mounted to the ceiling in the kitchen. His voice is gruff, rough and edgy, sort of like his appearance. Internally, I giggle with how dorky he is as he mock headbangs and acts as if he still has long black locks instead of a bald head. Dad's not a great singer, and he's definitely not a good dancer, but he is a good dad.

"How did you fall for him?" I whisper to Mom, even though I know the answer. There's something comforting in having the same conversations with someone you love.

"The better question is how did your father fall for me?"

My parents are exact opposites. She's delicate sunshine, and he's a thunderstorm with his broad shoulders, bouncer-for-a-bar physique and black goatee. Mom's poetry, art galleries, quiet days and poppy-seed muffins. Dad's football on Sunday afternoons, poker on Mondays, and a few beers on his tab with friends on Fridays.

"He loves you," I say. No one has ever loved anyone as much as

Dad loves Mom. Even though he's not particularly happy with her at the moment, the love is still there.

"He loves us," she corrects.

I couldn't agree with her more.

Dad remains focused on the waffles and allows me time to ease into my day before jumping into conversation. I'm not a diva, it's just that most mornings I wake with a pounding headache. Moderate pain days equate to a massive migraine that makes me feel as if a 747 is continuously landing on my brain. On terrible days, the pain is so bad, I can't make it out of bed.

But I didn't wake up with a raging headache, and I really did sleep well, so I'm quick to let Dad know it's a good day. "How did you sleep?"

Engaging with him this early is a gift, and the smile Dad flashes in my direction lets me know I couldn't have given him anything better. "I slept great. Are you ready for today, peanut?"

"Yep." Not really. I'd rather rip out my eyeballs than go to school orientation, but Dad's pretty adamant on this whole education thing. I don't want him going on the road worrying about me so it's easier to lie. "Are you ready for your trip?"

Dad leaves this afternoon for a five-day drive. "I think so, but you know me."

Mom and I giggle as Dad is notorious for forgetting things when he has long hauls. He'll forget toothbrushes, toothpaste, deodorant, shoes . . .

"He didn't sleep well," Mom whispers to me. "He tossed and turned all night."

"Why?" I ask, glancing at Dad to make sure he can't hear us over his singing and the accompanying air-drum solo.

Mom combs her fingers through my corkscrew short blond hair. Worry consumes her expression and the pain in her eyes hurts me. "He's concerned about you."

And she is, too.

Unable to stand either of their worries, I look away from Mom and notice the strawberries, blueberries and whipped cream—all of my favorite toppings—on the table. Dad loves doing things for me and with me. My throat tightens because I'm lucky to have a father like him.

Dad forks steaming waffles out of the iron, and his eyes fall on the fifty colorful, construction-paper turkeys I stayed up to make last night then taped to the wall. "Does this mean we're celebrating Thanksgiving again?"

"Yes."

"When do I need to be home?" Dad doesn't balk at my strange fascination with creatively celebrating holidays at a time other than the designated day. It's one of the many things I inherited from my mother.

A lot of people at school call me weird. People called my mom weird when she was in high school, too, so I do my best to view any taunts as a compliment. "I need to talk to Leo, Nazareth, Jesse and Scarlett and see what works for them. We should buy a huge turkey this time. I want lots of leftovers."

"Can you give me two weeks' notice on Christmas? I'd like time to buy you a gift that isn't from a gas station."

"Join the present day, Dad. Internet shopping. Two-day shipping. It's a thing."

"Won't Leo be leaving for college soon?"

The reminder makes me frown, and I change the conversation. "Are the new people still moving in downstairs today?"

"Yes, and they've been instructed to never knock if they need anything. They're to call me. If they break the rules, tell me and I'll evict them. I don't want them bothering you."

"Sounds good." Dad is gone several days at a time driving long distances, then home two to three days driving locally. It's a rotation that works well for us. Sometimes our renters will try to talk to me when they're impatient with waiting for Dad to return their calls and that pisses Dad off. "Who's moving in?"

"Someone from within town. It's a short-term lease. Rich people waiting for their house to be built in The Springs."

The fancy-schmancy neighborhood being built on the east side of town. If Dad and I saved every penny we made in the last ten years, we still couldn't afford a down payment for one of those overpriced, mammoth mansions.

"Their first month and deposit check is on the counter. Do you mind depositing it?"

"Sure." Because Dad travels, I handle our finances. Trucking is a small business, at least owning your own rig is, and there's a ton of accounting associated with it. Dad's been teaching me how to balance budgets since I was fourteen. He double-checks everything I do, but as I've gotten older he doesn't look over my work nearly as much.

"Did you tell them the house is haunted?" I ask.

"The house isn't haunted."

Oh, yes, it is. Dad's feeling left out because he hasn't seen the shadow people, but I have. "Then why did the Realtor tell you it was haunted?"

"Because people like to tell stories."

"You should tell him what you've seen," Mom whispers to me, and the guilt tastes like bile. "He'd want to know."

If I tell Dad, he'll overreact and go insane, and I'm not ready for what telling him will entail. "I'll tell him. Just not now," I say softly back.

"That may be too late," Mom continues in her hushed tone. "He'd want to know now."

I'm not ready to share my secret with Dad, even though it's an incredible burden to carry on my own. "You said you were fine with how I chose to deal with this."

"I did, but I'm not sure I agree with keeping things from your father. He loves you."

"He'll freak out," I whisper-shout. "He'll quit his job and he'll never let me out of his sight." That's not the life I want for me, and it's not the life I want for him.

"V, I don't think—" she starts, but I cut her off.

"Are you happy with how things went after you told Dad?"

Mom is crushed by my words, grief-stricken over what happened between her and Dad when she told him her secret. Even though she's pressuring me now, Mom told Dad that how I decide to handle the fallout of my diagnosis is my choice, and I'm guessing that's why Dad doesn't talk to Mom anymore—at least not in front of me.

Late at night, though, after he's checked on me to make sure I'm asleep, his anguish carries from his side of the house to mine. I can't hear what he says, but the sorrowful, mournful melody of his tone reaches my ears and breaks my heart.

I nibble my bottom lip and hope she understands. "There are things I need to do before I tell him. After I do those things, I'll tell him. I promise."

"Regret is a bitter thing," Mom says. "Be careful with how you play this hand. There are some decisions you can't take back."

Which is why I can't tell Dad what's happening with me, not now. Maybe not ever—despite my promise. I know Dad loves Mom and that Mom loves Dad, but there's this wall between them. Before I tell Dad my secret, I need to find a way to make things right between them, to give him comfort in the midst of my decisions, and to do it in a way that won't destroy my plans for this year and Dad's life.

"Are you ready to eat?" Dad asks, beaming.

"Definitely." I stand, and so does Mom, but instead of going to the table with me, Mom crosses the room and disappears up the stairs. Like always, Dad acts as if he doesn't notice her. While that cuts open my soul, I force a smile on my face and do my best to enjoy this moment with my dad.

SAWYER

Top five things I need to tell my mom, but I'd rather cut off my leg with a dull butter knife than say aloud:

1. She loves that I'm a swimmer more than I do. In fact, she loves most of my life more than I do. But she should, as she's orchestrated most of it.

2. I didn't break my arm by slipping on the deck of the pool at the YMCA like I told her, but instead by doing something stupid.

3. Even though I know what I do is the definition of insanity, I can't stop.

4. No, I'm not happy my cast comes off tomorrow as that cast is the only thing that's kept me from being stupid again.

5. My dad's current girlfriend is pregnant with their first child, and that's the reason I haven't talked to or visited

my father since the beginning of summer. He can hardly handle playing "dad" to us, so why have another?

Did I write any of that in my senior journal? Hell no. Our English teacher must live under a delusions-of-grandeur rock to think there's a single one of us who would share our deepest and most intimate thoughts in our Daily Top Five Forced (my addition) summer assignment.

I'm forty entries behind, and I have until six this evening to finish before turning the journal of doom in to my teacher at orientation. I'm aware it's not a good way to start the year.

In the driver's-side mirror of the U-Haul, I watch as my little sister runs in circles around my mother. Lucy's shrieking at the top of her lungs because she saw a bee. Her mess of black curls trails behind her like a billowing cape and her high-pitched scream mingles with my mother's frustrated pleas. Not sure how holding her coffee with two hands above her head helps a six-year-old in full panic mode, but Mom has an obsession with her morning coffee that wins over Lucy's fears.

Mom finally sets the cup on the porch then tries to contain my sister. For every half-hearted slip of my mother's arm around Lucy's waist, my sister zags. It's like catching air. From the way Mom moves as if stuck in wet cement, I can tell she's exhausted. Not sure if it's a didn't-sleep-well exhausted or I'm-a-single-mom-in-my-late-forties-with-a-demanding-full-time-job exhausted or just tired that it's nine in the morning and being responsible sucks.

Six years ago, my parents filed for divorce the day after Lucy's birth, and Mom and Dad gave me the choice of who I wanted to live with. My father had taken me out for dinner, put his hand on my shoulder and said, *Your mom needs you. She doesn't like to be alone, plus she's going to be overwhelmed with Lucy. Your mom will need an extra pair of hands and your little sister will need a permanent, loving big brother. I need you to be the man of the house now. I need you to take care of them.*

Decision made. Plus, considering Dad spent a total of ten minutes a night at home with me when they were married because he preferred work over us, choosing Mom didn't feel like much of a sacrifice.

A car honks and I try not to be annoyed by the sound. I'm blocking the end of the street lined by one-hundred-year-old towering oaks that bend as if the weather is too hot even for them. As far as I'm concerned, whoever it is can keep honking because I'm not moving until Lucy's safe. Besides, the house is the end of the road, the last of the neighborhood. Whoever it is can back it up since there is no more forward.

I roll down the window, and the August heat hits me like a jackhammer. I lean my head out and call, "Lucy."

My sister freezes in place and her big dark eyes blink as she slowly swivels her head in my direction.

"Hop in and I'll give you a ride."

Lucy squeals again, but this time in delight. In her favorite fluffy pink skirt and sequined unicorn shirt Mom bought her on their latest shopping spree, my sister races up the driveway toward me. I open the door, hop out and offer the car waiting on me an *I'm sorry* lift of my hand. The older man in the four-door Cadillac that's as big as a boat shakes his head as if pissed and decides to back into a driveway and head in the opposite direction.

With complete abandon, my little sister jumps into my waiting arms, and I place her into the truck. Lucy scrambles to the other side of the bench seat, and I close the door behind me. Even though we're only going a couple feet backward, I click her seat belt into place then put my hands on the wheel.

"Sawyer, you need your seat belt." Her innocent expression forces me to put it on.

Lucy can be Jiminy Cricket on crack, and most days, I need the additional conscience. I place the U-Haul into reverse, and the motor rumbles as I gently tap the gas. Seventeen isn't old enough to drive a U-Haul, but being a pharmaceutical representative, Mom has a way of talking until people listen.

My son is a doll. She dropped her million-dollar grin and fluttered her hand in the air when the guy at the U-Haul counter protested the idea of me driving. *Perfect to a T. He's going to win Olympic gold someday. You should see how good of a swimmer he is.*

Mom waves me back, in theory guiding me, but I don't watch her. I trust the mirrors instead. There's not a ton in the truck. Most of our possessions are in storage as we wait for our newest house to be built. It should have been done by now, but the contractor is late, the house we had been living in has been sold and now we're in short-lease-apartment purgatory.

Bright-eyed and grinning like I took her to the gates of Disney World, Lucy opens her door the moment I place the truck into park and jumps out. She senses adventure while I sense a train wreck. Mom has that grin that suggests she has something bad to tell me, but is intent to sell me the impending trauma as something good.

While you were at summer camp, I accidently forgot to feed your hamster, but wouldn't you prefer a turtle?

I dropped the leftover spaghetti dishes on your eighth-grade graduation suit you had laid out near the table, but wouldn't you rather skip the ceremony and spend the evening with me?

Lucy has the stomach flu and I have a huge meeting with clients, and if you stay home with her you don't have to take that reading test.

I'm slow leaving the truck and slower still as I cross the high grass of the front yard to join Mom on the crumbling front walk.

"You know, most people consider it a privilege to live on Cedar Avenue," Mom says. "The houses have been in families for generations. Aren't they gorgeous?"

I glance around, not really understanding the draw. It's a house. Not a waterfall.

The other towering homes on this street have manicured lawns that suggest the laser-sharp precision of a gardener. But this particular home is overgrown with bushes and wild roses that look like they haven't seen a sharp pair of shears in years.

Mom grew up in this small town. Until I was eleven, I lived in

Louisville. It was weird being a transplant at first, but I've learned to fit in.

Removing an elastic band from her wrist, Mom draws her done-by-a-master-stylist blond hair on top of her head into a bun. What Mom does for a living relies heavily on appearances. Her acrylic nails are always perfection, her makeup on point, her body the result of a daily onslaught of forty-five minutes on the treadmill then another thirty minutes of P90X.

Her black yoga pants and tennis shoes are a testament that she meant what she's said and she's going to pitch in and work. Sweat beads on her forehead and she brushes it away with the back of her hand as she looks at the monstrosity of a house in front of us.

In typical Mom fashion to save time, she signed a lease without a walk-through. "The house seemed cheerier in the photos."

"So do psychopaths."

The yellow house is three stories, was probably built in the eighteen hundreds and has a turret. The color alone should be inviting, but there's something dark about the house. Like the glass in the windows is a bit too thick, the air surrounding us too heavy, a pressure building that we aren't welcomed.

It doesn't help that the house sits at the bottom of a steep, looming knob and near the top of that huge hill is an aging, abandoned TB hospital that everyone in town knows is full of ghosts and demons, and it's where devil worshipers perform their ceremonies.

"Try being positive." Mom pushes my shoulder, but I don't budge.

"I'm positive psychopaths look cheerier in photos than they do in real life." A side-eye from Mom, and the hurt on her face causes a pinch of guilt. It's up to me to keep her going when things are hard.

I wink at her to take away the sting of my words. "You did good finding us a place."

Mom loves a compliment, and she accordingly glows. "I did *well*." She emphasizes the last word, a reminder she would like me to focus on my worst subject. There are subjects people get and subjects people don't. Math, I love. English is a constant struggle.

"We have the entire first floor and three bedrooms," Mom continues. "One for you, one for Lucy and one for me. There's a full kitchen and the appliances come with it. We can use the washer and dryer in the basement, we only pay half the utilities, and considering how much houses cost on this street, our rent is practically free. The best news is that we're only here until December."

When the contractor promised our house would be done.

"Did you tell your father about the move?" Mom's light tone is now forced. After all these years, the mere mention of Dad still causes her to flinch.

"Yeah." I'd begrudgingly sent him a text, but only to get Mom off my back about it.

"What did he say?" She puts on her designer sunglasses that are too big for her face.

There's no answer that will make her feel better. "Nothing much." And it's the truth. Mom glances over at my sister who's playing with a stick under the shade of the tree.

Where Lucy looks like Dad, with black hair and fair skin, I favor Mom. Our skin has a natural, year-round tan and our eyes are the same baby blue. My hair, though, is the original sandy-blond instead of her salon-bought platinum.

I'm tall, close to six feet and so is Mom. She was a volleyball player in high school and college. No volleyball for me, I'm a swimmer like Dad. A good one, too. If I can keep up my grades, my coach is convinced I'm on track for a state title.

"Are you sure you should be handling all these boxes with your arm?" Mom asks. It's the hundredth time she's asked this question in the past two weeks.

"The doctor went a week over to be safe, so I'm good."

"You're such a great kid. I don't know what I'd do without you. Our landlord and his daughter live on the second and third floors, but they won't disturb us. They have their own entrance. I think the daughter goes to school with you."

My head snaps up as this is the first time I've heard this part. "Who?"

Mom waggles her eyebrows. "Why? Thinking of having some late-night trysts?"

No. I don't like the idea of anyone from school having a bird's-eye view of my life, but saying that to Mom will only make her fish for an explanation. Mom laughs as she takes my noncommittal silence as an affirmative. She's always on the search for me to be her version of normal.

"Hannah helped me find this place. She said that Sylvia said that the girl who lives here isn't someone you all associate with." Hannah's a Realtor and one of Mom's best friends, and Sylvia is Hannah's daughter. Besides Miguel, Sylvia's one of my closest friends.

"Hannah also said that the man who owns the house is super nice. He travels a lot for his job, but is fantastic to his tenants."

"If Hannah said it, then it must be true," I mumble. Because of her job, Hannah knows more about most people than should be allowed, and happily dumps all the personal info she learns about her clients by the first round of drinks.

Mom ignores my comment, which is probably better for both of us. "By the way, I told Sylvia you'd invite her over to see the place once we unpack the boxes. Maybe you should take her out to dinner when you bring her over. Maybe a movie, too. I'll pay."

"Like a date?" I overly raise my brows in the hopes Mom might think before she speaks.

"Sylvia is a nice girl, and she thinks the world of you. Maybe you two could be more than friends."

"She prefers girls."

With a sigh, Mom drops the subject. "Ready to head in?"

Not really. "Sure."

Mom calls Lucy, and she races up the steps of the porch that need to be sanded down and stained. A few pushes into the electronic key lock and we're past the first door and into the foyer. We walk past the flowing staircase to another door with another electronic key lock. Mom has to check her texts to unlock this one and when she opens it, it's like the house exhales, and not in a good way.

The air is stale, the inside dark and when we walk in, I swear it's somehow darker. Lucy grabs on to my hand with both of hers and hides behind me. I turn on the ancient light switch with a loud *thwack* and a single overhead lightbulb flickers to life. The room has a dull haze now, like a slasher movie, and I'm betting Mom wishes she had done that walk-through.

"We need to open some windows," Mom says, but there aren't any windows in the living room as the bedrooms, kitchen and bathroom line the walls. "Lucy, come with me and we'll start in the kitchen. Sawyer, check out the bedrooms for us."

Translation—your sister and I are heading to the room with an exit while you check the bedrooms to see if there's a serial killer in the wings. I agree because I take care of my mom and sister, protect them, that's my job.

I inspect the right part of the house first. The area on the other side of the stairway is walled in. That area contains a bathroom and a big bedroom, which I assume will be Mom's. I re-enter the living room and check the small room running along the left side of the house. Maybe it was meant to be an in-home office. I then enter the bedroom with the turret and a circular window seat—something Lucy will love.

Even though the shades are drawn, rays of light peek through and highlight the copious dust particles in the air. I narrow my eyes at the rectangular-shaped object on the cushion of the window seat. I'm slow as I walk farther into the room, glancing multiple times over my shoulder as it feels as if there's someone else in here, someone staring at me.

I pick up the stack of stapled papers on the seat, flip through it, and it's nothing more than something that's been printed out, but it's wrinkled as if it's been well read.

DIARY of EVELYN BELLAK

1918

"To Evelyn from Maidy. A Merry Xmas & a Scrumptious New Yr."

"What's that?" Mom says from the doorway.

"Something left behind." I roll the paper into a tube, place it in my back pocket and open the shades. Bright, cheerful light pours into the room. "Hey, Lucy. What do you think of this room?"

She runs in, straight for the window seat, and the heaviness in my chest lessens at the sight of her smile.

"There are a few stipulations for living here," Mom says. My stomach sinks as this is what I'm used to, the kick following the good. She walks backward into the living room, and from the look on her face whatever it is she has to tell me isn't news she wants Lucy to hear.

I join her in the black heart of the building and cross my arms. "What?"

"We can only use the washer and dryer when the landlord isn't, and we aren't allowed to pester them. Not even if something goes wrong with the apartment. We have to call—never knock. The only exception is when we pay rent. We're to hand it to them personally, and we can't be late. And we have to do the yard work, but all the equipment we need is in the garage around back."

Which means I'll be doing yard work, but if that's the worst, I can live with it. "That's doable. Anything else?"

"Just one thing, and it's not a big deal. Small, really."

"What?"

"The house is haunted," Mom rushes out, then smiles at me. "So let's unpack."

VERONICA

The only reason people come to live in this small town is to hide or to die.

Nazareth's parents brought him here in seventh grade to hide. My father, on the other hand, uprooted me from our suburban, cushy, lower-middle-class, chocolate-chip-smelling home when I turned eleven for me to die.

There aren't many of us new people in town, so I've always been curious which reason brought Sawyer Sutherland to this forsaken land. Is he here because he's hiding or dying?

"It's bad enough Sutherland is moving into your house, but now it appears he's invading your mountain." Leo jumps onto the crumbling brick wall that runs along the concrete porch of the old TB hospital and looks down the hill. Sure enough, Sawyer Sutherland and his band of merry friends are walking through the thick bushes and tall, green trees up the narrow path.

Leo's right about Sutherland invading my space, but wrong on the hill being mine. Our backyard touches the property, but the hill and the sanatarium belong to the state. Leo doesn't come here as often as I do. We spend most of our time at Jesse's farm, but Leo's on a countdown to college and he wants to visit all his favorite places before he leaves. The hike up the hill is killer, but the view is breathtaking.

"Fantastic." Sarcasm in full effect. "I'm so happy he's feeling at home."

It's early evening, not quite nightfall, and the sky surrounding us is full of pinks and the dark blue of evening. Behind us is the massive porch where nurses would roll out patients in their beds so they could take in the fresh air. Back in the early 1900s, thousands of people lived here as they tried to "cure" themselves of TB by taking part in a fresh-air treatment. Many lived. Many more died.

Most people in town are terrified of this building. It has been abandoned for so long that not even the windows are in place anymore, leaving gaping, dark holes for all sorts of wild animals and undesirables to wander in. It doesn't scare me, though. To have fear for this place is to be scared of death and that is not a dread that I possess.

Leo drops to sit beside me and our legs dangle over the wall. His shoulder rubs against mine, and I'll admit my heart skips several beats. I wish it wouldn't, but it does.

He smells of sandalwood, and I hate how handsome he is— beautiful black skin, black curly hair that almost touches his shoulders and a smile that makes even the stone-cold people in the world feel included.

Maybe if Leo's eyes were misplaced on his handsome face like a Picasso painting or he had an alien popping out of his forehead or slimy tentacles attached to his back, I could find a way to not like him a little too much. But there's no alien, no tentacles, and I have feelings for Leo even though he has no idea I've fallen for him.

I have to stop thinking of Leo and feelings so I focus on the opposite of Leo and find Sawyer Sutherland leading the pack. Following him are a few guys and a few girls. The girls are huddled together and laugh hysterically when Sawyer turns his head toward them and surely says something witty.

That's what Sawyer does—talks. Laughs. For some reason everyone loves him. Girls want to date him, guys want to be friends with him, teachers want to hate him but he charms them regardless, and coaches fall over themselves to convince him to be on their teams. That is what popularity looks like.

Sawyer cons them all. He makes them all feel as if they're important—that is, everyone but me and my friends. He and I have been alphabetical buddies since he moved here, and he acts like I'm invisible. "Do you think he'll talk to me now?"

"No," Leo replies.

"That was blunt." Yet probably true.

"Starched button-down shirt, cargo shorts, Nike high-tops. He's got that same God-awful haircut everyone else has, and like the rest of the losers in town, he thinks he's original. People like him don't know how to see anything beyond themselves."

I wouldn't say God-awful haircut, but I'll agree on the unoriginal. Sawyer's brownish-blondish hair is cut into a low fade, longer on the top with the brush up that's popular among most guys of our town. He's on the taller end of the student population, has a swimmer's build, and he's as semi-good-boy-cool as they get. On the outside he checks all the boxes adults require to be a good boy. He says "yes, sir" and "no, ma'am" at the right times with the smile that hints at the mischief he's been up to, but he's the type to down a few beers with his "bros" on Saturday night and act like an ass.

But because I like to make life interesting . . . "What if it's a façade and there's really a rebel hiding underneath?"

Leo snorts, and even I have a hard time keeping a straight face. Sawyer Sutherland is as textbook cool-boy-with-money as one can get, and I gave up on anyone who's textbook years ago.

"I like your outfit." Leo gives me an appreciative once-over.

I waggle my eyebrows. "I do my best."

Today, I'm in a knitted see-through pink top with a black lace tank underneath, a layered black skirt that ends midthigh and striped black-and-green knee-high socks. I'm a real-life, vertically impaired anime character.

Four-foot-nine isn't an impressive height. Like, there are Charlie

Brown Christmas trees taller than me. And God help me, I look cute and cuddly. Like a stupid kitten with big blue eyes. I can't look mean and menacing even when I've tried, and trust me, I have. Anytime I've attempted to straighten my corkscrew blond curls, I've failed. They spring back into place.

Nazareth, one part of our small group of friends, pops out of the forest and climbs up the brick wall. Wondering if I've forgiven him yet, he offers me a questioning rise of his eyebrows. I'm already sad that Leo and our other friends graduated last year and won't be attending school with us anymore, and knowing that I'll be alone at school next year sucks.

Nazareth is supernova intelligent and will be taking college classes online at home to supplement his high school education. Tragically, this year, he and I will only share two classes. He won't even be there for lunch. A part of me is seriously pissed at the traitor. Yeah, I get it, the decision is best for him, so I'll hold on to a fraction of my anger and be passive-aggressive about it until he buys me tacos in repentance for his bad-for-me, yet good-for-him choices.

The past three years have been the best of my life. Now everything is changing, and not for the better. When it's clear I'm pouting, Nazareth clasps hands with Leo. "Hey."

"Not sure how long we'll stay. Sutherland and his friends are on the way up." Leo jacks his thumb in their direction then pulls his cell out of his pocket, no doubt texting Jesse to see if he's started his ascent since the popular people may possibly ruin our plans for the evening.

My cell rings. The caller ID informs me it's Glory, Jesse's older cousin and town psychic. She's been helping me avoid my fate, but I'm avoiding her so I reject the call.

"I started packing for school," Leo says as he pockets his cell, and my stomach bottoms out. Soon, Leo will be two hours away, and while he promises we'll hang out all the time, I don't believe him. When Leo went to a three-week-long camp for his college this summer, I didn't hear from him once. Typically when people leave this town for more than a month, they don't return.

Instead of accepting the inevitable, I intervene by dropping the news onto Nazareth. "Sawyer Sutherland moved in with his mom and sister into the downstairs apartment."

Nazareth isn't much of a conversationalist. He isn't much on showing emotions, either, yet his eyes widen. Nazareth has been my best friend for so long I can practically read his mind. *One of the most popular guys at school is living in the house of the girl voted most bizarre in the latest Tillman High's student Insta poll?*

"I know, right?" I make a funny face of twisting my mouth and crossing my eyes. Nazareth's lips turn up.

"Did you hear what happened to Sawyer's arm?" Leo asks.

No. School gossip isn't my thing. "I'm assuming the cast means he broke it."

"On how he broke it. He told everyone he slipped on the pool deck at the YMCA."

"So he's suing the Y?"

"No, he lied to his mom and the doctor. He didn't slip on the pool deck and his friends know he lied, but he won't tell anyone how he broke it. Everyone's covering for him, but they want to know what happened."

That's interesting, but nothing noteworthy. Sawyer Sutherland is known for playing it close to the edge in the search for a good time. In this instance, karma bit him in his cute butt. "Let's return to the real subject at hand. This guy is now living in my house. Doesn't that obligate us to talk? Before it wasn't awkward. We were two people who share the letter *S* for our last names, but now ignoring each other will be weird."

"Stay away from him, V," Leo says. "Guys like him don't know how to appreciate a girl like you."

A girl like me. Translation—misfit. Leo made the mistake once of calling me a misfit. I didn't talk to him for a week. Misfit suggests

I don't fit in anywhere. I do fit in. I just don't fit in easily with other people, and that's okay because I fit in fine with me.

Nazareth and I are kindred spirits in that way. Neither of us would ever change who we are in a fruitless quest for more friends. We're content being ourselves.

Like me, Nazareth has his own style. He recently had his mother cut his long hair and buzz it on the sides. He now wears it in a spiked Mohawk. He's a muscled guy, wears black thick-rimmed glasses that hide his dark green eyes, and he's taller than me, but who isn't? On his arms are a string of tattoos. Not common for a teen, but what's more fascinating is that every single one of those tattoos was inked at home by his mother.

"You're one of a kind, V," Leo says. "You deserve better than to put yourself out there for the unoriginal, and that kid is as original as a blank sheet of paper. He won't get you, and if you try to be friends with him, he'll make your life a living hell by being nice to your face then talking crap about you behind your back. That's how his group of friends work."

There's bitterness to his tone. Leo could fit in if he wanted. In fact, he used to fit in, but literally one day, out of nowhere in middle school he moved from a lunch table overflowing with people to sitting at the loner table across from me. My life changed then. For the better and I'm grateful.

The sound of pebbles bouncing along the floor of the empty sanatarium causes all of us to turn our heads. I strain to see into the darkness, eager to catch a sight of the shadow figures people have talked about online. Leo moves closer to a window then gives me a wide grin. "Want to go in with me?"

I'd love to, but the annoying giggles from below keep me rooted in place. I shake my head, and Leo disappears through the floor-to-ceiling window and into the darkness.

To be honest, Leo could have rocked smart, cool-boy over-achiever. A part of me believes that's who he'll become in college, and that's why he'll forget me. With Leo now a safe distance away, I finally release the air I had been holding. Nazareth gives me a concerned glance as he takes the spot beside me Leo abandoned.

"How are you?" he asks in that quiet way of his.

Only my closest friends are aware that pain is a part of my life. Sort of like how my arms and legs are attached to my body. But today is a good day and the pain level is minimal. More like a shadow of a memory of what it could become. "I'm migraine free."

"That's not what I'm asking." Nazareth swings his gaze from me to where Leo disappeared, and my chest aches.

I'm in love with Leo, and Leo doesn't know. Nazareth does. Jesse, too. Some days I wonder if I'm that good at hiding my emotions from Leo. Other days I wonder if Leo is blind. "I don't want him to go."

"Do you want him to stay?"

I shake my head. I'd never clip anyone's wings. Especially Leo's.

Nazareth pats my knee, and with that one touch, I lean into him and place my head on his shoulder. Nazareth is like my security blanket I used to drag around with me when I was a child. I'm not into him, and he's not into me so we're safe and easy with each other.

A ladybug walks along an overgrown bush close to us and it's clear she's headed for a spider's web. Nazareth, of course, reaches over and lets the ladybug walk onto his finger before gently depositing her onto the rock wall beside him. I smile; there's such a gentleness to Nazareth I'm not sure exists in anyone else. He literally lives the phrase *do no harm*.

"What about nature's balance?" I ask. "Didn't you just starve the spider?"

"The spider already has a meal and one waiting. She doesn't need three."

Because Nazareth is not only the kind of guy who cares to know what markings make a spider a male or female, but he also cares enough about a ladybug to save the day. Sure enough, the spider is weaving a web around a struggling fly and there's another fly caught in her sticky nest waiting for its turn to be spun.

Ice-pick pain spikes through my brain, and I shut my eyes and wince.

"V?" concern oozes from Nazareth's quiet tone.

Though the pain of that spike still reverberates through my skull, I force myself to lift my head and smile at my friend. "What?"

"You flinched."

"I yawned." My vision doubles and it takes a moment before the world refocuses. This is why I refuse to drive. I tell Dad it's because we don't need the additional cost of insurance, especially when living in the center of a small town, I can easily bum a ride or walk. But it's really because headaches like this can hit fast, and I don't want to ever cause an accident.

Nazareth broadcasts his doubt rather loudly through his tense jaw, but he does what I need and lets it go.

"I have an idea for our senior thesis," I say, ignoring the baby tremors of aches rolling through my brain. "It's a crazy idea, but I love it."

"I wouldn't expect anything less." Because crazy is who I am.

"I'm thinking we center our project on ghosts. Urban legends. Kentucky ones to be specific. It'll meet all the requirements we need to hit." I stick out a finger as I tick off each of the "rules" of the game our teachers have created. "We'll have to do extensive research, so we'll research the legends. We have to visit areas that deal with our project, so we'll visit the haunted spots. We have to conduct interviews, so we'll—"

"V," Nazareth interrupts me, which he rarely does. I fall silent, and it's weird that he won't meet my eyes.

"What?"

Nazareth rests his arms on his legs then joins his fingers together. For each beat of time that passes my stomach turns like the spin cycle of a washing machine.

"Because I'm on an accelerated schedule, they had me do my

senior thesis last year. I thought they'd let me do the thesis again and I'd partner with you, but they said no. I'm to focus on my college courses. I'm sorry, V. I'll help you if you want, but . . ."

But the project requires us to work in a group of two to four people and Nazareth won't count. My inhale rattles through me as I'm hollowed out. Jesse has graduated and is focused on his farm, Scarlett is already at college, Leo is leaving and Nazareth might as well be gone. The worst has happened. I'm going to be alone.

SAWYER

It's been weeks since I've had a release, and I'm wound damn tight. I glance around the huge monster of the building searching for something to impress me. Something to take my mind off the fact my cast will be off tomorrow and there will be nothing stopping me from seeking my high.

Here's the thing about the high: I want it as much as I don't. A constant push and pull, and I'm always on the losing end. I don't want to give in to the need for the high and disappoint and endanger myself. At the same time, just the thought of the high relaxes some of my always-twisted muscles. If the thought alone relaxes me, then doing it would be close to heaven.

Won't lie, part of the reason I suggested we all hike up here was in the hopes of finding a hint of the rush, but unfortunately, there isn't enough danger.

The guys fan out and start for the stairs that lead to the front door of the place. They're a mixture of the swim and soccer teams, and they're discussing a combination of baseball, football and Call of Duty. Miguel, the guy I'm closest with, is the one that leads the conversation and is the most opinionated.

Sylvia slides up beside me. With her comes the group of girls that follows her most everywhere she goes. Sylvia is a pied piper of people—just like my mom. I understand why—there's something about her that draws me in, like a light, and that's why she's one of the few I call friend.

I know a lot of people. A lot of people know me, and while I can put on a show that I'm outgoing, I consider myself private.

Sylvia stays by me as her friends follow the guys through the hole where glass for a window used to be. She tucks her honey-blond hair with done-by-hand curls behind her shoulder.

As she always does, she looks good. She wears designer jeans and a purple top that hugs all the right places. All bought on a shopping day with her mom, Hannah, my mom and Lucy. Not exactly hiking clothes, but it's not like she knew we would be tackling this adventure when she showed. In my defense, it's not like I invited anyone over—that would be Mom ignoring my request to give me some time to unpack. Mom feels I need to be social, twenty-four/seven, so she texted Sylvia, telling her to bring my "squad."

I wish Mom would learn how to back off.

"Do you remember when we came here freshman year?" Sylvia says as we scale the stairs.

"Do you mean when I jumped out from behind a door and scared the hell out of you and you peed your pants?"

She smacks my shoulder. "I didn't pee my pants."

"But you did scream."

She laughs because she did scream, for five solid minutes, then shook for a half hour after. I hop through the window first, and Sylvia's hesitant as she lifts one leg then the other to enter. Faint evening light streams from the open windows and the entire place has an eerie haze.

Our friends are scattered about the large lobby. Most of the girls huddle near a guy as they explore the rusting gurneys left behind. Someone turns on the flashlight on their cell and light dances along the tiled floor. Red and black graffiti decorates the dirty and peeling plaster walls, and I do a double take when I spot arm restraints in the corner of the room.

"So this year," Sylvia says with heavy apprehension, and those muscles forever tightened in my neck twist some more.

"So this year," I repeat with the same heaviness and search the place for something to get my blood pumping. Just being near this building puts people on edge, starts that leak of adrenaline associated with terror, but I can't find an inkling of fear. It's walls, floors, abandoned medical equipment, syringes left by junkies and runaway imaginations.

There's no such things as ghosts or demons. Probably the most dangerous thing in this place is tetanus from a rusty nail or encountering a raccoon with rabies.

Sylvia nudges the broken tile floor with the toe of her black Converse. "We have a real shot at winning the team coed state division in swim this year, but to do it, we need you."

She's nice enough to leave out that one of the reasons why we didn't capture the title last year, when we should have, when we were expected to, was because I was forced to sit out near the end of the season for academic reasons. The shame of letting my team down because I didn't keep my grades up still burns.

"Listen," she says with sympathy, "I know English is tough for you."

Reading is tough. I can get an A in math with my eyes closed and earbuds in tight, but reading is like being air-dropped into the middle of Japan and expected to be fluent day one.

"I was thinking, if we have English together, then you, me and Miguel should work on our English project."

The short, dry laugh is my answer. "I won't be in your English class." They're in advanced classes. Except for math, I'm not.

"It's a crazy world." Sylvia waggles her eyebrows. "You never know what can happen."

"Hey." Miguel walks toward us. "Are you two coming in farther or are you too scared?"

"Sylvia's scared," I say, and Sylvia pushes my shoulder again. I nail her with a side-eye. "You are scared."

She glares back because she is. "Not all of us were born without a fear gene. Which is weird, by the way. Like they should do genetic testing on you to see how that's possible."

True.

"I overheard you two discussing AP English, and I know where this is going," Miguel says. "You're not stealing Sawyer, Sylvia. He's going to be in my group."

This conversation is fruitless since I won't be in their class.

"You're going to be in my group and so is Sawyer," Sylvia says. "The two of you would be lost without me. You'd spend the first three months of the project talking video games."

Has she not caught on that I haven't been on a single honor roll since moving here? "You're better off with Miguel than you are with me."

"Did you hear that?" Miguel glances over to Sylvia's friends, and when Jada meets his eyes, he offers her a crooked grin. His deep and slick voice causes her to lean forward. "You're better off with me, *mi alma*."

Miguel is bilingual, and girls fall for the Spanish tidbits he drops. Miguel calls it his Latin charm. I tell him he's full of crap. He'll laugh then agree.

Sylvia fakes a gag as she presses her cell to life after it flashes with a notification. "Can you two go make out in a darkened corner and save the rest of us from having to witness this?"

Jada and Miguel laugh. The two of them have been nonstop flirting since junior prom.

Miguel and his sister older sister, Camila, are second-generation American. His father came to America from Mexico as a child, and Miguel's mother came here on a student visa for college. The two met, fell in love, got married and now run a successful we-bring-the-birthday-parties-to-you business.

"What do you think of the apartment?" Sylvia asks.

The question is for me as I'm the only one currently in rental living. One of the problems with my mom being best friends with my friends' moms is that my friends know too much of what's going on in my life when I'd rather be a closed book. It can work in the opposite direction, too. Sometimes information I'd rather keep to myself gets magically unloaded onto Mom. "It's fine."

"Our moms are going out later tonight." Sylvia focuses on her cell, typing in a comment to someone's photo. "I hope they start the party at my house first. Your mom is such a riot."

Yeah. A riot. Mom's plans means I'll need to hightail it out of here to watch my sister while Mom burns down the town.

Sylvia grins at Miguel now. "Did Sawyer tell you he's living in the apartment below Veronica Sullivan? Gives you chills just thinking about it, doesn't it?"

"No crap," Miguel says. "Twenty dollars there's dead bodies in the backyard."

"Has she done anything crazy yet?" Sylvia twists her face in mock horror. "Eat live bats in front of you? Bake small children into cookies? That girl is *Addams Family* insane."

"Not yet, but I did find this in Lucy's room. It's a diary or something." I pull out the papers I still have tucked in my back pocket. "Veronica Sullivan? That's who is living upstairs from me? The weird girl?"

Right as Sylvia is about to reach out to take the thick packet of paper from me, her gaze shoots over my shoulder and her eyes widen in fear. I whip around, half expecting to find someone wielding a machete, and I briefly float with the taste of the rush.

There's no machete, but a shadow slowly moving along the outside porch.

"Technically," comes a musical voice from the shadow, a voice I can't peg where I know it from. The shadow steps onto the ledge of the window opening and blocks the light of the fading sun. My stomach drops as I have a sickening idea of where this is headed. Standing in front of me are short blond curls, a beautiful face and scathing blue eyes. "*You* live downstairs from me."

Screw me—it's Veronica Sullivan.

"Is there anything else any of you would like to say about me?" she continues. "Because the proper thing to do would be to say it to my face."

Veronica glares at us, waiting, in silence. She doesn't enter the building, but stays atop the window ledge. She's bold enough to look Miguel straight in the eye, then Sylvia and then eventually me.

"We didn't mean anything by—" Sylvia starts.

"I don't care." Veronica's blue eyes are so cold that I'm surprised we don't see our breaths in the air.

I've got to admit, there aren't many people who can make me feel like crap, but she just did and it's an odd sensation to have in regards to a complete stranger.

"Where did you get that?" She jerks her chin toward the papers in my hand. From her tone, it's clear she's pissed.

The already strangling light is dimmed further when another shadow appears in the opening beside her. Nazareth Kravitz leans his back along the frame, watching us like he's bored. A sixth sense tells me he's actually sizing me up, which is bizarre because last I heard he's one of those peace-at-all-costs people.

"Leo texted," Kravitz says. "He was on the third floor and said we're going to have guests."

She glances at him, in a way that tells me something in his words bothers her.

"What's that supposed to mean?" I ask.

"Where did you get those papers?" she asks me again.

"I found them."

"Where?" she pushes.

"Is there a problem?" Kravitz's voice pitches low.

Before she can answer they both whip their heads toward the parking lot and main road.

"The police are here!" someone yells, and sweet blood pumps wildly in my veins.

Footsteps pound against the tile floor as people rush for the exits. Miguel and Sylvia immediately jump out the nearest opening.

Kravitz unhurriedly drops from his platform, and I look at Veronica again. She still stands there, watching me with that frozen glare, completely unaffected by everyone else running for their lives.

"Sawyer!" Sylvia calls. "Let's go! They arrest people who are caught here."

They do, but there's an unspoken dare with how Veronica stays in her spot. As if she's challenging me. As if she's letting me know that in a contest of nerves, she'd win. Truth? The longer she stays there, the more my skin vibrates with that sweet rush. I want to accept her dare, her adrenaline-induced challenge.

"Sawyer!" Miguel shouts. "Let's go!"

"Our parents will be pissed if we're caught!" Sylvia is pulling on Miguel's arm and her stare is yanking at me.

> Mom
> Lucy
>
> *I'm the responsible one.*
>
> Sylvia
> Miguel
>
> *I'm supposed to do what is expected.*
>
> *But I don't want to turn away.*
>
> Damn.

Veronica tilts her head at me with a knowing smirk that I envy. One that crosses my face whenever I stand on the edge of a cliff, the one I wear when my heart is pumping so fast it feels like it might burst out of my chest. My high.

Her smirk is an affirmation that she won this round and that causes my respect for her to grow. I didn't know this about her—I didn't know she had balls of steel.

I break off the connection with Veronica and bolt through the window. A single siren wails, the cops' only warning they're on their way. I'm running now, and I'm fast. Faster than Sylvia, faster than Miguel. So fast that I catch them and then become the leader on the way down.

When we're far enough away, safe in the thick foliage, I turn and look up at the looming gray building and watch in awe. Two police officers scale the steps of the entrance of the building and then three figures lazily drop from the brick porch on the opposite side. One of them has blond curls. It's Veronica, Kravitz and Wheeling. All of them walking as if taking a stroll through the park instead of being chased by police. Veronica seeming to be the least concerned.

No worries.
No fear.
Just courage.

Now that is impressive.

VERONICA

L

ave the new people moved in?" Dad asks over my cell.

It's late and my eyesight is blurry from exhaustion. After one of Sawyer Sutherland's merry band of mean friends was stupid enough to trigger an alarm and bring the police, Nazareth, Leo and I drove around town with the windows down and the music blaring. Of course, Nazareth being Nazareth, he saw a stray puppy with a collar and we had to find the owners, but it's fun to be the hero for a few minutes.

After that, they dropped me off at the Save Mart where I'm an assistant manager so I could help close for the evening since one of the other employees left early with the stomach flu. Dad and I are always hustling for money, and because Dad is preparing for the day I get so sick that he'll quit his job and his entire life to take care of me, he shoves a ton of what we make into savings. I do what I can to add to the pot.

I have him on speaker as I sit at the desk in our living room and search through file folders, searching for Evelyn's diary. It's a copy of a diary from a library in upstate New York. One my mother had heard about and asked to see, and they were nice enough to send. The same one I saw in Sawyer Sutherland's hands tonight, and I have no idea how he got it.

Those papers were securely placed in a hope chest in my room. No one knew I kept the diary there, not even Dad. I have ransacked nearly every part of my house in search of the copy, hoping against hope that, besides me, Sawyer is the only other person in the world who owns a copy. This riddle is driving me insane—how did Sawyer get his hands on my transcript of Evelyn's diary?

"V," Dad says. "I asked if the new people are done moving in."

"I guess." I shove all the accounting files for Dad's business back into the drawer.

Relaxing on the circular window seat and listening to me and Dad chat, Mom stares into the night. She's peaceful, as if there's not a problem in the world. I wish I could feel that way for thirty seconds. "I don't see them hauling in any more boxes."

Dad and I are close. From the way people talk at school, we're closer than most parent-child relationships, but I don't feel like telling him that the guy who moved in downstairs was making fun of me. As much as I hate to admit it, their words hurt. Plus, Dad will kill him for upsetting me, and it would suck to have to visit Dad in prison.

"All the gas receipts are officially scanned into the computer and logged," I say.

"Thanks." Dad sounds as drowsy as I feel. He drives long hours before taking the mandatory rest period the government insists truckers take. In the background, I can hear the TV in the sleeper of his cab.

Dad tells me about a character of a waiter he had at the truck stop diner and the story makes me laugh. As he talks, I check my school email and find a reply from my teacher.

I had nicely begged for permission to do the research project on my own. Her answer was short, simple and to the point: *No. One of the purposes of this project is to learn how to work with others. This is an essential skill you will need for your future.*

I disagree. Wholeheartedly. I have absolutely no intentions of doing anything in my future that involves me working with groups of people.

"Did you deposit the rental check?" Dad asks, drawing me out of my melancholy mood.

"Yep."

"Tomorrow, not tonight, as you need to get some sleep, can you set up all the new spreadsheets for these tenants?"

I've already started them. Rent, utilities, incidentals . . . "Yep."

"Have you turned on the alarm?"

"Yep. I'm home safe, Dad, and I'm okay."

There's silence on his end, and I allow it. He eventually clears his throat, but his voice is gruffer than normal. "I love you, peanut."

My heart warms. "I love you, too."

He hangs up, and I relax back in the comfy rolling chair that is pleather and has a high back. There's a lot of people my age who would be freaked out to be alone at night, but except when I was eleven and we first moved here, the dark doesn't scare me. In fact, there's a comfort in the blackness of night. A lot like a soft, heavy blanket. A lot like my mother's hugs.

Searching for a solution to my problems, I swivel in the chair. I need to find someone else to work with on my English project. Someone who has a car, someone who will be easy to meet with, someone who will willingly work with me and someone who is absolutely on board with what I want to research. This topic means the world to me—literally life and death.

My cell pings and I glance down at the text. Glory: You need to contact me. I'm seeing things in your future that concern me.

There are things that concern me about my future, too.

Out of the corner of my eye, there's movement. A shadow. I barely see the blur, and it darts from the living room toward the stairs that lead to the foyer on the first floor. My heart picks up speed. It's past midnight. The time when this house comes alive. Beyond shadows, I haven't seen the children since I was a child, and I'm hungry to see them again.

I'm up, out of my seat and I follow. A push of a few buttons, the alarm is disarmed and I open the heavy wooden door that separates me from the rest of house. At the top of the stairs, I strain to look down into the darkness. A faint light pushes through the thick stained glass over the main front door, creating shadows in the corner. There's silence. So loud that it almost hurts my ears.

The children frighten easily so I creep down the stairs, working hard to distribute my weight to keep the old steps from creaking and moaning.

What do the children see when they frolic around this old house? Do they see their own home, in their own time, back when they were alive? Are they lost in their happy memories? Because that's what I hope for death to be, lost in a dream of joy.

I lean my back against the wall, close my eyes and listen. At this time of night, at exactly this time, I hear their light footsteps tapping against the hardwood. Some nights, I'm lucky and can hear their giggles, and on rare nights, back when I was younger, I was offered the rare jewel of catching sight of more than just the hem of a dress.

I breathe in. I breathe out. The energy of the house surrounds me, and a child's high-pitched scream pierces the night.

SAWYER

Tuesday Jan. 1: Well, Diary, I'll introduce myself. My name is Evelyn. I'm 16 years old. I have tuberculosis and at the present time am in the Ray Brook Sanitarium trying to get cured. You must keep my secrets well, for I'll tell you things that I want no one to know.

— Evelyn Ballak, 1918

The girl is at a desk, writing into a journal. I stand at the doorway, watching, listening, confused by the look of happiness on her face. I scan the hallway and see the exhausted doctors, the worried nurses, the people deathly thin walking up and down the hallway. Someone coughs. It's a ragged, guttural, desperate sound. As if someone is drowning on dry land. And everyone stops and turns toward the noise.

A man stumbles out of his room and almost runs into me, and I jump into the girl's room—my heart in my throat. He holds his chest, clawing at it as if it won't work. He continues to cough, doubles over with it and then collapses to the floor.

He's sick, they're all sick here. They've been sent here to die and I turn back to the girl and she's still writing and she's still smiling.

"Haven't you been told?" I say.

The girl looks up at me and blinks like she's confused. Her innocence causes me pain. "Told what?"

That you can't be happy. You're dying. I should tell her. Someone should tell her. But why does it have to be me?

A scream. So loud that everyone moving around me stops. They turn and stare at me. The doctors, the nurses, the patients, the man on the floor. Their eyes wide, their mouths open, as if the scream is resonating from all of them, but it's one sound, one horrifying shriek and the real world slams into me.

Lucy.

My eyes open, and I shoot off the mattress resting on the floor of my new room. Evelyn's diary falls from my chest.

Adrenaline pumps through my veins. Someone's hurting my sister. Her scream ends for a beat then her shrieks continue. I fly through my room, grab the baseball bat by the door and swing it over my shoulder as I charge into her room.

The princess bed is set up in the middle of the room, the white sheer curtains hanging from bedpost to bedpost. Pillows at the top of the bed, pink sheets and comforter kicked back, but my sister is gone. Nausea races through my gut, and I fight the wave of dizziness. "Lucy!"

Footsteps behind me, multiple ones, and I spin searching for the threat. There's no one. Darkness. Only a smidge of light flows from the hallway that leads to Mom's bedroom. "Lucy!"

Cries. My sister's cries. Heart-wrenching cries. Desperate cries. And the panic throbbing through me makes me feel like I'm going insane. "Lucy, answer me!"

The door to our apartment bangs against the wall and I jump. A shadow rushes through it, and on instinct, I chase. Out to the foyer, my feet pounding against the floor. Pain in my chest at the sight of another shadow descending the stairs and the craziness in my head grows. "Lucy, answer me now!"

The front door to the house flings open, light from the streetlamps floods in and my heart stalls at the sight of my sister. She's in her long nightgown, her black hair tangled and her face red. She hyperventilates as tears stream down her cheeks. At the threshold, she starts to step out, and as the roar for her to stop reaches my throat, the shadow on the stairs leaps toward my sister.

My heart tears through my chest, Lucy screams and I sprint with my fingers tight around the bat, the intent to kill. Then there's a halo of beauty crouched in front of my sister, and I come to an abrupt halt. Short curls, delicate hands on my sister's shaking shoulders and that musical voice I had heard earlier today isn't reprimanding, but soothing. "It's okay. You're okay. Everything's okay. Just take a deep breath. You can do it. Try it with me."

Lucy chokes as she tries to breathe, and Veronica tucks my sister's hair lovingly over her shoulder. "Good job. Now try again. Can you tell me your name?"

"It's Lucy," I say as I lower the baseball bat. I scan the foyer, the corners, and the shadows. The hair on my neck stands on end in warning. Instincts nagging that there are eyes, unseen eyes, glaring at me.

"Hi, Lucy, I'm Veronica. Where were you going so fast?"

Lucy shakes from head to toe, and she tries to jerk out of Veronica's grip, but Veronica doesn't give. I'm grateful because I'm taking my time moving toward them. There's an eeriness in the air. A sixth sense that something's wrong, a something I need to fight.

"Let me go!" Lucy screeches, and that's not like her. She starts crying again, and her body convulses with the sobs. "We have to go! It's coming! The monster is coming!"

"Did you have a nightmare?" I ask, and though I'm only a few steps away, I glance over my shoulder again, toward our new apartment that's somehow darker than moments before.

The sobs stop, like someone flipped a switch and that causes a terrified squeeze in my lungs. As if the same energy that just pulsed through Lucy is now attacking me. Lucy's face goes white and taut, and my back itches as if I'm about to be shot. "What's wrong, Lucy?"

My sister methodically inches her head toward the sidewalk outside as if she already knows what she'll see, but is horrified by facing the actuality. Veronica glances in the same direction, then shoots up. Her hand slips from Lucy's shoulder to her elbow and with a firm grip she yanks her back, away from the door, and I'm moving again. On my toes, bat by my ear, coming in fast.

Veronica swings Lucy onto her hip, covers her hand over my

sister's head, shielding her from whatever horror lies in wait and dashes up the stairs. I push past them, willingly becoming their first line of defense, then disgust courses through my veins at the sight of a figure stumbling up the stairs of the porch. A trip on the final step, a collapse, then a thud of a heavy body, and I swear aloud as I throw the bat across the porch.

It's not a monster, at least not the ones from Lucy's nightmares. On the ground is my mother. She rolls to her back. Her hair covers her face as her giggles grow into a hysterical laughter. I hate it when she goes out with her friends because this is how she comes back—drunk.

"It's all right," I call out, but I don't sound all right. I sound pissed.

"Who is it?" Veronica asks.

Not exactly the way anyone wants an introduction to go. "My mother."

Silence on Veronica's end. I'm with her; there's not much of a decent response for that.

My mom's laugher subsides, and that's never a good thing. She moans, and I know what that means. I wish my cast were already off because odds are she's going to puke, and with the way my luck goes, she's going to puke on me. The cast can get wet, but it retains toxic smells.

Lucy's shuddered breaths are a sign she's calming down but is still upset over whatever bad dream started this whole debacle. There's one of me and two people who need help, and God help me, I don't know who to take care of first.

I glance over my shoulder at Veronica who is hugging my little sister close. "Do you mind taking Lucy into our apartment?"

On the second landing where the staircase turns, Veronica leans over to get a good look at my mom just in time to see her roll to her side with a dry heave. Veronica's lips thin out, then she rubs a hand along Lucy's back. "Would you like me to take Lucy to my place? I can get her something to drink, let her watch TV and give you time to deal with . . . this."

Do I want what she's offering? More than I want eyes to see, but pride is a fickle beast as I'm the one who takes care of this family. That's the job Dad left to me.

"I promise I won't bake her into cookies," Veronica says in a flat tone, and my shoulders drop with the reminder of how much of a jerk I am. "I already had a few Girl Scouts for dinner so I'm good for a few weeks."

I deserved that yet I can't bear to look at Veronica as I accept her offer. "That would be great if you could take Lucy." I suck in a deep breath as I lift my mom into my arms. She's a bit heavier than air, but with my cast on, she feels like dead weight. "Thanks."

I hear a mumbled "welcome" as I carry my mom through the foyer and into the apartment. I kick the door shut behind me then head straight for the bathroom. Using my shoulder, I flip on the light, and when I set her on the floor, she barely makes it to the toilet before she vomits what's left of her liver.

Mom makes ugly sounds as she retches, and grabbing an elastic ponytail holder, I draw her long blond hair back even though she's already vomited on several strands. I drop my ass to the floor and lean against the cold tile wall.

I've never had a girlfriend. I've kissed a few girls, but no one steady. It drives my mom crazy and maybe this scenario is the reason why. I can't comprehend a world where anyone would want to do this for someone they loved. It's bad enough I have to do this with Mom. I don't need nor want to do this with anyone else.

A few more dry heaves that contain fluid, and Mom moans as she places her head on the toilet bowl. I wince for her—we haven't cleaned since moving in this morning and who knows what flesh-eating bacteria was on there from the previous occupants.

"I'm sorry, Sawyer," she says in a rasp. "I didn't think I drank that much."

"I told you that you should have eaten dinner with us."

"What can I say other than you're right?"

Not much. "Is everyone this drunk? And if so, how did you get home?"

"Jennifer called an Uber to take us all home."

Which means Mom's car is still at whatever restaurant or home she left it at. When I stare blankly back, she offers me a pathetic smile. "It was Vivian's birthday." But then her smile fades and tears well up in her eyes. My forehead furrows as this isn't my mom. She's the happy type, especially when there's alcohol rolling in her veins.

"What?" I lean forward, wondering if she's going to puke again.

Mom closes her eyes, pressing them so tight that crow's feet form. "My credit card was denied tonight, and I had to pay cash. I was so embarrassed."

Of all the issues we've had in life, money hasn't been one of them. "Did someone steal your card?"

She rocks her head against the porcelain. "Your dad didn't send the child support check."

My mouth opens in shock, but it doesn't take long for rage to boil up from my gut. "What?"

"He hasn't sent anything for the last few months. I make enough money to support all of us, and I didn't want you guys to be disappointed in him, so I didn't say anything, but then I had to pay a few unexpected bills, your medical bills, and I forgot that I'd have to pay our mortgage at the old house and a first and last month's deposit here and then there were costs associated with selling the house and the new house . . ."

Sweat breaks out along Mom's forehead, and my stomach turns as I try to understand where this is all headed. Mom's body shakes as goose bumps form on her arms. "I didn't realize how much I had put on the card or how low the checking account has become. I'm afraid that the check for this apartment is going to bounce. Our landlord said his daughter was going to deposit it soon. I'll be fine when I get paid again, but . . . I'm sorry, Sawyer. I'm sorry."

And as Mom opens her mouth to say something else, she lifts her head and vomits into the toilet again.

VERONICA

Lucy's brother is a jerk, their mom is a Dumpster fire, but Lucy is the shining star of the family. After she saw my old dollhouse in the corner of the living room, Lucy quickly forgot her fears. She played for a few minutes, and now she sits at our high kitchen table and swings her legs as she surveys the room with wonder. "There're a lot of turkeys."

"There are." I fish out a box of crackers from the pantry. That's what little kids like, right?

"Who made them?"

"Me. Would you like to make one?"

"Sure." Her grin is mostly baby teeth. After opening a package of crackers and sliding them to her, I pull out everything she could think of or need to make a paper turkey—construction paper, crayons, markers, glue, tissue paper and the golden grail of glitter. It takes a few more minutes for me to dig into the bottom of my Tupperware drawer to find safety scissors. I finally find a pink pair, and Lucy seems satisfied with the tubes of glitter she holds up to the light.

"I like it here. It's happier than downstairs," Lucy says. "Why do you have so many turkeys?"

"I think the better question is why doesn't everyone have turkeys hanging on the wall?"

Lucy tilts her head as if my answer was profound then eats a cracker. Crumbs fall from the corner of her mouth.

"How old are you?" I ask.

"Six," she says through bites. "How old are you?"

"Seventeen."

"My birthday was in July," Lucy declares. "When's yours?"

"May."

"I have one brother and no sisters."

"I don't have any."

"That's sad." And her little brown eyes show how serious her words are. "I like having a brother. He's fun."

I'm sure he is.

"I'm going to have a new brother or sister in a few months."

My eyebrows rise. "Your mom is pregnant?"

Lucy shakes her head so fast that her hair flips across her face. "No. The new girl Daddy dates is having a baby. Mommy doesn't know yet. Sawyer said he'd tell her. I'm glad I don't have to. I don't like it when Mommy cries. If Mommy cries, it's usually during the week. Mommy laughs more on the weekends, but that's when she gets sick. I don't like that, either."

Fantastic, our new tenants aren't just a dumpster fire, but a wild-fire inferno. "So why were you so upset earlier?"

Lucy slows her cracker chewing and sorts through the construction paper until she finds a sensible brown. I purse my lips, and she notices. "What?"

"Brown is a fine choice, but why make a turkey everyone else makes? Why not make your turkey a Lucy original?"

"Because turkeys are brown."

"But they don't have to be."

"But if you see a real turkey, they're brown."

"Maybe they're brown because everyone keeps telling them they are. Maybe we need to stop labeling the turkeys and set them free."

Lucy glances around at my colorful array of turkeys then sorts through the construction paper again. This time she picks purple. I pick out blue and we begin the process of cutting, gluing and coloring in silence. As I tear up green tissue paper and start the daunting task of twisting the ends and gluing them to the wings, Lucy says, "Sawyer won't believe me."

I only allow myself a quick glance at her because if I seem too interested she'll shut up. At least that's what I would do. "What won't Sawyer believe?"

The sound of scissors cutting paper ceases, and I look up again to find Lucy staring at me. Sheet-white, her little eyes as big and round as saucers. "You won't believe me."

"What if I do?"

Her throat moves as she swallows, then she whispers, "I saw a ghost."

I watch her for a few more seconds to see how serious she is, to see if she's testing me, to see if her brother put her up to some sort of joke as there have been rumors about this house. When the fear doesn't leave her eyes, when her tiny fingers fist the scissors tighter, I know this isn't a con. "What did the ghost look like?"

"A girl. Like me, but in a dress. Her dress looked weird."

"Weird how?"

"Not the kind of dress I've seen anyone wear. It was longer. Past her knees."

"Did she hurt you?"

Her forehead wrinkles as if that wasn't the question she was expecting. "It was a ghost."

"Yes, but did she hurt you?"

"No." A pause. "She scared me."

"Did you ever think that maybe you scared her? I mean, according to my mom, the little girl has lived here a long time, and she's used to me and Dad, but you"—I point at her with the tip of the glue—"are brand new. How do you think a ghost would feel when they strolled into their old bedroom and surprise! You're in there and screaming. I know I'd freak out. The proper thing to do would have been to introduce yourself or at least say hi."

Lucy twists a ribbon from her nightgown around her finger then sticks the ribbon into the corner of her mouth, nibbling on it without thought. "But ghosts are scary."

"Says who?"

She leans forward on the table to impress upon me the soberness of the situation. "Everyone."

"Well, Miss Lucy, I'm here to tell you that this 'everyone' you speak of is usually wrong on a lot of things. And ghosts are one of them. Ghosts are only people who had to leave their bodies, but they aren't ready to leave home yet."

Lucy's lips turn down and the sight causes my lungs to pinch. I put down the tissue paper and curse that my fingers are so sticky with glue that if I touch Lucy, I'll be stuck to her forever. "What's wrong?"

"I miss my home."

I exhale slowly as I remember my first night in this house and how I sobbed in my mother's arms as I missed my home, too. "I'm sorry. If it makes you feel better, the ghosts here won't hurt you. I promise."

Wetness lines her eyes and her cheeks flush red. "How do you know?"

I do a quick wash of my hands at the sink then stand in front of Lucy. She's so heartbreakingly young, so desperately scared, so innocent that it's wrong to keep my secret from her.

But that's the thing, this is my secret. My secret no one else knows and a secret I want to keep to myself. But who I am to let this poor girl hurt? "If I tell you a secret, my most private secret, do you promise to never tell anyone? And if you keep this secret, I promise in return to let you come up here whenever you want, make as many crafts as you can dream of, eat my food and watch my TV as long as I'm here."

Lucy nods, and I guess that's the best I can hope for. I tuck her hair behind her ear, just like my mom did for me. "There are ghosts in this house, and they won't hurt you. I know this because . . ."

Courage. Take courage. "Because my mom is one of the ghosts. She's watching over us, and I promise she'd never let anyone or anything hurt us, ever."

Lucy's expressions softens, like she believes me, and the relief inside me is akin to joy.

"Can I tell you another secret? I mean, some of it's a secret, but not."

"Okay."

"I'm going to do this English project that's going to prove to the world that ghosts exist. I'm doing it for my dad. He doesn't see the ghosts, and I think it's because his mind isn't open to believing so I figure if I do my project on ghosts and prove to him that they're real, he'll see the ghosts, too."

"Can we show Sawyer your project when you're done?" Lucy asks. "I want him to believe, too."

"Sure. The more who believe, the merrier."

SAWYER

Thursday Jan. 3: Weight 119 Diary dear, I met a new fellow this morning, a friend of Sue's from Amsterdam. He's real nice looking . . . Oh dear, I want a letter from Jack. I certainly did miss him tonight. I've gained three pounds this week. Hope it keeps up. I sure have the blues tonight.

Mom collapses onto her mattress in the middle of her bedroom, and I lay a sheet over her. I only had time to put Lucy's bed frame together today. Mom's frame is first thing on the list tomorrow after she wakes. I place a towel near her head and one on the floor in case she's not done barfing then close her door behind me.

In the living room, our furniture is haphazardly placed in the middle and the mountains of boxes line the walls. With the lights on, the eerie sensation from earlier is gone, and I shake my head at myself for being whipped into a frenzy. I need more sleep, and so does Lucy. It'll help when we don't live in a two-hundred-year-old house, but we're months away from that reprieve.

I leave our apartment, climb the stairs and hesitate at the old wooden door. The muscles in my back tense with how terrible the last twenty-four hours have been and the torture isn't done yet. Two quick raps on the door and I hear footsteps on the other side.

The beep of buttons being pushed, a chain rattling as if it's being undone, a dead bolt being pulled, and then the knob rattles as I'm assuming that's also being unlocked, then the door only opens a crack.

And there's the pissed-off blue eyes I remember from earlier to-day. "Yes?"

Yes? Like it's a question as to why I knocked. "I'm here for Lucy."

The door squeaks as Veronica opens it wider. She watches me like she's a hawk and I'm a field mouse as I walk in. A fast survey of the room and I'm quick to jealousy. This place is a hundred times better than the dump downstairs. The walls are a sky blue, the trim a bright white, and the lighting from this century.

The entire floor is open. The kitchen is to the right of the door. Before me is a couch, a recliner, and a small flat-screen TV is mounted to the wall. To the left is a semicircular window seat in the turret along with an office area filled with a desk, a computer, bookshelves, filing cabinets and a piano.

On the couch is a sprawled-out lump covered with a blue velvet blanket. That lump is my sister, and she looks completely at peace with her eyes closed and little chest moving up and down in even breaths.

Veronica leans back against the counter in the kitchen and watches me. She's in cotton shorts and an oversized T-shirt that has Mickey Mouse on it. Her arms are crossed, and she's definitely not impressed with me.

"You should have left the chain on before you opened the door all the way to check who was knocking."

Veronica points one finger, and I follow to see a small television on the kitchen counter. The image is separated out into several shots, and one of the pictures is of the steps at her door.

Okay then. They have a security system. A fancy one at that. That's smart and makes me uneasy. Guess she'll have a nice view of our dysfunction for the next couple of months.

"Thanks for taking care of my sister." The sincerity is real, and the suck part is, I feel like I should be able to say more to Veronica, but I don't know what to say or how to say it. I shove my hands in my pockets because that's wrong. There's a lot to say, I just don't like saying it. "I'm sorry about what you overheard between me and my friends. It wasn't right and—"

"Thank you for the apology." Veronica cuts me off, and that brings me up short. As I helped my mom, I had come up with a plan, with a speech, and one part led to another part that was going to end with me somehow convincing Veronica to give us a few days until she cashed our deposit check, but she blew that plan to pieces.

Veronica continues to watch me. She's waiting for me to gather my sister and go, and that's exactly what I want to do, but I need to try and make life easier for my mom.

"I really do appreciate your help with Lucy, and I hate to do this, but I was wondering if it was possible for you to take a few days to cash the—"

"Just so I know how to handle this situation, does your mom have a problem with alcohol?"

"No." My answer is immediate, and Veronica tilts her head as if she doesn't believe me.

"Really? Because your sister said she gets sick on the weekends. I'm assuming 'sick'"—she uses quotation marks with her fingers—"is a loose term for the drunk I saw earlier."

"She has a few drinks with friends on the weekends. Sometimes they go out and have a few too many, but she never touches anything during the week." Why I feel the need to defend Mom, I don't know, especially when I'm pissed that I currently smell like vomit.

"Your mother's check bounced," Veronica says in an even voice.

My eyes briefly shut. Damn. "Does your dad know?"

"Not yet."

Can this girl give me anything or is she going to make me beg for everything? "We'll have the funds on the fifteenth." A week from now and that feels like a lifetime away. My brain races—I have a job as a lifeguard, but that's barely minimum wage and we haven't gone grocery shopping yet and Lucy needs school supplies and I'll start swimming again tomorrow and that means fees for the Y, for my coach, for the school league, for my outside swim league, for . . .

Her deadpan expression is one of the most paralyzing things I've come across, and I'm the guy who does death-defying feats.

"Do you have a car?" she asks, and I'm stunned as I try to understand why she'd ask that.

"Yes."

"Your sister is welcome in my part of the house whenever I'm home." It's unspoken that I'm not. "You have until next Friday to give me another check that won't bounce. You'll need to add forty dollars to cover the fees we incurred. If that check bounces, then I'll have no choice but to tell my dad. Not just about the check, but about what I saw here tonight."

She's dismissing me, but I'm stuck in place. "Please don't tell anyone about my mom." My tongue feels thick. "About the check or what you saw tonight. I get that you might have to tell your dad, but you won't as I'll get you the money. But if people find out . . . that would embarrass her." And me.

"I'm not the type who gossips. There's enough people in our town who like to say mean things so I figure no one needs my help in that department."

I wince. Message received loud and clear. She hates me. It's okay. I hate me, too.

"Thanks," I say again. "For Lucy." I walk over to the couch and gather my little sister in my arms.

"I'm curious," Veronica says, "about the diary you had at the TB hospital. Where did you find it?"

In my arms, Lucy's a hot, sweaty mess, yet snuggles closer to me. "I found it on the window seat of the front bedroom." This entire time I've been trying to break through Veronica's wall, and it's with that answer that there's a flicker of emotion other than hate. "I assumed it was from the last tenant. Is it yours? Do you want it back?"

Veronica looks over at the empty window seat of her living room and then back at me. "Are you reading it?"

When she says it like that, reading it seems wrong. Like I shouldn't be prying into someone's words—dead or alive.

"It's okay if you have. It's what it's there for."

I nod.

"Then keep it. For now at least. You can give it to me when you're done." Veronica opens the door, and I leave.

Mom woke up with a hangover, Lucy woke up whining about not being able to find her toys and each time they opened their mouths, my skin shrank. And it kept shrinking. To the point that my bones started to feel as if they were being crushed into dust.

I finally settled Lucy in front of the TV with two boxes of her things, Mom resting on the back porch with a thick novel, her sunglasses and sunscreen, and I got the hell out.

A quick doctor's appointment, my cast is off, I'm free and that's not a good thing.

The speedometer of my car rises higher and higher as I press harder on the gas. Rocks and dust fly behind me as I take the sharp curve too wide. It's a dirt road, one that was closed a few miles back. There were NO TRESPASSING signs. Many of them along the route. But I don't care. That only adds to the growing high.

At the top of the old rock quarry, I slam on the brakes and throw the car into park. I toss the keys onto the passenger seat and push open the driver's-side door. I rip my shirt over my head, take the shoes and socks off my feet and toss them and my wallet onto the seat.

I slam the car door shut and my pulse pounds in my ears as I stalk to the edge of the quarry. And that's where I find my zone. My toes hanging off the rock, pebbles that had shifted under my weight falling and plummeting to the water below.

The water below . . .

It's a safe jump, it's why I picked it. Forty feet. Not as many rocks in the water as other jumps. Forty feet. Safe. "Damn."

I run a hand through my hair, pulling at the strands to create pain, and force myself away from the edge. Safe. There's nothing safe about this. It's stupid. That's what it is. It's how I broke my arm.

I did a bad dive. I jumped at another quarry that was too high and into water that was too shallow. I almost drowned. I almost died.

"Dammit!" I yell, and my voice echoes along the walls of the empty quarry.

But I need this high. I want this high. I want to feel the surge of adrenaline in my veins as I step off the ledge. I love the way my stomach rises, how the wind rushes over my body, and the complete feeling of freedom as, for a few seconds, I'm flying. And then there's the hit. The pain of my body coming in contact with the water. The shock of the cold locking up my muscles. My lungs burning as I go deeper and then the panic as I fight for the surface. The moment of terror when I think I'm never going to taste air again and then the overwhelming feeling of triumph as I break through to the surface.

But I almost died.

                                                              Died.

But that was a higher jump. A more dangerous jump.
This jump isn't as high. It's safer.

                                                              Safer.

Mom's voice plays in my brain,
I'm sorry, Sawyer. I'm sorry.

                                        The sound of Lucy's screams.
The pure hate in Veronica's eyes.

                                                        How I fail.

At school.
At home.

                                        How I never meet expectations.

With friends.
With family.

                                                        With . . .

Swim, Math
English, Projects, Papers
Moving . . .

                                                        Bounced checks.

My father.

                         No control.

Out of control.

                         Spinning.

My muscles lock.

                         My head swims.

My blood runs hot.

                         Runs fast.

I'm boiling alive.

                         I need to cool off.

I need a release.

                         I need it.

I need.

                         Need.

I'm addicted.

                         Addicted.

And I hate myself for it.

                         Loathe.

I'm running. Toward the cliff and all the voices screaming in my head go silent as I take one step too many and jump feet-first into the abyss.

VERONICA

✍

My body hums with nervous energy. Leo is close, so close tonight. Maybe that means something. Maybe that means he's also feeling the weight of our time running short. Maybe he doesn't want to leave without saying and doing all the things that need to be said and done.

A few feet from us, Jesse's red hair sticks out from his sleeping bag and the rest of him is buried deep within the material. Nazareth, on the other hand, the guy who runs forever hot, is stretched out on top of his sleeping bag. His arms and legs tossed about during a restless sleep. The bonfire that was raging hours before has tapered off to a slow, glowing burn.

We're on Jesse's land, acres and acres from civilization. This place is like a second home to me. The stars above me, a blanket. The thick grass beneath me, pillows. Every inch of me smells of burning wood and of Leo. Tiny thrills run through me as I never want to smell of anyone else ever again.

It's very late at night. So late that I can almost taste the dew of dawn on the tip of my tongue. I typically love sunrises, but I never want this sun to rise. This is the night that needs to last forever. Tomorrow, today, Leo leaves.

Leo and I sit on his open and laid-flat sleeping bag, watching the dying fire. We sit tight, shoulder to shoulder, leg to leg. The air is heavy with moisture, warm from the summer, yet has the coolness of night. On our legs is the thin blanket I brought. My eyes are heavy from exhaustion, but there's no way I'm giving in to my body's urge for sleep. My desire to be with Leo is much stronger.

The only other downfall of the evening is my headache. It's an ache that keeps growing in intensity, but I do my best to ignore it. My brain is not going to ruin my last moments with Leo. But for the first time tonight, a spike of pain blasts through my skull. My hands shoot up, and I cradle my head.

"You okay?" Leo asks.

I force my hands down. "Yes."

Leo pops his knuckles, inches away from me and won't look me in the eye. My stomach sinks. Leo's nervous and it's over my pain. That's the one thing I would change about Leo if I could—he gets awkward whenever anything with my head is brought to attention.

I watch the fire and give Leo time to get over whatever goes on in his mind whenever my head aches. Fortunately, it doesn't take too long for Leo to reclaim his spot. When his bare skin touches mine, I close my eyes as I shiver with happiness.

"Can I ask you something?" Leo says.

Anything. "Sure."

"What's it like to have a brain tumor?"

My eyes snap open. Anything. He could have asked me anything, but he had to ask me that? Disappointment feels a lot like anger as I fall back onto the sleeping bag. I rub my eyes as they're watering. I could say it's from the bonfire smoke, but it's not. Leo, like always, breaks my heart.

I clear my throat, and when I finally peel my hands off my face, I find Leo lying on his side watching me. I don't know what it is Leo wants me to say. Besides doctors, he's one of the few people who know about my tumor and he knows all that anyone needs to know. Like bullet points, if I were to write about my tumor in my English journal:

- *I have a brain tumor.*

- *It's small and, since finding it, it has never grown.*

- *According to the doctors it's "harmless."*

- *It does give me migraines, but due to the location of the tumor, the doctors feel that surgery or any other course of treatment is a risk they aren't willing to take at the moment.*

- *Our course of treatment is called "watchful waiting," which means annual MRI scans.*

"My head hurts at times," I finally answer and do my best to sound lighthearted, "but other than that, I don't know it's there."

Leo looks past me and into the night. His eyes are red, remnants of the many beers he had earlier this evening. "That's not what I mean. Do you wonder if what happened to your mom will happen to . . ."

Me.

Leo trails off and it's like he stabbed me with a knife. The pain in my chest is worse than the one in my head.

"Yes," I say as a hoarse whisper. "I wonder."

My mother's tumor was malignant. Mine is benign. My mother died, and I'm still alive. The wound of her loss is still fresh, and I don't like discussing her tumor or how she died. I swallow to help the tightening of my throat. "But I also know that what happened to Mom won't happen to me."

I won't allow it.

"Because your tumor is different?" Leo asks.

Is mine different? "Yes." Is that why it won't happen to me? No.

Before Mom died we had very long talks. Deep discussions about her choices, my choices and how I was free to choose the same path or a different path from hers *if* my tumor changed from something benign to something disastrous.

My mom's demise was long and torturous. In return for more time, she gave in to a life stuck in bed in the hospital. It's what my dad wanted. It's what he begged her to do. It's what he would expect me to do, and I don't want it. Not now. Not ever.

I'm not an idiot. I'm quite aware that seeing my mother's ghost may signal a change in my tumor, but then again, does it? Our house is haunted. Like Lucy, when I was younger, I also saw a child in the first-floor bedroom. For years, I've heard the footsteps, the cries, and the laughter.

My mother loved me, and she loved my dad. Is it too much of a stretch to think she'd stick around to make sure that the loves of her life are okay?

Besides seeing Mom, there have been no other changes. My headaches and migraines are the same. There have been no other physical signs or symptoms from the telltale list I memorized since being diagnosed at eleven: dizziness, tingling, problems with sight, numbness or seizures.

If I tell Dad about Mom, I'll be in a hospital so fast I'll suffer from whiplash. Dad will quit his job, he'll watch me twenty-four/ seven and he'll ruin both of our lives. And then I'll be just like Mom—I'll die in a hospital, filled with every possible poison to fight the cancer.

My next MRI is in June. If my tumor has grown, Dad will find out then, but I have almost a year between now and then to live life completely.

"The only reason this world has anything redeemable in it is because of you," Leo says. "Promise you'll never stop being you, V."

"As long as you promise to not forget me while you're away."

"I could never forget you." But his eyes are sad, as if he's already grieving me—because he's leaving, because when he looks at me he only sees my tumor and my impending death.

"I don't care for a lot of people," Leo says softly, with an expression that I must misread. One that suggests, as his eyes linger on my lips, that he'd like to kiss me. I'd love for him to kiss me, but what I'd really love is for him to love me. "But I care for you."

Cares. Not loves, but the way he looks at me, as if I'm the most desirable girl in the world, softens the blow.

We've done it—kissed before. It's a game Leo and I have played many times over the years, and each time the rules keep changing. He leans in, kisses me, my heart explodes and then he runs. Far and fast. Making us friends again until he, once more, takes a risk on me.

Leo reaches over and his fingers graze my cheek. Just a whisper of a movement that causes my heart to stutter. Kiss me, Leo. Please, kiss me.

But he rips his gaze away, sits back up again and his face hardens as he stares at the fire. I'm left cold and empty.

"Maybe, next year, when you leave town and go to college," he sputters out, and while his words don't make sense, I understand what's happening. He's running again. ". . . maybe you'll go to my college . . . maybe . . ."

"Maybe," I whisper.

"I hate that you're sick."

He had given me the gift of his touch then snatched it back so quickly that he left an emotional scrape. "I'm not sick." Not as long as I don't tell Dad and end up weak and puking in a hospital bed.

"You know what I mean. I hate your tumor."

Me, too, and I hate that it keeps him from loving me. I wonder what life would be like if I didn't have a tumor or if I had the presence of mind in middle school, way before I fell for Leo, to never have told him about the foreign entity in my brain. Would we be kissing right now? Would I have lost my virginity to him? Would we have gone to dances together and have pictures of each other up on our bedroom walls of us locked in an embrace? Would he be currently holding my hand, holding me close, whispering that he loves me?

But I did tell him and that was the right thing to do. It would be unfair and selfish of me to allow someone to fall in love with me when my forever won't last nearly as long as theirs. And once they know the truth, no one in their right mind would fall in love with someone like me, and I don't blame them.

I force myself to sit up next to Leo, and this time, I'm the one who makes sure there's distance between us. Leo's still stewing, but then he brightens as if he found the answer to our problem. Unless he's figured out how to wrangle a miracle, there's no solution.

"In a few weeks, you, Jesse and Nazareth should visit me. I'll want everyone to meet my best friends."

Best friends is all I can ask for from him, and that hurts. "That'd be great."

"It will be epic."

But I'm not holding on to the epic visit as a friend. I'm holding desperately on to his faint promises of *maybe*.

SAWYER

Thursday Jan. 10: Weight 118 lb. Cured 4 hours today. Isn't that great?

I'm starting to drink milk again, because I lost this week. That will <u>never</u> do.

Wrote to Maidy today. Hope somebody hurries up and writes to me. I'd like to get some mail.

Had cocoa this afternoon, but ate a big supper anyway.

Frank came over tonight, and played cards with Sadie, Carolyn and myself. I s'pose he'll ask me to sit with him at the movies. I wish he wouldn't, then maybe I'd get a chance to sit with Mr. K. Wish I could.

Reading comes slow for me so I don't read unless forced, but something about this diary has drawn me in. Each entry is short, simple, but says so much. What Evelyn often wished for and her reality were two different things.

That I get.

So much was happening to her—sixteen, diagnosed with TB, sent to live in a sanatarium to "cure," which meant lying outside in a bed for hours. She tried to create a life there—friends, boyfriends, jobs . . . But I can't help but wonder, did she feel trapped?

I do.

Often.

Most of the time, my life makes me feel as if I'm trapped inside a nailed-shut coffin that's already been buried six feet deep, and I'm running out of air. I'm not trapped in the ground, but I am in the school library with my headphones in so I can block out the world. Though I shouldn't feel like I'm suffocating, when I suck in a deep breath, my lungs don't inflate all the way.

Today is the first day of school, and after picking up my schedule, I discovered I'm in AP English. I can't read worth a damn, and I'm in AP English. When I tried talking to my counselor, she told me to talk to my mom. That answer was the equivalent of someone taking a chainsaw to my leg.

Mom is like a snowball that's thrown at a mountain teetering on an avalanche. She tries to "fix" my life, without my consent, and ends up burying me in more problems. I'm terrified to ask her what she's done now. My fingers tap against the table, my knee starts to bounce. The muscles in my neck tighten, and I'm swamped with the need to jump.

My cell pings and Coach's words are read to me through the text-to-talk app: Great job at practice yesterday! Keep up the good work! Make school a priority this year. Remember the state title is the goal!

Since breaking my arm, I had been doing physical therapy to keep in shape. Yesterday was my first day in the pool. I didn't clock my best time, but I did beat some guys on my team. Swimming is natural for me, just like breathing and jumping off cliffs.

Another ping. Mom: Are you sure our landlord is okay with the bounced check? People usually aren't that nice.

Yeah, I agree, but the girl who thinks I'm trash is that nice. Me: AP English?

Mom: Sylvia and Miguel agreed to work together so you can join their group. This way you'll get a good grade in the class.

Agreed . . . so you can join . . . like I'm a charity case. I roll my neck to help ease the tension, but it doesn't work. The same thought circles my brain—jump, jump, jump, jump, jump.

But I don't want to jump. I promised myself I wouldn't do it again. Not after this weekend. But then the idea of feeling that rush again . . .

God, I've got to stop. But how do I?

A slamming of a hand on the table, and I flinch. My right earbud falls out of my ear, and I press pause on the music I had been trying to lose myself in.

"I saw your schedule and you and I are in the same English class. Because of that, you're going to be my partner for the senior thesis paper." Veronica stands in front of me, glaring. If I hadn't seen her smile with her friends, I'd think her expression was set on permanently pissed. Evidently, that look is reserved for me.

A quick scan of the mostly empty room, and no one is paying attention to us. The few other people in here are lost on their phones or asleep. The bell to head to first period won't ring for another five minutes. Most of my friends are hanging out in the cafeteria, but I wasn't in the mood to pretend I'm in a good mood when I'm not.

Veronica is in blue jeans that are more tears than material and layered underneath are black lace tights. Her black T-shirt with the name of a death metal band on the front has been cut so that it hangs precariously off one shoulder. Beneath her shirt is a spaghetti-strapped, black lace tank top. It's a sexy look not one other girl at this school would dare to rock.

"How did you see my schedule?"

"I rooted through the stack on the secretary's desk until I found it. She was making copies at the time."

Wow.

She plops down in the seat in front of me and tilts her head as if she's waiting for me to speak, which I guess she is, but I'm not sure what to say. My family and I currently have a roof over our heads because of her, and the last thing I want to say is no. But what she doesn't understand is that my life is complicated. "I don't think you want to work with me."

She bobs her head like she agrees, and I don't know why, but I find her honesty amusing. I take out my other earbud and slide back in my seat.

"You're right, I don't. I don't like you, you don't like me, but since I'm not allowed to work by myself, I figured we should work together."

This I have to hear. "Why me?"

"One, we live in the same house so it will be easy to meet up. Two, you have a car and I don't. This paper requires a lot of research and personal interviews, which means travel."

"You can do research online and the interviews over the phone."

For the first time, at least in my direction, Veronica's eyes spark with joy and that draws me in. "Not for what we're doing our paper on. We'll need firsthand experience."

"Yeah? What's the topic?"

Veronica leans forward, and she's absolutely hypnotizing. "Ghosts. Do they exist?"

Is she kidding? "Ghosts?"

"Ghosts."

Damn. She's serious. "Why ghosts?"

She falls back in her chair. "For starters, the house we live in is haunted."

"There's no such things as ghosts."

Veronica offers me a slow daring grin like she knows secrets I don't. "You'll change your mind after living there a few weeks."

Sure. As much as I've enjoyed this conversation, there's still a reality to this situation. "While that sounds interesting, I meant what I said before. You don't want to work with me."

"Why?"

I drum my fingers against the table and a million plausible reasons flood my brain as to why she wouldn't want to work with me. My instability—my addiction to jumping off high cliffs—that nobody knows about is a good reason for her to ditch me, but the truth—that my mother has different expectations—isn't what I want to admit.

I could snatch any reason, give it to her with a full dose of bull, but it doesn't feel right. Not for the person who helped my sister when she was in need. Not for the person who is letting the bounced check slide.

The longer I take, that spark that was there before fades and that's a shame. Veronica pushes away from the table and stands. "Screw it. I'll save you the burden of having to say no to me because I'm too weird to work with. Weird, right? Isn't that what you and your friends said?"

Dammit. "Wait."

But Veronica is fast, very fast, and I'm out of my seat chasing her. "Veronica!"

She's close to the doors of the library and if she gets into the hallway, I'll lose her for sure. "Veronica, wait!"

Last second, so abruptly that I almost run into her, she spins on her heels. "What?"

"I have a form of dyslexia."

Veronica's face twists up like I told her there's a rabbit popping out of my ass. "So?"

So? "When it comes to reading, researching and writing papers, it takes me longer. Is that what you want to deal with when working with a partner on this project?"

Her anger slips away as she gives me a slow assessment. A look down and a look up. "Of all the things that could or ever would bother me, that's not one of them."

There are hundreds of voices in my head. All of them always talking at the same time, but for a brief few seconds the voices stop. Silenced because whenever I tell someone this truth, they're uncomfortable. It's not a secret, I've never kept it a secret as the dyslexia is a part of me. Like the way I was born with my eye color. Some people don't know how to handle something different. But this girl doesn't even blink.

Wonder what she'd say if I told her I jumped off of cliffs for a high? Internally, I chuckle. She'd probably help by pushing me off the edge. "Ghosts? That's a research paper?"

"Yes."

"I have to get a good grade in this class to help my GPA or I can't swim. Researching ghost stories sounds like the easiest route to an F."

"The way I see it, you owe me, and I won't hold that over your head to work with me, but I will ask you to take me to one of the places I want to research this weekend. If you don't want to do the paper with me after our visit, fine."

I do owe her, and if she wants me to drive her someplace as a thank-you, I'll do it. "Sure, but that doesn't mean I'm doing the paper with you."

Veronica snatches my cell from my hand, and with a few quick swipes and taps, she enters her number into my cell then hands it back. "We have until Monday to decide groups, and I have a feeling you'll choose me." Then she's out the door.

I follow and watch as she glides down the hallway. Her blond curls bounce near her shoulders, her hips have a gentle sway as she walks. The girl is gorgeous, sexy, mesmerizing, and has the biggest, brightest personality I've ever encountered.

In a world where most doesn't impress me, I'm impressed.

VERONICA

I'm the last person out of school as I had to stop twice to puke in the bathroom. I hate migraines. Hate them. I once had a teacher tell me that *hate* was a bad word. I agree. It is a bad word and so is the word *migraine*.

I step outside, and the sunlight is like a demon sent from hell to torture me. I shield my eyes using my hand, and my heart soars that I don't have to walk home. Leaning against the hood of his Chevy Impala, Nazareth waits for me in the student parking lot. I never asked for him to come for me, yet I knew he'd be there waiting because that's how Nazareth is.

With my backpack dragging from my fingertips, I stop in front of him and barely have the energy to lift my head to look him in the eyes. He doesn't ask how I am, nor does he ask where I want to go. His gaze flickers over my face, and it's as if he understands all that's happening beneath my skin—the normal exhaustion of school, the ugly pit in my stomach at being alone after he left, including and especially lunch, and then the pièce de résistance, the typical first day of school category-five migraine that causes blood-draining nausea.

With an incline of his head toward the passenger side, I slide into his car, lean my head against the window and close my eyes. Nazareth doesn't turn on music, nor does he say a word. He just drives, letting me rest. The headache, though, becomes worse instead of better. My stomach churns, and I try to focus on my breaths to keep from vomiting on the floorboard.

The car eventually stops, and when I open my eyes, the sunlight is so bright that I'm temporarily blinded. Still, I slip out of the car and follow Nazareth to the aging, tiny blue farmhouse. My head feels as if it is a lead ball and my feet move as if there are one-hundred-pound weights attached to them.

Nazareth opens the back door of his house for me. The hinges squeak, the sound like a jackhammer to my skull. The world tunnels, and the darkness in the periphery of my sight starts to close in on me. I stop at the bottom of the steps as I refuse to go any farther.

"You always have permission to enter my house," Nazareth says, and that gives me the okay I need. One should always be careful who they invite into a house because once you give death permission, you've lost the battle and the war.

"Why are you friends with me?" I don't quite understand why the question has tumbled out, yet it has. It's like I've lost control. "I mean—other people don't want to be my friend, so . . . why?"

"Because you're you and I'm me. We work. Plus you've never asked who my real dad is or why Mom and I moved here nor will you ever. You take me exactly as I am. Nothing more. Nothing less."

He's never told me that before. "Jin is your real dad."

Nazareth gives me one of his rare grins. It hurts my heart because while it's sweet, it's also sad. "Go in before you pass out."

Inside the tiny kitchen, my stomach flips when the smell of something cooking on the stove hits me wrong. All sounds drown out thanks to the roaring in my ears. I waver on my feet, then there are hands on my face. Nazareth's mom's kind, dark eyes bore into mine, and while I can't hear what she's saying, I can read her lips. *Will food make you sick?*

I nod.

Like she's a faded voice of a not-quite-tuned-in radio station, I barely make out the *Let's make you feel better and get you to bed. I grew a plant just for you.*

Greer takes my hand and leads me out the front door to her garden house. There I sit at the picnic table she uses to pot and repot her flowers and plants. On the opposite side of the table from me is Nazareth. He's hard at work placing dried leaves onto a rolling paper. Once done, he rolls the paper into a thin strip then licks the edges to seal it shut.

Nazareth stands, grabs a lighter from the top of a shelf that's filled with tons of potted plants, most of them spices, and he straddles the bench I'm on to sit beside me. He lights the joint, sucks in a few puffs then gently blows the smoke in my direction. Nazareth doesn't hold his breath in the search for the high. Instead, he continues to inhale and release until I'm surrounded by a cloud.

I close my eyes and breathe in the oddly sweet scent. There's a light pressure on my hand and I crack open my eyes enough to take the joint from Nazareth. I put it to my lips, suck in and hold the smoke for so long that my lungs might explode. I shake my head to help hold it a bit longer then let it out in a fast stream and pray that the high comes fast and it comes strong.

The sound of a door opening causes me to roll over in Nazareth's bottom bunk bed. I open my heavy lids and lift my head. My sleep was deep and peaceful, and my limbs are gloriously lazy. Unruly red hair pokes into the room. It's Jesse. He holds a cell to his ear, and whispers, "Yeah, she's here. V, it's your dad."

The room is dark thanks to the heavy curtains, and I glance over at the digital clock on the dresser. It's seven and my head drops back onto the pillow. Dad. I forgot to call Dad. I reach out my arm and wiggle my fingers in a "gimme."

"Hold on." Jesse looks guilty as he walks in and hands me the phone. "Sorry for waking you, but he was worried. Just hearing you were here wasn't enough."

"Don't be sorry." My voice is thick with sleep. "I want to talk to him." I should have called him earlier or at least had Nazareth text him, but I couldn't think beyond my pain. Odds are my cell is still in my backpack on the floorboard of Nazareth's car.

Jesse leaves, and I stretch as I place Jesse's cell to my ear. "Hey, Dad."

"Hey." The concern rolls off his voice in waves. "How are you doing, peanut?"

"Better."

"Migraine?"

"Yeah."

"A bad one?"

"Yeah." One of the worst. "I was able to get through school, though. Nazareth picked me up and brought me to his house. Sorry I didn't call, but I crashed as soon as I got here."

Dad's silent for a few beats as he knows that means I smoked pot. The migraine medication my doctor prescribed doesn't put a dent into my bad migraines, and when Dad told the doctor this, the other rounds of medication prescribed had terrible side effects or tore holes in my stomach. Maybe not literally, but it sure felt like it.

While my father admittedly smoked pot when he was a teen, and he knows that smoking pot can help with the symptoms of my migraine, he's still a dad. The years of having it shoved down his throat that drugs are bad and you're an even worse parent if you allow your kid to do drugs, makes him feel like crap. Doesn't help that anything involving me weighs on him like he's holding the entire universe.

So the two of us have an agreement—I only smoke when the migraine is tearing me apart and I tell him the truth when I do smoke up.

"Tell Jesse I'm sorry for calling him, but I tried contacting Nazareth and . . . well . . ." Dad trails off.

Nazareth didn't answer, and he didn't call Nazareth's parents because no one has their numbers except their children. Even if Dad had their numbers, they wouldn't answer. While Nazareth isn't as disconnected from the world as his parents are, he still isn't the type who follows social rules. He only carries his cell when he wants to, it's often on silent when he does have it on him, and he has a habit of not checking it for days.

"I'm sorry," I say. "I didn't mean to worry you."

"I know. It's okay. Can you do me a favor?"

"Anything." Especially after worrying him.

"I want you to start keeping track of your migraines on the calendar in the kitchen and number them from one to ten for your pain level. They seem to be coming faster."

My lips squish to the side as Dad on high alert isn't going to fit into my plans. While I'm hiding the presence of Mom's ghost from him, I won't lie to him about my migraines. I promised Dad and my mom I'd always be truthful to him about that. "Okay."

"If you're having too many, I'll ask the doctor to bump up your MRI."

I hold the cell away as that idea causes my eyes to water. I don't like going to the doctor, having MRIs, having twenty gallons of my blood drawn and being held captive under a microscope, and I also hate how Dad has to rearrange his life for this nonsense.

"I'm okay. It's the first day, and you know I'm always like this at the start of school. Give me a few weeks and I'll be normal again." Normal for me.

"I know, but you can't blame me for worrying."

I can't, and I hate that he worries.

"Was it a good day?"

Nope. "I'm making a new friend." Blackmailing Sawyer into helping me. Same thing.

"Good. Listen, I'm driving, and Jesse said Greer made some soup for you. I'm going to get off so you can eat. Text me to let me know if you go home or if you decide to stay there."

"I will. I love you, Dad."

"Love you, too." Dad hangs up, and I rub the wetness and exhaustion from my eyes. It's going to be okay. I'm going to be okay.

I'm not going to get sick like Mom, and I'm not going to end up in a hospital hooked to a machine that breathes for me. Nor will Dad have to make the decision to take me off so I can finally die.

I glance around at Nazareth's narrow, attic bedroom he shares with three of his siblings. The room is simple: two bunk bed sets pushed against the wall and each bed is covered by a quilt Greer made for each of her boys. Nazareth's section of the dresser is littered with guitar picks and books, and in his corner of the room are three guitar cases.

Pushing back the heavy curtain of the small window, I spot the sun setting along the rolling green hills. Nazareth's family owns a small farm, not even close to the size of Jesse's farm, but about thirty acres. They grow their own food in a large garden and have chickens, pigs, goats, two cows and three horses.

Greer's voice drifts from the kitchen. "Jesse, I think you should turn your farm into a farmer's market—like a pick-your-own-vegetables-and-fruit type place. You could bring in schools for field trips and teach them the importance of organic farming."

"It's a thought," Jesse answers, which means, no way in hell, but he likes Greer so he's respectful.

A bit foggy from the pot, I'm cautious going down the stairs, and when I step onto the first floor, I look to the left to find the living room that's filled with desks for homeschooling. I then look right for the dining room and find Jesse sitting at the long wooden picnic table. Long enough that it easily sits ten people. Jesse feasts on a bowl of soup and a hunk of homemade bread. My stomach rumbles, and Jesse looks up as if he heard it.

"Hey, V."

I hand back his phone. "Dad said he's sorry he made you find me."

"No worries. It would help if someone actually used his phone." He gives a side-eye to Nazareth who is in a chair in the middle of the kitchen.

In jeans, Nazareth has his shirt off and his mother buzz cuts the sides of his hair. There is a new tattoo on his muscled chest, and I'm curious what the significance of that one is. But odds are he won't spill. Something haunts Nazareth and not something kind like my mom. Even with a demon who hounds him, he's still the gentlest person I know.

Nazareth raises an eyebrow at Jesse's comment then lifts the right side of his mouth.

"I'm not a hypocrite," Jesse mutters, and I laugh. Jesse is also terrible at answering his texts.

As his mother continues to trim his hair, Nazareth cradles a baby rabbit in his arms and is feeding it with a syringe. The sight warms my heart. There's no one else in the world who loves the world around him as he does. "Where did you find this one?"

"In Jesse's field," Nazareth says, and I look over to Jesse for him to finish the story as Nazareth isn't into filling in blanks.

Jesse puts down his spoon to butter a slice of bread. "He heard the cries and found it. It looks like a coyote got ahold of the mom and the rest of the litter. Besides being scared, this one seemed untouched."

In the high chair, Nazareth's little sister, Ziva, bangs her tiny fingers against the tray and squeals. She's a cutie with her mother's nose and smile, and like the rest of her full brothers and sisters, she has her father's Chinese features. Jin obviously isn't Nazareth's biological father, but they love each other as if they were flesh and blood.

Greer sets down the clippers on the island in the kitchen, hands Ziva a sippy cup, then heads to the stove. I love this home. With the rustic feel, tons of plants and herbs living in pots on the shelves and hanging from the ceiling to dry, this place is warm and welcoming.

Nazareth's mom walks back toward the picnic table, places a bowl of chicken soup on the table across from Jesse as well as several slices of bread so hot it has steam. She settles her authoritative yet kind gaze on me. "Can you eat?"

"Yes."

"Then sit and eat, and I expect you to eat it all. You need some good food in you instead of that frozen stuff you always eat. It's a wonder you all don't have migraines with the amount of preservatives you put in your bodies on a daily basis." She tilts her head as she examines me. "How are you feeling, sweetheart?"

Greer is beautiful. There are no other words to describe her. Even with her chestnut hair in a ponytail, even in worn jeans and a blue T-shirt that has a spit-up stain on the shoulder, even with no makeup—she's movie-star gorgeous.

"Better." My favorite non-answer. "Thank you for the food."

"You're welcome."

I sit like she commanded, and the first bite of the homemade soup is like heaven. Anything Greer makes is from scratch and typically grown on this farm—meat included.

Nazareth is the oldest of seven children living in a three-bedroom farmhouse. If he didn't have so many siblings, Jesse and I would live here. Literally. Well, then again, maybe not. Neither Jesse nor I want to live with Nazareth's mom. She's great, but a little overzealous in her homeopathic beliefs. Plus, on the scale that includes Tarzshay to designer, Nazareth's parents would be considered dollar-store drug dealers.

They don't grow an exuberant amount of pot, nor do they sell to many people. They only sell to people like me, for medical reasons (since I'm considered family, I'm never charged). Then they also grow stuff for themselves that has a bit of a kick.

If maybe Nazareth only had three siblings, we'd be here every night for dinner, but there are nine people in this family living in this small house so we don't hang here much. Which makes my slow mind catch up. "Where is everyone?"

"Because the boys thought it would be smart to prank me with putting crickets in my bathtub, they're mucking out the stalls while Jin took the girls horseback riding. We wanted to make sure you got some rest."

My cheeks burn that the entire family would rearrange their schedule to let me sleep.

"How was school?" she asks.

"Okay. I think I found someone to work on my senior project with me."

"Who?" Jesse asks.

"Sawyer Sutherland."

Except for Ziva's baby babble, Greer's scissors clipping away at the dead ends of Nazareth's longer hair on the top of his head and my scooping a spoon into my soup, there's silence. I look up to catch Nazareth and Jesse staring at each other in that pensive way of theirs that means they don't agree with my decisions.

"I don't remember asking your opinion," I say to them.

"What am I missing?" Greer asks.

"Sawyer Sutherland . . ." Jesse starts but then flicks a glance at me. "He's one of those rich, popular guys at school."

"Uh-huh." Greer flips Nazareth's longer hair from one side to another. She stares at it as if in contemplation, then obviously satisfied with the results, she pats Nazareth's shoulder to let him know she's done. "Why is this a problem for the two of you?"

Greer has a stern stare for Nazareth as he stands. His only response is a shrug as he rolls his strong shoulders back. The body language is clear—there is a decent reason, but he's not telling. She then throws the same expression in Jesse's direction, and he yanks his baseball cap on as if to hide.

"Sawyer and his crew talk crap about me," I say to save my friends from the third degree.

"This boy talks bad about you, yet you want to work with him and he's agreed to work with you?" Greer asks.

"It's complicated."

"Can you handle him if he gets out of line?"

"Are you asking if I can kick him in the balls?"

Greer grins. "Yes, and can you handle it if he continues to talk badly about you?"

I've been handling people talking trash about me since moving here. It hurts, but I can deal with it so I nod.

"Then you boys need to trust her judgment." Greer grabs three open notebooks and pens. She tosses one in front of me, one to Jesse and the other to the spot next to me and gestures for Nazareth to sit. "The three of you—you're seventeen and you act as if you're forty. This is your last year before the world forces you to be adults, and I want you to write down all your hopes and dreams for the year. Then we're going to head out to the bonfire, talk about them and then place them in the fire to be freed into the universe so it can help."

Nazareth's head drops as we all walk into his family's weekly feelings bonfire. He hates it, but I think it's fun. Jesse starts to stand. "Scarlett is going to be calling soon, and I need to get some work done on the farm before she calls so I'll—"

"Sit, Jesse," Greer demands, and he sits.

"I'm eighteen already, and I graduated. I'm adulting. Daily."

"True, but you're still doing this."

I smile, Jesse scowls and Nazareth places the baby rabbit in a box cushioned with towels then pulls a T-shirt over his head before taking a seat at the picnic table. Jesse will write something about his farm and spending time with his girlfriend, Scarlett. Nazareth will either write down the preamble to the Constitution or write out a bunch of the numbers to pi, but I embrace the moment for what it is.

Dad's correct—my migraines are getting worse and there's a sinking in my stomach that the next MRI will mean a fight between me and him. If I only have a few more months of living, I need to live it right.

I write the number one on my paper and make a list of everything I need to do as soon as I possibly can.

SAWYER

The required health class I took my freshman year talked about this meeting when we went over the unit on addictions, and I'm here on a Hail Mary pass. Or I'm here because I've officially lost my mind. Both. I'm here for both reasons.

With my arms crossed and my legs stretched out, I'm slumped in the seat that's the farthest from the podium of an AA meeting in a town thirty minutes from mine. People stand and talk about alcohol, drinking and being thirsty. I don't have the same problems they have. There's no substance I crave in my veins to keep my motor running, but I do have this itch to jump. Ten miles down the road from this place is a nice drop into a pool of water. I was heading in that direction, but then guilt got the better of me. So here I am, in a room I don't belong in because if I leave, I will literally jump off a cliff.

If anything, I'm hoping the meeting will last long enough that it will be too dark for me to jump and that will force me home. But I still want to jump . . .

School sucked. Miguel and Sylvia didn't act shocked to see me in English, which makes me think I'm on the losing end of discussions about me. Swim practice went well, but then Coach started talking about his hopes for me and that sucked. Mom's work meeting ran late and she forgot to pick Lucy up from school and then Lucy called me in tears. That definitely sucked.

My muscles under my skin tighten, and I shift uncomfortably in the chair. I should have gone to the cliff. It's not a bad jump. One I've done before. The high dive at the Y is taller than the cliff. The jump is safe even. Not a big deal. Yeah, there're rocks everywhere and there're unseen ones under the surface, but—

"Hey."

I glance up, startled to find a guy about the same age as me, maybe a few years older. He's in jeans that sag, a white T-shirt that's too big, and there are blue Converse on his feet. His blond shaggy hair makes me think he's a surfer from California. "Hey."

"First time?" he asks.

"Yeah." I scan the room and people are standing around, chatting in groups. I must have missed the ending of the meeting.

He takes the seat next to me. "Do you have any questions?"

How do I ignore the urge to jump from cliffs? Even better, can you tell me how to kill the urge altogether? "No."

"You sure?"

I clear my throat then rake a hand through my hair. "I don't think I belong here."

He tilts his head like he hears what I'm not saying. "Yet you're here."

Yet I am.

"I'm Knox."

"Sawyer."

"Nice to meet you, brother." He even has a slow way of talking that reminds me of a stereotypical surfer, but considering we're hundreds of miles away from an ocean I find that unlikely. "I had about a dozen first meetings before I had the balls to actually talk to someone. Even after that, I needed time to sit in the back and soak in everyone else's words. If you need this to be one of those first meetings or if you need time, I'll let you have your space, but if you need to talk to someone, I'm here."

About a dozen first meetings sounds good. A hundred sound even better, but . . . "What if I don't belong here?"

"I haven't met anyone yet who doesn't belong here. I started coming when I was sixteen, and I've been sober for five years. When I first started coming I didn't think I belonged, either. All these people coming in and talking about broken hearts, loss of control and mistakes? I remember thinking that I wasn't one of those fools, until one day I realized I wasn't one of them—I was worse."

That I get. I'm hesitant, but why not? It's not like I'm coming back, and it's not like I'll ever see him again. "How do you stop doing what you crave when it's all you think about?"

"I come here. I work the program. I call my sponsor when the craving hits, and I take it one day at a time."

Sounds stupid. "I really don't think this is for me."

My response doesn't ruffle him in the slightest. "Fair enough, but I do think you're wrong. If you change your mind, I hope to catch you here again."

We both stand. He turns away, but then says over his shoulder, "Don't answer me this, but to yourself. I hear what you're saying about this place not being your thing, but if you weren't here, what would you be doing right now?"

He walks from me then, leaving me rooted in place because it's scary how he read me when I didn't think I was readable.

If I wasn't here, I'd be jumping.

VERONICA

Leo: What the hell are you doing? Sawyer Sutherland?

It's Friday night—my favorite day of the week. Dad will be home later tonight, and tomorrow we'll have waffles. I should be riding the impending waffle high, but I'm having to deal with an angry Leo. He hasn't texted me once since leaving for college and when he does reach out, it's because he's pissed. Lovely.

I don't have to ask Leo how he knows about Sawyer. The next time I see Jesse and Nazareth I'm going to deep fry them both. Me: Why is this a problem?

The irony of the situation is that I'm riding shotgun in Sawyer's Lexus. Lexus. The check for his rent bounced, yet he drives a Lexus. How does that quite work?

Anyhow, we're on the way to our first interview for the project, and I can't decide if I prefer a ticked-off Leo or the stoic silence of Sawyer.

Leo: The guy is a jackass. He ignores you for years and his friends talk crap about you. I know these types of guys, V, and he's no good for you.

I stretch my fingers as I want to throttle him. Me: I'm doing great. Thanks for asking. How's college?

It takes him longer to respond, and I can't decide if I like that I threw him off or if I'm uneasy that I might have pushed him over the edge. I glance over at Sawyer, and he quickly looks away, playing it off like he wasn't watching. "Where do I turn?"

"Right on Cedar Avenue. The house we want is the third one on the left."

Sawyer drums his fingers on the steering wheel. "And who is this guy again?"

"A ghost hunter." If I was going to grow up, I think that would be a fascinating job.

"You told me, but how do you know him?"

"He's a family friend."

"Of course he is," Sawyer mumbles, and I choose to ignore his sarcasm.

Leo: I just got done texting with Jesse and he said you needed a partner for the senior paper. I'll call Jenna and Marie. You can work with them.

Like I need someone making playdates on my behalf, and those two were whispering about me in math. Me: Do it and I'll drop kick you into next week.

Leo: They're better than Sutherland.

Me: My life, Leo. Not yours. If you were honestly so concerned, I would think you would have contacted me before now.

I drop my phone into my lap and ignore it when it chimes. Then when it chimes again. Two stop signs later, there's another chime. Sawyer peeks at me from the corner of his eye. My cell then rings, and as much as I want to hear Leo's voice, I really do not want to have this conversation with him.

After five rings, there's silence and then my cell starts ringing again. Annoyance rushes through me, and I angrily accept the call. "What?"

"Don't be mad."

My eyes close at the sound of Leo's voice, and there's an ache inside me with how much I miss him. "I'm not."

"You are. I know I'm a bastard for not keeping in touch, but

things have been busy between classes, working a job and then getting to know people. College is different from high school. By the
time I have a moment to text, I know it's too late and I don't want
to wake you. I promise I'll do better."

Nothing from me.

"This whole Sawyer thing has made me realize how much of a
jerk I'm being. I'm concerned about you. I don't want you getting
screwed over by some guy because I wasn't there to help. I care
about you, V, and I'm worried."

Sawyer looks straight ahead, but there's no way he's not listening.
One, I'm right beside him. Two, I totally would eavesdrop. "I know."

"Short answers. Does that mean you're at work?"

No. "Yeah."

"I'll call later and we can talk."

"Not about this."

Tense silence on his end. "Fine, but I'm calling." More silence. "I
miss you, V. Life's weird without you."

I soften, and a bit overwhelmed, I fiddle with the hem of my
skirt. "Okay. Thanksgiving is September twenty-ninth. You're still
coming, right?" It's the day Leo picked before he left.

"I told you before I left I would. I'd never break a promise to you."

"Okay."

"I miss you."

I miss him more. "Same. I'll talk to you later tonight."

"Later." He hangs up.

Sawyer takes the right onto Cedar. "Everything okay?"

"Why wouldn't it be?"

He shrugs one of his massive shoulders. "I don't know. You
sounded off."

"You know me well enough to figure out when I sound off?"

"I guess not." Another drum of his fingers against the steering
wheel. "You celebrate Thanksgiving in September?"

"Yep."

Sawyer doesn't call me strange, but it's painted all over his face.

He turns into the driveway of the correct house and cuts the engine. The house is one of those brick ranches with two huge trees in the front yard. I dig my notebook and a pen out of my backpack as well as the folder that has the thick packet of information for the project. "You ready?"

"Sure." I wonder if he eats sarcasm for breakfast so he can vomit so much of it during the day.

We leave the car, walk up to the stoop and after only one ring of the bell, Max opens the door. He has a welcoming smile when he sees me, and I hug him. "Max, this is Sawyer. Sawyer this is Max. He's a good friend of my dad's. Max is a ghost hunter."

Dad and Max have beers together on Fridays and play poker together once a month.

"I'm actually an accountant, but I like doing some ghost hunting on the side." Max shakes Sawyer's hand, and anxiety twists my muscles. Max needs to say the words, he needs to invite me in and I breathe out in relief when he says, "Come in, come in."

Needing to be invited into someone's home is one of my many quirks.

The only place to sit is the couch built for two and a recliner. Max takes the recliner so that leaves the couch for me and Sawyer. I sit, Sawyer drops beside me and I have to scramble to keep from falling into him. Even though I do keep myself upright, our knees bump. The touch surprises me and it must surprise him as well. He jerks away, as do I, but there's really nowhere for either of us to go.

Good thing I'm small otherwise I'd be on the floor.

"So which one of you is possessed and needs me to exorcise them?" Max asks then adds as he chuckles, "Just kidding. What can I do for you today, V?"

Sawyer's head shoots in my direction at the mention of V. That's what my friends call me, and Sawyer's not a friend so he probably hasn't heard this before.

"We're going to do a project on whether or not ghosts are real, and I was hoping you could tell us how to prove they exist."

Max readjusts glasses that seem to be permanently lopsided on his face. "I did a vinegar and baking soda volcano when I was in school."

"That sounds boring. Now tell us what to do."

Max goes to the closet and returns with a crate and a duffel bag. He explains about how before we do an investigation of a place that we need to do some research about the possible spirits that could be there and how that will help us connect with the ghosts. "You need to understand the difference between local legend and fact. If ghosts are there, they might be there for a purpose. Be willing to listen to them with an open mind instead of approaching them with a mind-set of what everyone else has to say."

I lean forward, enchanted with the idea of connecting with a spirit, at least one who isn't my mom. Sawyer, on the other hand, keeps crossing and uncrossing his legs and looks as comfortable as a lobster about to be put in a boiling pot.

"Did you know that Thomas Edison once said in an interview that he tried to build a ghost phone?" Max says. Sawyer shakes his head, and I'm writing in my notebook.

"Most spirits don't have enough energy to create audible sounds like we do, but some can muster enough energy to leave a sound on a recording," Max continues. "Some people believe that a ghost can't talk, but can gain enough energy to alter the static near the coil of the microphone to create a voice to communicate with, which is why you can't hear the voice with your own ears. This type of communication takes a great deal of energy, which is why most EVPs—or electronic voice phenomena—are very short."

"But there are ghosts that people can see and hear," I say. "How's that possible?"

"Full-bodied apparitions are rare events, but it can happen. Those ghosts are very strong." Max opens his duffel bag and takes out a recorder. "I like using digital recorders so I can run the recordings through the computer. Ghosts are in another dimension than ours, which means that they communicate on a different frequency than we do. They could be communicating faster than us or slower. We can use the computer to find those different frequencies."

Sawyer's lips flatten in disbelief, and Max notices. "What's on your mind?"

Sawyer's fingers move like that's an answer, but then he says, "It sounds like you're creating evidence for what doesn't exist."

"Wait until you hear the direct response to a specific question on an EVP. You'll be a believer then." Max then goes on to explain how to capture an EVP and then shows us different types of what he calls ghost boxes. Skepticism seems to be a hardwired DNA trait for Sawyer, and a part of me sinks as I realize this isn't reeling him in like I need.

"What I hear you saying is that we have to spend money to do this project," Sawyer says.

Crap. The boy who drives a Lexus and couldn't pay his rent won't be interested in a project that will cost him anything. Fan-freaking-tastic.

"Typically, yes," Max answers. "But in the case of the two of you, no."

Sawyer's eyebrows rise, and I'll admit to being stumped. "How's that possible?"

"I'm going to let you borrow the equipment you need to do your assignment." Max slides to the edge of his recliner, and the chair tilts forward with his weight.

He looks at me, and that stomach sinking goes to a whole other level as he gives me the sad, pathetic pity-eyes. Oh, God, he knows, and horror causes me to become paralyzed.

"Max," I try, but my tongue is twisted. My heart is beating too fast, and he either doesn't hear me, understand my desperation or doesn't care because he doesn't stop.

"V, your dad told me about your brain tumor, and I can't even begin to tell you how sorry I am. Whenever I see you, you put a smile on my face with how you live life—full throttle. As if there isn't something foreign in your brain. You give me courage, and I want you to enjoy this project to the fullest."

SAWYER

Sunday Feb. 10: Didn't cure at all today. Didn't even have my blankets out.

Oh Diary dear, I'm in the awfullest fix. Both Frank and Harry are at me. Harry wants me to sit with him, and only him. Frank doesn't say anything, but he keeps up a "hurt silence" that makes me feel worse than if he'd get good and angry.

I wish Veronica would have gotten angry with me. Really, I wish she would have stopped. But she didn't stop. She walked home and that didn't sit well with me.

I had hauled the crate of Max's equipment and the duffel bag to my car, placed it in my trunk, and there she was, leaving. I hurried, drove up beside her, but she told me to leave. I agreed with what she said to me, it wasn't a far walk, but I'd brought her there and it seemed like the right thing to do to be the man who drove her back, but she asked me to leave, even adding a please.

It was the way her blue eyes ached with the please that caused me to leave. She had said a total of six words to me, but I wanted more. Needed more. But her hurt expression told me to go so I did, and now I feel like an even bigger ass. I let a girl with a brain tumor walk home alone.

Evelyn lived over a hundred years ago and I understand her completely. Sometimes silence hurts more than words.

A shove of my shoulder and Sylvia sits in the patio chair beside mine. "Hey, stranger. What are you reading?"

"Nothing." I roll Evelyn's diary into a tube again. I've done it so often that the sides are starting to curve on their own.

We're at Sylvia's house, hanging in the backyard. Miguel does a front flip from the diving board into the in-ground pool. When he hits the water, there's a round of shouts and cheers of approval from our group of friends who are either lounging by or in the pool.

There's about twelve people here. The combination of the group of guys I hang with and the group of girls she hangs with creates what my mom calls my tribe. At the grill, Sylvia's dad cooks sliders, and through the open patio doors of the kitchen my mom, Miguel's mom, and Sylvia's mom are laughing as Mom pours all of them another glass of wine. Several other moms hover around the main three, jockeying for position to have their glasses filled and to be closer to the gossip.

It's late, probably nearing midnight, and the pool is lit up by multiple lights within and around the pool. In the shallow section of the water, Lucy jumps from the steps leading into the pool, but then quickly doggie paddles back to safety. She has water wings on her arms as she is equal parts fascinated with pools and terrified of them. Strange since the only love affair I have is with water and jumping.

"I can't wait for you to move into the neighborhood," Sylvia says. "It's going to be like this all the time instead of just on the weekends."

Mom's laugh is so loud that several of my friends turn to look at her. Lucy frowns at the sound then sits on the stairs of the pool and plays with her mermaid doll.

Sylvia grins ear to ear as she watches the commotion in the kitchen. "Your mom is the best. I want to be the life of the party, too, when I'm knocking on the door of fifty."

Sylvia told everyone our sophomore year that she's a lesbian at a get-together just like this. I already knew the news, so did Miguel, and we told her in eighth grade it didn't change our friendship. When she told everyone else, we stood beside her, shoulder to shoulder in support. But her declaration hit everyone else like a shockwave.

The adults in the room were frozen, like we were all stuck in the Ice Age, but then my mom walked across the room and hugged her. That one hug woke everyone else up, including Sylvia's parents, and ever since then, Sylvia's been a loyal supporter of my mom. Oftentimes more friend to her than she is to me. I get it, but it can be annoying.

It doesn't help that while Sylvia's parents love and support her, they still have conversations with her about whether she's "sure about her choices" or if she's "really given guys a chance."

I don't tell her my mom tries to get me to go out with her on a biweekly basis. With the way she worships Mom, that'd break Sylvia's heart.

"I hope I have a body like hers, too," she continues. "Your mom is ridic with how fit she is."

Sylvia looks over at the other girls in swimsuits and readjusts the spaghetti straps of her bikini like she's unsure how her body compares, which is stupid. She's on the girls' swim team, could swim laps around my mom and is one of the few who can keep up with me in the pool. So she has muscles—that's a good thing.

"Your mom said she's not going to put your pool in until next year," Sylvia says.

"Yeah."

"Now that you're finally back to swimming again, I need someone to challenge me in my workout. Want to do laps together this week?"

"Sure."

"You didn't go to swim practice today. How come?"

"I had things to do." I was learning how to communicate with ghosts, and then I spent time driving around trying to wrap my head around life. Actually Veronica's life. She has a brain tumor, and from the way that guy talked, at least talked around it, it sounds like it's bad.

"You're quiet."

Brain tumor has a way of shutting me up.

"Why aren't you in the pool now?"

I nod in Lucy's direction and watch as she tries to put on goggles. I'm tempted to help as the straps need to be adjusted, but I give her space to see if she can figure it out on her own. "She needs a set of eyes."

"Yeah . . . but typically you swim with her."

I shrug. "Not in the mood." Brain tumor. God, what is that like?

Sylvia fiddles with the undone button of her jean cutoff short-shorts. Underneath is her bikini bottom and I wonder if this means she's going to hit the water again. "I told your mom you'd be upset."

That causes my eyes to jerk away from Lucy to Sylvia. "What?"

"Don't play it off. We've been friends for too long for that. I told your mom and my mom that instead of making this big plan behind your back to make sure you're in a good group for the senior project that we should have been up front. You're aware you need good grades to stay on the swim team, and you know how tough this project is going to be. But your mom thought you'd be offended. That's stupid, though. Why wouldn't you want us to help? There was no reason for your mom to go behind your back. I told her you'd figure it out, and that she should have been honest from the start."

Not at all why I was quiet, yet my eye ticks. "Why didn't you tell me the plan?"

She fiddles with her button again. "Your mom asked me not to."

Once again, I wish there was separation in my life between my mom and my friends.

"She didn't want you to think she didn't believe in you."

She doesn't believe in me, and obviously, Sylvia doesn't, either. "So you all had a big meeting about me and didn't feel I should be invited?"

"That made you sound whiny. Everyone was here, hanging out,

and you weren't. It's not like we were sent a coded message and had to stay up late at night with our decoder rings figuring out when we could meet in private to discuss you. Why you weren't here? I don't know, but don't think I haven't noticed how you've been pulling back from everyone since you broke your arm. And neither Miguel nor I believe the whole you-broke-your-arm-on-the-pool-deck."

I bristle with the correct accusation. "I was lying in pain on the pool deck, wasn't I?"

"Miguel and I had been doing laps together all day and we never saw you there."

"I had just gotten there."

She levels her pissed-off glare on me. "You're lying."

She's right, I am, and I look away, back to my sister.

"What's going on with you, Sawyer? You used to be like your mom, the life of the party, and now it's like you turned yourself off."

Grades, swim, Mom, Dad, Lucy, jumping, not jumping, AA, moving, money, brain tumors . . . "I can do the project."

"I never said you couldn't. We expect you to take part of the project . . ." She trails off, and my skin twists around my bones. I shouldn't have continued this conversation. There are some things better left unsaid. "It's just that there are times that the project is going to move super fast. It's better that you're with me and Miguel so we can plow forward and do those parts of the project and then you can do the other parts."

The easy parts, she means. I work my jaw. Who wants to be told they're a charity case? To have so many people talking behind my back makes me feel like crap.

"Please don't look like that, Sawyer. You have to admit that this is a huge project and that you struggled all year to keep your English grade up last year. None of us want to watch you go through that again. Your mom wants the best for you. We all do."

By not even letting me try to rise to the challenge. "This decision was never yours or my mom's. It should have been mine." I stand, put the diary in my back pocket and Lucy glances over at me with the movement. "Ready to go home?"

Lucy takes off her water wings like that's what she's been praying for me to say and starts up the pool stairs. I grab a towel, but before I step toward my sister, Sylvia scurries to her feet and catches my arm. "Don't be mad at me. I told them you'd be angry, and it's the reason I'm talking to you about this now. If we would have talked to you about this from the start, you would have understood."

Would I have? "I'm not mad."

"You are, and I understand why, just don't be mad at me, okay?"

Hurt flashes over Sylvia's face, and that makes the annoyance grow that I have to, once again, suck up my emotions to make someone else feel better. But she's been my friend since I moved to this town, and she's had to deal with enough people's animosity and judgment so I swallow down my anger. "I'm not mad at you."

She nods like she's accepting my answer even if she doesn't believe it. "Mom said something about lighting the bonfire. Are you sure you don't want to stay? We can roast marshmallows with Lucy. I know how much she likes that."

Mom laughs loudly again, and my skin crawls. I need to get out of here because I'm tempted to confront Mom about her lack of faith in me, but I know that's the worst route to take. Yet Sylvia's looking at me with expectation so I do my best to soften the blow. "It's late, Lucy's had a long week and she hasn't slept well." She's woken up with a nightmare nearly every night. Not as bad as the first night, but she still wakes in tears.

"Will you swim with me tomorrow?"

"Yeah." Because that will make her feel better, but it's the last thing I want to do as I need space.

Lucy's dripping from head to toe so I wrap her like a burrito, then because it makes her laugh, I toss her over my shoulder. Friends shout good-byes as I go into the house, and Mom and Hannah, the moment they see me, stop their intense conversation that included lots of giggles.

"Yes?" Mom asks like I'm a pest.

"We should leave. Lucy's tired."

"Lucy, do you want to go home?"

I readjust Lucy so she's on my hip. Her thin arms wrap around my neck, and she nods as she places her head on my shoulder.

Mom sighs as if annoyed, but then Hannah reaches over and pats Mom's hand. "Let them go. I'll take you home later or you can sleep over in my guest room." Hannah winks at Mom. "We have to finish our medication so we can make it through the week."

They cackle as if that was the best private joke in the world. About to tell them to go to hell, I snatch my backpack off the floor, spin on my toes and go for the bathroom in the hallway.

"Don't be like that," Mom calls out. "Come back and at least stay for a hamburger."

"Yeah, come on, Sawyer, stay," Hannah joins Mom in a singsong voice, and I feel like the butt of too many jokes. There's whispers then more laughter.

I hand Lucy her nightgown to change into, nudge her into the bathroom, and wait for what seems like a lifetime for her to change. She eventually emerges with her wet bathing suit in her fingers, her dry clothes on her body, and her arms held up to me in an unspoken plea.

She's getting too big for this, but she's my little sister and she's tired. I swing her up on my hip and she nuzzles into me as we head for the front door.

"God, he's been so moody," Mom says as I step out into the night and away from her.

VERONICA

What a crappy day, and my English teacher's response to my email isn't making it better:

> Veronica,
>
> I'm sorry you're having a difficult time finding a group to work with, but I am adamant about you being a part of one. I understand you have a topic that you're passionate about, but maybe once you do join a group you could persuade them to switch to your topic.
>
> If you don't have a group by Monday, I will assign you to one.

I hate my life.

It's nearing midnight, and I'm sitting on the steps of the front porch. I put down my cell and take my first drag off my lit cigarette. It's a nasty habit. One people like to tell me will kill me, but their words of wisdom make me chuckle. I'm going to die regardless.

I don't do it often—rarely really. As in close to never. Only when life has become a bit too much, Dad is gone and loneliness has gotten the better of me. The cigarettes are easy to find. Dad used to smoke like a chimney then quit when Mom was first diagnosed, but he still has one or two when he plays poker with friends.

To be honest, I think that's why I smoke them. At least just light them and then have one or two drags. I don't like it enough to actually smoke the entire thing. The smell makes me think of Dad, and right now—I want my father. Really, I would love to hug my mom and have a good cry, but she's not around tonight. Today flat-out sucked and the loneliness hurts.

Yes, I'm having a pity party, for once. Tomorrow, I'll pick myself back up, dust off the nastiness and start all over again.

I look at the glowing cigarette then sigh heavily. This isn't making me feel better. Nothing will, and smoking only creates guilt and will cause a headache later. I grind it out on the sidewalk then smash the rest out with my boot.

Our street is dark, quiet. The moon creating a silver sheen over the old houses. Down the block, a car turns in my direction. It slows as it approaches, then parks. That's Sawyer's car, and in the backseat is the silhouette of a child in a car seat.

Sawyer exits the car, gathers Lucy from the backseat and carries her up the walk. She's sound asleep, her body dead weight in his arms and she rests her head on his shoulder. I stand, move ahead of him and open the main door.

As he passes, our gazes briefly meet, but I quickly glance away. He knows my secret, and I'm not okay with that. His car keys jingle as he tries to shift his sister and punch in the code to his apartment. Taking pity upon him, I ease past and enter Dad's code to unlock the door.

Why he seems surprised, I don't know. Technically, I'm more owner of this house than he is. Sawyer mumbles a thanks, and as I go to leave, he quietly says, "Will you stay?"

Seriously? Stay? No, I really don't want to, but I guess it's better that we get this conversation out of the way. "I'll wait on the porch."

"In here," he whispers. "I can't be far from Lucy. She's been having nightmares."

"You need to invite me in," I say as dread fills my stomach.

"What?"

"I won't come in unless you invite me."

With an expression that screams he thinks I'm crazy, he says, "What are you? A vampire?"

"Maybe."

He rolls his eyes. "You can come in, and when you do, hit a light for me?"

I enter first, flick the switch on the wall and notice the mounds of boxes lining the walls. It's not at all homey, and I can see why Lucy has knocked on my door twice this week. Her brother and mother, though, called her away before I could let her in.

Sawyer goes into the front bedroom, the one with the turret, and I have no idea what to do with myself. The soft light flicks on in the room, and I'm drawn in by the pink tint. I bet Lucy's room is cute yet instead of heading that way to find out, I peek into the kitchen in the back of the house. It, too, overflows with boxes, and then I wander to the other side of the house to where the bathroom and other bedroom is. That room is filled with lots of dress clothes hanging on portable racks and a huge sleigh bed with too many pillows. This must be where his mom is crashing.

I return to the living room and make the conclusion that the narrow room that lines the side of the house, the one originally built for a small library or office, is Sawyer's. Inside is a mattress on the floor and an open suitcase of folded clothes—like he doesn't believe he'll be here longer than a week.

Murmurs from Lucy's room, and I lean upon the arm of the couch, acting as if I'm not spying, but I am. A smile crosses my lips at the wonderland inside. Lucy has a canopy princess bed. The kind that nearly every little girl dreams of. Beautiful sheer and sparkly material hanging from pole to pole. Butterflies meander across her ceiling thanks to a rotating nightlight and there's an entire zoo of stuffed animals in and surrounding Lucy's bed.

Lucy's like a limp rag doll as Sawyer helps her into bed. They're saying prayers, both of them reciting something about God's protection and then on to a list of people they want God to bless. He kisses her forehead and as he starts to pull away, she leans up and hugs him tight.

It's a sweet sight, and I'm confused how this guy has the ability to act like a jerk at school yet be so loving to her. Not wanting him to know I was watching, I pretend to be staring at something fascinating on the floor.

Sawyer leaves Lucy's door open a crack then turns to face me. "Sorry it took so long. She's been having nightmares since moving in so I try to make bedtime as pleasant as possible in hopes it'll help."

"It's okay."

"Would you like something to drink?" He goes for the kitchen. "We don't have much to choose from. We have milk, orange juice, Mom might have something diet in here and—"

"Did you tell your friends or anyone else about my brain tumor?" I cock a hip against the door frame of the kitchen as he opens the fridge. He stares into it longer than needed then shuts it.

"No."

"Are you going to?"

He shakes his head then meets my eyes. "Not my news to tell."

I should feel relieved, but I don't. He could be lying to me now or he could change his mind later.

"Is it fatal?" he asks, and his straightforwardness throws me off guard.

"Are you asking if I'm dying?"

Sawyer places his hands in the pockets of his jeans. "Yeah."

"Yes."

His eyes practically pop out of his head.

"We're all dying. In fact, I have some theories about this. Have you ever considered that maybe we could live forever if we found something we could breathe other than oxygen? I mean, what if oxygen works, but at the same time, it's slowly killing us? What if we aren't meant to age, but it's oxygen that's the poison?"

He mashes his lips like he's annoyed, and I really don't know why he is. I didn't invite him into my personal business.

Footsteps behind me, and Sawyer's gaze snaps to over my shoulder. A cold shiver down my spine, and I'm dying to look and see if the little girl is there, but I know she isn't. She's playing with me and she's playing with Sawyer.

"Did you hear that?" he asks.

"Yes. I told you this house is haunted."

"Ha."

"My tumor is small and it's benign." I change the subject because he's not ready to believe. "It can cause headaches, but other than that, I'm fine."

Sawyer's eyes flicker from the living room to me, back to the living room and then to me again. "Is that why you act different all the time?"

My spine goes rigid. "Is your lack of a brain tumor why you're an ass?"

I don't know why, but he grins. It's not a huge one, just a minor lift of his lips, but it's strangely adorable. "That would answer a ton of questions as to what's wrong with me."

I fight it, yet I smile. I push off the door frame and enter the kitchen. On the wooden table with four chairs is the box and duffel bag Max gave us. I pick up the digital recorder and point it in his direction. "There're a few things I should mention if you do agree to work with me."

"What's that?"

"There're places I want to visit that may not be open to the public so we might have to be creative on how we do our investigation. Meaning I want to do a thorough investigation of the TB hospital up the hill, and it's a risk since the police like to visit it often."

"Are we going to break in? Past the lobby? Past the wooden barriers?"

The ones the authorities put in place to keep teenagers from exploring the rest of the hospital. It typically works. Most people find enough of a thrill by just attempting the climb and then walking in. A few though, like Leo, will risk danger and go further.

I bob my head. "More like asking for permission to enter only if we get caught. Actually, you'll be trespassing and then inviting me in because that's how I roll. So are you in or out?"

There's a daring glint in his eyes that I find appealing. Maybe there's more to Sawyer Sutherland than I originally suspected. Maybe he's just as hungry to live as I am, and if that's the case, the next few months will be a wild ride.

"I'm definitely in."

SAWYER

It's Monday, and I walk in the moment the last bell rings. My English teacher gives me a disapproving glare, but can't say anything as I'm technically on time. "Cutting it close, Mr. Sutherland?"

"More like perfect timing."

She grins, and I can tell she likes me, which is good because I'm going to struggle in this class. Me and reading comprehension tests aren't friends. Especially the timed ones.

Miguel and Sylvia smile at me, and I take a seat next to them in the middle of the room. I glance over at Veronica. She's in the back corner staring out the window as if having the best daydream. Her short blond curls fall around her shoulders, and with how the beams of sun hit her hair, she looks like an angel with a halo.

Miguel asks if he can have a ride to practice, and I tell him yes. Sylvia starts in about some drama that happened at her pool party on Friday. A guy talked smack about his girlfriend's best friend and the girl is rightly pissed. Now the two friends are fighting because the girlfriend is defending the guy instead of her best friend and the drama has carried over to social media.

"Lunch is going to be tense." Sylvia slumps in her desk like this fight is the end of the world. "Both of them expect me to sit with them, and I don't know how to choose."

I don't get dating and why people want to do it. When I was a kid, I once heard Dad yell at Mom that he was sick of her nagging. She yelled back that she was sick of his irresponsibility. When they weren't yelling, Dad worked or watched TV while Mom took care of me. In public, they'd pretend to be in love. Couples at school act like they're in love for a day then fight for months. Relationship love is a ton of bull that tears the people around them apart. "Don't sit with either of them."

Sylvia's head jerks up. "I have to. They're my friends."

"If they're your friends, then why are they making you choose?"

She doesn't have a chance to respond as Mrs. Garcia brings the class to attention. She's a twentysomething, overenthusiastic, slender woman with straight black hair and a big smile. In fact, that smile gets bigger as she announces that we will continue our top-five senior journal project. My groan is internal while there are several others who loudly voice their distaste for the assignment. I wonder if other people's agony is how she gets her kicks.

"All right." Mrs. Garcia claps. "Now is the moment of truth. I need to know who your group will be. After you tell me, sit with your group, and I want a list of possible project ideas turned in to me by the end of the hour."

No one volunteers, and when I look back at Veronica, she's still stuck in a daydream. Figuring the easiest route will be the fastest, I put my hand in the air.

"Mr. Sutherland, who will you be working with?" Mrs. Garcia asks.

"Veronica Sullivan."

"What?" Sylvia says, and I can't ignore the other whispers going on in the class.

When I glance back again, I finally have Veronica's attention. Her blue eyes meet mine, and there's curiosity as if she's been caught off guard. Veronica is a challenge, a puzzle I can't quite figure out, and I have to admit I like it.

Mrs. Garcia moves the class forward, gathering the names of the other groups, then dismisses us to work. I gather my notebook and folder, stand to head back toward Veronica, and Sylvia wraps her fingers around my wrist. "I thought you said you weren't mad?"

Her question is barely a whisper, but Miguel is turned around in his desk and he's also waiting on an answer. There's lots of noise in the room. Desks squeaking against the linoleum floor, the low rumble of conversation starting, but I feel like her accusation was a shout.

"I'm not."

"Then why aren't you working with us? Your mom convinced the counselor to put you in this class so we can help you with the project. Otherwise you wouldn't be in here."

"Sylvia," Miguel says in warning.

"It's true," she shoots back at him. "And he knows it. I told him everything Friday night. He said he's not mad, but he obviously is and it's causing him to make bad choices."

"Maybe I don't want to be a charity case."

Sylvia flinches. "You're my friend, not a charity case, and have you stopped to consider how mad your mom is going to be?"

Yeah, she probably is. "I need this project to be my choice. Not hers."

"It's not too late," Sylvia continues like I didn't speak. "Go tell Mrs. Garcia you made a mistake."

"Sylvia," Miguel reprimands. "Let it go."

I use that as my cue to leave and drop into the desk facing Veronica. I slam my notebook onto the desk and look up in time to spot Sylvia glaring at me, but then she turns away.

"Something vexing thee?" Veronica asks in an Old English accent.

"I'm good."

"You sure?" She resumes her normal soothing tone then circles a finger in Sylvia's direction. "Because that looks like a lot of something. Nothing good, but a lot of something."

Agreed, but it's nothing I can't handle. "What's going on with our project?"

"Deflection. My favorite defense mechanism as well."

"What?"

"I'm taking AP Psychology, which probably isn't good for anyone. Deflection—when you deny your emotions, but then again you could be taking part in sublimation. That's where you pour your feelings into doing something else, which will be fantastic if that means you're going to pour yourself into this project."

I stare blankly at her as I got nothing.

"I have good news for you," she says. "Your mom's check cleared."

"Never thought it wouldn't." I'm lying, and it should bother me, but it doesn't. Lately, I lie more than tell the truth.

"Tell me something about you," she says.

"What?"

"We're going to be working together, and before you moved into my house, we'd never said a word to one another. It feels like we should at least attempt to pretend to be cordial."

Right. "I swim."

"I don't."

"The pool at the Y is pretty good, and it's not far from your house. I'm allowed a guest if you'd like to—"

"You don't understand. I can't swim."

"Did you have a bad experience?"

"I've never learned. I'm assuming that would equate to sinking like a rock. That doesn't sound like fun so I don't swim."

Wow. "How is it possible you've never learned?"

"The impossible is always possible. Any-hoo, back to the project. There're a couple of places I'd like to visit. There's this covered bridge that is said to have the ghosts of people who died when their car missed the bridge and went into the river. Then there's this stretch of road where a girl died, and she walks along the road waiting for someone to pick her up. If you do stop, she'll get in the backseat and then disappear when you pass where she actually died."

"Are you for real?"

"I'm dead serious." Her lips twitch. "Did you get the pun?"

When I remain deadpan she giggles, and the sound moves something inside me. The tension in my muscles eases, and I lean forward on the desk. "Dead people on bridges and then on a road. Anything else?"

"That sounds like a messed-up Dr. Seuss book. 'Could you, would you, on a bridge, see them, see them, on a ridge. Maybe in a park, not in the dark. I do not like ghosts, I'm not a fan, I do not like them, Sam-I-Am.'"

I actually chuckle. Damn, she's funny.

"Of course, I want to investigate the TB hospital."

The idea of trespassing gets the juices going in my brain. The same way it does when I jump off a cliff. Not nearly as intense, but it's a good substitute. "I'm game."

"We'll need to research the actual background information of the place then also investigate the legends. I thought about what Max said about understanding the difference between fact and legend. I think that should be part of the angle of our paper."

It all sounds good to me. "I've heard about the TB hospital. All sorts of weird stuff went down in that place. Experiments, torture and satanic rituals. I've heard that sometimes the ghosts hurt you when you go into certain areas."

First time I've seen skepticism on Veronica's face. "You believe?"

"Not at all."

"That's what I figured." Veronica studies me, and I shift as her intense gaze makes me feel as if I'm on display. "Have you read it?"

"Is there a how-to book on how to catch Casper the Friendly Ghost?"

"No. Evelyn's diary. How far in are you?"

I shrug my shoulders. "Probably not as far in as anyone else would be."

"What do you think of it?"

I think of the last entry I read—while she had been making a life for herself at the hospital, she was sick and tired of the place and longed to go home. She wanted her life as it was before her diagnosis.

Sometimes I wonder what life would have been like if Dad had been more interested in being a father and a husband over his devotion to his job, TV or video games. Would I be as hungry as Evelyn for my life before the divorce? Even though our circumstances are different, I understand her. She wanted to live and to be happy. So do I. Problem is—how do we do that? Especially when she faced TB and I can't stop jumping off cliffs?

There's a sick sensation in my gut as I'm not sure I want to read to the end. When you struggle daily to gain a pound, what is the end result? "Did anyone survive TB once they were diagnosed?"

She nods, but isn't answering what I want to know—if Evelyn survived.

I go for a change in subject. "Listen, I'll be able to hold my own on this project. I may need more time than you on reading and writing, but I can do this." English has never been my best subject, and I'll admit that last year, I gave up. I got tired of everything having to be so damn hard, but I'm not giving up again.

Veronica's wink unravels the knots gnarled in my chest. "Are you trying to make me feel better because I have a brain tumor? I sat in front of you in math last year, and you're a math god. Shocking, I know, that we shared a class, since you ignored me."

"It's not like you talked to me," I counter, but there's something in how she looks at me without blinking that makes me wonder if I'm wrong.

"I was surprised you aren't taking the math AP course this year," she says.

Me, too. Along with discovering that Mom had placed me in AP English, it turns out she also switched me from AP math to another class. We fought over the change, but like always, she won. "My mom and Coach are worried about me keeping up my grades so they didn't want me to overload my schedule."

"My dad was like that when I was first diagnosed, but he got over it pretty quick."

"You proved him wrong?"

"No, I can be a real bitch when I want to be."

I laugh and the sound causes several people to look over at us.

Veronica touches a flower barrette in her hair and a hint of sadness tarnishes her beautiful face. "It helped that Mom was on my side. Dad always listened to her." She shrugs like what she said didn't mean anything and tries to smile. "Anyhow . . . life happens."

I want to ask about her mom. I've not seen a woman at the apartment yet, and I can't help but wonder if her parents are divorced, too. I don't ask as I don't want the question turned around on me. "Does the tumor make things harder?"

She fiddles with her pen, and as I'm about to take the question back, she says, "I have bad migraines. Some are super awful, and I can hardly function. I'll miss school over them, but when there's something important happening, I try to fight through the pain and show. I promise I won't let my migraines get in the way of the project." She drops the pen then plays with the edge of her notebook, and I can tell that admitting that wasn't easy. "The headaches are out of my control, and sometimes they take over my life."

I understand something taking over my life—being all twisted up until you can't breathe.

"Thanks for not telling anyone," she says. "I don't want to deal with people's pity and whatever else they'd say about me because of the tumor."

We're in the corner of the room, isolated from everyone else, yet I have a hard time wrapping my head around having such a deep conversation with so many people near. At least for me. I don't like having people in my personal business, but she's sharing and it feels wrong not to share as well.

"Having dyslexia . . . sometimes people think I can't do things. When people find out I have it, I see how their face draws down like they feel sorry for me, and I hate it. Dyslexia sucks, it's not something I'd choose, but it doesn't make me less."

"What's dyslexia like?"

"It's different for everyone. What I experience isn't what another person with dyslexia might experience. We can all be different. For me, the letters jump around in a word, and it's not like once they jump they stay that way. They keep moving. I can read, but it takes a ton of concentration. I can understand what I'm reading, too, but it takes so much time to read that I can barely finish reading a passage on those damn reading comprehension tests before time is called.

"I have an IEP—Individualized Education Program. Sometimes it helps because I do get more time, but sometimes it doesn't help. Sometimes I have teachers who forget I have an IEP, and sometimes I don't feel like having to remind them. It brings more attention on me, and sometimes I get tired of it."

I take a moment as the past tugs at me, not good memories. "It took until my freshman year to be diagnosed. I remember one time in elementary school, in third grade, we had to answer introductory questions about ourselves and draw a picture. You know, the typical stuff—what I like to eat, sports I play, favorite movie. The teacher put up our posters of ourselves on the bulletin board in the hallway for open house. I remember coming home and crying, begging Mom and Dad not to go to open house because I didn't want them to see my poster next to everyone else's. Everyone's handwriting was perfect, the words spelled right. Mine looked like a mess and hardly anything was spelled correctly. I was embarrassed and then Mom got mad when she saw it because she didn't think I was trying hard enough. Here's the thing, I was. I gave that poster everything I had and it still wasn't good enough."

I go quiet, and Veronica allows me time. She doesn't have a look of pity on her face, just understanding. Then she does something unexpected. Veronica leans forward and places her hand over mine. Soft fingers, a delicate touch, and my entire body sparks to life. As if I had been in darkness—the world was black and white—and then the switch was flipped into color.

"Thank you for sharing that." God, she has a beautiful voice.

"Besides the counselor who diagnosed me, you're the only person I've told what it's like for me to read," I say.

She unleashes a beaming smile, but unfortunately takes her hand away from mine. "So what you're saying is that I'm special."

I chuckle. "I guess so."

"What?" She mock gasps. "Sawyer Sutherland, the most popular guy at this school, likes me? You better watch out. If you hang with me for too long, people are going to talk."

"I'm not popular." And they talk anyhow.

She overly rolls her eyes. "Please. You're the king, and you know it, and the king likes me." She sings the last part like she's five. "Sawyer likes me."

She playfully nudges my foot with hers, and my heart skips a beat. These reactions aren't something that normally happen to me, and it's confusing. Her gorgeous blue eyes dance, and I wonder how it is that I've been around her for the last few years and have never stopped to notice her eyes before, or her mesmerizing voice.

"Five minutes left, people," Mrs. Garcia says, and Veronica smiles at me before she opens her notebook and begins to write.

I rub the back of my head, stretch, and I'm shocked to find my heart beating faster.

Get it together, Sutherland. Get it together.

VERONICA

L

"You can't let her in," Mom whispers in my ear, and her warning causes my blood to freeze. It's Monday evening, and I watch on the security monitor as Glory enters the foyer of the house and starts up the stairs.

Where people in town think I'm weird, they think she's insane. Yet that doesn't stop them from going to her house and paying her money for a psychic reading. She may not be invited to the fanciest parties in town, but Glory's laughing all the way to the bank.

"If you let her in," Mom says, "she'll make me leave."

My gaze darts to hers, and there's fear in her eyes. "Why would she do that?"

"Because that's why God gave Glory her gift to see spirits. She's to usher those of us who linger in this realm to the next one. Remember what I told you, V. Be careful of who you invite into your home—once invited in, death is too powerful to stop."

I jump when there's a knock on the door. I don't want Mom to go. I need her here with me, but . . . "Should you go? I mean, I don't want you to go, but will you be happier in heaven?"

There's this twisting hope in me that's nearly strangling: I want so desperately for her to say that death isn't terrifying.

Mom tilts her head then reaches out and cups my cheek. I close my eyes with the brief, feathering touch and wish I could hug her. For some reason, we can do light touches, but we can't hug. That's one of the things I miss the most—her tight, safe hugs. She'd always smell of roses and baby powder, and no matter how cold it was outside she was warm.

"Why would I want to leave you and your father? There's no place I'd rather be than with you."

Glory knocks again, and my pulse quickens as she calls out, "I know you're in there, V. Quit stalling and open the door."

"What should I do?" I ask.

"Ignore her."

"Glory can't make you leave, can she? If you want to stay, can't you stay?"

Another knock, but louder this time. "Take a look at the camera, V, and I promise you'll open the door."

Glory holds up some sort of thick, wrapped stick, and my mom flickers. Honest to God flickers. Like she's there and then not there and that causes panic to rush into my veins.

"I've been told to use this if you don't open this door," Glory calls.

"Open it." The anxiety in Mom's tone heightens mine. "But get her to leave. Quickly. She'll lie to get what she wants. Her instincts are to force spirits to move on, but she doesn't understand that some of us need to stay."

Then Mom disappears and the suddenness causes my lungs to squeeze. I scan the room and it's empty and that makes me strangely hollow. Footsteps upstairs, and I find the ability to breathe again. She's not gone, just someplace different.

I undo the locks and open the door. Glory has waist-length, sandy-blond hair that has a wild natural curl. She wears a long, layered, light blue skirt and an off-the-shoulder white blouse. In her hands is the bundle she held up, and in the crook of her arm is a wicker picnic basket.

"Hello, V," Glory says. "Are you going to let me in?"

Don't want to, but . . . "Sure."

Glory enters and surveys my home with wary eyes. "You skipped our monthly healing session." She pins me with her gaze. "Twice."

"Sorry. I've been busy."

"Hmmm." Glory walks farther into the room, each step more hesitant than the one before. "I've been dreaming of you."

"All good things, right?" My smile feels fake, and I'm betting it looks that way, too.

"No."

Crap.

She lifts the bundle in her hand. "Do you know what this is?"

Not really. She's used it around me before when I've gone to her home for psychic healings and when she's cleansed my aura. "Some sort of expensive pot?"

"Sage, and it's used to rid your body and your home of unwanted negative energy."

"That sounds good."

Glory walks toward the turret and there's a sinking in my gut as she brushes her hand along the pillows of Mom's favorite spot. She then looks over at the piano. Mom's piano. Where Mom had been sitting before Glory came to the door. "I remember when I first met you, you used to play the piano all the time. Beautifully if memory serves correctly."

I did. Mom taught me how to play. The music belonged to me and her. After she died, I stopped.

"I'm curious," Glory continues, "why in my dreams you're smudging this house, and when you do it, you're doing it in fear?"

"Smudging?" I ask innocently.

She waves the stick in the air. "The act of lighting this to rid a house of spirits. Now tell me why I saw what I did in my dreams."

"I have no idea."

"An even better question, why did I have an angel visit me this morning telling me that you've chosen a very dangerous path? One that will affect your health, your family, and one that includes you messing with the spiritual realm?"

We stare at each other. Me trying to hide my guilt. Her in disapproval.

"Spill," Glory demands, and my shoulders sag.

"It's not a big deal. I'm doing my senior thesis paper on whether or not ghosts exist."

Glory grimaces as the picnic basket slides from the crook of her elbow to her wrist. "And how are you going about this project?"

"I'm going to do some research and"—I twine and untwine my fingers—"I'm going to visit haunted places."

"And communicate with the spirits there?"

I nod. Glory tsks me like I'm a toddler then walks into the kitchen and sets the basket on the table. "From the moment I met you, I told you to be careful with spirits."

"Technically"—I hold a finger in the air—"you told me to avoid the first floor, and I do." At least until recently.

"Because you're an antenna." Rare frustration leaks into her tone. "Spirits are naturally drawn to you, and when you start communicating with them you're inviting them to attach themselves to you. Not all spirits are good ones. Some aren't spirits at all, but demons. You're not trained to understand the difference, and what are you going to do when something negative attaches itself to you and you drag it home?"

"I'll call you?"

"Yes, you will, but you don't need to drag anything else into this house. Whatever lives on the first floor likes to play games with people. You and your father are protected, I've seen to that, but this entity draws in prone people and then it takes advantage of their weaknesses. The last thing you need is more negative energies in this house and possibly creating a situation I can't control."

"I don't think the spirits downstairs are as bad as you think."

"Because you think it is a child."

"I know it's a child."

"And I'm telling you that there is more than just that child. Something else lurks there, and I don't understand why you're choosing to be naïve. You're too smart for this, V, and I'm curious as to why you're avoiding me, why you're taking on this project and why you're lying to me about being downstairs. This house is alive, it talks, and I'm aware you spent time in the living spaces on the first floor. In fact, this house is screaming at me—so many things all at once, and there are so many voices I can hardly understand what any of it means."

She places a hand to her head as if it aches, and I understand how she feels.

"I'm sorry you're in pain," I say, and my guilt becomes a weight on my chest. "I know how much you hate being here."

"I worry about you. Otherwise I wouldn't be here at all." Choosing to ignore her pain, Glory lifts her head. I can tell because I do it all the time. "I need to smudge your house, and I need your permission to do it."

"Why?"

"I need to rid the house of the spirits it has collected over the past few years, and I need your permission as someone has allowed these spirits to stay here. I'm assuming that person is you. While I understand that a good majority of these spirits have come to the house attached to the different tenants you've had in the apartment downstairs, they have stayed when the people left because your energy creates a welcoming environment."

Everything in this house has always been friendly. Maybe Mom is right. Maybe Glory doesn't understand that it's okay for spirits to linger.

"I first smudged the house when you became friends with Jesse, and I've continued to do it over the years. I wasn't able to force everything out since I've been doing it around the house and I didn't have you or your father's permission to smudge. I have been able to minimize the negative energy's impact and power, but I had no idea how much the energy had grown since my last visit. There's something evil lurking downstairs and you need to let me force it out."

I wrap my arms around myself as I think of my mom. What if Glory accidentally forces her to leave? "Dad will be home soon. He's making deliveries in the area this week, and I don't think he's going to be happy to find you walking around trying to burn down his house."

"My angels told me you'd say that." She goes silent, waiting for me to respond, but I don't have anything to add.

"You're playing a dangerous game," she says, "but I'm here for you if things spiral out of control. In the meantime," she opens the basket, takes out another smudge stick and a seashell, "I'm leaving these with you. When you are called to do this, open the windows and every door to the house, closets included. Light the sticks and go through the entire house, and you have to command the spirits to leave. Once you're done, put out the sticks by crushing them into this shell. Then call me and I'll do a follow-up. Do you understand?"

I nod because Glory has always been awesome to me and lying to her doesn't feel good. Glory places the smudge sticks and shell on the kitchen table then crosses the room to me.

"You aren't helping anyone, living or dead, by giving spirits a place to stay," she says. "They need to move on."

"Why?"

"Because we're meant for more than here. Earth isn't our final destination—it's preschool. Death is a graduation from this place to another. Plus, if the spirits don't move on then neither do we." She tucks my hair behind my ear, like my mother used to do. "Jesse told me your headaches are getting worse. I brought crystals: amethyst and tourmaline. They will help. I spotted the hammock in the backyard. Let's go there and I'll perform a healing. The house is too loud for me to stay in."

"Okay." But I don't move. Instead I'm stuck in place. Dread fills me as I think of Mom, how Sawyer said Lucy's having nightmares and how the activity in the house seems to be growing. "Why am I a magnet for spirits?"

"One, you believe."

True.

"Then there're some people who share a rare place between the living and the dead and you happen to sometimes be there."

I say what she dances around. "Because I'm dying."

"Not anytime soon if I have anything to do with it. Come, let's call on some angels to do their job." Glory takes my hand. I clasp on to her as if I'm a child and follow her out the door and down the stairs.

SAWYER

Wednesday March 13: Nothing much doing today. Cured a little, but Diary, I really am neglecting my cure. But I simply cannot compose myself enough to keep quiet on the cure.

Harry and Joe came over and sat with Tillie and I. I certainly was angry with both of them. They acted too silly for words.

But probably I was disagreeable because I had the most terrible pleurisy. Painted my side with iodine.

Pleurisy—an inflammation of the inner chest wall of the lungs. My Google search on a word I didn't know brought up pictures of people in pain. Can't imagine painting iodine on skin helped, but it was 1918. Don't imagine there was much that helped at all.

Neither can I imagine curing—lying outside in the open air. Even when it was cold. Even when it was hot. Lying still, being quiet, doing nothing . . . for hours. Sounds like hell. I imagine I would have been a lot like Evelyn. I would have gone there because that's what I was told to do, but then would have done a crap-ass job with what was expected.

In the living room, Lucy sits on the floor, zoned in to cartoons and using the coffee table as a place to eat. If Mom finds out she'll go nuclear, but I need the break. I put Evelyn's diary on the coffee table, grab the pot and scoop more box mac-n-cheese onto Lucy's plate.

I walk into the kitchen and place the pot next to the stack of stuff to be cleaned. I've helped Lucy with homework, played dolls until I thought my brain was about to crack and made her dinner. At the kitchen window, I do a double take and spot Veronica lying in a hammock while the town nutcase/psychic hovers near her head.

My cell pings, and my eyebrows draw together when I spot Dad's name. I put in one earbud and listen using the text-to-voice app: It's time for me to hang out with you two again. When would be a good time for you to drive up so I can see you and Lucy? You pick—this weekend or next?

Never. How's that for an answer? I talk into my phone to text back: How about you pay your child support?

There's a purring engine and Mom's shiny Beamer flies into her marked spot on the big space of blacktop. There's a garage in the back big enough for the semi without a rig that pulled in here early Saturday morning. We aren't allowed to park in or near the garage, but only in one of the two spots designated on the side of the garage or on the street out front.

My cell pings two times in a row. It's Dad, and when it chimes a third time, I turn my cell off. I don't have the patience for Dad's bull excuses.

I'm betting with how Mom slams her car door and rushes the house, Sylvia told Hannah about English and Hannah told Mom. Or maybe Sylvia snitched in person. The back door flies open, and Mom yanks off her sunglasses. "What the hell is wrong with you?"

I lean back against the counter and fold my arms over my chest. "Want to pull back on the language? Lucy's in the living room watching cartoons, eating the dinner I made her that you promised to make tonight. And thanks for picking her up from day care like you also promised. I had to split from practice early to get her. We owe more money on the day care account now for the late pickup and the director was ten shades of angry. And Coach is pissed at me again, and because you sweet-talk him, he blames me not you."

Mom jerks like I threw a baseball in her face. "I didn't promise you anything."

"Yeah, you did. Last night before I went to bed, I asked if you would pick her up and make dinner since I had late practice."

"You must be remembering incorrectly as I wouldn't forget that."

The muscles in my neck tense. "I walked into your room last night at ten and I said—"

"Enough!" she shouts. "I don't want to hear it. I would remember, you're wrong and none of what you're saying has anything to do with the real problem. How could you refuse to work with Sylvia? Do you have any idea how many strings I had to pull to put you in that AP English class? Do you have any idea how much time I spent?"

My vision tunnels and my pulse pounds in my ears, but I keep silent because it won't matter what I say. It never matters what I think.

"And now I look like a fool and you're risking your grade and your swim career in order to prove some sort of point?"

Miguel
Sylvia

               Mom

Lucy
Dad

"And what point is that, Sawyer? I don't understand why you would do this to yourself. Why you would do this to me?"

Senior papers
Swimming
I'm not wrong on pickup

             My head pounds

Veronica
School

                                     My hands become clammy

AA meetings

                                            I can't breathe

"Explain to me exactly what it is you're trying to prove by deciding to do the project with the weirdest girl at school!"

"Weird?" I repeat.

"Sylvia told Hannah about this girl—how she does weird things and dresses strangely and hangs out with that delinquent Jesse Lachlin and that hippie Nazareth who stopped traffic last week for a cat. They're losers, Sawyer, crazy even, something I refuse to let you become!"

"That loser is the girl who lives upstairs and is the one who is keeping from her father, your landlord, the fact that your check bounced. She cashed it, and she knows we didn't have the money and she agreed to give us the extra time. I'd think twice on how you talk about Veronica, because she's the reason we have a place to live, and how about you check yourself at the door before you walk in yelling at me again."

I yank my keys out of my pocket, and as I go to walk past Mom she tries to stop me by placing a hand on my arm, but I'm too fast and too strong and I just don't give a damn.

"Sawyer," she calls out, following me, but I'm quick to slam the door to my car. I start the engine and my tires squeal as I back up too fast then tear down the driveway.

                          I take turns too quick
I know what I asked Mom   *I know what I heard*
I know I'm not responsible for everything

                                      She's wrong
                  I hit eighty at the state road

I'm heading out of town
                                  Toward a jump
Toward a cliff
                                  Toward death

own the hallway, near English, Sylvia and I briefly lock eyes. She's still mad at me and I'm mad at her. I hate it, but I don't know how to make this standoff end. She's one of my best friends, but that doesn't give her permission to be mad at me because I don't go along with Mom's plan. I'm grateful we have to sit next to partners in English. That means one less class we have to actively avoid each other in.

"She's pissed," Miguel says as he walks up beside me, and Sylvia enters class.

"You think?" Sarcasm in full effect.

"Sylvia feels like you betrayed her."

Same.

"I should know better than to get involved in this, but don't you think you two have been friends for too long for this?"

I turn on him. "So I should give? Because, to be honest, I don't know what I did wrong."

Miguel moves in front of me, cutting me off from heading into class. "Agreed. You chose a different partner. It doesn't hurt my feelings, but it did hurt hers. She doesn't see this as a project, she sees this as you picking Veronica over her as a friend. I don't understand why Sylvia's upset, but I will say this—why are you willing to hurt Sylvia over the weird girl? Someone you've been friends with since you moved here as compared to the freak who will probably slit your throat in the middle of the night."

"She's not weird," I say as anger leaks into my tone. "And don't talk like that about her."

Miguel's face contorts as he slips to the side, waving me into class. "You lost that portion of the entire argument."

My head drops as I walk into English. Veronica's dressed in fairy wings, a torn-up white fairy dress, and there's fake blood spots all over her outfit, body and face. She texted me last night that today was Halloween, even though it's September, and told me to dress up. I declined that offer, but accepted the invitation to bring Lucy up for Halloween treats.

Our class is a combination of staring at her, whispering about her and flat-out just talking loud enough about her so she can easily hear. It's not right, but Veronica makes herself an easy target year after year. I don't understand why she makes life hard on herself.

Sylvia still watches me like I should have something to say. We've been friends since I moved here, but friendship should work both ways. Not just me having to give all the time. At some point, I'd appreciate it if anyone in my life got that.

Sylvia deflates when I walk past her. What she doesn't understand is that it hurts me, too, but I need Sylvia to side with me for once. Not with Mom.

I collapse into my seat and Veronica assesses me. "No costume?"

"It's not Halloween."

"But that's the magic, it could be. Someone else told you it wasn't Halloween, and you chose to believe that."

I stare blankly at her and she looks thoughtfully back.

"What are you supposed to be?" I eventually ask.

"A fairy."

"Why the blood?"

"I'm a bad fairy."

I guess that makes sense—at least it does in Veronica's world. With Sylvia glaring at me, Veronica's world seems a lot more appealing than mine, so maybe she's the one living life right.

The bell rings, and Mrs. Garcia hands out papers. She places our thesis plan paper on my desk and points at the red A-plus. Her eyes smile with pride.

I do my best to not react, but as soon as she turns away, I slide the paper closer and my mouth lifts with her encouraging comments. Damn, that feels good—especially in a class like English. I did half the research and half of the writing for this paper.

Veronica peeks at the sheet we turned in on Friday. Since then, we've been nervous about whether or not Mrs. Garcia was going to tell us we were now going to be subjected to weekly drug testing. Evidently, Mrs. Garcia has a flare for the unique.

Mrs. Garcia is talking already, going over our lesson for the day, which means we're supposed to be paying attention, but instead I hand the paper to Veronica. She flat-out beams, and I could sit and watch that pretty little grin all day. Even with the fake blood spots on her face, Veronica is beautiful with that halo of curls, but what I love the most about her is that she zigs when I think she's going to zag, and I like being kept on my toes.

Earlier this morning, I ran my earbuds through my sweatshirt to hide that I've been listening to music while my teachers talk. I put in the left earpiece, and I'm greeted by a text. Having not turned off my text-to-voice app, the text is read to me.

Veronica: You know there's a no-cell policy at school, right?

I smile and fight the urge to look at her. That may tip off our teacher that we aren't listening. I place my hand over my mouth and whisper into the microphone. I'm doing research by binge watching Supernatural. Evidently, when we go ghost hunting, we should bring a shovel to dig up a grave. Also a good idea to carry salt and a blowtorch at all times.

Veronica: You're killing me, Smalls.

Me: Is smart-ass a learned or a genetic trait for you?

From the corner of my eye, I catch her lips turn up. Both.

I whisper into the mic again: I read a USA Today article. Did you know 45 percent of people surveyed believe in ghosts? 18 percent say they've been in the presence of a ghost.

Veronica: I believe it. I think the statistic is higher, but people are scared to admit it.

Me: I don't. I think that's the 18 percent who cook up meth on a daily basis.

Veronica: Our house is haunted.

Sure it is. I meant to text your dad. I found Bigfoot taking a shower in our bathroom.

Her smile is close to blinding. You're just flirting with me now. ;-)

I wasn't before, but I am now. You're a cute girl. Flirting's going to happen.

Her cheeks turn bright red. Cute?

Me: Would you prefer hot?

Veronica: Only if you mean it.

Me: I mean it.

Veronica blinks like she doesn't believe the words on her screen, but I couldn't be any more serious. She texts again: I'm serious about our house. When you're courageous enough, meet me at midnight on the stairs.

Nice to know that if I fluster her, she'll change the subject. Who's flirting now?

She smiles again. Me. Definitely me.

"Mr. Sutherland," Mrs. Garcia calls out in that tone that indicates she's aware I'm not listening and that she's about to call me to the stand to testify. "What is the answer?"

Homonym, says Veronica through the text-to-voice, and that computerized voice is welcome because I don't have to look down at my cell to find the answer.

"Homonym," I say like a man who had been born knowing the answer.

Mrs. Garcia raises an eyebrow because I must be right and she has no idea how that happened, yet she continues with the lecture. I sneak a peek at Veronica and she's fighting a smile as she stares straight ahead. What is one more amazing thing about this girl is that she can type without looking at her phone: Nice save.

Me: Thanks for giving me the save.

Veronica: No problem. That's what friends are for.

Friends. I glance over at her again, she winks at me, and that sends me high—almost as high as standing on the edge of a cliff. The sensation is a lot like falling, though not through the air. It's confusing, but it's a rush and I like it.

VERONICA

"Veronica," Sawyer says in a quiet voice, and there's a light, warm touch on my hand. "We're here."

I lift my head off the passenger's-side window and blink away the drowsiness of the unexpected nap. There's a pleasurable awareness along my skin as his hand remains on mine. As if him touching me is natural, destined. It fills a cold, black hole I didn't know was there until I experienced his warmth. Just as I'm starting to comprehend how nice his hand feels, he removes it. I frown, and Sawyer's eyebrows draw together with my reaction.

It's late September, and it feels like a lifetime has passed since Sawyer and I received official project approval from Mrs. Garcia. Trying to find time for us to meet between his swim practices, his work as a lifeguard and my work schedule has been tough, but today finally works.

When we left the house earlier, I had a mild headache that had been threatening to become more. I got up early to do research on our paper, and reading on the computer strained my eyes. Then my shift at the Save Mart was long, busy and loud. Once home, I had enough time to eat a granola bar before meeting Sawyer and Lucy on the front porch.

Lucy was nonstop chatter as Sawyer drove her to a friend's house for a sleepover. I talked along with her, but then we dropped her off, leaving only me and Sawyer. Music was on, but it was low and, after a few pleasantries between us of "how are you" and "I'm good," we fell into silence. I had meant to talk to him about the research I had done on the bridge, but then I had rested my eyes. It was only supposed to be for a second, but . . . I obviously fell asleep.

"Sorry for touching you, but you weren't waking up."

"It's okay." I liked it, and I sort of would like him to do it again. "I can sleep deeply."

I stretch and my muscles are stiff from the weird sleeping position. I gently search my hair and find my fake sunflower barrette that shifted during my nap. I take it off, clip it to my off-the-shoulder T-shirt then stretch again. "I'm sorry for falling asleep."

"Don't worry about it." He gestures with his chin out the windshield. "What do you think?"

There's an awe that sets in as I realize we're here—the covered bridge. The narrow wooden bridge looks barely wide enough for one car to fit through, and if a car was brave enough to drive over it, the only thing keeping it from plunging into the water below is several layers of wooden planks. The aging shingles of the bridge have a foreboding feeling as if they're thunderclouds imprisoning all that's inside.

"I think it's brilliant," I say. "You ready?"

"For lions and tigers and bears? Sure."

We exit the Lexus Sawyer parked off to the side of the road on a dirt clearing. We're north of Lexington, and there's a hint in the west of the fading sunset. A warm breeze carries the scent of the rich forest surrounding us, and the world has a grayish tint as the day gives in to night. Soon, the sky will be deliciously dark. No lights, and ghosts will be hiding in the shadows.

I join Sawyer at the hood of the car and fiddle with the digital recorder in my hand. "Once it's completely dark, we'll go to the middle of the bridge and turn on the recorder. We'll ask a question, give the spirit time to answer and then ask another question."

The skepticism on his face tells me he thinks I'm batcrap crazy.

"Do you know how far that drop is into the river? It's big, and I'm not sure that bridge is safe."

"I agree. It's not safe." I point to the CAUTION sign behind us then follow along the road to show the curve before the bridge. "A driver lost control of the car, missed the bridge completely due to the curve then went over the edge into the river. The people in the car drowned."

"Two teens, right? On the way home from a dance?" Sawyer glances over at me with a knowing smirk on his face, and I smile because he's correct.

"Someone's been doing their research."

He shrugs one shoulder and goes for the backseat of the car. Sawyer opens the door, tosses his cell in, pulls out a fancy camera and starts for the river. I refuse to let him off the hook. "What's the camera for and what else did you find out about the bridge?"

"I have to take pictures for my photography course. As for the bridge, I read about some teen who hung himself in the middle of the bridge and a woman who was walking through the bridge who had a heart attack and died halfway through. There are some sketchier earlier stories about people who would go in the bridge and never came back out, but I couldn't find too many references to support that."

"Do you know the ghost stories?"

"I assumed ghosts were your area of expertise." Sawyer pauses near the steep river bluff, puts the camera to his eye and takes a few snapshots. "I have a hard time believing we're going to see ghost headlights behind us on the bridge and then headlights shining from the river up into the bridge, nor do I think we're going to hear people calling from the river for help."

"Aren't you optimistic?"

He snaps a picture of me and waggles his eyes. "That's my nickname."

Sawyer continues to take pictures, each step taking him closer and closer to the edge of the stone cliff until his toes literally hang off.

"As you mentioned earlier, that's a big drop," I warn.

"I know."

The river below is fast moving, deep, murky and feels evil. As if Satan himself had taken the time to create this place. "I think falling into it would suck."

"I've jumped from higher."

"I haven't. I don't swim, remember?"

"I still don't see how that's possible."

"Easy. If you don't go into the water, there's no reason to swim. When you download the pictures onto a computer, we should look through them for spirit orbs."

"I think you meant dust particles."

"Someday, you're going to piss off a ghost and he's going to rip out your heart."

"I'll keep that in mind."

Not liking the strange dizzy feeling of being near the drop, I sit on a rock by the edge and watch as Sawyer continues to point and click with his fancy camera. I place my cell and recorder on the ground behind me and take in the world.

My eyes tell me that the place is beautiful and that I should be relaxed as I become one with nature, but there's this sixth sense that tickles the back of my neck. Like a spider landing on my skin. It's extremely uncomfortable, and it's hard to stay still and not run back to the car, but I force myself to remain seated.

The wind blows my curls in front of my face and I take the hair clip from my shirt. My fingers fumble, the clip falls from my hands and I lunge forward in a vain attempt to catch it, but fail. "No."

It drifts to a rock a few feet below me. Dang it. Mom gave me that barrette. I roll onto my belly and ignore the sickening gravity trying to yank me over the rocks and into the river. I reach and nothing. I crawl forward a little more and pebbles roll and bounce down the embankment. My fingertips barely brush the area of the rock near the barrette. So close.

Just another inch. A few centimeters more and my stomach drops as the ground beneath me gives.

"Watch out!" Sawyer yells.

My heart shoots up to my throat as I scream. My body tumbles forward. Pain as I hit rocks, burning as I slide. I grasp wildly for anything to steady myself, but everything's moving, everything's shifting, and there's a huge boulder ahead. As I try to roll to keep my head from the impact, I'm caught.

A grip on my arm. My body whiplashes as I move up and my feet come around toward the river. I'm drawn into something strong, and when I look up, solid blue eyes bore into mine. "Hang on to me."

Sawyer has me by my right wrist and snakes his other arm around my waist. I swing my arm around his neck and clutch him. Carrying my weight, Sawyer vertically rolls us against the rock to place me against the ledge with him prone to the edge. His arm, a steel belt, keeps me securely to him. Our bodies are pressed tight, and I'm surrounded by his warmth.

"Are you okay?" Sawyer asks.

Am I? My skin burns from the slide, but the pain is bearable.

"Veronica," Sawyer says softly, his breath against my ear. "Are you okay?"

"Yeah." My eyes widen with how far we fell, and by the knowledge that in order for Sawyer to be here he had to have fallen, too . . . or jumped after me.

Sawyer releases my wrist, and I flatten myself against the rock wall. All I can see is me falling down another fifteen feet into the dark water. Around us, shadows edge forward as we lose the last of the gray daylight.

Sawyer scans the area and there's nothing but a rock ledge on either side of us. On the other side of the river, there's a sloped clearing. Too bad we aren't over there. I think of the two teens, of their car hurtling down this cliff, and I think of what it must have been like to hit the river, to struggle to breathe, to only take in water and for the last thing they saw to be the murky blackness. I'm not scared of dying, but I don't want to die this way.

A comforting touch on my shoulder and Sawyer brushes his fingers lightly along my arm. Pleasing goose bumps form, and I shiver.

"We're okay." He misreads my reaction. It's shocking how in control and calm he sounds. "I've been in worse positions than this."

My head snaps up. "You've what?"

"Do you have your cell?" he asks as if I haven't spoken.

My hand goes for my back pocket and my fingers twitch. It's up top and not with me. Now, I panic. "This is bad, this is—"

"We're fine. I could swim my way out of this, but you don't swim, and that's easily a fifteen-foot drop into deep water. I've heard about this river and it doesn't run shallow for another couple of miles. How's your upper body strength?"

For the first time in my life, I wish I would have done a chin-up.

Reading my expression, Sawyer tilts his head then rubs my arm again as if saying my lack of strength doesn't bother him. He tests the area near where we fell and the dirt gives. Pebbles and earth plummet down the side then start to rain on me. My blood pumps wildly as my arms shoot up to cover my head. I'm going to be knocked down by a boulder and drown.

Heat and solid warmth as Sawyer wraps his body around mine, gathering me into his chest. He uses his shoulders and head as a shield. I take in a deep breath, and I'm consumed with his scent. It's a comforting combination of a pool and a sweet, dark smell. I keep breathing slowly in and out as I listen to the pebbles and rocks continue to slip and slide and bounce down the rock wall.

When the downfall halts, Sawyer straightens and I'm confused by how unfazed he is, whereas I feel as if I could literally vibrate out of my skin. Sawyer stares down at me, not blinking, and the reality of our situation is written plainly all over his face: we have to jump. "There's no going up."

Fear dries my mouth out. Death, I'm not afraid of. Dying by drowning—I'll admit—scares the crap out of me. "I told you, I can't swim."

"But I can. In fact, it's about the only thing I'm good at, besides math. If we jump, I'll hold your hand, and I won't let go when we hit the water. I'll help you reach the surface. Once we do, I'm going to have to let you go for a second and then I'm going to come up behind you. I'll put an arm underneath your arms and then you'll need to trust me enough to let go of your body to float. I'll get us to the other side, okay?"

"No."

"We're on a deserted road at nightfall with no cell phones. Give me our other options, and I'll give those a try."

My eyes flit from the shoreline on the other side that now looks a mile away to the cliff wall behind us that's impossible to climb. Truth—maybe we could climb it, but if we fail and I fall, I'll drown. At least by jumping, Sawyer will be holding on to me.

Another deep breath in. I'm not a coward. I never have been, and I won't start now. Go big or go home, right? Or is it go big so I can go home?

Defiant of my fate, I raise my chin. "Okay. We jump."

"As soon as you hit the water, kick your legs. That will help with keeping you from going deeper. Hold your breath, and I need you to fight any panic that will set in. Your instincts are going to scream for you to do everything it takes to survive. You'll be desperate to find something solid and then push down on it to keep you up. That solid thing is going to be me. Don't grab on to me, and if you do, don't fight me and don't push me down. When I take hold of you, just go with it and then do everything I tell you to do. Trust me to get you to safety."

He extends his hand to me palm up. I hesitate before placing my fingers in his and stare straight into his eyes. "I swear to God, if you let me drown I will haunt you until the day you die, and I will be the nastiest ghost you've ever met."

His eyes dance, like he's amused, like he's looking forward to what's about to happen. "Promise?"

"You're crazy, aren't you?" I say.

"Yes. Now let's jump."

SAWYER

Veronica places her hand in mine, and it's warm and soft. The softest skin I've ever touched. I rub my thumb over the top of her hand, and she squeezes my fingers. Something in my chest moves, and it's a light feeling, the tiptoeing of wings. This jump scares the hell out of her. It's there in the back of her eyes, but she holds herself as if she can take on the world and win. She's strong, she's courageous, and for some reason, she's trusting me.

"Jump out," I say, "away from the rocks."

"Okay."

"On the count of three," I say. "One . . . two . . ."

"Three," she says, and I have to move quick as she makes the leap of faith.

The fall is electrifying. It's too short, but the thrill of the complication of doing it with someone else creates that rush that I crave. We hit the water and the current is faster than I thought. Veronica's hand becomes slick, her grip loosening as she panics. She drifts away from me, and the pull of the racing river threatens to tear her away.

I kick. She's kicking and I open my eyes. There's nothing in the dark water. Veronica's body jerks, she starts to become deadweight, and holding on to her tightly, I fight for the surface. I break free, gulp in air, and automatically tread water as I yank her up.

Veronica emerges, and she takes in an audible gasp then coughs as if choking. She's kicking too fast, not in a rhythm and her arms are slapping at the water. I let go of her wrist, her eyes pop open and she thrashes as the terror of going back under takes over.

Her body starts down again, but I go under the water, swim behind her, and surface while slipping my arms under her armpits. "Veronica! I have you."

Veronica's legs stop kicking, but her arms continue to flail. Treading water with only my legs, I turn her to the shoreline and in the last seconds of daylight, she calms at the sight of our destination. "I'm going to remove one arm and wrap it around your waist. Then I want you to float with me as I swim us to shore."

"I can't float," she says.

"That's weird because you seem to be doing a good job of it now. Just keep doing what you're doing. If you think you need to help me swim, don't. The water is going to keep you buoyant, plus I'm strong enough to get us both to shore."

Using a side stroke, I fight the swift current and swim. The moment my feet hit ground, I stand, help Veronica to her feet then keep an arm around her as she staggers out of the river. We reach the grass, and Veronica collapses to the ground.

Her wet hair is plastered to her face, and she shivers as she leans back against the trunk of a tree. The night is warm, the breeze cool and while my juices are flowing, Veronica appears exhausted.

"Thank you," she says, and the sincerity in her eyes causes me to look away.

"Thank you for trusting me. Besides, you did the hard part. It takes a massive amount of control to suppress thousands of years of survival instincts. Most people would have tried to push me down to keep themselves up. You kept your cool in a hard situation."

"How are you so calm?" There's awe in her expression, and I don't deserve it.

"It's not calm, it's stupidity," I say then, switch the subject because I don't want to linger on that topic. I'm ashamed that I like the adrenaline high I'm currently experiencing, especially since that high scared her so much. And I'm even more ashamed that I want to do it again. "I guess we're going to have to cross the ghost bridge to head home."

Her forehead furrows. "You don't want to leave now, do you?"

"Don't you?"

Veronica's eyes glint, an adventurous spark that speaks to my soul. Her reckless smile follows suit, and I'm officially on board for whatever she has planned. "No way. This place is definitely haunted. We're staying and we're investigating."

VERONICA

M y jeans are wet, my T-shirt is soaked, but the worst part is my soggy shoes. My feet squish in my socks, and I contemplate taking them off as Sawyer and I walk through the thick forest for the bridge.

"What do you mean this place is definitely haunted?" Sawyer asks.

The glance I throw him is incredulous. "Seriously? We almost died. Several people have died here. Do you think that's coincidence?"

"What are you suggesting?" Sawyer is as drenched as I am, but he seems more comfortable than me in our current saturated state.

"That the bridge, the river, maybe an entity of some sort, wanted us to fall."

"I think we've had a lot of rain this summer and that loosened the ground where you sat, and I don't think we were anywhere close to death."

A disagreeing *pssh* leaves my mouth and that causes Sawyer to smirk. It's crazy, but the cocky swimmer boy has been growing on me by the day. So much so that I look forward to every adorable, arrogant smile and his self-assured quips.

We reach the road and the bridge looms before us. The half-moon's light creates an eerie haze over the roof of the bridge and only highlights the black void we must cross to reach Sawyer's car, our cell phones and hopefully the recorder. A cool breeze drifts over my arms, but that isn't what's causing my skin to prick. There's a growing uneasiness in my blood, and a voice inside me screams to run.

"Do you feel it?" I whisper as my chest compresses with an invisible pressure.

"Like a serial killer is waiting for us in the middle of the bridge? Yeah."

Surprised by his admission, I glance over at him. "So you agree this place is haunted?"

"No. We're in the middle of nowhere. When we had light, I didn't properly check the bridge. There might be some deranged hermit who lives in the bridge for shelter, and it's really going to piss me off if I have to punch him in the jaw because he touches you."

I roll my eyes. "It must suck to not believe in anything."

"I believe in things."

"Like?"

"Things. Are we crossing the bridge or what?"

"Oh, we're crossing." Definitely crossing. I start forward for the dark opening and Sawyer's right beside me. So close that his arm brushes mine. "If you don't believe, then why are you scared?"

"I'm not scared," he says.

"I think you are. I think you're walking close to me because you need me to protect you from the big, bad monsters."

"You're right. I was actually considering using you as a human shield for the serial killer. Or I could be close because we're crossing a wooden bridge that was built over a hundred years ago. The back deck at my old house barely stayed together after two years. So maybe if the termite-eaten boards beneath us crack, I can grab you before you fall through to the river."

That thought causes my heart to beat faster, especially when the boards beneath us do creak with our weight. I have no intentions of going into that river again. "People drive their cars that weigh thousands of pounds over this bridge."

"People also do meth, but I don't recommend it."

I breathe in deeply as we pass the halfway point of the bridge, and the scent is of the wood. The only sound is the tapping of our shoes against the planks and the rushing water below. I glance wildly around, but I don't see anything—just blackness.

Sawyer's not touching me, but I sense his solid presence beside me. As if the heat of his body has the ability to reach out and envelop me in a protective hug. It's odd because while fear creeps along the back of my neck and I sense the impending hazards around us and spirits lurking in the shadows watching us with curiosity, I also feel protected. As if Sawyer is a natural shield against the dangers of the supernatural world.

A loud snap behind us, I jump and glance over my shoulder. Sawyer snakes his fingers around my wrist and holds on to me.

"Hello?" I call out as I edge toward the safety of the exit. There's another tapping. Like footsteps and Sawyer pulls on my wrist, encouraging me to move faster.

"It's probably an animal," Sawyer says.

"Maybe." But I don't believe that. "But animals don't make that type of sound when they walk. We need to get that recorder."

Sawyer knows how to make a fire, and I'm impressed. He mentioned something about having remnants of stuff in the car left over from a camping trip with friends over the summer, but bonfire building without gasoline isn't nearly as easy as one would think. While he gathered sticks and kindling, I kept it to myself that Jesse taught me how to build a fire before I was fifteen. I wanted to see if Sawyer would succeed, and keeping with the theme for the day, he has surprised me once again.

Near the fire, Sawyer is examining the camera he discarded when he jumped down the rocks after me. It doesn't appear worse for wear, and I'm relieved when he points the camera at the fire and it flashes with the shot.

"Do you think it's legal to build a bonfire near a covered bridge?" I ask.

We're not right next to the bridge, but closer to his parked car in a clearing of the woods. "Probably not, but are you going to tell?"

"Nope." I'm a bit disappointed. I've been asking questions into the recorder for the past half hour, and when I've played back the audio, not a single ghost has talked to me.

I walk back to the bridge and step inside. Sawyer's watching me from the fire. His serious expression tells me he's ready to leap to his feet and save me from the river again if the need should arise. He raises the camera to his face and takes another picture of me.

I turn on the recorder again and say, "What's your name?" I stay silent, giving the ghost time to respond, and then say, "Are the two teens who went into the river in their car here?"

More silence and then I turn off the recorder. Still wet from our wild ride down the hill and into the water, I shiver with the cooling night air. I head back to the fire and sit next to Sawyer so I can watch the bridge. Hopefully, we'll see ghost headlights.

"How did you do it?" I ask, as I can't stop replaying what happened. "How did you remain so calm and how were you able to think so clearly?"

"I don't know." Sawyer tries to readjust his still damp shirt, and when it doesn't do what he wants, he yanks it over his head. My cheeks grow warm at the sight of his chest—his very, very beautiful, muscled chest. I comb my fingers through my hair to try to dry my curls and to distract myself. Yet my gaze drifts over to him again.

Stop it. My friends are fit. Leo is fit. I see them without their shirts all the time. This isn't anything new. This is just a guy. A guy who called me weird. A guy who has ignored me for years . . . a guy I text daily. Not only text daily, but eagerly await our flirty banter. A guy who makes me laugh even when my head is hurting. A guy who seems to want to make me laugh in those painful times. A guy who looks in my eyes as if I'm the only person in the room and not at my skull as if he's trying to see what's wrong with me. A guy who risked his life to save mine.

But that doesn't have anything to do with how I watch him as he stands and drapes his shirt over the low branch of a tree. I'm entranced by the way his shoulder blades stretch as he reaches up and with how each movement pronounces another way his body is glorious.

Maybe I hit my head and I'm concussed. That has to be what's going on. Yet I still don't glance away. Not even when Sawyer turns and catches me openly gaping. He raises an eyebrow, and that cocky, lopsided grin grows. God, help me, I smile with him.

"Can I help you with anything?" he tauntingly asks.

"You have to be aware you're beautiful," I say. "And I know for a fact I'm not the first girl to notice."

"Maybe. But I like you noticing."

I overtly roll my eyes. "Because you like the attention."

"No, because it's you." His grin moves from cocky to adorable. The warmth in my cheeks spreads to my chest and butterflies flutter their wings along my rib cage.

Sawyer settles next to me again, closer this time. So close that when he exhales his arm touches mine, and I can hardly breathe with this strange, building excitement.

We stare at the flames dancing in the night and watch as the popping embers shoot toward the stars. We're silent, but it's not uncomfortable. In fact, it's so comfortable that I don't want it to end.

A tickling touch near the crook of my elbow and my pulse kicks up a notch at the sight of Sawyer's finger slowly tracing a freckle on my skin.

"It looks like a tiny kitten," he murmurs.

I laugh because it does. He circles the spot again, and I wish I had the courage to look at him and see what he's thinking. To see if he finds me as attractive as I find him, but I stare at my arm instead.

What would I do if his blue eyes had that heavy hooded expression of desire?

Kiss him. It's a whisper in my ear, a caress along my skin. A wish, a hope, a temptation.

Good God, kissing Sawyer Sutherland. I bet he'd be an excellent kisser.

"I didn't know freckle imagery was a thing," I say, and my voice is softer than normal.

"It should be. Would you like me to decipher any more on you?"

I laugh louder this time as he waggles his eyebrows. "You're funny."

"So are you. I like being around you, Veronica. A lot."

Me, too. "You can call me V, if you'd like. That's what my friends call me."

His eyes stray away from mine to my lips. "I can, but I like Veronica. It suits you."

I blush, he notices and we both look away as if we're unsure middle-schoolers at a dance.

He clears his throat. "Plus, I'm not interested in being like everyone else."

Neither am I. Because of that, I tackle this head-on. "Is this as awesomely weird for you as it is for me?"

"Do you mean the fact we're becoming friends or that I'm attracted to you and would give just about anything to pull you close and kiss you until you can't breathe?"

Heat rushes through me like liquid fire at the idea of my body wound tight to his. "Both."

"Do you understand what's happening?" Sawyer asks.

"No," I whisper. "But I like it."

"Me, too."

Another round of silence, but this time Sawyer reaches over and places his hand over my mine and my heart nearly beats out of my chest. I swallow to help my dry mouth. If I don't speak, we might kiss, and as much as I want it, I'm equal parts scared of what feelings kissing might create.

"Tell me something I don't know about you," I say quietly into the night.

"You like this game, don't you?"

"If it makes you feel better, you're the only person I've played this game with."

Awe flashes over him and he quickly averts his gaze to the flames. I watch him as the firelight dances across his face, curious what he'll share with me next. Maybe that he likes peanut butter in his vanilla ice cream like me or that he, like his sister, has seen a ghost.

"My dad told me once I had to be brave," he says.

"Sorry?"

Sawyer doesn't look at me, only the flames. "You asked me earlier how I remained calm. When my mom and dad got divorced, he told me I had to be brave. He told me that my mom needed me and that Lucy needed me and that I had to be the man of the house since he wasn't going to be around anymore. He said that if I let Mom know I was scared that she would be scared and then so would Lucy so I needed to find my courage and not show fear."

That was heavy. "How old were you?"

"Eleven."

"And you listened?"

Sawyer rubs the back of his head, but keeps his gaze trained straight ahead. "I had to. My mom was working her way up the sales force with the company and the company told her she had to move here to cover this sales route. Mom's parents died a long time ago, and while she knew people here, she didn't know anyone well enough that they'd help us. After Mom worked all day, she had to come home and take care of us. Lucy was a baby, and while I always struggled in school, I had yet to be diagnosed with dyslexia. Mom lost her temper a lot and would cry as soon as she put us to bed.

"I felt bad for her and figured Dad was right. Watching Mom be scared and hearing her cry made me feel terrible. I figured my fear was making her worse so I decided to be brave."

Brave. People use the word all the time, but I'm not a fan of it. "When my mom was first diagnosed with cancer, all sorts of people came out of the woodwork. Old friends and family members. Mostly people who felt guilty for things they had done and wanted forgiveness to feel good about themselves before she died. Most of them would show up and then leave just as quick, but my mom had this sister who had completely disowned her when she married my dad because who would marry a truck driver, right? Like that's the most scandalous thing.

"Anyhow, my aunt stuck around and I hated this lady. She would try to talk to me as if she had the right to tell me what to do, and she'd come into our house and rearrange things because she said it would make our life easier, but she didn't know anything. She used to tell me all the time to be brave and to not cry in front of Mom."

I pause as my throat burns with the memory of standing in the hallway of the hospital. Of how I hated the sanitized smell, how small I felt as doctors and nurses passed by and how I hated the thought of seeing my shrunken mother in a bed hooked to all sorts of machines.

But then Mom called my name, my heart leaped and as I began to run into the room, my aunt had grabbed my arm, squeezing my bicep so tightly that it left a bruise. *Don't you dare cry in front of her. She has enough to worry about. You're old enough to be brave.*

Yet that's all I wanted to do. I wanted to throw myself onto the bed, I wanted to be cuddled in my mother's arms and I wanted to cry until I couldn't cry anymore.

Moisture in my eyes and I rub at them, hoping Sawyer doesn't see.

"Being brave didn't save her and neither did all the poison they pumped into her. She died in a hospital bed, too weak to even turn her head. All Mom ever talked about was wanting to see sunflowers again, but her treatments were so intense that she couldn't leave the hospital."

"I'm sorry," he says. "About your mom. I didn't know."

"Most people don't. I'm barely an afterthought so why would they care about my mom?"

Sawyer is nice enough for guilt to flicker over his expression. "What type of cancer did she have?"

I nibble on my bottom lip and it's tough to tell him the truth. "Brain cancer."

There's silence on his end and I hate it. "Of course there can be inherited genetic factors that causes people to have the same type of tumors and cancers, but Dad thinks it's because we used to live near this industrial plant. A lot of people in our neighborhood got sick. Quite a few died of cancer. Lawyers visit Dad, but I don't want to know what's happening so he keeps the class action lawsuit to himself. But that's why we moved here—to be away from the city."

"Are you scared the same thing is going to happen to you?"

Daily. "Mom fought for every second of her life. She went through every course of treatment available. Even when the doctors told her that doing so wouldn't add much more time. But Dad didn't want her to stop. I remember hearing him beg her to do the treatments even though they made her so sick that she couldn't get out of bed. They made her lose weight, too. She looked awful, and she felt awful.

"Sometimes I couldn't be around her because her immune system was compromised and they were scared I'd make her sick. The treatments helped her live longer, but it was terrible, and I don't want that. I never want to die like her. If my tumor ever grows and becomes malignant, I'm not doing a damn thing to stop it. Instead, I'm going to live every day to its fullest until I drop dead. I want quality of life, not quantity."

"How old were you when she passed?" he asks.

"She died when I was fifteen." I touch my hand to my hair. I lost Mom's sunflower barrette and the pain in my chest rivals the one that's often in my head. A lump forms in my throat. "Mom was diagnosed when I was eleven. I was diagnosed a few months later."

The sympathy on Sawyer's face is real. It's not pity, it's understanding. He nods at me, as if telling me it's okay. That he understands there are some hurts that don't go away, as if he knows that somehow at eleven, we were both changed forever.

"You okay?" he asks.

I nod, a little too fast. "Yeah. I lost my barrette in the fall. I'm a little sad about it, but it's a barrette so whatever." I need to change the subject. "How did you become brave?"

Sawyer's mouth curves up. "I killed a spider."

"What?"

"I was terrified of spiders and there was this huge one in Lucy's room. One of those big hairy wolf spiders. I swear to God that thing was the size of my palm."

"And how did you kill this Australia-sized spider?"

"A shoe. Scared the crap out of me, but I did it. So I figured if I could do that, then maybe I could be brave forever if I tackled my biggest fear."

"What was that?"

Sawyer lowers his head like he's embarrassed, like he's sharing secrets he never intended to share. He lifts his head again, and when he looks me in the eye, there's a bond that's created between us. An energy that's so tangible it feels as if I can reach out and touch it.

"I jumped," he said.

"You jumped?"

"From the high dive. I've been jumping and swimming ever since."

A swift breeze blows from the direction of the bridge and it's cold. An odd and eerie sensation, especially since the night is warm. Taps come from inside the bridge and Sawyer's head shoots in that direction. "Did you hear that?"

I did, and it's the most beautiful sound. I scramble to my feet and Sawyer joins me.

"Grab your camera," I whisper, and he does.

As we approach, a chill tingles the base of my neck, and Sawyer rubs his arms as if he is also affected. I stand on the edge of the bridge, and it's like I entered the air of an electrical storm. Sawyer steps farther in than me, scans the area, but I know what he sees—darkness.

"Take a picture of the inside of the bridge," I whisper. "Three pictures in quick succession, but before you take them, ask the ghosts to be present in the photo."

His entire face contorts. "Do what?"

"It's like picture day at school. Everyone likes to run their fingers through their hair before sitting. If we want a ghost to show, we have to give it time to work up enough energy to take the photo. Plus, how would you feel if some stranger showed up and started taking pictures without asking? If you think about it, it's sort of rude."

"I . . . um . . . am going to take your picture now," Sawyer calls out, and I cringe with how it's apparent how stupid he feels. "If that's okay."

Not the most eloquent, but it will do. Sawyer raises the camera, takes several photos in a row, changes position and does it again.

I pull out the recorder and extend my arm into the black of the bridge. "As I said earlier, we aren't here to hurt you, but to talk to you. Are you trapped on this bridge?"

Knowing the drill, Sawyer goes completely still and we wait a few seconds to see if the ghost responds.

"If you're trapped, what do you need us to know so you can be free?"

More silence from us again.

"Is there anything you think I should know?"

I wait some more, and then turn off the recorder. Stepping off the bridge to the fire, I use the light there to find the folder and play back what I just asked. Sawyer's also walked off the bridge, but he's near the edge where I fell and that gives me shivers. It's as if the boy has no sense of self-preservation.

On the playback, I ask my first question. No response. I ask my second question. More nothing. I ask my third and I jerk as if shocked by electricity. I back it up, listen again, and my hands shake with excitement.

Me: "Is there anything you think I should know?"

A whispered voice: "He's hurting."

SAWYER

Veronica laughs as I bust a modified move in the driver's seat of my car. It's late, and we're both slaphappy. I like to dance. It's something most guys avoid, but it doesn't bother me to get on the dance floor and move with the music.

After her fit of giggles, Veronica returns to singing along to the song and throwing out some passenger-seat moves herself. I'd love to get on the dance floor with her. I bet the two of us could bring the house down.

I turn onto Main Street and the song ends. She relaxes in her seat and rolls her head to look at me. From the unexpected river bath, her hair is dried, but it is wild and unruly. Even in the dark of night, she's brilliant sunshine and she has a way of thawing me out like no one else. There's something comforting in being in her presence and it's something I want more of.

"I'm going to download the audio from the recorder tomorrow and see if I can slow the recording down. Sometimes ghosts will communicate on a different frequency than us. Maybe that will help us hear something we didn't before."

I think she's going to be sadly disappointed, but I'm game to help. Honestly, I just like being around her. "Still trying to convince me ghosts are talking to you through a recorder?"

"Not convince, Sutherland. Prove. And you heard the ghost."

"I heard something." The recording was faint and it was nonsense. *He hurts.* What does that mean?

"You'll hear it better when I get it downloaded on the computer, and what are you going to do with yourself when I prove to you ghosts are real?"

"Probably rock in a corner and then cry myself to sleep every night."

She laughs, and I smile along with her.

"Text me when you're ready to go over the recording, and if you're okay with it, I'll come up," I say.

"Okay. You should bring Lucy, too. I need help making more turkeys, and I also need to start making decorations for Christmas. I think I'll do that in October."

Veronica's done this for years—celebrate holidays at weird times. And it's not just that she celebrates it in private and it somehow gets leaked. She goes all out. Her clothes, decorating her locker, decorating her friends' lockers, even handing out gifts to teachers. When she was younger, she sometimes gave invitations to people who would never come. Instead they made fun of her, making her the topic of jokes for weeks. When the teasing eventually died down, she would do something crazy again.

"Lucy will love that," I say, and it's the truth.

I want to ask Veronica why she does it, but don't. Doing so could bring down the mood. Tonight has been one of the best I've had in months, and I'm not ready to let it go.

"Would you like to come?" Veronica asks as I turn onto our street. "To Thanksgiving? It's a week from today. Dad makes this huge turkey and I make the sides and you should see all the desserts. You can bring Lucy and your mom if you want. Dad wouldn't mind. In fact, he'd probably like getting to know you all since you're living downstairs."

She squishes her lips the side, and I'm completely drawn in. "Actually, it would be awesome if you came. Since Dad travels for his job, he gives me a lot of room and trust, but he expects me to be honest with him about what I'm doing and who I'm doing it with. He'll want to meet you."

She peeks at me then, from under long eyelashes, and it doesn't matter what she would have asked, the answer is, "Sure." A pause. "Don't worry about Mom, though. She travels in the area for her job, even on Saturdays, but Lucy and I will come."

That smile she unleashes is close to lethal. "Great! This is going to be so much fun! We play games and we have a question at the dinner table that everyone has to answer and there's going to be pie! So much pie you'll think you died and went to heaven."

I pull up in front of her house, and there's a strange combination of sadness and nerves. Something I'm unfamiliar with. I'm not ready for this night to be over. But it's late, I have a curfew, and even though Veronica wears the most beautiful smile, there are dark circles under her eyes and her skin is a bit too pale—as if she needs to sleep for a week.

I turn off the engine, and there's silence as we both stay seated in the car. I wonder what it means that she hasn't jumped out yet. Maybe it doesn't mean anything, but there's a part of me that wants it to mean something because as weird as it is to admit—I like her. "I had fun."

"Jumping off a cliff was fun?"

I smile to take the sting out of the truth. "That's my every Friday, Saturday and Sunday night. I try to fit jumping in during the week when I can, but school often gets in the way."

"School ruins everything," she says.

"Yeah." A pause on my end. "I meant what I said earlier. I like hanging out with you."

There's something in how her blue eyes soften that causes me to feel lost and then found. "I like hanging out with you, too."

My head tilts, as I almost forgot. I dig into my jeans pocket and pull out her flower barrette. "When you were trying for EVPs that last time, I went over to check out where you fell and I found this."

Her gorgeous mouth pops open into an adorable O. "Where did you find it? I looked everywhere on the ground for it."

I shrug one shoulder like it wasn't a big thing as she sweeps locks of her hair up to fasten the barrette into place. "It had fallen down the cliff. Not as far as we fell, but down a bit."

"And you went for it?" Her voice rises in pitch as if she thinks I'm crazy. I am, but that would be news for her.

"It wasn't a big deal. As I said, it wasn't nearly as far down as we went and—"

I don't get a chance to finish my sentence as Veronica launches herself across the console at me. Her arms around my neck, her soft body pressed to mine, the sweet scent of her hair and perfume filling my nose.

"Thank you," she says against my neck. Her hot breath causes me to become warm, and the air surrounding us grows rich with electricity. "You have no idea how much this means to me. It's like you've given me the world."

I'm hesitant, so slow in moving because I don't want to do anything that she doesn't want, but I've been going crazy with the need to touch her nearly all evening. And with her arms still wrapped around me, with her head nuzzled intimately on my shoulder, her breath against my neck, I weave my arms around her and allow my hands on her back.

She sighs then, as if she's happy, and she relaxes further into me. I close my eyes and hold on tighter. I never knew a hug could feel like this. Every cell in my body buzzes, and I'd give anything to turn my head and kiss her.

Veronica slowly edges back, but she doesn't pull completely away. She keeps her hands on my shoulders as her eyes bore into mine. "You shouldn't have done that. The ground could have given way again and you could have fallen into the river and it was pitch black and what if you had hit a rock on the way down and passed out and drowned and—"

"But I didn't," I cut her off. I glance down as I tell her more than I've ever told anyone else. "Sometimes a good adrenaline rush makes me feel alive."

The humor in her eyes tells me she thinks I'm joking. "That's insane."

"That's me."

A renegade curl breaks loose from the barrette and bounces near her eye. I hold my breath as I capture the lock of hair and tuck it behind her ear. The air around us pops and sizzles as my fingers barely brush the skin of her cheek and neck.

Her eyes darken and she wets her lips. She stares down at my mouth as if she also feels this heat. As if she's also been thinking about touching and kissing me.

Movement over her shoulder, outside of the car, and my gaze snaps and narrows on the figures on the steps of the porch. Veronica turns her head to look, and she gasps. "No way."

A click of the door handle and she darts out of the car then shoots across the yard. My gut twists as I watch as Leo Wheeling lazily drops one foot then another down the steps of the porch. He wears a satisfied smirk as he wraps his arms around Veronica.

He hugs her, she hugs him, and jealousy taints my soul. At a deliberate and methodical snail's pace, I leave the car, walk up the yard and make direct eye contact with the two other guys on the porch. One is Jesse Lachlin, the other, Nazareth Kravitz. Jesse leans against the support beam, Nazareth sits on the top step. Neither of them are the type to glance away. Lucky me. Guess the three of us will have a nice staring contest for as long as it takes because I'm not giving in.

"What are you doing here?" Veronica says as she pulls back from Wheeling, and I hate that she acts as if it's Christmas.

Lachlin disapprovingly looks to Veronica, and so does Kravitz. That makes me curious. Which one of us are they unhappy about? Me or Wheeling? And if it's Wheeling, why? The four of them have been friends for nearly as long as I've lived in this town.

"I was bored and thought about how much I missed hanging

with you so I drove home." Wheeling touches her, his fingers playing with the ends of her hair, and I want to sock the cocky bastard in the stomach. But I won't because she's glowing.

Here's the sad thing, I have no reason to hate him—other than he just interrupted the best night I've had in months. Can't explain what I'm feeling right now because I don't do relationships, but I do know that I like Veronica and this guy is getting in the way of my time with her.

"I didn't think I'd have to wait a few hours to see you, though," Wheeling says.

"We were working on our project, and I turned off my cell to make sure it didn't interfere with anything."

"Good thing you did, too," I speak for the first time. Wheeling glares in my direction, and he's as happy to see me as I am to see him. "Otherwise you would have been pissed if your cell rang as you talked to the ghosts."

I get what I want, Veronica's smile in my direction. "You're right. That would have made me angry. By the way, Sawyer, this is Leo. Leo, this is—"

"I know who he is."

Yeah, I'm sure he does. We know a few people in common. He even dated a few friends of mine. No one has a bad word to say about him other than he chooses to hang with this group over anyone else. I used to think that was a bad thing, but after spending time with Veronica, I'm understanding I need to reevaluate a few things about life.

"Play nice, Leo," Veronica mutters under her breath, and the ticked-off glare she gives him gives me a fantastic high.

"Text me when you want to go over that recording, Veronica," I say. "I'll be downstairs when you're ready." She didn't kiss me tonight, maybe she'll never kiss me, but unlike him, I'll see her Monday and each day after that. And Wheeling? He'll head back to college.

From over Veronica's head, Wheeling's eyes flicker with rage and I can't help the smirk as I jog up the stairs.

I go inside, unlock the door to my apartment, flick on the living room light and my high takes a nosedive. A curse word leaves my mouth as I spot the television on, a corkscrew on the coffee table, two bottles of wine and a lipstick-stained glass that contains a backwash amount of red liquid. On the couch, Mom is a passed-out and snoring lump.

She's in her white silk dress shirt and black dress pants with high heels off. Hair falls out of her slicked-back bun and her mascara is smudged. I pick up one of the bottles, shake it and it's empty. The other one is empty as well.

"Great," I say under my breath.

Mom's eyes open. They're bloodshot and it takes a moment before there's a glimmer of recognition. "Sawyer?"

Her voice grates against the ashes of my good mood and a muscle in my jaw twitches. "Rough day?"

Mom either doesn't catch on or ignores my sarcasm as she struggles to sit up. Seeing her such a mess creates a sickening shame. She doesn't look like the top salesperson in the state, but like a damn broken bobblehead.

"Tell me if you're going to get sick," I snap, "because it will really piss me off if I have to clean the couch."

Mom successfully sits, but when she goes to stand, she tumbles like a tree that's been chainsawed at the base—headfirst and aiming for the corner of the coffee table. I snatch her before her skull collides with the wood, and as she goes limp, I swing her up in my arms.

She mumbles incoherently as I carry her to her room. Something about how she loves me, loves Lucy and she's not that tired. But the only words I listen for when she single-handedly finishes multiple bottles of wine are "bathroom" and "vomit."

Mom holds on to my shirt as I lay her on her bed, and for someone who barely has control of her body, she has one hell of a grip.

"Are you going to get sick?" I ask. "If so, you need to tell me now."

"Don't be angry at me," Mom slurs. "You're like your dad that way. So angry."

"I'm not angry." That's a lie, but it's easier than the truth.

"You're angry."

There's no point in responding. It's not like she'll remember this conversation anyway. I spread a blanket over her, go to the bathroom and grab a couple of towels. I return to the room and lay them out for Mom.

"Sawyer," she croaks. "Please don't leave me alone."

I hate being around her when she's drunk. I hate the stench of alcohol breath, hate how she breathes out of her mouth, hate how her hands are clammy when she touches me, and hate the sound of her gags as she dry heaves.

"Please," she begs, and her voice breaks as she's close to tears.

I hate my life. I hate it when she cries, and I hate more that I love her.

I slump to the floor, lean my back against the bed and Mom touches my head to confirm I'm there. It's a light touch, but the weight of taking care of her suffocates me. I often wonder if this is why Dad left or if she's like this because he did. I never ask because it doesn't matter. This is my life, and knowing the answer won't change my situation.

I'm never falling in love. Besides Lucy, after I'm out of this house, I'm never taking care of anyone in my life ever again.

VERONICA

✒

It's two in the morning, and I'm sitting on the bottom branch of a tree on Jesse's land. I point at Jesse as Nazareth, Leo and Jesse's girlfriend, Scarlett, all clap and cheer at my success of making it six feet off the ground on my own. "You owe me twenty dollars, Lachlin."

Jesse shakes his head, but he's smiling. We're all smiling. That's what happens when our family is all together again.

"Forty dollars I can go higher than you," Jesse says as he slips his arms around Scarlett from behind her. She leans back into him as if being that close to him is like returning home.

"Sixty that Scarlett can beat us all," I counter, and from the light of the bonfire that's a safe distance from the tree I can see Jesse hang his head in defeat.

"I'm game." Scarlett kisses Jesse's cheek then sprints for the trunk of the tree and jumps up, grabbing on to branches and climbing as if she were immune to gravity.

"I didn't take the bet," Jesse calls, yet he chases after her, taking branches at such a speed that I'm in awe. It took me ten hard-earned minutes to make it to this branch, and they're passing me like I'm a narcoleptic turtle on the interstate.

Soon, Nazareth is making his way up. Leo, too, but I'm done

tree climbing. I'd love to join them, but there's a nasty spike of pain that's been bothering me for the past hour and the most recent one caused a bout of double vision. Last thing I need is to be twenty feet in the air and get dizzy.

I slip over the side of the branch and fall to the ground, landing in a crouch. As I stand, I'm startled when Leo jumps from the branch I was on to land beside me.

"You're not going up?" he asks.

I wink at him. "All the cool kids are on the ground."

"True." Leo doesn't say anything else, just stares at me as if he's waiting on a witty response from me to keep our conversation going, but I don't have one.

I fiddle with my bracelet as I'm riddled with nerves. It's not the good kind of nerves—the type that's created by butterflies. No, it's the sickening type. Leo left, he promised he'd keep in touch and then he practically dropped off the face of the planet.

But he's here now, looking at me as if there hasn't been stone-cold silence between us for weeks. I'm angry, I'm hurt and, oddly enough, I'm thrilled to see him again. But more I'm scared. Yeah, tonight has been fun . . . as a group, but where he and I used to be inseparable, we're now like magnets that repel, and I don't like the feeling. It's confusing and maddening.

Leo surveys me and he doesn't bother hiding his concern. "You okay?"

"It's been a long day, and I'm pretty beat." Fantastic. Relying upon physical weakness to distract from the fact that being alone with him is creating pressure—that will help chill things between us.

"Then let's sit." Leo inclines his head toward the bonfire and we walk back to it. Once there, I drop onto the blanket and sitting doesn't help as Leo stands there watching me. Nope, this isn't uncomfortable at all. Talk, V. Just talk.

"I had homework, a shift at the Save Mart and then Sawyer and I went and investigated this haunted bridge north of Lexington." I'm rambling now and can't stop because this silence is awful. Dear God, send a lightning bolt and kill me. "I sat at the cliff of the river, the dirt gave way, I fell, but then Sawyer caught me and got us safely on this ledge, but then we couldn't climb back up so we had to jump and—"

"Wait." Leo throws his hands in the air as he sits beside me. Not right beside me like the last time we were on a blanket together, but a safe foot away. "You don't swim."

I don't know why, but I smile. One that lights me up like I'm a firefly. "I know, but as I said, we couldn't climb back up because the ground was unstable so Sawyer said it was safer to jump. At first, I was like, no way, but then Sawyer talked me through how we would jump and how he would help me in the water and he did. It was terrifying, yet pretty cool. Then we investigated the bridge. Do you think I'm too old for swim lessons?" I frown. "I've only seen little kids do it at the Y, but I think I'd like to try it. I mean, I totally kicked ass at floating."

Leo watches the bonfire, and I can't quite decipher his expression. He picks up a stick then tosses it into the fire. "What's up with you and Sutherland?"

"I needed a senior thesis partner." It's the truth, but there's a strange fluttering in my chest at the thought of seeing him again. Yeah, he's hot and he's super fun to hang out with, but what I wasn't expecting was the sweetness . . . or the urge to kiss him.

Leo draws up his knees and rests his arms on them. There's that heavy silence again, and it's smothering. Finally, Leo is the one to talk. "I didn't think it'd be this hard."

"What?" Even though I'm in full agreement.

"Being gone. It's weird."

"Weird good or weird bad?"

"Both. I'm meeting tons of new people, and they make me different, and I have to be honest, I like it. But then I come home and see you and I want everything back to how it was. As I said, it's weird."

Sludge enters my veins and my insides become gross and disgusting from the filth. "Oh."

"You know what I like about you, V?" Leo asks.

Does he even notice how emotionally sick I sound? "What?" As if I'm distant—far away.

"You never get down. I meet all these girls at school and after you talk to them for longer than five minutes they start into whatever problems they have. It's like they have no idea how to have fun. I mean, you have this tumor in your head that causes you to be sick and could possibly kill you and you never get down."

Because that's what I am to Leo—fun. Sometimes being fun all the time is exhausting.

"Then the girls who aren't all drama want to be serious after a few dates. Saying stuff like if I really like them, then I shouldn't be talking to other girls. I wish more people were like you—I wish they lived in the moment instead of always worrying about the future."

The blood drains from my face. Dates. With an *s*. Multiple. Girls. Leo's dating other girls. Not that he shouldn't, but before he left he said *maybe* we could try, even if that *maybe* was for next year. I briefly close my eyes to hide the wince at how stupid I was to think *maybe* meant anything.

"You and Sawyer looked like you were having fun when you pulled up," he says.

My face contorts as I have no idea how he could change the subject so fast. "What?"

"When you and Sawyer pulled up in front of the house. You looked like you were having fun and then you guys looked . . . serious." His voice dips with the word "serious." Like it was a curse.

My spine goes rigid. How is that his concern? Especially for a boy who is dating girls—with the emphasis on the *s*. "What's that supposed to mean?"

"It means that looked a lot deeper and more intense than a senior thesis partner."

"What's your problem with him?" My tone comes out fast and sharp.

"I've told you my problem with him. He's the type of guy who will be nice to your face and then talk crap about you behind your back."

"Maybe, but that's my choice."

His eyes narrow on me like he's mad. "And your choice is wrong."

"I never asked your opinion."

"Maybe you should."

Is this how he wants to play this out? "Then that would require you to talk to me. Last text you sent was over a month ago."

"I could have gone to a party with friends tonight and I didn't. I came home to see you, and when I do, you're not even home."

"Oh, I'm so sorry I'm not sitting at home waiting on you to show."

"You're changing."

I blink. Multiple times. "I'm changing?"

"Last year, you would have never hung out with someone like Sutherland and now you're all about him. Throwing yourself at him across the seat."

"Excuse me?" Somehow, in that split second, something does change. I don't know what it is exactly that changes, but it happens. It's a subtle shift, but it's one that feels a lot like that morbid feeling when you realize you forgot something important.

Me. I forgot me, but it's okay because now I'm remembering. "What does that mean?"

"I'm sorry I brought it up." But he doesn't sound sorry. He sounds like someone who opened up Pandora's box and then got irritated that Pandora didn't smile and nod like a good little girl when he didn't like the contents of the box.

"You did bring it up, so I guess you're out of luck. I'm pretty sure that this is how our conversation has been going—you're mad that last year I had three friends to hang out with at school and this year I have no one and that I took on an English thesis partner who, for some messed-up reason, you don't like. What do you want me to do, Leo? Fail English? Be a hermit? Wait for you on the porch? And as for throwing myself at him, I hugged him. I didn't have sex with him in the front seat. And as if it's your business who I hug or screw because last I checked, I don't have a *boyfriend*. And even if I did, I would never answer to him or to anyone!"

"But you don't have to be hanging out with Sutherland." His voice drips pure venom.

"What difference does it make if it's him and why do you think you have a say? You left and dropped off the face of the earth except to pop back in at random to criticize my choice of project partner for the year!"

"So you chose him to get back at me for being busy?"

"I chose him because he lives downstairs from me and he has a car. I'm going to ask again, what is your problem with him?"

"Why do you keep defending him?" he shouts.

"Because I like him!" I yell so loudly that my voice echoes across the open field.

"Exactly," he shouts. "And that's why you're changing!"

We're staring at each other, both of us breathing hard as if we've run a marathon. My exhaustion takes on a whole new level and consumes me. I rub my eyes and then my temples as I try to fight off the pounding now overtaking my brain. "I don't want to fight with you."

Leo's posture deflates. "I don't want to fight with you, either. That's not why I came to see you."

There's a few more beats of silence as I continue to rub my head.

"I'm sorry, V," Leo says like he's torn up. But here's the thing—I'm torn up, too. So much so that I swear bruises are forming all over my body. "I don't know why I'm so angry."

"Then can you cool off about Sawyer?" I say. "He's my partner for the year. That's not going to change. I hear everything you're saying about him. I'm not stupid. I know who he is and who his friends are and I'm well aware of the risks I'm taking. But I'm also telling you I'm a smart girl who can handle this situation. How about a little trust?"

"I know what I saw," Leo says. "You were going to kiss him, and he's not the kind of guy you need to be kissing."

Sawyer was warm and solid and with him I felt good and I felt happy. Sawyer's easy to talk to, easy to laugh with, making it easy to forget that there's a ticking time bomb in my head. His hands were hot on my skin and I welcomed each and every touch, and I wanted to kiss him. I wanted to be kissed. I wanted to bask in the feeling I have with him—feeling alive.

But then I saw Leo and I remembered . . . I'm supposed to be in love with him.

"He doesn't care for you," Leo says.

How many times did I wish Leo would be here beside me? But instead of making me feel alive and happy, he's making me feel guilty and unlovable. "Maybe he does care for me."

"Not like you deserve. He's chasing after you because you're fun, exciting and different. Living in the world he has, he's been told what to do and what line to follow his entire life. Meeting someone like you is like seeing the sunrise for the first time."

Leo swears under his breath as he lowers his head. "He's not going to treat you right. He's going to hurt you, and I don't want that for you. That's what guys like him do. Once his hands get slapped for stepping out of line, he'll hurt you in order to appease the people in his life."

His words cut me so deep that I feel as if I'm bleeding from my chest. "Why are you saying this?"

"Because I care for you. It takes a strong person to be with you and he's not strong enough."

Leo's type of care is causing my eyes to burn with tears. "Maybe he is strong enough to be with me."

His sharp glare flickers to my head, and I'm sick. I've seen that look thousands of times over the years. My brain tumor. Leo doesn't think anyone will ever be strong enough to love me past the tumor.

"Oh," I say so softly that it is barely audible, and I hate how Leo's shoulders relax as if he's relieved. Like it was a burden for him that I wasn't catching on to what he was trying to say. A part of me wants to ask him if it's just Sawyer I should avoid or love altogether, but I don't. Hearing his answer might very well crush me.

"Listen . . . V. The reason I came home this weekend is because I can't come home next weekend."

My forehead furrows. "But that's when I'm planning Thanksgiving dinner."

"I know."

"You've never missed Thanksgiving dinner."

"I know," he says again. "But there's something real important I need to do next weekend."

"And this is important to me. I scheduled it for next weekend because you said that date worked best for you."

"I know."

"You promised."

"I know."

"Are we even friends anymore?"

His cell pings then. A text.

Leo stares at me, I stare at him. I will him not to check his phone. In fact, every cell inside me is reaching out and begging him to ignore whoever it is that's trying to reach him and answer me.

His phone rings. A ringtone I'm unfamiliar with and when Leo digs out his cell I catch sight of a picture of a girl. A beautiful girl, and a lump forms in my throat. He's dating someone and it's not me. He's making new friends and I'm no longer one of them.

He accepts the call and it's like he's impaled me in the heart with a sword.

"Hey," he says with a gentle voice into the phone. "Can you give me a second?"

He means a second to deal with me, but I don't need to be dealt with. I force myself to my feet even though my knees are weak. A tug on my hand and Leo's expression is pained repentance. "It's just a friend going through a tough time."

"Is that what it is?" I demand.

The way his eyebrows draw together tells me it isn't.

"I guess I got my answer on if *we're* friends anymore."

"That's stupid. You're my best friend. You always will be. I came home to see you." His thumb swipes across my hand, but I don't feel anything.

"Give me a few minutes and we'll talk. Really talk. You're my best friend, V," he says again. "That's why I came home. I don't want that to change."

"Sure." But I don't want to be here anymore, and I definitely don't want to listen to him talk to another girl. He walks off into the night, and I wish for the first time in my life that I had a car and could drive. Pain crashes through my brain. A jackhammer to the skull. I stumble, and as I put my hands on my knees to keep myself upright, there's a hand on my elbow.

"V?" It's Jesse, and I hate how scared he sounds. "You okay?"

No. "I want to go home."

"Do you want to lie down?" he asks. "You can crash here tonight."

"No." A sharp slicing pain that causes dizziness. The swirling overtakes me, and I grip Jesse's arm so hard that I'm concerned I'm drawing blood. "I want to go home. Now, Jesse. Just take me home."

"Okay. We'll get you home."

Jesse pulls into my driveway and sighs heavily as he shifts his truck into park. His cell rings again, and we both glance over at its spot in the cup holder. Leo's face is on the screen. Jesse reaches for his cell, and I'm thankful he ignores the call as he checks the slew of texts. With an even deeper sigh, he powers off his cell.

Ten minutes into our way home, my cell had started pinging with texts from Leo, and when I ignored those, the calls had begun. I turned off my cell, then Jesse's cell had started in on the avalanche.

"Leo wants to talk to you," Jesse says.

"We've talked." It's weird how empty I sound. "Whoever this girl is, is he in love with her? You aren't breaking some bro-code if you answer. I know about her. At least enough." Enough for it to hurt.

Jesse's head falls back and hits the headrest with a thump. "I don't know. He came home because he's confused."

I snort and it's all bitter. I try to find something funny to say, but there's nothing funny in me. I'm heavy, all over, as if I did sink into the muddy river, and I drowned.

"He met her at his camp this summer and they've been talking since then. She wants things to be more serious between them." Jesse readjusts as if uncomfortable, and I hurt for him because it has to be tough to be caught between two friends. "He doesn't want to hurt you, and he doesn't want this to affect your friendship. I know he cares for you, more than a friend, but he's struggling with his feelings for you. He's always struggled with them and—"

Heat rushes along my neck and I want to vomit. "Stop."

"V," Jesse starts, but I don't want to hear any more. I want life as it was six months ago. I want my life before my mother died. I want any type of life other than the one I have right now.

My head is pounding so badly and my stomach is churning so quickly that I bolt out of the truck and focus on getting up the stairs of the porch. Jesse's door groans open and tears well up in my eyes.

"Go home, Jesse." I hate how my voice breaks. My hands shake as I push in the code for the lock of the main door. I don't want to cry and I don't want to cry in front of Jesse.

The door to the foyer opens, and I'm briefly blinded by the bright lights. I blink, and when my vision focuses, I watch as my father races down the stairs. His face is as hard as steel, and he's barreling toward me like a freight train. "Where have you been? I've been calling you for the past half hour. You said when I called from the road earlier that you'd would be home by one. I bust my ass to get home and I roll in and find the house empty! Do you know how worried I've been? Do you—"

It's my dad, and he's angry, and he's still yelling and that should bother me, but the pure relief of seeing him causes me to finally let go of the sob I've been shoving down since walking away from Leo.

I force my feet forward, and Dad stops yelling as I stumble into him and bury my head into his chest.

"I've lost him," I sob. "I've lost my best friend."

The migraine becomes overwhelming and I cry, shoulders shaking and tears soaking his T-shirt.

SAWYER

Thursday March 21: Cured almost all day. Weight 121 ½ lb.

One more beautiful day. Oh, I do hope this weather lasts, tho I'm afraid it won't.

I was examined by Dr. Ryan today. Some encouragement, I got. I'm still positive and he doesn't know if I can go home in September or not. Oh Diary, sometimes I don't believe the game is worth the candle. I'm not improving in lung condition, so I can't see what good it does me here.

Don't believe the game is worth the candle—I had no idea what that meant and looked it up. It means whatever the situation is, it's not worth the work put into it. Evelyn felt that way about staying at the TB hospital. That's how I feel about taking care of Mom on the weekends, and I especially feel that way about our current conversation.

"Sylvia doesn't have a date to the homecoming dance yet," Mom says. "Hannah and I think you two should go together—as friends, of course. It's time you two get over whatever silly little feud you have going on."

"Homecoming's still over a month away. I'm not her type and she'll find a date." I tuck Evelyn's diary into a notebook and return to the sink. Because this place doesn't have a dishwasher, I'm elbow-deep in suds. I got creative tonight and made lasagna with Lucy. It was good, she had fun, but I won't do it again. Too many damn pots to clean.

"That's not the point." Mom's at the kitchen table. Frustrated with me, she rubs her temples as if I'm giving her a headache, but she woke up with it and it's made her a witch. "You haven't joined us at Hannah's in forever, and it's noticeable you're avoiding Sylvia. You're breaking her heart and that's not acceptable. I'm still shocked that you chose that Veronica girl over her. You need to get over yourself and apologize. I raised you better than this."

"Sylvia's not an angel in any of this." Like how she talked about Veronica with her friends in English last week. Loud enough that Veronica had to hear.

The gossip isn't just reserved to that one moment in English or limited to Sylvia. It's everywhere, incessant, and I hear my name being discussed in hushed conversations. The latest gossip I've been waiting for Mom to jump all over me about—I must be hanging with Veronica because I'm using drugs.

"But you probably said worse things and I bet you deserved whatever she said to you. I'm not asking. I'm telling. Make up with Sylvia."

My response is the sound of me dropping more dishes into the sink. They clank together and Mom winces with the sound.

It's Sunday evening, Lucy's two doors down with a friend from school and Mom's at the kitchen table taking a break from working to check my grades online. Since elementary school, this has been my least favorite day of the week.

"How is it possible for you to have a D in photography? Are you even bothering to take photos and turn them in?"

"I'm taking photos and I'm turning them in."

"Then why do you have a D?" Mom pushes.

"Because my teacher doesn't like my pictures." Irritation leaks into my veins. I take a hundred pictures a week, pore through them and find three that I think she'll like. Each time she sighs heavily like I'm a toddler that missed the toilet bowl when taking a piss.

They aren't capturing emotion. Translation—she doesn't like me and we're both screwed because it's too late to drop the class.

"Try harder," Mom says. "I put you in that class because it was supposed to help your GPA. You're lucky you're pulling a low C in English, otherwise, you wouldn't be able to swim."

I have a low C thanks to my project work with Veronica, but I've been screwed over by a book we're reading in class. The audiobook was checked out of the public library and Mom refused to spend the money for the one I could buy online. I'm reading, but I'm behind, which has made the quizzes impossible. Pride's been keeping me from talking with Mrs. Garcia. If my grade drops to a D, though, I'll be begging for her to give me more time to read.

"Your first meet is this week." Mom's voice has hit an annoying high-pitched tone that must be used for dog whistles. "How would you feel if you missed it because of your grades?"

Bad. She knows this, and her being on me isn't helping.

"You know the school's rules. Two D's in a class and you can't participate in athletics."

I have the entire school policy memorized.

"Sylvia has had a tough time dating since coming out." Mom switches the subject, and I can hardly keep up. "She should have great memories of her senior year. Who better to go to homecoming with than you?"

I scrub the hell out of the pan I cooked the hamburger meat in. "How about a girl?"

Mom sighs heavily like I'm stupid and not getting the point. "You know what I mean—as friends. You two are close and she'd have a good time with you. Be a good boy and ask her. While you're at it, be a great boy and get me the other bottle of wine from the fridge."

I pick up the empty bottle of wine from the dinner table and toss it into the trash can, but ignore her request. If she wants to drink until she's so drunk that I have to carry her to bed, then she's going to have to get up and do it herself. First it was Friday nights, then

Saturdays and now Sundays seem to be moving from a two-drink limit to three or four.

"Sawyer," Mom says. "The wine."

The scowl on my face speaks more than any words could.

"What? You're punishing me because I had a bit too much to drink last night?"

She said it. Not me. I rinse a plate and put it in the drying rack.

"I work hard, and I work constantly," Mom continues. "You were gone and so was Lucy so I made a sandwich for dinner. Excuse me for making the mistake of having a low alcohol tolerance and committing the crime of not having enough in my stomach. I didn't realize I raised you to be so judgmental."

"Funny, I thought you did."

"You need to get over yourself. Your attitude is awful."

I agree. It is.

"You treat me terribly, you're treating Sylvia terribly, and I'm betting you're treating others the same. It will be a wonder if you have any friends left when you graduate."

She pulls herself away from her laptop, opens the fridge, and gets the wine out herself.

"Will you please set up a weekend to see your father?" As soon as Mom sits, her cell pings and she immediately taps a response. "He's accusing me of keeping you and Lucy from him, and he's threatening to take me to court. I already have enough things to worry about, and you're making my life more difficult by not taking care of this for me."

"Maybe he'll pay child support if I don't go."

"Maybe he's holding the child support because you haven't gone. I do very well for myself, but you and your sister's extracurricular activities are expensive. That money from him would be helpful. Plus, if you don't go, then I have to drive Lucy myself, which means time away from work for me. Do you want me to attend your swim meets? Do you think Lucy would like me to watch her at ballet practices, and then be at her monthly Girl Scout meetings? Don't you think I'd like to be here for dinner more often?"

I mash my lips together because she knows the answer. Yes, we do want her with us.

"Then I have to work so I can take that time off. You realize you haven't seen your father since this past spring, which means Lucy hasn't seen him. I've got too much going on between work and the two of you to stop everything I'm doing to drive Lucy the two hours to see him. If I have to rearrange my schedule to take her, that means I can't make it to the important events, so do us both a favor and arrange a time and go see him."

"Why can't the bastard come see us?" I pick up the lasagna pan from the table.

"Because your dad doesn't want to see me."

I throw the pan onto the counter and it clanks loudly against the wall.

Dad

                                       Mom

Lucy
Visitation

                                     Money

A click I'm unfamiliar with. I turn to see Mom has shut her laptop and her cell is on the table. Her full attention is on me. "What's going on, Sawyer? This isn't like you."

Only it is me. I'm typically better at hiding it. Jumping would feel damn good right now. The adrenaline rush like last night. The tingles I had from that jump with Veronica stayed with me through the night, but I woke up this morning weighed down after feeling high and I now crave more. "I'm fine."

"I know you and your dad aren't close, and I know how he treats you and Lucy like you're houseplants that need to be watered on occasion is upsetting, but he's still your father and that money he sends is helpful. I can't make a case against him on the money if he can make a case against me that I'm withholding visitation."

I try to focus on cleaning the dishes, but my thoughts are so scattered I can't concentrate.

"Tell me you'll take Lucy and you'll visit him," Mom insists.

There's a huge abandoned quarry a half hour from town. It's got a drop the size of Manhattan. It's the kind where I lose my breath before the impact with the water.

"Tell me."

"I'll take her."

"Good. Now that's resolved, I want to finish our conversation about your choice of partners for the English project. I understand you probably said yes to this girl because she did us a favor with our rent check, but Sylvia is so hurt over this, and with your photography grade in the gutter, I think we should rethink the situation. It's a yearlong project and I'm betting most groups haven't gotten that far. Plus, I'm hearing rumors. I've heard that the only reason anyone hangs out with this group of people is to do drugs. Should I be concerned about this? Should I take you to have a drug test done?"

"I'm not doing drugs."

"But you're acting so erratically. Maybe that's the problem."

"I guess you trust Sylvia more than you do me. If that's the case, tell me where to get tested and I'll go and prove you wrong."

"Maybe I should," she pushes. "All of your problems are because of this girl. Can't you see this? She's hurting you, changing you, and it's destroying all that's good in you. I had a long talk with Hannah about this, and I think she's right. I'm going to contact the school and demand that you be switched into Sylvia and Miguel's group."

I spin, not caring as suds fly across the room. "Can you leave one damn thing in my life alone? Or do you enjoy treating me like a puppet?"

Mom's mouth gapes, and someone knocks on the front door. A curse flies out of my mouth as I leave the kitchen, stalk across the living room and yank open the door. I'm dumbfounded as a tall man, a real-life moving force of boulders, stares me down like he's the reaper and I'm the one who just took my last breath. He's in dark jeans, a black T-shirt, and black work boots meant to kick ass.

"Yes?" My shoulders roll back, prepared to take a swing if he tries to walk in.

"I'm Ulysses." Our landlord. Veronica's dad. Crap. Did our check bounce again? But then he extends his hand. "Are you Sawyer?"

"Yeah." I shake his hand and don't miss how he squeezes to let me know that if he wanted, he could crush every bone in my body. I'm a strong guy, though, and have enough balls to squeeze back. "I'll get my mom."

"Actually, it's you I'd like to speak with."

Stunned, it takes me a beat longer than it should to step back and let him in. Ulysses walks in and glances around the living room, taking in the stack of boxes I've better organized lining the wall.

"Hello," Mom says, and Ulysses introduces himself. I forget that they've never met face-to-face—only dealing with each other via calls, texts and emails. Mom brings on her patented charm. They exchange a few pleasantries, and Mom invites him to sit at the kitchen table.

He waves off her offer for something to drink, and the moment Mom and I sit, he's pinning me with his gaze. "I won't take much of your time. I wanted to talk to you about my daughter, V."

If it's my attention he wants, he has it. "She okay?"

"She's dealing with a rough headache, but she's asleep and she typically feels better when she wakes."

I nod because Veronica mentioned having headaches with her tumor.

"V and I had a long talk, and she told me how you found out about her brain tumor."

Mom twitches with the news, news I never told her, information she didn't know, but she recovers quickly. "Sawyer and I are so sorry and have been praying for you and your daughter since finding out."

"Thank you." His eyes flicker from Mom to me. "V is private about the tumor. She'd prefer for people to focus on her and not on it. I hate that it was a friend of mine who told you. V said you won't tell anyone else, and that it appears you've kept your promise. But as her father, I need to hear that guarantee myself, especially since I'm part of the reason you found out."

"I told Veronica I wouldn't tell anyone, and I won't."

Ulysses nails me with a glare as he silently communicates what torture lies ahead for me if I tell anyone Veronica's secret. Satisfied he's let my imagination figure out the ways he'll make me bleed if I upset his daughter, Ulysses leans back in a chair too small for him and strokes his black goatee. "I appreciate your discretion."

"Of course." Mom pops into the conversation. "I'll admit, out of respect for your daughter, Sawyer hasn't told me much about her tumor."

He crosses his massive arms over his chest. "The tumor is small, benign, and for now there's no course of treatment because of the position of the tumor in the brain. Besides migraines, she's fine, but the doctors keep a close eye on the tumor in case anything changes."

Mom leans forward on the table like she's honestly concerned. "What happens if things change?"

Doesn't take a genius to see that question makes Ulysses uncomfortable. "That depends upon the change, but more than likely surgery followed up with extreme doses of chemo and radiation. At least that's what my wife went through. The treatment will be tough. My wife was bedridden and sick the last years of her life."

Something in how he says "tough" makes me think of a living death.

Mom's head tilts, and there's a pit in my stomach that this is now gossip for her. As she goes to open her mouth to dig for more, I intervene. "Veronica's been amazing on our project."

Ulysses doesn't smile, yet he beams with pride. "She's enjoying it. In fact, that's another reason why I dropped by. V said you two were going to work on your project today, but I'm putting a hold on that. V didn't go to bed until late last night and she needs to sleep."

I glance at the clock on the stove. It's six in the evening. How long can a person sleep? As if reading my mind, he says, "When she gets bad migraines, she's been known to sleep for close to twenty-four hours. I know it was tough with V's friends graduating and Nazareth on a different track than her to find a partner for the project. She said you've been good to work with, and I appreciate that. There will be times when her migraines will take her down for a day or two. V's smart, smarter than what she gives herself credit for, and she'll make sure that this project is perfect."

It already is. "That's no problem."

"I also came to tell you I'm pulling V from school for the week. We'll leave tomorrow morning. It's not something I normally do, but it's been a while since V and I've had a vacation. I've got a haul down to the Gulf Coast. V loves the ocean and she needs the time." The sorrow in Ulysses' voice causes something protective to coil inside me.

"Is Veronica okay?"

Ulysses doesn't answer, just stares at the table. My mom touches my wrist and shakes her head at me as if I'm an idiot for asking the question. "Ulysses, Sawyer and I will watch over the house while you're gone, and of course, we know Veronica will do a great job on the project. Tell her not to worry about taking whatever time off she needs."

"Thank you." His voice is gruff. "V also mentioned that she told you about dinner next weekend. As of right now, she decided to put that on hold for a while."

"Dinner?" Mom pipes in.

Mom won't understand early Thanksgiving. I don't pretend to get it, but I like Veronica so I go with it. Mom will judge. "She invited you, me and Lucy to have dinner with them next week so we could all meet."

Mom's face softens as if she's surprised someone like Veronica would do something like that. "That was nice of her. Tell her we hope she feels better soon, and that we'd love to reschedule dinner when she's up for it."

Ulysses stands. "Will do." As Mom and I move, he says, "I can see myself out. Thank you for your time."

From my seat at the table, I watch as he walks across the living room, opens the door then shuts it behind him. Thoughts race as to what could be wrong with Veronica. Yesterday, she was fine. Better than fine. She was brilliant sunshine, comebacks, and a daredevil. She was an unsinkable ship, but the way Ulysses looked when he said, V *loves the ocean and she needs the time*—it's as if she's dying.

A pang of guilt lashes along my spine. What if she got hurt because I convinced her to jump? What if jumping messed something up in her brain? What if my decisions hurt her?

My brain cracks into two halves and both sides have slipped into madness.

The silence between me and Mom is deafening as I dread whatever might come out of her mouth next. Beyond being pissed I didn't join Sylvia's group, Mom'll now be angry I'm partners with a girl who has migraines and a brain tumor and misses school.

For the second time tonight, Mom reaches over, places her hand over mine and gives my fingers a squeeze. "I get it now."

"Get what?"

"That I raised a great boy." She pats my hand, grabs her cell and then stands, leaving me feeling off balance.

Any lingering feeling of the high I had from yesterday's adrenaline rush flees. God help me, I want to jump again.

What kind of monster am I that I'm filled with this need? But then another monster looms in the back of my brain, and I yell out, "Don't tell anyone, Mom! Don't you dare tell anyone about Veronica's tumor!"

I'm at war with myself. Pissed because I don't belong here. Pissed because I have nowhere else to go. Pissed because the place I want to go—to any cliff with a dangerous jump—is no good for me.

I'm in the back of the room of the AA meeting. My knee

bounces so hard I'm shocked no one has tried to punch me. Listening is hard, concentrating is harder as the speakers get up and talk about the challenges, failures, and successes of their week. I'm not sure if I had any successes this week, but I'm racking up the failures left and right.

Some people share the overview of their dismal affair with alcohol. Their stories are a mix and match of alcohol-induced scenarios that lead to losing jobs, marriages, kids, friends and family. People clap when a guy finishes sharing. Knox the Surfer Dude stands from his seat and goes to the podium. When he looks up to speak, he nods his chin at me to let me know he sees me. I nod back, even though I don't like being seen.

Knox talks about family complications—how his mom and dad drink and don't understand why he doesn't, and because of that, he's moving out, even though he can't afford it. He talks about trusting God with this choice, and that sounds like a lot of faith for someone who admits he doesn't have enough money.

He wraps up, and the person who led the meeting asks if anyone else wants to speak. There's a part of me that does. I want to yell. Scream maybe. If I do, maybe that will make me feel better and I won't want to jump anymore. Maybe if I can let go of all the things wound tight inside me, I wouldn't be so messed up. But I can't because my problem isn't with drinking.

The meeting is dismissed, and I equal parts want Knox to talk to me and for him to stroll right on by like I ain't no thing. Knox makes eye contact with me again, and it appears like he's heading in my direction, but takes his sweet time as he stops by every damn person to make small talk. Right when I feel like my bones are about to pop out of my skin if I don't leave, Knox finally slow-strides his way up to me. "You came back."

"Yeah."

"You ready to talk?"

I scan the room, wondering if someone is watching, if someone is judging, if someone knows my truth. Wondering if they know

Mom and they'll tell her where I've been and then the rest of the world will know all my secret weaknesses.

"Brother," Knox says. "There's nobody here who's going to judge you. We leave that nonsense to everyone outside this room."

I shove my hands into my pockets. "You still live at home?"

"Not much longer. My parents asked me to move in last spring to help with bills. It sounded good at the time. I'm in college, working a full-time job, and things were and still are tight for me on my own. But then I moved in and remembered why I had to move out to begin with. Living with my parents is like playing Russian roulette with a fully loaded gun. Maybe someday they'll change, but that someday isn't now."

I'm playing with that gun every time I jump, and the guilt that walked me through that door tonight is a boulder in my stomach. "I put someone in a dangerous situation so I could feel high, and I can't do that again."

Knox sizes me up. "Anyone get hurt?"

"I scared her." Because that's how normal people would react.

Veronica's fall was a freak of nature, my jumping after her was a gut reaction the moment I heard her scream, but being on the ledge with her was where the lie began. We possibly could have climbed the rock wall. The ground was unstable, but the risks between going up and going down were equal. I should have made it her choice, but I wanted to jump and I wanted to jump with someone in my arms who couldn't swim because it heightened the danger.

But I'm haunted now, in ways I've never been before. The pure look of fear on Veronica's face when we surfaced after the jump was a damn kick in the balls that won't stop hurting. She was scared, is probably traumatized, and that's my fault. "She's physically okay, but I'm a bastard for putting her in the spot that I did. It could have gone wrong in a lot of different ways. If I had messed up even a fraction, she could have died."

"First step in all this is to admit you have a problem," Knox says.

"Yeah." That much I read on the website. A small voice screams inside me that jumping isn't as big of a deal, but then I think of Veronica shaking in my arms, her pale face, her wide eyes. I can't do that again. Not to her. Not ever. "I don't drink. I have these urges for an adrenaline rush. I find dangerous cliffs and jump into water, and it's getting tough to stop. You still think this place is for me now?"

Knox is quiet, and I prepare for him to turn me away. "Truth? Until I can find you that specific support meeting, which I'm not sure exists, you're stuck with me."

"You sure?"

"Do you want to jump off a cliff right now?"

I nod.

"Then yeah, you're stuck with me. Want to go get some food?"

Not at all. I really want to get in my car, peel out of the parking lot, find a jump and feel the sweet rush of flying through the air and then the slight pain of hitting the water. But I also don't want to do any of that because as much as the rush will feel good at the time, the guilt of being so weak that I couldn't stop myself will eat me in the morning. "Yeah."

"All right, brother, let's go eat."

He starts for the door and when he notices I don't follow, he glances over his shoulder. "You all right?"

"Why are you doing this?" I ask. "Why are you taking me on?"

"Simple answer—because someone took me on and saved my life. Complicated answer—there are a ton of things wrong with what you just told me, but there's one that bothers me the most. You're more concerned that your friend was in danger than you are that what you do will get you killed. I was like that once, right before I bottomed out. Maybe I'm wrong, but I think you need a friend. Am I right, brother?"

Yeah, he might be.

VERONICA

I wake with a jolt. As if someone had said my name, the way one does when it's important to be awake, but as I glance around, I'm alone. Not even my mom is in my bedroom. The room is dark except for the moonlight rolling in through the slats of my still-open blinds.

Rolling from my side to my back, I hesitantly elongate my muscles as my body is stiff. The type of stiff where I could easily stretch my calf into a charley horse. I can sleep for days when I take the migraine prescription, staying so still that Dad says he puts his ear to my nose to confirm I'm breathing.

Last time I was awake, I was leaning against my dad. I cried, he held me. I cried some more and he hugged me. I eventually calmed down and we talked. The good type of talk. Where I told him everything going on in my life from start to finish. Almost everything—I left out seeing Mom, but other than that he knows it all—down to me jumping into a river and me hugging Sawyer then almost kissing him in the car to Leo falling for someone else.

I talked until I had nothing else to say, so Dad picked up where I left off because Dad gets me. He understands I don't want to analyze my feelings or have a frank discussion about where I should go from here, but instead I want to forget so he mumbled in a low tone about his week.

The boring stuff, the mundane. The trivial that makes the world feel normal and safe. I listened to every word as my eyelids grew heavy. Sometime, at some point, I fell asleep, and Dad must have carried me to my room.

The jackhammering of my skull is gone, and in its place is a rare moment of silence. The digital clock on my bedside table reads midnight. Twelve with two zeros exactly. I swing my legs over the edge of the bed and a smile creeps along my lips as I realize some-one had said my name to wake me. Just not someone I can see.

I exchange my old jeans and T-shirt for a pair of cotton shorts and a tank top and frown in the mirror at the rat's nest of blond, unruly curls bouncing along my shoulder. There are so many tan-gles and picking them out after a shower will definitely suck.

In the hallway, I peek into Dad's room and my heart lifts when I spot Mom lying next to him. He's in a deep sleep, and Mom's eyes are closed as she's snuggled close. His arm is outstretched over her and his hand touches hers. They look peaceful, in love, and I pinch myself on the arm. Pain at the prick and I breathe out in relief. This isn't a hallucination. It isn't a dream.

Dad's body is curved protectively around the love of his life so he must know, at least subconsciously, that Mom is with him and that brings on a sense of warmth. Dad doesn't see her because he doesn't believe ghosts are real. Like how Sawyer couldn't clearly understand the EVP. But the more I prove to them that ghosts are real, the more they'll be able to see beyond what only exists in this realm. That way, when I die, I can join Mom in this house and then Dad will be okay because he'll never be alone.

Light taps come from our second-floor living room, and I silently curse that I don't have the recorder. That would be amazing—to catch an EVP in my own house. I've thought about asking Mom to play along, but I can never bring myself to do it. That feels too private for others to listen to and pick apart.

Loving that the house is coming alive, I'm quick yet light on my feet as I go down the stairs in search of the little girl who loves to play.

SAWYER

I walk along the long corridor, looking into the rooms as I pass. The rooms aren't what they were before. They don't seem so dark, so gray. There's laughter echoing around me, nurses chatting with patients, patients talking with one another—helping with the staff. The rooms are bright, filled with personal belongings. The windows are wide open, a warm spring breeze blowing in.

There's a girl my age at a desk reading. I pause at her door, walk in and read what she does.

> *Saturday March 23: Took a whole day today with Peg and Sade. We went out this morning and got a ride in a Ford. Oh, it was great outdoors. I hated to come in and go to services, but I did.*

> *Had a date with Harry for tonight, but he sent word that he was sick. Now, Diary, he wasn't sick at all but he just wanted to go to the Match Pool Game. Never mind, he'll get one grand bawling out from me.*

She glances up at me. "She's lying to you."

My forehead furrows. "Who? Who's lying to me?"

"*She* is. You like to visit here." She scans the room then out into the hallway. "The hospital, I mean. Not many people like to come here. Why do you like to visit? Aren't you afraid?"

Feeling discombobulated, I shove my hands into my pockets. "Afraid of what?"

"Death."

I don't know. Am I? Is that why I'm drawn to Evelyn's diary? Am I scared of death? I'm scared of hurting Lucy and my mom, but do I fear death? Naw, that doesn't feel right—at least it's not why I read the diary. I read it because . . . "Reading about Evelyn . . . I don't feel alone in all my problems. What I face sucks, but what Evelyn faced was worse and yet she still tried to find a way to be happy."

The girl jumps as if startled and grabs my hand. "You need to get to Lucy. She's not safe."

My eyes snap open, and I shoot up with Lucy's shout. "Sawyer!"

She screams and the sound sends a sickening chill down my spine. I'm out of my room and into hers. My little sister sits in the middle of her princess bed, drenched in sweat. Her hair sticks to her face, her light nightgown clings to her body. Tears fall down her face.

Nightmares. Like clockwork, they hit her at midnight. That crap got old the first week here, but there's not much I can do other than be here for her. Mom suggested giving her sleeping pills, and I reminded Mom that the only way that was happening was if she got the certified approval of the American Academy of Pediatrics. That doctor's visit would mean another day off for her, so that was a no-go.

Lucy sniffles and chokes on the sob, and when she doesn't put her arms in the air for me to hold her, I realize she's still in the middle of the dream, but living it out in our reality. At least this time, she stayed in bed.

I smooth her hair back from her face and gently ease her onto the pillow. "Shh. It's okay, Lucy. I'm here."

Lucy allows me to mold her back into bed, and she grabs on to the covers as I lift them to her chin. "There's a . . . a monster." She hiccups midsentence.

"And I scared it away. Just like I always do." Just like I always will.

She takes in a quivering breath, and I'm encouraged by the longer exhale and how she snuggles down into the pillow and closes her eyes. I sit on the edge of the bed and mumble-sing the wrong lyrics to a lullaby because I never tried learning them right. Lucy reaches out, places her hand over mine, and for a moment the constant barrage of chaos stalls. She loves me, and I love her back.

Taps on the wall of her room, and my head jerks up. Another tap, then another, and my eyes follow the sound as it continues along like it's making its way to the front of the house. Something dangerous coils within me as I realize—those aren't taps, but footsteps in the foyer.

Careful not to wake Lucy, I creep to the window and spot nothing moving outside. More steps rap along the opposite side of the wall, a door closes somewhere in the apartment, and I whip my entire body around to spot nothing in the room.

I'm on the move and out into the living room. My bedroom door is open, the bathroom door open, the closet doors still closed. I make my way down the hallway and dim light shines from beneath Mom's closed bedroom door. She murmurs something I can't make out, and I shake my head. Great. She's probably talking in her sleep now, too.

Footsteps upstairs and the creaking of the heavy door from Veronica's apartment and my heart pounds. What is going on? I sprint for our front door, and my mind trips over itself when I notice the lock undone and the door not closed all the way. No. No way. I checked that mother before I went to bed.

My pulse beats in my ears as I open the door the rest of the way and strain to look out into the darkened foyer. The faint light from the stained glass around the main door to the house casts intimidating shadows into the corners that grow darker with each second that I stare.

A few more taps, the gentle sound as if someone is walking toward me, and the blood drains from my face as the sound expands and magnifies. A cold gust of air, and I shiver as a frigidness peels back my skin and leaves frostbite on my bones.

Overwhelming sadness rolls through me like violent waves from the ocean, nearly driving me to my knees. Wave after wave pummels me, and the more that I fight to stay standing, the more that I lose the ability to breathe.

"Sawyer?" A familiar voice, and it's as if someone threw me a life raft from this pit of despair.

The sight of beautiful blue eyes snaps me back to reality. Veronica stands at the bottom of the steps, appearing like an angel in the midst of a nightmare, and looks awestruck as she watches me. "You heard it, didn't you? You heard and felt the ghost?"

I rub my hands along my arms, searching for warmth, for some grasp of the situation. As I go to tell her no, I'm struck mute. Veronica offers a hesitant grin. "That's okay. I didn't know what to say either the first time it happened to me, but it gets easier."

I cock an eyebrow at "easier," and she giggles. "Once the ghost finds you, she'll visit again."

Again.

Again.

I jumped with Veronica because I wanted to feel the rush *again*. That wasn't okay. Not at all. "Are you okay?"

Veronica tilts her head as if she's confused. "Me? I'm fine. We're talking about you."

"The jump," I practically spit out. "Are you okay from the jump? Your dad said you weren't feeling okay, and I was worried that maybe something had happened from the jump."

Veronica recoils and that makes me want to pound my head against the wall. If I hurt her with the jump, that's on me. That's—

"No, that's not what made me feel bad."

Silence in my head, but then my brain starts to race again with the possibilities of what hurt her.

"Do you want to talk about it?" Those words coming out of my mouth stun even me. I'm not the guy who talks feelings. "Or we can just talk. About anything."

Veronica nibbles on her lower lip and glances back up the stairs. "Sure—on the anything. On the front porch maybe? I don't want to wake Dad. He hasn't slept well recently and he's sleeping great tonight. I don't want to ruin that for him."

I don't, either. I want to know what's upset Veronica, but I also need to be the one talking. I did something wrong and she needs to know. I need to be held accountable for my actions, and the thought terrifies me. "Will you take a ride with me? I want to show you something."

Veronica glances up the stairs again and then down at her clothes. She's tempting in a spaghetti-strapped tank top and low-cut cotton shorts. "Can you give me a few? I need to grab my phone and leave Dad a message so he won't worry if he wakes."

I push a hand through my hair as I wasn't thinking straight. "It's late, don't worry—"

"No, we'll go. My dad won't care. He just wants to know what I'm doing and who I'm doing it with. He only gets mad when I'm not straight with him on things."

"Okay." A slice of guilt needles me as I watch Veronica scale the stairs. I should go in and do the same with Mom. But she wouldn't understand, and at the end of the day, as long as I don't get into trouble that would make her look bad, I don't think she'd care.

Besides, this isn't the first time I've snuck out at night to go to this place, but it is the first time I've taken someone with me. Question is, will doing so cost me the one person I want to be around? Maybe, but I need to start doing some things right, and Veronica is the one to do them right with.

VERONICA

A twenty-minute ride later and Sawyer turns off the engine. He doesn't say anything as he takes the keys out of the ignition and exits the car. Sawyer comes around the front, like he's going to open my door, but I've beat him to it. Still, he places his hand on the door as I ease out.

I scan the area in the moonlight, but I don't see much other than rocks, trees, what appears to be a black abyss ahead and the stars in the sky. The ground beneath my feet feels solid, like stone, and that's confirmed when Sawyer turns on the flashlight of his cell.

"Where are we?" I ask.

"One of my unfortunately favorite places."

"'Unfortunately'?"

"It's an abandoned rock quarry." He flies right past my question. "I should mention we're trespassing, and that you're the first person I've brought here."

"I admire how you admit bits and pieces of truth, but then breeze through a shocking part with another shocking part in a way meant to confuse the mind."

Sawyer's lips tug up in that cocky way of his. "I've learned from the best." He winks at me. I mock gasp and put a hand to my chest as if I'm offended, but quickly smile, because yeah, I do it, too.

"Which part was shocking?" he asks.

I tap my finger to my chin. "Hmm. Let me think. Your 'unfortunately' favorite place is an abandoned rock quarry, we're going to be arrested if caught and I'm special. I've never been arrested so that could be fun."

"You skimmed over the best part," he says.

"What's that?"

"That you're special." His eyes meet mine then and the intensity of his gaze steals the air from my lungs.

I quickly glance away because this is the reason I'm here with him in the middle of the night. Because I like feeling this way. I like how my blood is flooded with this exciting pins-and-needles sensation whenever he casts his gaze in my direction, how he makes me laugh in the most unexpected moments and how he finds me funny when I mean to be. I like the ease of our conversation and the supreme ease of our silences. I just like him.

A swift cool breeze blows through the trees. I run my hand along my arms and curse that while I had changed into jeans and a short-sleeved shirt, I didn't bring a jacket. September has been warm, but we're nearing October, which means cooler temperatures.

"Are you cold?" he asks.

I could lie. It's my natural instinct to not rely on anyone besides Nazareth and Jesse, but I don't feel like pretending with Sawyer. I did that too much with Leo and it got me nowhere. "Yes."

Sawyer rummages through his backseat, pulls out a blanket and then hands me a sweatshirt. I hold it out and it's his high school sweatshirt. Our bland colors of maroon and baby blue. It's so big I could wear it as a dress. Another gust of wind turns my skin into icicles so I pull the sweatshirt over my head.

The fleece on the inside is warm and the first inhale brings the rich scent of Sawyer. I turn my head and fit my nose along the seam of the sweatshirt to take in the dark, spicy smell again before I draw the rest of the sweatshirt down along my body.

"Thanks," I say, then grin when the end of the sweatshirt falls just above my knees. "Has anyone told you you're too tall?"

I expect a "you're short" crack back, but instead he gives me a glorious smile. "Yes. My mom always told me to quit growing, but I'm not good at listening."

That makes me laugh, and he's gorgeous with how he brightens, as if I'm the one who gave him a gift. I follow him as we walk toward the edge.

"We're not jumping again, right?" I ask as a tease, and it's unsettling how he grows grim.

"Not in the game plan."

A few feet away from the edge, Sawyer spreads the blanket, but he doesn't sit. Instead he walks scarily close to the drop-off, so close that the toe of his athletic shoe dangles off the edge. He shoves his hands into his pockets and stares down into the pit. "There's water down there. About a high dive's distance away. The pool is deep, but it's not the safest jump. If you jump wrong, you could end up hitting the rocks that jut out of the water."

"Have you jumped from this place before?"

"Yes." Something in his tone makes me ache for him. I'm slow as I walk toward him, as if I'm scared if I make too loud of a noise that he'll lose his balance and fall. I reach out and touch his arm, the spot right above his elbow, and Sawyer immediately turns toward me, away from the edge. Our eyes lock, my heart reacts and my fingers trail down his hot skin until I can lace hands with him.

"Are you okay?" I ask.

Sawyer's silent for a beat then squeezes my fingers. "When I'm with you, I am."

His admission warms me from the inside out, which is totally unlike me. But maybe that's what I like about Sawyer. Being with him causes me to explore unknown things about myself, learning things when I thought I knew it all.

"What made you feel bad?" Sawyer asks.

"Same old, same old. A baby brain tumor that can cause mi-graines."

"Yeah, but something in how your dad looked when he talked . . ." He trails off. I really need Dad to stop talking about me. I sigh heav-ily, and as if sensing my inner turmoil, Sawyer lightly tugs on my hand and leads me to the blanket.

We sit and he doesn't let go of me like I expect, but instead he scoots so close that we're able to rest our joined hands on our outstretched legs. Sawyer's hands aren't quite what I expected. They aren't super rough, not super smooth, but a strong and gentle in-between. While he holds my hand as if I'm fragile crystal, there's power in his grip. As if even his hands are as precisely muscled as the rest of him.

I skim my finger along the top of his hand and Sawyer sucks in a small breath as if I surprised him, as if he likes my touch. The idea causes a pleasing sensation to course along my veins so I do it again.

"You're quiet," I softly say.

"I'm giving you time," he answers.

"For?"

"To decide whether or not you want to tell me why you were upset."

"What if I don't want to tell?"

"Then you don't, but I'll be sad if you stop touching my hand."

I smile, so does he, but then he turns serious. "To be honest, I need to tell you something, too. Something private. And I'm using the time to work up my own courage."

"There's nothing you need to tell me," I whisper.

"Yeah, there is. I don't want to, but I have to, and there's no doubt it'll change how you look at me so I'm okay if you decide to talk first or if you want more time."

Time. It's such a weird concept. Three hundred and sixty-five days in a year. Twenty-four hours in a day. Sixty minutes in an hour. Sixty seconds in a minute. Fifteen breaths per minute.

How many breaths do I have remaining? How many more mo-ments will I ever have like this in my life? To be pain-free and alive as I am right now? When will I ever sit on this quarry edge and live this moment again? Never. Probably never.

What do I tell Sawyer? That I was sad because I was once in love with Leo, and I realized that sometime, someway, without conscious thought, that I fell out of love with him?

That for well over a year, if not longer, I've known that Leo has been in love with me, but he was never strong enough to love me past my tumor. I convinced myself he was oblivious to my feelings because that was easier than seeing the truth—that the tumor made me unlovable.

Do I tell Sawyer that I finally understood my feelings changed because I now have feelings for him? I can't tell him that though. How can I start something with him when I'm going to die?

Sawyer knows I have a small tumor, a tiny tumor that causes headaches. Leo saw my mother's slow and excruciating death. Sawyer has never witnessed my debilitating migraines. Leo's watched me writhe in pain from a distance as Nazareth has smoked me up to help with the agony. Leo knows my fate. Sawyer doesn't. He deserves to know, but I want to be selfish, just for tonight. I deserve that. I deserve, if only for this heartbeat, to live.

Tonight, Sawyer looks at me with possibility. Tomorrow, Sawyer can join Leo in viewing me as something that could have been.

"I don't want to do this," I say.

"Do what?"

"This. If you want to do this, have this conversation about why I was upset, about why you're upset, we will. But once we do, at least once I talk, nothing will be the same between us again and I'm not ready for that yet."

Sawyer's gaze flickers around my face as if he's trying to find the secret way into my brain so he can read the thoughts I so desperately want to keep hidden. "I don't understand."

"You don't? Because I do and I think you do, too. You're holding my hand and I'm holding yours and we've snuck out in the middle of the night to be alone to share our deepest thoughts, but we're both terrified that those deep dark secrets are going to mess every-thing up so why share them? Why share them now when, if your eyes hadn't tracked over my shoulder to Leo, you would have kissed me and I would have kissed you. We can talk another time, Sawyer. Whatever it is you have to tell me will still be there in the morning. But tonight, I need you to kiss me."

SAWYER

My heart beats wildly. Kissing Veronica is my dream, but I never thought it could be a reality and I try hard to focus on rational thought instead of this driving need. "Are you sure?"

"Yes," she says as she angles herself toward me.

"But we do need to talk." I need to do the right thing.

"We will, but can you let me have tonight and then we'll worry about the rest tomorrow? If you don't want to kiss me—"

I cut her off as I cup her face with both of my hands. Her skin is so incredibly soft. Her mouth beautifully perfect. I've never wanted anything more than her lips against mine. I look straight into her eyes as doubts war within me.

If I kiss her then I talk to her, will she regret it? If I talk to her and she does change her mind, I'll regret that I let this moment slip through my grasp. I lean forward and her lips are so close to mine. I take a breath in, and her sweet scent envelops me.

"Veronica," I murmur in a plea to help end this torture of my indecision or to give her the opportunity to run.

"Let's live tonight," she whispers as if she can hear my internal struggle. "I want you to kiss me, Sawyer. You. It has to be you."

And it has to be her. I close the distance between us and press my lips to hers. An explosion in my chest, in my brain, and heat races through my veins with how warm she is, with how soft. Her mouth moves with mine. In question, in hunger, and when she takes my bottom lip into both of hers, I'm lost.

Our mouths open, our tongues dance and her arms twine around my neck. I caress her cheek and then allow my hands to roam. Along her back, into her hair and down her sides. Veronica shivers under my touch and presses tight to me, crawling onto my lap, leaving no space between. Her lips leave mine, graze down my cheek and we're both breathing at a frantic pace.

"Let's keep kissing," she whispers in my ear then nips my earlobe. A new type of rush enters my system and it's stealing all thought from my brain. "Just kissing, nothing more. But I don't want to stop. Not yet. I just want to keep doing this."

I nod my agreement. Her hands find my hair and her fingernails lightly scrape along my scalp as she presses her lips to mine again. A maddening heat rolls through my bloodstream—a rhythmic current begging and pleading for more. With the way Veronica holds on to me, she's feeling the same driving pulse. I could kiss her forever and that's exactly what I do.

VERONICA

Sawyer held my hand on the car ride home. We didn't say much. We listened to the radio, we kept smiling at each other, and we kept holding hands. His fingers would slide against mine, I would trace his knuckles, and my heartbeat would rise with just the mere thought of kissing him again.

Taking the corner toward my house, I catch a glimpse of myself in the side mirror. My lips are swollen from the hours of kissing, my hair rumpled in way that shows I've been properly kissed and I'm almost terrified to look at my neck as I'm ninety-nine percent sure there's a hickey there since I'm one hundred percent sure there's one on Sawyer.

"Stay here," he says as he parks in front of the house. It's four-thirty A.M. and the world is still asleep. I should be, and considering school starts in a few hours, so should he, but he doesn't seem to care we've been up all night and neither do I.

Sawyer leaves the car, rounds the front and opens the door for me. The action makes me joyous and causes me to be a bit shy. It's a stupid reaction, I guess, but it's real.

After he closes the door, Sawyer shines down at me as he takes my hand. We go up the walk and then he patiently waits at my side as I unlock the main door. Once inside, I close the door, relock it and have to stifle a giggle when Sawyer immediately uses his body to back mine up against the wall.

He's solid and strong, and he feels so right against me. My hands wander up to his chest as his hands rest on my hips. If I stretch to the tip of my toes and kiss his lips, how long will we spend making out near the stairwell? Minutes? Hours? Days? An eternity?

"If we start this," I murmur, "I don't think it will end."

Sawyer leans forward, nuzzles the hair behind my ear with his nose and pleasing goose bumps form. "Is that a bad thing?"

No. Not at all, but then I sigh. "It is if my dad finds us like this. He's awesome, but he's not that awesome."

But that doesn't stop Sawyer from nibbling on my ear then placing delicious kisses along my neck, nor does it stop my fingers from curling into his shirt and dragging him closer to me. He draws me in for another round of kissing, and my slow and hazed mind decides this is one the most brilliant ideas I've ever had—sharing this night with him.

"Do you want me to stop?" Sawyer asks between kisses.

I gasp as he kisses the sensitive spot behind my ear. "No." Yet I uncurl my fingers, place my hand flat against the hard plane of his chest and lightly push. Because Sawyer's a real man, he immediately backs away and gives me my space.

He hitches his thumbs in his pockets and he looks so adorable that I want to drag him back into me again. But daylight will be breaking soon, our proverbial midnight, and we'll both be forced to return to reality. Him being Sawyer Sutherland, popular, cool guy, and me being the weird, quirky girl who lives upstairs from him.

"Thank you for tonight," I say.

"Does it have to end?" he asks.

"The daylight about to break says yes. I, at least, get to sleep on our way to Florida. You have to go to class."

"That's not what I mean." He shrugs his shoulders like he's unsure of himself, which catches my attention because Sawyer Sutherland is the definition of confidence. "I mean what happened tonight between us. Me and you. It just started. Does it have to end?"

What Sawyer is suggesting is so sweet, so beautiful, but impossible. "What do you see when you look at me?"

"Is this a trick question?"

"Maybe."

Sawyer is hesitant as he steps toward me, giving me the room to reject his advance, but I stay still because his being close creates sensations in me I want to feel again. He touches one of my curls and the slight pull on my head sends pleasurable shivers down my spine.

"I see beauty." His voice is so deep, so sincere that it vibrates along my insides. "I see someone who's intelligent, funny, confident, and unique."

I search his face, his eyes, desperate to see if there's more, waiting for him to bring up the tumor like Leo would, but he doesn't. Probably because he doesn't understand my situation, not like Leo did. Leo saw the agonizing way my mom died. He saw how it affected me, affected my father, how it tore our family apart and turned our lives upside down.

"I see someone I like being with," Sawyer continues, "and I hope someone who likes being with me."

My heart stutters because I like being with him. So incredibly much, and it warms every part of me that he feels the same. He knows I have a brain tumor, but he doesn't understand what my future holds and what his future holds if he cares for me.

I don't want this to end, but if he and I get any more serious than we already have, I'll be forced to tell him the truth—that I'm dying. By the grace of God, Sawyer doesn't see my tumor, but me, and I selfishly don't want to lose that.

Nerves feast on my stomach as I don't know what to do. With or about him. I don't know if I should run away to save us both from pain, or maybe it would be better if I don't run at all.

"I like being with you, too," I say, and while that's not a new declaration, there's something in how I become shy as I say it and how his eyes glint with happiness that makes this moment absolutely sweet and terrifying.

Footsteps on the stairs and Sawyer glances over his shoulder. My pulse quickens as there's no one there, but we both hear the footsteps continuing down each step. Sawyer moves to stand in front of me, as if he can protect me from the unseen.

"Who's there?" he says, but no one answers.

"It's four forty-five," I say. "It happens every morning at this time. The same as at midnight, but these steps are always heavier, darker than the ones at midnight."

We both stare, seeing nothing, but the hair on my arms stands on end, and when I look down, Sawyer's skin is prickling as well. He feels it, the energy, the ghost. My mouth turns up as I run my hands along his arms. "Do you believe now?"

Sawyer raises an eyebrow as he returns his attention to me. "I believe it's an old house that settles with the changes in air pressure."

I seductively tilt my head with a pout. "Is that what you believe?"

I love how Sawyer's eyes darken as he watches my lips. "Which answer gives me the greater odds of kissing you again?"

I laugh, and as he leans in for another round, the door at the top of the stairs opens and Sawyer and I jump.

"I see you on the monitor," Dad says, and I swear to God I blush from head to toe. "You need to come up, and Sawyer needs to decide what type of man he's going to be."

"Great," I whisper, but I give Sawyer major credit when he offers me his hand. I take it, and we walk with our fingers linked together up the stairs.

"Sir," Sawyer says as Dad stands at the door indicating for us to walk in. Once inside, I see Mom at the piano bench. She turns her head, and when our eyes meet, a strange electricity hits me, headfirst. I'm stunned and then the world turns. Fast, too fast. Dizzy, I waver.

"Veronica?" Sawyer says, and there's a strong arm around me. I don't respond, I can't respond. It's like my tongue has become too big. Sawyer talks, Dad talks, there's buzzing and then there's complete and terrifying silence. The floor beneath me gives and I fall. Like a feather, down a hole and then I'm caught.

Sound returns, as if someone literally flipped a switch, and I'm able to blink, able to talk, able to function. As I go to regain my footing, I feel something soft beneath me. The couch. I'm on the couch. I sit up, and there's immediately hands on my shoulders keeping me in place. Dad. It's Dad. His scared eyes bore into mine.

"You okay, peanut?" he asks in a low tone. A conversation meant just for us.

"Yeah," I say, and then do something I swore to Mom I'd never do. I lie. Directly. About my health. I promised. I know I did, but she also promised she'd be okay and she wasn't and now if I don't lie, I will lose what I've found tonight, and I can't let that happen. Not yet. "Ice-pick headache."

Dad eases down onto the coffee table, and I'm impressed it doesn't collapse under his weight. He rubs a hand over his face as if he's tired and then stares straight into my eyes. I work on trying to look normal. A breath in, a breath out, blink.

"You know how these headaches are," I say. "They hit hard and fast. I should have probably stayed in bed for longer than what I did."

"You can say that again." A war wages within him, and I pray he believes me. I need him to believe me. With a sigh, he gives his verdict. "But it is what it is. Thank you for being man enough to face me with her, Sawyer." Dad holds out his hand to him. Sawyer hesitates before extending his arm and accepting Dad's shake. "A boy would have sent her up the stairs and run.

"Next time though"—Dad's grip visibly tightens—"I'd appreciate it if you brought her back with fewer marks on her body like the one currently on her neck."

Sawyer turns bright red. "I'm sorry, sir."

"Yeah, well, it's time for you to head home." Dad doesn't sound angry, just tired, and he returns his concerned gaze to me.

I don't want Sawyer to leave. Not like this, not yet. Not with him having seen me like this. Not with me going out of town tomorrow. "Can Sawyer and I say good-bye?" And I become very brave. "Alone."

Dad's eyebrows shoot up. "Alone, eh? I think you two had plenty of alone time to say good-bye, but because I'm a good sport, I'm going to make some coffee, in the kitchen, and you two have a few more minutes for good-bye. Words, mind you."

It's the best I'll get, and I'm aware how awesome my father is. I know of no other parent who would be even close to as cool as Dad's being. True to his word, Dad heads into the kitchen and offers us his back to allow us privacy. Sawyer moves in front of me and crouches so that we're eye to eye. "Hi."

"Hi," I say in return, and it's strange how fascinatingly shy I feel.

"You okay?"

"Yeah. Just a headache. A weird headache, but a headache. When you hang with me strange things will happen."

Sawyer flashes me his adorable, cocky grin. "That I know."

I'm flying.

"You didn't answer me earlier," Sawyer whispers, but there's no doubt Dad probably hears. "Is this something we can continue?"

I nibble on my bottom lip then whisper back, "There will be rules."

"Rules. I can do that. Tell me what they are."

I glance over at Dad, and he immediately returns to pouring cream into his mug.

"We're fun," I whisper as silently as I can, in a way that Sawyer can hear and not Dad. "We can be us, together, but there's no pressure. We just enjoy each day, okay?"

Sawyer tilts his head as if he's not convinced, and I quietly continue. "We're seniors and a lot can happen next year and I want to have fun, not be in an awkward relationship where we become jealous and fight all the time. We hang out, we laugh, we . . ." I sneak a peek at Dad, he looks away again and I mouth the word, "kiss."

Sawyer's eyes laugh and then he takes my hand. "I'm game for fun, and I like having fun with you. But if we kiss, I'm not into sharing."

"Okay." I'm happily flustered as he slides his fingers along my arm.

Sawyer is fine with keeping us chill, but wants a kissing-only-each-other commitment, and he's basically agreeing that this is a senior-year-only thing. That's good. It's beyond good. It's great. We enjoy our senior year, graduate, and then he'll go off to college, I'll have my MRI and then that's when I'll battle Dad over being sick.

Sawyer leans forward, briefly kisses my lips then stands. Dad tells Sawyer good-bye and he walks out the door. My father grabs his coffee mug and settles on the other end of the couch. He looks over at me and I at him. "A normal parent would ground you for what you pulled tonight."

I nod because they would. "Are you going to?"

"That would require us to be normal. Sometimes I wonder if I'm doing wrong by you, but your mom told me to trust you and I am. But if you lie to me, that trust goes away and so does my patience with waking to find notes telling me you left."

"I hear you," I say. "And I won't break your trust."

SAWYER

Monday June 17: Nothing at all doing today. Cured a lot.

M. is polishing over in the MacDonald Solarium now, so I spose I'll see quite a lot of him. I won't mind very much, I don't think. Oh, Diary, I like him. I think that he is a gentleman.

Oh, Diary, I want to go home so badly. I wish I would hurry up and get well, if I'm ever going to.

I suppose I'll see a lot of Veronica, too. And I like her, as well. I also wonder if I'm going to get well—if when Mom pisses me off I won't want to jump. Like now.

In a reusable shopping bag by Mom's feet on the floorboard of the passenger side of my car are three bottles of wine. On the phone with Hannah earlier today Mom laughed and said she's bringing a bottle for every bad day she had this week. Don't know why, but each word was the equivalent of sticking my hand into a working blender.

Those three bottles of wine would be the reason why I'm driving us to Sylvia's for another Saturday night potluck dinner. Lucy's strapped into the backseat, singing a song she's made up on her own. Most of it is about unicorns and how she loves macaroni and cheese.

Veronica returns sometime tonight, and I'm equal parts dying to see her and going slightly insane. I lost myself in kissing her and in the dream kissing her provided. Veronica and I agreed to a committed, chill relationship, which is good because the idea of that intense bullcrap love I see everywhere else in the world rubs me wrong.

What's really wrong is for me to have committed to her without telling her the truth about the night we jumped into the river. But how do I tell her? How do I keep her yet be honest?

Mom looks over her shoulder to Lucy. "Are you excited to move into a house in this neighborhood?"

Lucy stops singing and scans the huge, new houses with lawns that don't have a single weed. I expect a swift answer from her, but instead she strokes the hair of the mermaid doll she refuses to get into the pool without. "Do these houses have ghosts?"

My eyes snap to the rearview mirror and catch sight of my sister's white face. "Does our current house have ghosts?"

"You're both silly," Mom says. "Ghosts aren't real."

Lucy hugs the mermaid to her chest as if she disagrees and stares out the window. I guess she doesn't feel like singing anymore.

I park in front of Sylvia's house since the driveway is already filled. Leaning toward the backseat, I grab Lucy's backpack and Mom touches my arm. "Can we talk?"

Uh . . . there's no part of me that wants a conversation that starts with that mixture of sweetness and inferred guilt. "Sure."

Her gaze bounces between me and Lucy. "I told Hannah about the insufficient funds with our first rental check."

I'm quiet as I gauge where this is going. Sometimes, conversations with Mom are like testing ice on a pond after the first warm day of spring. "Okay."

"I also told her how your dad's not paying child support."

My heart sinks, but I stay silent. Mom's free to talk to her friends about whatever she wants. But while Dad and I have problems, I've never liked how Mom and her friends dog my dad. *I* can be pissed at him—he's my flesh and blood. Mom can even be mad at him. He married her, knocked her up twice, then ran. But when her friends get going, cackling around Hannah's kitchen table, calling him names like they have the right, it irritates me in ways that make me want to rip my arms out of their sockets.

"I told Hannah that my check didn't bounce because of insufficient funds but because of a bank error—a technological issue." Mom picks nonexistent lint off her pressed khaki shorts. "So if the subject comes up, I'd appreciate it if you'd keep it to yourself that our check bounced because we didn't have enough money. I don't want anyone to think I can't handle my finances or that I don't make enough to take care of the two of you. I make plenty of money. More than enough. It was just a weird week. What I'm saying is that if for any reason it comes up, I don't need your dad's child support and any issue we had was a bank error."

I glance back at Lucy, wondering if she understands anything Mom's saying. Lucy's braiding her mermaid's hair, not paying attention. That's for the best. But then Mom reaches back and places a hand on Lucy's knee. "Do you understand? Don't talk about Mommy? Okay? What happens in our home, stays in our home."

Like our apartment is a drunken, weekend bender in Vegas. Lucy nods and then Mom looks at me for confirmation that I, too, will keep my mouth shut.

"Will you keep quiet about Veronica's tumor?" I ask.

Mom scowls. "It's like you have no faith in me at all."

That's the thing, I don't.

"Promise me you'll keep quiet," Mom pushes.

I cross a finger over my chest because I want out of this car. That does the job and Mom finally exits with her bottles of wine. When she shuts her door, Lucy and I study one another.

"You okay?" I ask.

"I don't like being here," Lucy says. "It's not fun."

Because she's wary of deep water and because being the youngest there with no one else anywhere near her age, it can be boring for her. "I'll swim with you."

"I want to go to Bridgett's. She invited me over and Mom said no."

"I'll take you there tomorrow, okay?"

"Our house has monsters."

Quick switch-up in conversation and that confession from my sister creates an uneasiness in my gut. Veronica has been telling me since the start that the house is haunted, but somehow the words falling from Lucy's lips is chilling. "Is that why you have nightmares?"

"The little girl doesn't scare me, but the man does."

My spine straightens. "What man?"

"The one who comes in at night. He can change what he looks like. Sometimes he looks the same, most times he doesn't." Lucy hugs her mermaid closer to her chest, and she drops her voice like she's terrified someone will hear her and she'll get in trouble. "Sometimes, he peeks into my room. One time, he walked in and stared at me."

My blood turns cold. "What did you do?"

"I screamed before he could touch me and he left. Then you came and sang to me."

That could be any given night since we moved in. I don't understand why her nightmares are so bad and include random men. The idea creates a sickening sloshing in my stomach.

"Does Daddy not love us?" Lucy asks, and her question causes my lungs to squeeze. "I heard Mommy say that to Hannah."

A knock on my window, I jump and spot Sylvia smiling and waving at me. Before I can respond, Sylvia opens Lucy's door and undoes her seat belt. "How are you doing, Luce?"

"I don't know. Mommy says we aren't allowed to talk."

Sylvia's forehead furrows, and I'm swamped with the urge to bang my head against the steering wheel. Instead, I get out of the car, shoulder Lucy's backpack and watch as Sylvia picks up my sister, giving her a huge bear hug accompanied by a ton of kisses.

It's a comfort to watch, but I'm also cautious. Sylvia's been ignoring me since I publicly picked Veronica as a partner. Which has been fun considering we share the same friends and have swim practice together every damn day.

Lucy giggles and squeals when Sylvia gives her a raspberry on her cheek. Sylvia then sets her on the ground, reaches into the car for the mac-n-cheese and hands it to Lucy. "Go take this to Mom. I need to talk to your hardheaded brother. And, Lucy, you better not eat it all!"

Lucy laughs as she tells Sylvia that she will eat it all, and Sylvia mock pouts.

"Stay away from the pool until I'm there," I call out, and Lucy responds with, "Okay."

Once Lucy's inside, Sylvia leans back against the car. "Hey."

"Hardheaded?"

"Would jerk work better?"

"Probably."

She smirks then uses a finger to poke my bicep. "You okay? You look a bit out of it."

"I'm good." I rub the back of my head. I could tell Sylvia about the string of weird conversations I just had with Mom and then Lucy, but then figure Lucy's right—we aren't allowed to talk. "I had to teach the toddlers' swim classes today and then I've been working on homework. I'm brain dead."

Sylvia notices the folded diary and snatches it from my back pocket. "What's this?"

The instinct is to take it back, but the bigger deal I make out of it, the harder it will be to pry it from her hands. "Research."

"On your ghost project?"

"Yeah. It's a diary of a girl who lived in a TB hospital in upstate New York in 1918."

Sylvia flips through the pages. "You carry this around with you everywhere you go. I catch you sneaking in reading all the time." She glances at me and it's uncomfortable on my part. "I see you more than you know, Sutherland."

She's right, I carry the diary with me all the time, read it every chance I get. There's something in Evelyn's simple, everyday life that calls out to me—her underlying loneliness, her need for peace, to be part of something, to go home, to be cured of something she can't control . . . and her need to live.

"Miguel and I are talking in circles about what our topic should be." She hands the diary back to me. "Did you know that neither Miguel nor I like compromise?"

"Yeah."

"How many of the toddlers held on to you and wouldn't let go?" she asks with the knowing smile of someone who's also taught two-year-olds.

"One in every class. I even had a crier. Didn't stop the entire time. Wailed and screamed and strangled my neck. The kid has a serious water fear. The mom never once offered to help."

"Was she on her cell the whole time?"

"Yep."

"Parents are worthless."

True.

Sylvia deflates. There's a shadow of hurt in her eyes, and all the anger I've had with her vanishes. "You okay?"

She shakes her head. "Mom and Dad tried *talking* to me again today."

Damn.

Regardless of the fact that we've been mad at each other, Sylvia's my friend. My best friend. I wrap an arm around her shoulders and she leans into me.

"They aren't telling me that I shouldn't be attracted to girls, but they keep questioning me in this nice way. It's like a backhanded compliment. Saying things like, 'We support you and we love you, but are you sure you've thought this through?' Mom and Dad think I can't say for sure I'm a lesbian unless I kiss a boy."

"That sucks." No one has ever told me that I should kiss a boy to be sure I'm into girls.

"Mom and Dad suggested that I try kissing you."

"You know you want to kiss me," I tease.

Sylvia places a hand on her chest and dramatically dry heaves. "Excuse me while I vomit out my pancreas."

The light moment ends when she sighs heavily. I rub my hand up and down her arm. "I'm sorry . . . for a lot of things."

"Me, too . . . for a lot of things as well." A pause, then she continues, "I wish my parents were more like your mom. She accepts me. Like you do. Like Miguel does."

I rub my hand up and down her arm again because I can't bring myself to tell her that my mom pushes me to date her.

"I think that's why I was so angry with you about Veronica. You chose to work with her over me. I guess there was a part of me that was scared."

"Scared of what?"

"I don't know. I guess I was scared you were switching one weird girl for another. That I'd been replaced. Because who could be friends with more than one weird girl in this town without losing their minds over the stupid gossip?"

"You're not weird." A pause. "And neither is Veronica."

"We live in a small town where I can count the number of gay people on two hands. Most people around here consider me weird."

"But you aren't."

She rolls her eyes and pulls away. "Whatever. So here's the thing, Miguel and I need a favor."

"What?"

"Because we haven't agreed upon a topic, Mrs. Garcia told us that we need to join another group. Miguel and I talked and we'd like to join your and Veronica's group."

I warily eye Sylvia then shove my hands into my cargo shorts. "You don't like Veronica."

"Well . . . you seem to like her so maybe I'm missing something about her. Plus Mrs. Garcia showed us the list of project ideas she's approved. I have to admit, your ghost idea is far-fetched, but it's also the most interesting."

A pit forms in my stomach. "If this is my mom maneuvering for a good grade again—"

"It's more than that," Sylvia cuts me off. "I don't want to get into another argument, but can you trust me that there's more to this than just your grade? Without overanalyzing and asking a billion questions, can we go back to being friends? Can you let us in your group?"

I can't imagine Veronica is going to be anywhere near okay with this, but Sylvia is my friend and I can't let her down. "Okay. But there's something you should know."

"What?"

"Veronica and I are dating."

VERONICA

"You had a seizure last week." Mom is on the window seat in my bedroom, looking out beyond the glass to the world below. "It wasn't a major one, but a seizure nonetheless. You promised him you'd tell him if you ever had a seizure."

"It wasn't a seizure. It was an ice-pick headache."

"You're lying and you should tell your father." The phrase has become her personal mantra.

I finish tying my boot. "And I'll be in the hospital before my toast pops up from the toaster. No, thank you. I had my heart set on strawberry jam today."

I pick through the curls in my hair and do a last look of myself in the mirror. Thanksgiving was a bust so I'm moving on to Christmas. Red plaid, pleated short skirt, white, lace tank as this fall is going to be the hottest on record, red-and-green-striped socks that end above my knees and black combat boots. I look good, very good. Sexy and ready to kick ass.

"You didn't tell Sawyer how serious your brain tumor is. It's growing. You know it is. Leo, at least, understood the implications of being with you. Are you being fair?"

I sigh because Mom's persistence on these matters is starting to get annoying, and it's really difficult to be mad at your mother's ghost. "Dad went and visited Sawyer and his mom before we left for Florida, opened his big mouth again, and told Sawyer about your agonizing death and how the same fate awaits me when the tumor grows. As far as I'm concerned, Dad's already told Sawyer all he needs to know. I'll find out today if, after having time to think about it, that officially freaked him out and has driven him away."

It's Sunday. Dad and I returned from our trip last night. We drove to the Gulf Coast, dropped off his load, had two days to play, picked up another load, took it to Daytona, spent time there, then picked up another load and headed home. Overall, it was fantastic. I just wish that Mom wasn't tethered to this house and she could have been with me.

Today, I'm dressing to break all sorts of hearts. But it's really Sawyer's heart I want to pound a bit harder. If he's going to run for the hills, I at least want him to sort of regret it. After brunch with Dad, because I slept too late for breakfast, Sawyer and I are meeting to work on our project. I texted him last night asking if he would be willing to go over his photos and my EVPs. He texted quickly back yes. I'm choosing to see that as an encouraging sign.

"You look nice," Mom says, and I grin at her tone. She means what she says, but she's also hinting that she's aware of my hidden agenda. "I'm sure Sawyer will like it."

My stomach flutters with butterflies at the thought of seeing him, and I put a hand there in an attempt to tame them. Chill. This is a chill, kissing-only, hardly-any-emotion relationship. "Did you ever kiss a boy when you knew no serious emotions were going to happen?"

Mom shakes her head, but not in reprimand. "My mom told me to never do such things, but I like that you're more adventurous than I was. It's a quality you inherited from your dad."

She unfolds her legs from underneath her to touch her toes to the floor. "The question is, how does kissing a boy who you don't have feelings for make you feel?"

Her question causes hesitation, and I stop fussing with my hair to join her on the window seat. As I sit beside her, there's an ache because I miss her warmth and her smell. Whenever Mom walked in the room I would immediately breathe in the scent of roses. I have a rosewood candle in my bedroom, but it doesn't quite smell like her.

"I kissed a couple of boys just to kiss when you were sick. I thought it would make me feel better." That it would help me forget.

"Did it?" she asks.

My throat tightens at the memory of the boys pawing at me. "No." I don't think there was anything that could have made me feel better when Mom was so ill. "But when Leo kissed me after the eighth grade dance, I liked it. And when Sawyer kissed me this past weekend, I liked that, too."

Mom reaches out like she's going to touch my cheek, but then stops just a breath's distance away. Since the ice-pick headache, Mom's stopped touching me. I don't know why. Maybe she's punishing me for not being honest with Dad. But the loss of her touch has created a gaping, bleeding hole. I miss her, so incredibly much.

She withdraws her hand and lays it on her lap. "What's important is that you're comfortable with your body and how you decide to use it. If you want to kiss the boy and he wants to kiss you, then you kiss. If you don't want to kiss the boy, you don't. Kissing is magical, but it's not magical enough to make your wounds heal. Only time can do that."

I know that now, and it was a hard lesson. A lump forms in my throat. "I miss you."

Mom gives me a sad smile. "I'm right here, peanut."

"I know." And I'm grateful for that. The last few weeks of her life, Mom was so sick she slept all the time. When she was awake, she was barely coherent and whispered about the past.

When she died, it wasn't anything like I thought it would be. It was so still . . . so quiet. A breath in, a breath out and then she wasn't alive anymore. It felt wrong. Her dying should have been huge. There should have been violent storms and earthquakes. But none of that happened. She slipped away and the world kept turning. As I said, it felt wrong.

I had stood by her side, silent tears streaming down my face as I lost my best friend, my rock, my mother. "I love you." So much. I'm not sure any daughter has loved her mother as much as I love her.

"I love you more."

"V," Dad calls. "Brunch is ready!"

Mom goes back to staring out the window. I stand, walk across the room, and at the door, I pause and look back at Mom. I hate that she died, but I'm so grateful she chose to stay here with me. I need to convince Dad about ghosts. I need him to believe and then he'll see her. And when I die, he'll never be alone because he'll see me, too.

"Great news," I say as I head down the stairs. "I don't have a headache . . ."

My lungs squeeze when I hit the last step. Lights. There are lights strung everywhere. Orange lights, white lights, and all the paper turkeys I had taken down before we left for Florida are back up. Stranger? There are more than there were before. The one with large googly eyes hanging from the stairs' entrance causes me to smile.

The large, long table Dad keeps in the basement is set up, covered with a white tablecloth and set with Mom's fancy china and crystal. My mouth waters at the sight of so much food, and it's such an odd combination. Waffles and bacon and sausage and eggs . . . and turkey and dressing and green beans and rolls.

Complete awe overwhelms me as Jesse, Nazareth, Scarlett and Dad step into my view from the living room. My eyes burn. They're giving me Thanksgiving. "You did all of this?"

"We helped," Dad says, then gestures toward the kitchen, "but he did most of it."

He?

"Surprise!" Lucy jumps out from behind the couch. She's in an orange shirt that has a turkey on it, black leggings and a bright orange tutu. "Sawyer says it's Thanksgiving!"

She runs to me, and I gladly pick her up and accept her warm hug. A quick kiss to my cheek and she shimmies back to the ground, takes my hand and guides me to the table. "I made the turkey."

"You did?" I say, and that's when I scan the kitchen and find Sawyer watching me.

His hands are in the pockets of his khakis, and he's beautiful in his pressed, button-down blue shirt. There's wariness there, but also hope. He's waiting on me, on my reaction, and as Lucy continues to talk nonstop about all the food she helped her brother make, I let go of her hand, and approach Sawyer. "Hey."

"Hey."

"You did this?"

"I had help." He keeps his baby blues on me, and my heart flutters. "You know, you're not dressed correctly. Christmas isn't until the end of October."

The laugh bubbles out of me, and he gives me his brilliant smile, the sunrise after the darkest night. He lifts his hand, cradles my face and I lean into his touch. His eyes darken, the same way they did when he kissed me the other night, and my blood starts to tingle. Gravity pulls me toward him, him toward me, and right as our lips are about to meet my father clears his throat. "While I like that my daughter is happy, do you mind if you took your hands off of her?"

My heart pounds and we separate so fast we could both be track stars. Dad gives Sawyer the evil eye, puts an arm around me and guides me to the table. I glance at Sawyer over my shoulder. Even though he has red cheeks, he's grinning from ear to ear. So am I.

This is the best Thanksgiving ever.

SAWYER

Thursday Aug. 8: Weight 112 ½ lb.

Nothing much doing today. Cured quite a lot.

Was weighed today. Still keep on losing. It makes me sick.

Morris was over tonight. Oh Diary, I'm still crazy about that kid. I certainly have hung on for a long time, but I like him exactly as well as I did at first.

Yeah, I get it, Evelyn. You're into Morris and I'm into Veronica. It's a great feeling when that person is into you, too.

Brunch is done, the dishes are washed, the kitchen cleaned, the table folded up and put neatly back in the basement. Ulysses then had me, Jesse and Nazareth help bring up the heavy prelit Christmas tree from the basement along with the boxes of ornaments Scarlett and Veronica deemed necessary as they hunted through the massive amount of stuff in the basement storage. Lucy skipped around the commotion singing Christmas songs at the tops of her lungs.

As everyone was packing to leave, Ulysses asked me to stay. He told Veronica to go out onto the front porch and Ulysses and I had a talk. More like him staring at me for an uncomfortable twenty minutes before finally saying, "Don't hurt her."

I received the message loud and clear: the man is going to kill me if I do. He never said the words. He never had to. It was all right there written in his death glare.

Glad I survived that round, I step out onto the front porch and Veronica glances up at me. "Your mom's home and she called Lucy in. I told her you were helping Dad with some boxes."

"Thanks." I settle onto the step beside her. "Did you have a good time?"

"The best. You know, I've never had a boyfriend before. I'm assuming that's what we are now—a chill boyfriend/girlfriend. As in we kiss with none of the clingy drama."

"We're definitely boyfriend/girlfriend. If it helps, I've never had a girlfriend."

Her eyes widen in disbelief. "I don't believe you."

"It's true. I've never wanted to be in any type of relationship. Taking care of Lucy and Mom is enough responsibility for a lifetime. But this"—I take her hand and love how her breath catches with my touch—"I can handle."

"Whatever." Her smile is tempting and teasing. "It's well known you've dated. Plus your kiss screams experience."

"Dated. Mainly to get Mom and my friends off my back. And how far down the who-I've-kissed rabbit hole do you want to go?"

"Not far," she admits.

Since she brought it up. "What about Leo? There were rumors at school you two were an on-again, off-again thing. I meant what I said. I'm good with a chill relationship, but I'm not into sharing people I kiss."

Veronica nudges the ground with her shoe. "I was in love with Leo, for a long time, but I fell out of it. I don't know when I fell out of it, but it happened. But even during that time, while we flirted around a relationship, we mainly stayed in the friend zone. And before you ask about kissing and Leo, ask yourself how far down that rabbit hole you want to go yourself."

"Not far at all."

"Good, but here's the truth." She takes her hand from mine and places her fingers to the side of her head to point out the problem.

"He didn't know how to see past the tumor. It was always there with him. He saw it all the time. He saw it before he saw me."

Fear forms in her eyes—am I like Leo?

Naw, I'm nothing like him, and the honesty of the situation is I'm not much different from Veronica. She has a tumor in her brain that's waiting to grow out of control. I have this addiction in my blood that can set me off, cause me to go over that ledge and end up impaled by sharp rocks. If I don't get this under control, my life span could be shorter than most. The miracle here is that she cares for me.

To calm her anxiety, I take her hand that's pointed at her head, link her fingers with mine and lay them on our knees. I lean toward her and brush my lips to hers.

Her breathing hitches, and with the brief taste of her, my heart beats faster. Knowing that my mom could walk out, that her father could storm out, I pull back, yet rest my forehead against hers. "All I see is you."

She exhales as if relieved. I kiss her forehead, and reluctantly pull away, but keep her fingers laced with mine. The happiness of being with her fades as my own fears fester in my gut. "I need to talk to you."

Veronica studies my face. "You don't need to. Not if you don't want. I'm fine with how things are between us."

I let go of her and scrub my face with my hands.

"You're allowed to have your secrets," she whispers. "Just like I'm allowed to have mine."

She's right, but Knox and I talked and I need to start being honest. With myself, with her, with so many areas of my life, and that's not easy. I could start with Mom or Sylvia or Miguel, but it's not them I want to be honest with. It's her. It's because she's one of the few good things I like in my life. The one thing that purely belongs to my choices and not anyone else's. If I tell her and it messes things up, then it does, but at least I was honest. At least this part of my life won't be tainted with this need to jump. "I go to AA meetings."

Veronica twitches beside me as if shocked by a lightning bolt. "You're an alcoholic?"

"No, I jump from cliffs."

Veronica blinks, and I release a long breath as I'm aware that made no sense.

"It's the reason I took you to the quarry. I thought it would be easier to explain there. See, my sponsor said I needed to be honest with you in order to start being honest with myself. I . . . uh . . . have this problem. I love jumping. The more danger associated with the jump the more of a rush I feel. I like the adrenaline high, and I've chased it for years. I used to hitchhike rides from strangers when I was too young to drive. Sometimes, I broke into the Y at night to jump off the high dive when no one was around. Since I've been able to drive, it's worse. I'll search online for hours to find the biggest, scariest jump."

I give her time, give her space to process. In reality, I'm giving her time to leave. When she stays put, I doggedly continue, "I started taking bigger risks because some of the jumps had become boring. I want the high, crave the high, and then I did a jump and it went bad." I show her the scar on my leg. It's two inches long, right below my knee and it stung like a bitch when I hit the rocks. "You'd think when I hit those rocks and saw blood gushing from my leg that would have been enough to get me to stop jumping, but it didn't because I'm stupid."

It's strange how her blue eyes are inquisitive, as if what I'm saying isn't shocking and instead curious. "Is jumping how you broke your arm?"

"Yeah. I went to this place about an hour from here. Another abandoned quarry, but higher than the place I took you. The rocks there are spawns of Satan. It's so dangerous that even other adrenaline junkies online warn people to stay clear. But I went and it was the best damn jump of my life. The rush I felt as I was in the air . . ."

Just the memory brings on a rush in my blood, but then I attempt to breathe away the sensation. I don't want the high anymore. I don't want to die.

"Even though I knew it was dangerous, I kept returning. The time between visits shortened and shortened until one day, the jump went wrong. I clipped an outcropping—a rock ledge about halfway down—and it changed my trajectory. I hit water, but slammed my arm against a sharp rock under the surface. My bones cracked and my arm became jelly. The pain disoriented me and I ended up losing air and taking in water. I panicked and was sinking and I should be dead right now."

I choke on the last words and have to clear my throat.

"It's okay," Veronica whispers. "You aren't there now."

But I am. That's what she doesn't understand. When I'm not jumping, I often feel like I'm still stuck under that water. "But I got it together, fought the fear and kicked my way to the surface. I landed far from flat land, and it was the longest, hardest swim of my life. The drive to the Y was worse."

"The Y?" Veronica exclaims, and I wince with how her tone calls out my stupidity.

"Besides having an arm dangle in a way that wasn't natural, that's how I knew I had a problem—I was more interested in lying to get myself out of the situation than taking care of my arm. I didn't want anyone to know what I did so I went to the Y and faked a fall on the pool deck. It was a crap thing to do. I know it. I'm trying to stop so I started going to AA meetings."

She tilts her head in disbelief, and I bitterly chuckle at her incredulous expression.

"There's this guy a few years older than me, and he knows my problem. Even though I'm not an alcoholic and don't drink, he's taken me on. He's my sponsor, I'm going to weekly meetings and I'm going to kick this. I'm going to stop jumping off of cliffs because if I don't, I'll die."

Veronica's eyes flicker about my face, searching for something, and I hope to hell she finds it. "Is it really that hard to stop?"

Her question digs into my soul. "Yeah. I'd love to go now. I'm wound as tight as I can get. Every part of me hurts. But when I jump . . ." Just thinking of the high makes me hungry . . . *thirsty*, as Knox would say. A deep breath in and then another out.

"I get it if this is too much for you," I say. "You're the only person who knows about my need to jump besides my sponsor. I haven't even had the courage to talk at the AA meetings yet."

"Why are you telling me this?" she asks.

"Because you need to know I'm a real bastard. On that night, even though the ground was loose, we may have been able to climb back up the cliff. But I didn't want that. I wanted to jump, and I wanted the added complication of jumping with you." Anger at myself pummels my muscles and it's chased by a shot of shame.

"I was stupid," I say. "Careless and wrong. I could have hurt you and that pisses me off. I get it if you think I'm crazy and want to walk away."

"Sawyer," Veronica says slowly.

I glance over at her and she's not looking at me like I expect—as if I'm the world's biggest jerk, but instead with gentle understanding. This girl continuously trips me up.

"You don't think I'm already aware you like a good rush?"

My mouth drops open to respond, but confused, I snap it shut again.

"How do people not see that about you?" She speaks in a slow way, as if testing out the words, like she might offend me. "If anyone bothers to take a good look at you, it's obvious you like situations that get your heart pumping. I saw it that day at the TB hospital when the cops showed. You were willing to go toe to toe with me for as long as it took."

My forehead creases as her words churn in my stomach. Do other people see it and say nothing or do other people in my life not see me at all?

"I don't think liking extreme sports is a particularly bad thing, but I do think it crosses a line if you're knowingly putting yourself into danger for the rush. Jumping out of planes with a parachute—not a problem. Jumping off of dangerous cliffs and into rocks because you can't stop yourself—that's a bit much. But I also give you credit for getting the help you need. Bonus points for the creative use of an AA meeting in your pursuit to make it right."

"You should be bothered that I put you in danger."

"First off, you didn't put me in danger. I'm the idiot who tried to reach down for a barrette. I fell and you came after me to help. If you had wanted the jump to begin with, you wouldn't have grabbed for me like you did. I felt the tug as you tried to drag me back up, but the pull of the landslide was too great."

True.

"Two, I'm a smart girl and if I'm going to be offended by anything it's going to be that you thought I hadn't taken the climb into consideration before choosing the jump. I don't let anyone talk me into anything. I saw the loose ground, and I also thought we could make the climb, but then I also considered the fact that if the climb did prove unsuccessful and the ground beneath us gave, we would have fallen into the water anyhow. Then you wouldn't have been in the position to help me swim."

I'm dumbfounded. So much so that I can do nothing more than stare at her.

"I don't have room to judge you, Sawyer, if that's what you're waiting for. You've been doing something incredibly stupid, but you realize that you have an addiction and you're getting help. For me to come down on you would be the same as someone getting mad and disappointed in me for having a tumor."

"It's not the same."

"It is," she says. "There's something in your genetic makeup that makes this a struggle for you. Same as there was something in my genetic makeup that made me sensitive to whatever chemicals that company poured into the ground near our home. That doesn't mean you give in to the cravings, but it does mean that it's a fight that you have that not many people will ever understand."

"But my fight and your fight are different. You didn't choose the tumor."

"And you didn't choose the addiction."

My throat's tight and I can't look at her, only at the cracks along the sidewalk. She's too nice, too forgiving, and she's wrong. She has to be. I'm the one who's weak, and I'm confused how she doesn't see it. "I promise you, no more cliff jumping." For her, I'll do it.

"What if you do?" she asks. "Will you tell me?"

I don't like her question, it eats at me wrong, but it's an honest one that deserves an honest answer. It'll suck if I let her down, but . . . "I'll tell you."

Veronica holds out her pinkie. "Swear?"

I chuckle yet link my pinkie with hers. "I swear." Then roll my neck because while she's been understanding about this, I'm not sure she's going to be on the board for the following. "I have more bad news."

"You're a vampire?"

She'd probably like that better. "No, Sylvia and Miguel asked to join our group and I told them they could."

And that's when Veronica gets pissed.

"You kissed her," Mom says the moment I close the door to our apartment. She says it as a statement, a fact, but the look she gives me from the couch is full of accusation. "I saw it myself, from Lucy's window, so please don't deny it."

It's late—ten at night. Veronica finally stopped being angry over the additions to our group by me pointing out I'd accept Kravitz and Lachlin if the situation was reversed. I get why she doesn't like it, and I'll admit to being hesitant, too.

Then, after a few minutes of kissing on the porch, the two of us went to her apartment and sorted through the photos I had taken of the bridge. We then went through the audio until I had to head to the Y for an evening staff meeting. To top it off, after the meeting, I did a few laps.

During our research, I'll admit I heard, "He's hurting," and I'll also admit that there was a strange ball of light in some of the photos, but I'm still not convinced about ghosts. Not like Veronica clings to the hope. To me, there's probably some scientific reason. Some logic that I'm not smart enough to know.

"Yes, I kissed her," I answer.

Mom has weekend-bloodshot eyes. She had more than a few too many last night at Sylvia's and she's been drinking by herself again tonight. Thank God tomorrow's Monday and I'll get at least four evenings where our conversations aren't alcohol induced.

I walk past her and check on Lucy. She's sound asleep in bed. I head to my room, dump my clean clothes from my basket onto my bed then pull the wet stuff out of my duffel bag and place that in my basket to wash later.

My hair is wet, it seems like my hair is always wet now. Since meeting with Knox, I swim. All the time. Before and after practice in the morning, after my shifts as a swim coach and lifeguard at the Y. In the evenings, I bring Lucy with me and do more laps. Knox calls it trading one addiction for another. A new addiction that's less likely to get me killed.

Knox's preferred addiction over drinking is long-distance running and painting. He laughed when he told me he sucks at painting. Knox's theory is if we stay busy, we're less apt to do the thing that brings us down.

"Are you dating her?" Mom stands in the doorway of my room, and I start folding clothes and placing them in my dresser.

Mom not saying Veronica's name works under my skin. "Did Sylvia tell you that?"

"She doesn't need to when I see you two kissing."

"Yeah, I'm dating Veronica."

"Is that wise?"

"Why wouldn't it be?"

"Because she's . . . a distraction."

That causes me to pause in mid-fold of a T-shirt. "What's that mean?"

"It means you already have enough going on between swim and school and this project."

"I thought you wanted me to date."

"Yes, but you should be with someone who is less . . . complicated."

My spine straightens. "Does 'complicated' mean brain tumor?"

"Yes, no, I mean . . . I don't understand . . . there are so many other girls in your group who would be better suited for you. Girls who are more like . . . you. This girl is just so . . ."

"Different," I finish for Mom. "Yeah, she is, and I like it. So you know, I think it'd be wise if we drop this topic of conversation."

"I'm concerned about this. I think she's a bad influence."

I cock an eyebrow but keep any comment to myself as I return to folding laundry.

"Since you've been spending time with her you've been so moody." When she enters my room, she's unbalanced on her feet.

"That's not because of Veronica."

"You've been letting down your friends and not hanging out with them as much and yelling at me, and you've been missing practices."

"I won every race I had at last Saturday's meet, so don't worry about practices."

"That's not the point," Mom pushes. "I'm not saying you shouldn't be friends with her. I'm proud that you are, that you are good enough of a boy to take on someone like her for a project when no one else would, but dating her seems—"

"I set a date to see Dad." I cut her off, changing the subject to another one that sucks because if she keeps up on her problems with Veronica, we might have a screaming match so loud that Veronica might hear and that's the last thing I'd want.

"He won't stop texting me," I continue, "as he thinks my doing this is me wanting some sort of relationship with him. And you should know, because he seems intent to stick around for this one, his girlfriend's pregnant."

Mom's posture crumples as if I'd hit her. "How far along is she?"

"Dad said she's due before Christmas." I pick up my jeans and fold them in half.

Her entire body flinches and her cheeks go red. "How long have you known?"

"Since the beginning of summer."

"Were you going to tell me? In fact, when were you going to tell me he had a girlfriend?"

I pause mid-fold. I seriously hate my life. "He's always dating someone."

"And you never told me?"

"What do you want me to say here, Mom?"

"You should have told me."

Irritation leaks into my veins. "Why? The only thing it was going to do was upset you."

"You think I can't handle it?" Mom shouts.

"No, I don't!" I shout back. "I also didn't tell you because I didn't feel like listening to you and your friends chatting it up every Friday night like my feelings about it don't matter!"

"Sawyer?" Lucy's groggy voice stops us cold. She rubs her eyes then shuffles into the room.

"Did you have a bad dream?" I ask.

"No. I'm thirsty."

So am I, for a jump. My cells itch with the need, but I breathe out and instead take my sister's hand. Without looking at Mom, I thank God for Lucy's interruption and walk her into the kitchen. I take out my phone, look up Knox's number, and as soon as Lucy's back in bed, I'll call him. He said any day, at any time. I sure as hell hope he means it.

VERONICA

Interview number two: Dr. Kelly Wolfe, professor of history at Transylvania University, with personal interest and knowledge in Kentucky history, local folklore and ghost stories.

I write down all Dr. Wolfe just said about EVPs, then look up to find Sylvia doing the same. She glances up, catches me staring and offers an I'm-trying-here smile before returning her attention to Dr. Wolfe.

"Miguel and I are new to the project," Sylvia says in a cheerful voice. Not one that's fake, but real, and I like her for that. "So forgive us if we don't quite understand all the ghost terminology like Sawyer and Veronica."

Sylvia is a beautiful girl, stunning really. She's smart, studious, so far has a flare for details and she's nervous around me. I'm not nervous around her, and I think that freaks her out more. If I were in her shoes, I'd probably be uncomfortable, too. She's been forced to join another group, to work on my chosen topic, and the last conversation we had, she told her friends that I eat Girl Scouts.

In the chair beside me at the coffee house in Lexington, Sawyer stretches out his legs and lays a hand along the back of my chair, his fingers caressing my shoulders. Sylvia's eyes follow the motion. Not angry, not jealous . . . more like confused.

We're all jam-packed together—five of us at an intimate table meant for possibly three. Considering everyone at this cramped table, except for me, was sired by giants, we're all up close and personal.

Sawyer and I are particularly squished together. Our legs and arms brush along each other's with every inhale. Each touch sending little zaps of electricity into my blood. For someone new to the whole boyfriend/girlfriend thing, he's very relaxed touching me in public—as if we've been dating forever and have had time to become very aware and comfortable with every part of the other. I'll admit, I'm loving every delicious second. I feel so very . . . alive.

But it's time for me to focus on our project and not how Sawyer's fingertips are tracing seductive circles along one back of my neck. I turn my laptop around to show Dr. Wolfe the pictures Sawyer and I took at the bridge.

"Here are the pictures I told you about," I say in reference to the email I sent her that helped with her agreeing to this interview.

Dr. Wolfe's eyes narrow as she studies one picture then moves on to the next, studying the next one with the same excruciating precision. "I agree. These definitely look like orbs."

I'm riding so high that it's practically a miracle that my toes are touching the ground. I glance over at Sawyer and while he still wears skepticism like a second skin, he smiles at me.

Orbs are round balls of light anomalies that can represent spirits. We caught several in the same spot in the middle of the bridge, but my favorite picture is the one with the orb hovering next to Sawyer when I stole his camera from him. He looks so cute, as skeptical as he does now, and it's brilliant that a spirit rode shotgun on his shoulder.

Sawyer, of course, dismissed it all as particles of dust, but the shapes are too perfect, too round, too bright. But even he, when we played the EVP of "He's hurting" on the computer, had no explanation other than stunned silence.

Dr. Wolfe pushes the laptop back toward me. "I have to say I'm very impressed. It's very difficult for even the most seasoned ghost investigator to capture actual active spiritual evidence like you have. Most times, people believe they are making contact, but instead are caught up in a residual haunting."

Now everyone at the table is focused on Dr. Wolfe as I'm betting they are as lost as I am.

"What's a residual haunting?" Sylvia asks.

"A residual haunting is when an event that is so traumatic, so emotional, happens and the energy created from the huge outpouring of emotion, most likely negative emotion, imprints onto the area. That emotion becomes a loop, replaying over and over again. It's not an actual spirit, it's a memory."

When it's clear we're all dumfounded, she continues, "Think of the hauntings often associated with widow's walks by the sea. Those ghosts appear at the same time of day and the apparitions do the same thing—whether it be they just appear staring out at sea or they walk along the same stretch of area then disappear. Sometimes there isn't an apparition involved. Sometimes it's the same sounds at the same time of day. Like the slamming of a door or—"

"Footsteps going down stairs," Sawyer says.

We all glance at him. His smile is gone, his eyes serious, and I can tell he's thinking of our house.

"Yes," Dr. Wolfe says. "There is no communication with these phenomena as it would be the same thing as trying to have a conversation with people who belong to a memory in your head. Your memories, to you, are alive. You see them play out in radiant color. Sometimes you remember something so vividly that you can almost taste the air, feel a touch, or sense a presence. That's what a residual haunting is like, only we all see the memory being replayed."

"What I hear you saying," says Miguel, "is that something so powerful happened that it can't be forgotten?"

Dr. Wolfe looks at each of us before answering. "Yes, and it was so powerful that it literally reshaped the world surrounding it forever."

Because Miguel has an SUV and a full tank of gas, he drove us into Lexington and then into Louisville. He and Sylvia in the front seat. Sawyer and I in the back.

I've been silent mostly, absorbing their easy banter with each other. Sort of like how Nazareth, Jesse, Leo and I used to be before Leo left for college. Their gentle jabs at each other, the jokes—the new and private ones, their laughter, the way they argue yet have each other's backs makes me miss my friends.

It's not like I don't see them. I do, but not as much as they're busy with life, and then there's how I haven't responded to Leo. Even though he still texts daily, begging for us to be friends again.

Sawyer squeezes my hand and I lift my lips as I look at him to let him know I'm okay. I give him and his friends credit, they've tried to include me, but they've been friends forever. I'm new, plus I'm the weird girl they gossip about. I officially have a better appreciation and respect for how Scarlett was brave enough to waltz back into Jesse's life.

"Tell us more about this place." Miguel takes a left when the light changes to green then looks at me in the rearview mirror. "What ghost are we hunting tonight?"

"Sometime around 1950 there was a couple who were going to a dance and they crashed their car when they missed the curve on Mitchell Hill Road. The legend says that people see a girl walking along the side of the road in a prom dress. She's also been seen walking in the cemetery that's at the top of the hill."

"Why are there so many stories of teenagers dying in car crashes and then of the girl walking along the side of the road?" Miguel asks.

"Probably because they crashed due to the boy's stupidity, and then the boy was too lazy to go get help so she had to do it herself then died of disappointment," Sylvia says.

I laugh. "Good one."

"Thanks. I asked my parents about this place as Dad grew up in Louisville. He said that when he was a teenager, he had heard that if you saw the girl and pulled over she'd get in the backseat of the car and then disappear when you reached the cemetery."

"Your dad knows about this?"

Sylvia turns all the way around, her long blond hair falling over her shoulder. "Yeah. He's weirdly happy I'm doing this project. He said that one time in high school he and four of his buddies drove along the road trying to see the ghost and were hoping to pick her up."

"And if they found her where was she going to sit?"

"Dad said he volunteered to let her sit on his lap."

Our combined laughter, including me, feels good. As if I'm somehow part of their group and they want me there.

"Papá said he and his friends once went to Pope Lick trestle in Louisville to try to find the goat man." Miguel follows the instructions on his GPS, turns onto Mitchell Hill Road and we begin the ascent up the hill. "I've heard all sorts of crazy stuff about that trestle. Why aren't we checking that place out?"

"Because a goat man isn't a ghost but a man who is part goat," Sawyer says. "We're trying to prove ghosts are real, not goat people."

"True, true," Miguel adds, and we fall into silence as Miguel's motor lightly strains as we continue up the winding and steep hill.

We lost the friendly porch lights of neighborhoods over a mile ago. With the climb up, the foliage thickens. The limbs, heavy with the start of fall leaves, lean over the road, as if threatening to collapse and crush us.

The sky is dark, thick clouds racing along the windy night. A sudden break in the trees reveals the Louisville skyline in the distance and the miles and miles of neighborhoods below. It also discloses the steep, rocky drop. Miguel jerks the car more toward the center of the road as Sylvia gasps and holds on to the armrest of the door.

"Be careful," she whispers. "Another car could whip around the curve and hit us head-on." And push us off the road and over the cliff.

Miguel goes from driving one-handed to two.

The cliff. Sawyer's drawn to the drop-off, his head resting upon the glass. I squeeze his hand, and when he glances over at me, I spot a glimpse of the war being fought inside him. I squeeze again, to let him know that while I don't understand what must run through his head in moments like this, I can guess that it's hard.

He leans away from the window, toward me, and we sit shoulder to shoulder. His lips gently brush against my temple as he squeezes my hand back.

"Can you imagine what it must have been like for the couple who died?" Sylvia says. "To have been going to a dance? To have spent all of that day excited, the hours spent picking out the dress? The anticipation of the magic that was going to happen and then the fear they must have felt when they realized they had lost control?"

"Don't get too serious," Miguel says. "None of this is real."

"That's where you're wrong," I say as I watch the side of the road for the girl. "The couple and the accident were real. There's documentation in the county records about it. Sarah was a real girl and so was her boyfriend. They really did die in a crash on this road. Her family owns the cemetery at the top of the hill. Both she and her boyfriend are buried there."

A heaviness descends upon the car. Sylvia glancing over at Miguel, him looking back quickly, the exchange saying that this is more than what they signed up for. Their fear, palpable.

"How do we want to play this out?" Miguel's voice is deeply serious.

"The cemetery is at the top of the hill," I say. "Park near there and we'll look around."

We take a hairpin curve and a large white blob shoots in front of the car. Miguel curses, Sylvia screams and the brakes of the SUV squeal as we whiplash to a stop. A strong arm slips in front of me, keeping me safely against the seat.

"What the hell was that?" Miguel shouts while Sawyers asks, "Is everyone okay?"

No one answers either question as we're all stunned. Because whatever it was moved quickly, moved stealthily, and as fast as it appeared, it disappeared and no one wants to admit the fantastic obvious—that we just saw a ghost.

SAWYER

"Is everyone okay?" I ask again, as my pulse pounds in my ears.

Veronica's eyes flash with excitement. "I'm great."

Because she believes she saw a ghost. I don't have to ask to know she's now on level-ten-ghost-hunter mode. My friends, on the other hand, are shaken. "Sylvia, Miguel, are you okay?"

"I'm okay," Sylvia says as she rubs her hands up and down her goose-fleshed arms.

"Yeah," Miguel answers then mashes his lips together. He edges forward in his seat to look beyond the hood of his car and then toward the thick forest. "You saw that, right? I'm not losing my mind? There was something in the road."

"I saw it," Veronica says.

"Me, too," Sylvia adds.

"It was probably a deer." I lean my arms forward on the front-row seats and point at the road ahead. "We've all seen them before. The cemetery's right up there. Park off to the side and we'll get out and look around."

"All famous words at the beginning of a slasher film," Sylvia mutters.

Miguel parks off to the side, and Veronica's out of the car in a shot, digital recorder in hand. Miguel and Sylvia, however, turn to look at me.

"Are we going to die here, *vato*?" Miguel asks. He's kidding, and he's not.

Veronica's already across the street, in the cemetery, and I've already lost her in the darkness. Veronica has one mode—headfirst. While I typically respect that, I only love that quality when I can follow. "Stay in the car if you want."

"And have Veronica tell the teacher that she did all the work?" Sylvia says. "No way."

"Veronica's not that way." But it doesn't matter what I say as Sylvia's already out of the car. Miguel follows. I grab the camera and soon the three of us are knee-deep in high grass in a creepy-ass, dew-ridden cemetery at midnight with Sylvia skintight next to me. Sometimes, I question my life choices.

"Sawyer," V calls. "Over here."

I trudge forward through the wet grass and it doesn't take long for my Nikes to become soaked. Veronica shines the flashlight of her cell down onto a broken gravestone. "This is Sarah's stone."

Beside me, Sylvia shivers. "What happened to it?"

"I read on blog posts that someone vandalized it," Miguel says, and we all turn to stare at him. "Don't look so surprised. I want an A as much as the rest of you."

Without being asked, I call out into the night. "Sarah, Sarah's boyfriend, whoever else is here, we're not here to hurt you. We're here to help. I'm going to take your picture if that's okay."

"Have you lost your mind?" Sylvia mutters. "Are you talking to ghosts?"

Veronica bounces on her toes. "Good job. Take some pictures around here, and I'm going to walk around the cemetery. There's supposed to be a statue here that drag racers visit before they race down the hill. If you touch the statue's hands and they're cold, someone in your party is going to die."

"I read about that, too," says Miguel. "I'll come with."

"That's stupid," Sylvia says. "The statue's hands are always going to be cold."

Veronica doesn't respond as she skips into the darkness, eager for the next discovery.

"Miguel," I say. We stare at each other, a brief moment, and he nods his understanding. I care for Veronica and it will really piss me off if she falls down some deep, dark hole or is whisked away by some mountain man who has never seen a girl before. Miguel just promised to have her back.

I raise the camera and take a few shots of the tombstone with the flash on and then with the flash off. Then I start taking random shots throughout the cemetery.

"What are you doing?" Sylvia asks.

"Trying to capture spirit orbs."

"Do you really believe in all of this?"

"No." *Click, click, click.*

"Then why are you doing this project?"

"Because it's what Veronica wanted to do." I take a shot of Sylvia, and she's not amused. I release a long breath and glance around to make sure Veronica's nowhere near. "Why are you doing this project? You obviously aren't happy here."

Sylvia holds herself tight with her arms wrapped around her chest. "It's scary."

"What's scary?"

She huffs like she's annoyed. "Death, okay? Death is scary. Dead people are beneath our feet. Like, bones and decay, and those people were once alive and now they're dead and I don't know what happens to us when we die and I'm seriously uncomfortable with it all. Plus, it's creepy that Veronica would want to do this project to begin with."

I lower the camera, confused and unsettled. "What's that supposed to mean?"

Sylvia looks away from me, like she got caught, but I'm not letting it go. "What do you mean you think it's creepy that Veronica is doing this project?"

"It's a creepy idea is all."

"And you think she's weird regardless so that's not what you mean." Anger rolls through my veins. "Why are you part of my group, Sylvia? And don't give me that bullcrap answer about you and Miguel not being able to pick a topic."

Sylvia stares at the broken tombstone as if the sight breaks her heart. "Sarah deserves better than a broken tombstone."

"She does, but that doesn't answer my question. Did my mom tell you? Did she tell you what nobody else should know?"

Sylvia's head whips to stare at me and the answer is plain on her face. I curse under my breath, and Sylvia touches my arm. "Don't blame your mom, okay? She saw how upset I was about you choosing Veronica over me, and she told us to help me understand why you did choose Veronica. She told us to help me."

My vision tunnels. "Us? *She told multiple people?*"

Sylvia flutters her hands in the air as if that will calm me. "Just me, Mom and their close friends. They won't tell anyone. They promised. Your mom said Veronica's dad was adamant about that."

My hands shake, and I have to put the strap of the camera around my neck so I don't smash it into the ground. "That wasn't her business to tell."

"Don't you understand? She told me about Veronica to help me. I was so hurt and when I found out about Veronica's tumor, I was relieved. You didn't choose her as a friend over me. You're just a really great guy who is helping someone who is going through something horrible. And to be honest, I don't get why Veronica doesn't tell everyone that she has a brain tumor and not just any brain tumor. The type of one her mom died from. I didn't even know her mom died recently. Do you have any idea how life would be different for her if people knew?"

"Why?" I have to work to lower my voice so Veronica doesn't

hear. "So people can pity-like her? Is that what you'd want? For people to only like you because you have a tumor? Shouldn't they try to like her for who she is and not something she can't control?"

"I won't tell anyone, okay? And neither will Miguel. I think it's a stupid decision, but we'll respect it. And stop jumping down my throat. I'm part of this group to help. To help you. To help her. To help. I'm not heartless, and I really don't appreciate the fact that's how you're making me feel."

"She doesn't want anyone to know!" I whisper-shout.

"I get that," she whisper-shouts back. "But it's not my fault your mom told me. I know about the tumor. I'm glad I know, but I'm not to blame because of what someone else decided to tell me. I won't tell anyone else, and I won't tell because I understand having a secret. Remember?"

I scrub my hands over my face. I do remember. I remember her fear as she told me she likes girls, not boys. How she was terrified I would reject her and then how she begged me to keep her secret. I did, and now I'm questioning my best friend whether she could do the same. "I'm sorry."

"So am I," she says. "But none of this changes the fact that I'm terrified of death and she's not and now I'm the one standing over a dead person's body waiting for a bony hand to reach out of the ground and pull me under."

"That won't happen," says Veronica, and my stomach drops as she walks into the light of Sylvia's cell. How much did she hear and is she going to blame me? She should. It seems just knowing me is a train wreck no one in my path can avoid.

I study Veronica, searching for any sign that she overheard us. She gives nothing when she's upset, but that doesn't mean she did or she didn't. Veronica is a queen at masking.

"We found the statue." She jacks her thumb over her shoulder, and there's adventure in her tone. "Come check it out."

Veronica's curls bounce and her red plaid skirt swirls around her thighs as she turns away from us. She wears a heavy jean jacket, one that appears too large for her, and black-and-white-striped leggings with combat boots. She's damn sexy and with how she looks over her shoulder at me and winks, she's aware of what I'm thinking.

"Do you think she overhead us?" Sylvia whispers.

"I don't know." I follow after Veronica and Sylvia stays by my side.

"Are you going to tell her? That Miguel and I know?"

My insides feel like a garbage pit. There's no win in this for Veronica. If I tell her then she knows that other people know and pity her. Plus she'll figure out my mom's a nuclear waste dump of gossip. If I don't tell her—that feels wrong, too. "I don't know yet. Probably. But not now."

Miguel's face is lit up by the screen of his cell phone he's currently scrolling through. "So I found two stories about this statue. The first story is the one we told you about earlier—if you touch Mary's hands and they're cold then you die."

"Super," mumbles Sylvia.

"The other is that if Mary's hands are folded and she's looking down then everyone here is going to live." Miguel continues to read from his cell. "But if Mary's arms are outstretched and she's looking up to heaven, then at least one of us is going to die."

Sylvia holds herself tight as if the sweatshirt she's wearing isn't big or warm enough. "FYI, I hate every single one of you. Stories about religious statues that move aren't okay and I'm never going to sleep again."

"So are you guys ready to see how she's standing?" Veronica asks with an evil little smile, and I can already guess the results.

"Nope." Sylvia turns her back the moment Veronica shines the light on the statue. "I don't want to know." She looks at me. "What's the statue doing? No, I changed my mind. Don't tell me. Her arms are stretched open, aren't they? Forget it, don't tell me."

It's hard to hide my smile, and when it appears anyhow Sylvia glares at me. "You are not cute."

"I never said I was," I say, and glance over to find Veronica and Miguel smiling from ear to ear as there is just something amusing about being worked up over a statue.

"Her hands are folded," Veronica says.

Sylvia locks eyes with me. "For real? Are they? Because if I turn around and her arms are outstretched, I swear to God I will punch you in your stomach."

"Hands folded," I confirm.

But as Sylvia starts to turn, Miguel gasps, "She just moved!"

Sylvia pauses in terror and when her eyes land on the statue and she sees the hands are still folded, she throws her pissed-off glare at Miguel. "You're dead."

Miguel starts backing up as he's quite aware Sylvia is faster than him. "Then I guess it's a good thing I'm at a cemetery."

She's off, so is Miguel and their shouts and laughter carry off into the night.

That leaves me and Veronica. She's smiling, which is beautiful, but a part of me is heavy. I hate that there are things I should tell her that she doesn't want to know. I raise the camera and take of picture of her.

"Hoping to find a spirit orb attached to me?" she asks.

"Just like taking pictures of you."

"Hmm," is her only response. Veronica pivots on her toes and studies the statue of Mary. "I have to agree with Sylvia. The statue is creepy. Being Christian and all, I guess I should find some sort of peace in a figure of the mother of God, but I don't. Something about this statue feels . . . off."

I have to agree as I snap a few pictures of the statue. The energy of the cemetery is nothing like it was at the bridge. There's something here that feels darker, heavier, as if there's something looming behind gravestones, in the trees, watching, waiting . . . attaching.

As if there's a coat of slime right above the layer of my skin and the longer we stay here, the thicker it becomes. "It's because it's cloudy tonight and a thunderstorm is supposed to move through later this evening. It's the energy in the atmosphere messing with us."

"It's energy all right," says Veronica, "but it's not the weather. I think it's the spirits here. The ones at the bridge felt more open and inviting after we took the fall, but here . . . I feel as if they want us to leave."

Veronica reaches out her hand and a shock of electricity rushes through me when her fingers come in contact with Mary's hands. I take a picture, several of them, and I'm surprised to find my own hands shaking when I lower the camera. Veronica isn't touching the statue anymore, but she's stretching her fingers as if they're stiff and ache.

"You okay?" I ask.

She doesn't respond immediately, just stares at the statue.

"Veronica?"

"I'm good." She turns in time to see Miguel and Sylvia laughing and smiling as they walk back toward us. "We should take some EVPs, and maybe try the ghost box."

VERONICA

The four of us sit on a grassy knoll on the edge of the cemetery and take turns asking questions into the recorder. Some silly, some serious, all with a level of respect. Something is a bit off here, though. Something beyond the normal, almost as if we're the ones being watched.

"What would you do if a girl in a prom dress walked around that curve?" Miguel asks as soon as he turns off the digital recorder.

"Honestly?" Sawyer asks.

"Yeah."

"Run."

The two of them laugh while Sylvia and I glance at each other. We've picked nothing up on the recorder, nothing we can hear with human ears, and I'm growing restless as I feel that Sarah isn't the one making the skin at the base of my neck prickle with unease. There's something else here, the something Glory has been warning me about.

"I think Sarah's ghost must be a residual haunting," I say.

"What makes you say that?" Sawyer asks.

"Most of the stories we read have one thing in common—they see Sarah walking along the road and cemetery. As Sylvia said earlier, think of all the emotion that probably went into preparing for the dance. All the joy and hope and nerves and then for it to end with such disappointment and fear? That seems like a ton of powerful emotion and it seems plausible that emotion would imprint onto the area."

"If it's a residual haunting," says Miguel, "then why haven't we seen it?"

"Maybe we did when we took that curve," I counter. "What we saw was a white flash. Unless there are albino deer on this hill or a massive, dinosaur-sized rabbit, that wasn't Bambi or Thumper crossing the road."

Sylvia shivers and wraps herself tighter into the blanket she found in the trunk of Miguel's SUV. "I still think this is too creepy."

"You're looking at death and ghosts all wrong," I say. "Why does any of it have to be scary? Why can't it be the same as taking a breath in and then taking a breath out? A part of living that we do without overthinking?"

"She's got a point." Sawyer stretches out beside me on the grass, holding himself up by his elbows. "If residual hauntings are real then that means ghosts are nothing more than intense memories on replay so there's nothing to be scared of."

"I didn't say ghosts aren't real." I'm quick to nix that train of thought. "I think residual hauntings and ghosts are real. Remember the EVP and the picture of the spirit orb?"

"Yeah, Einstein," Miguel says, "explain that."

"That's not the subject at hand." Sawyer is quick in his retort, and I have to say that I love how he doesn't bat an eye to debate something he believes to the core is silly. "Veronica's saying there's nothing to be scared of and I'm agreeing. We should think this haunting through and determine for the paper whether or not we believe this is an actual haunting or a residual haunting. Fact one: someone named Sarah died in a car crash. Fact two: she's, in theory, buried a few feet away from us. Fact three: there are reports of a girl walking along the side of the road in a prom dress. Has anyone here read anything about the girl interacting with anyone?"

None of us speak up. The one thing I've learned about Sylvia and Miguel is that they take their grades seriously. They've researched this hill nearly as much as I have.

"I'll take that as a no," Sawyer continues. "This haunting, if it's real, is a residual haunting. The emotion of the car accident was so intense that it imprinted on this time and space. My guess is that Sarah's not really walking around here, but at peace. The only thing that would be left behind is the fear she felt due to the crash."

Sylvia pulls the blanket closer. "Still creepy and not making me feel better."

"Why does death scare you?" I ask. It's not a question meant to hurt or to even pry, but the look on Sylvia's face, the pure fear, makes something deep within me hurt.

"Why doesn't it scare you?" she spits out like she's mad, but all I see is fear. "In fact, why am I the only person here freaked out?"

"I'm quaking in my boots," Miguel says, but he looks about as calm as Sawyer. "At least the deer-slash-possible-ghost portion made me piss my pants."

"Seriously?" Sylvia bites out. "I'm the only one who's scared of death?"

"I'm not exactly a fan of it," Miguel says.

Sawyer sits up, draws his knees to his chest, and rests his arms on them. "I'm not scared of dying as much as I don't want to die. Sometimes I think of the stupid things I do and how it would be easy for it to go wrong and then question what would happen to Lucy if I was gone."

Sylvia blinks several times, as if she's shocked to hear that come from Sawyer.

"Are you scared of what happens to you after you die?" Sylvia asks. "Like, are you scared you'll be trapped in your own body? As in you can hear, but can't move or breathe or . . . you know . . . didn't do it all right and end up burning in hell?"

The ends of Sawyer's lips inch up. "I wasn't before, but thanks, because I am now."

We all giggle, but he's right. It's all there now in the forefront of the brain.

Miguel runs a hand through his black hair and mirrors Sawyer's position. "Does any of this make you wonder what your residual haunting would be?"

"What do you mean?" I ask.

"If you were meant to die in your worst moment, the one moment that had such an emotional impact that it would stick around forever, what would it be?"

It's a tough question, an honest question, and I hate that I know the answer so quickly.

"It's not your fault, Miguel," Sawyer says as Sylvia reaches over and places a hand on Miguel's shoulder. The pain radiating from him causes me to shrink.

For so long, I thought of these three people as the enemy—the untouchable popular kids who never felt a thing, but sitting here, witnessing this moment of support, I realize that pain is more universal than I had given it credit for. Sylvia slides next to Miguel and places her head on his shoulder and wraps her arms around him, reminding me of me and Nazareth.

"Mine would be after Mom and Dad first split," Sawyer says. "Lucy was a baby and cried all the time, I was miserable and used to complain how much I missed home. I was mad at my mom. So mad. I didn't understand why Mom couldn't make it work with Dad. They fought all the time and it was Mom always doing the yelling and I thought if she could have just stopped maybe they could have made it work."

Sawyer lowers his head and it's like the world quit breathing.

"I was at Mom all the time, every second, telling her it was her fault she and Dad split. Telling her it was her fault Lucy cried all the time, and then one day, Mom broke. We were in the kitchen and I was at her like I always was and she bowed her head and cried. I never saw her cry before and it scared me. Bad. Then she kept crying. She cried in her bedroom, she cried in the bathroom, cried in the shower. She kept crying. She broke and I realized I was to blame."

"Oh, Sawyer." Sylvia breathes out, and Sawyer shuts his eyes like her sorrow for him causes him pain. I get that. Pity doesn't make anything better, but often makes it worse.

"Mine would be when my mom died," I say while I keep my eyes on Sawyer. He finally opens his, and I see the raw gratefulness that I took the spotlight away from him. "She didn't want to go through the last two rounds of treatment. She barely wanted to go through the two rounds before that, but she did, for my dad."

My throat constricts and my palms grow clammy with the memory. I wipe my hands along my skirt. "My mom was life. When she walked into a room you could feel the breeze on your skin, taste the honeysuckle of a summer's day, and smell the roses in bloom. She lived and she loved and she laughed and then she was sick. So sick. We all knew she was going to die, but instead of dying with a smile on her face, doing what she loved the most, she died weighing eighty pounds, so sick she couldn't even eat. Her skin and muscles so sensitive that my touch brought her pain. Watching that, seeing her, seeing my father fall apart . . . that was hell."

I close my eyes as I try desperately to erase the images of her so weak, so broken, and there's a touch. My hair lovingly tucked behind my ear—just like my mom used to do. When I open my eyes, I see Sawyer loving me.

"My grandma told me that I'm going to hell," Sylvia says in a whisper. "In front of my mom, in front of my dad, in front of my brother and sister, in front of my aunts and uncles, in front of all the people who are supposed to love me. She told me that I'm a sinner, and if I don't repent, I'm going to hell."

"Your grandma is going to be seriously shocked when she dies and finds out God loves gay people," I say, and Sylvia laughs. Really laughs, and soon Miguel does and Sawyer, too.

"If a residual haunting is remnants of the bad," Sylvia says. "Maybe that means that the only thing that we carry with us when we die is the good."

"Amen," Sawyer says. He and Sylvia share the type of smile that best friends do. "I'm fine with all the bad being left behind."

Miguel glances around. "I don't know about everyone else, but this place is heavy. Since we got here I feel like something's watching me. Something bad."

I like ghosts, but it's as if there's something sinister hiding in the shadows.

"It's because of the energy surrounding us." All of Glory's warnings are on repeat in my mind, and I wish I hadn't left my cell in Miguel's SUV as there's a part of me that believes she's texting me right now, calling me, cautioning me that I've stumbled upon the danger she was desperately terrified of. "If it's a residual haunting then we're feeling the effects of its negative energy, and I know exactly what we need to do to cleanse ourselves of it."

"Is this going to include some sort of crystals with weird chanting?" Sawyer asks with a cocked eyebrow that tells me he's half serious, half joking.

"Oh, I heard Glory Gardner does those," Sylvia says. "Aren't you friends with her?"

"Yes." It's unsettling how not one of them has ever mentioned Glory to me before, but it's in this moment that her name is dropped. Even more upsetting? Is how the trees sway with her name, the gust of wind from the west that causes leaves to fall, twigs to snap and branches to bend. "But this is more serious than Glory's cleansings. This cleansing will only work if everyone is on board and has an open mind."

"I'm in," says Miguel.

"Me, too," chimes in Sylvia, leaving the three of us staring at the skeptic.

Sawyer rolls his neck. "Fine. What's the strange thing I have to do?"

I waggle my eyebrows at him. "You have to buy us chocolate milkshakes."

SAWYER

꧁

Tuesday September 3: Oh, Diary, I got my first real kiss tonight. Morris was over to say goodbye and he kissed me. O, but I'm going to miss him alright.

Reading Evelyn's first kiss brought me unexpected joy. Facing death, watching death, being right next to death—she lived. And I'm living. Right now, with Veronica by my side.

Veronica has a playlist that includes opening songs from cartoons, Disney and Nickelodeon shows, and one-hit wonders, and I've never seen Sylvia so happy. She's in the passenger seat joining along with Veronica, who's in the backseat with me, in some dance that can somehow be done with the arms more than the feet and it's hysterical how in sync they are with the melody and the movements.

Sad part? We're listening to a cringy, one-hit wonder that Miguel and I not only know, but we're singing along with. Veronica leans over, bumps my shoulder, a nudge for me to dance along with her. With how she moves her hips and can move her body, I'm game. She angles toward me, I angle toward her. Our arms are in the air, and I match the way she dances with the beat from side to side.

Sylvia glances at us from the front seat and cracks up laughing. A belly laugh I've rarely heard from her for over a year. Miguel flashes a quick glance at us, too, from the rearview, and he also releases a gut laugh. One I haven't heard him do since the end of our freshman year. Don't get me wrong, they laugh, but haven't really laughed. Not since their residual hauntings took over their lives.

Veronica meets my gaze and her blue eyes not only dance, but have a seductive shine. One that promises kissing, touching and holding each other very close. Catching on to the dance, to the rhythm, I move right as she moves left and then we meet in the middle, allowing our arms to flow perfectly with each other.

The song comes to an end, a song from a cartoon that I watched as a child starts, and Sylvia claps with joy. "I loved this show!"

I did, too, and when Miguel and Sylvia start singing along, I lean forward, cradle Veronica's face and kiss her lips. She's warm, she's soft, she tastes like heaven and the moment she kisses back, every cell in my body comes alive. The kiss isn't sweet, it isn't slow. It's hot, it's intense, and it's all my emotions pouring into her.

Against the driving need to keep kissing, to keep touching, I pull back and Veronica gives me a dazzling and daring grin. "What was that for?"

I rest my forehead against hers. "For creating this moment."

"You were the one who bought the milkshakes," she whispers.

"Yeah, but this is happening because you're you."

The car slows and Sylvia boos. "We should go around the neighborhood again."

"No," I say. "Five laps were enough." It's time for me to have some time alone with Veronica.

Miguel places his SUV in park, and Sylvia takes off her seat belt so she can reach back and give me a hug. Veronica's a bit shocked when Sylvia hugs her, too. Miguel and I share a shake, and he offers Veronica a fist bump. She accepts and then we slip out of the backseat.

We hold hands as we walk toward the house. In the distance, bolts of lightning dance across the sky, brightening the huge, growing clouds. The storm all the weather people have been raving about this week will finally hit tonight, but it doesn't bother me. Lucy's safe at her friend's, Mom's staying the night at Sylvia's house,

Miguel and Sylvia will be home before the first drop of rain hits the blacktop, and Veronica and I are home.

The air is full of electricity and has that deep rich scent of the promise of rain. Charged atoms preceding a storm. But that's not what's causing the buzz in my blood. That's due to the force of nature beside me. Veronica lets go of my hand to start tracing her fingernails along my arm as we make our way up the porch and at the door she gives me a slow, wicked smile.

Her fingers slip along my collarbone to my chest, causing the breath to catch in my lungs. Her touch tickles, it teases and when she glances up at me from behind long lashes, I'm undone. I place both of my hands on her hips and back her up against the house.

Veronica fists the material of my shirt and drags me into her. She's smaller than I am and while I don't mind leaning down to kiss her, tonight, being that close isn't close enough. I want to drown in her.

In a swift motion, I lift her and she giggles. The sound filling me with joy. She weaves her arms around my neck and her legs around my hips. We fit perfectly together, and each of her slight shifts to be comfortable creates sensations I want to feel again and again.

Veronica shines. Her blond hair glows against the porch light, her blue eyes sparkling, and the smile on her face is glorious. She's pure bliss and it's a world I want to be lost in forever.

I rest my forehead against hers and revel in the gravitational pull that's between us, in the way her breath teases the skin of my neck, the way her chest rubs against mine as she breathes out and I breathe in. My heart beats faster in anticipation with the awareness that the moment we start, neither of us might want to stop.

"What are you waiting for?" she whispers in amusement. "Are you going to kiss me?"

I don't have to be asked twice. I kiss her and the ground beneath us rumbles and shakes. The vibration racing through my toes, up my legs and along my body. She presses into me and I press into her as our kisses become deeper, hungrier, and our hands begin to roam.

Veronica breaks away, kissing along my neck, then whispers into my ear, "Inside."

Her apartment or mine, I don't know and I don't care as just the idea of inside is the most amazing idea I've heard. With her still in my arms, I move us toward the door and Veronica's soft laughter is an addictive drug making my head spin.

When I fail at entering the code, Veronica reaches out and does it for us while still focusing on kissing me. The lock gives, we're through the door, we pinball down the foyer hallway to my door, and then I'm able to navigate that lock with no problem.

Once in my room, we fall onto the mattress, into each other, and we give in to the warmth, the joy, the heat, the touches, the sighs, the kisses, and time stops as we lose ourselves in each other.

Thursday September 5: Weight 113 ½ lb.

Cured a lot today. It was a nasty rainy day.

Got a nice long letter from Maidy today. She sure is a cheerful cuss.

Oh, Diary, had 99.3 temp. tonight. Why, oh why, doesn't it go down? Am I <u>ever</u> going to get well? I'm just about discouraged.

And I'm <u>so</u> lonesome. Oh, dear, but I wish Morris would come back. Really, Diary, I care for him lots more than he does for me I know.

"Why are we doing this?" I ask as Knox opens the door for me to an old one-story, fifties-style church that hasn't seen a paintbrush or new furniture since the 1970s.

"Because our AA meeting is huge, and you like blending in. It's your comfort zone. You need smaller and you need to learn how to be you."

"I am me," I grumble.

Knox stops in front of the door labeled for the meeting. "And who is that? Are you the popular athlete who everyone loves because you become what everyone wants? Or are you the guy who jumps off of cliffs? Because those are two different personalities, brother."

I roll my neck, uncomfortable with how easily he sees me. "What if I don't want to be either of those?" I pause. "Or what if I'm a little bit of both?"

Knox stretches out his arms. "See, brother? One minute in the building and you're already starting to ask better questions. Now let's go."

He opens the door, waves me in and I decide to keep my mouth shut as he's the master swimmer in this scenario and I'm the lowly kid hanging out in the guppy class. Annoyance hits me as the first thing I notice is a circle of maybe a dozen chairs and not that many people in the room.

As I take a step back, Knox places a hand on my shoulder and pushes me forward. If I won't willingly go out of my comfort zone, my sponsor will physically drag me—got it.

As always, everyone knows Knox. Sort of how I am at school. The difference between us though is that my act at school is a show. Between nods, handshakes, and hugs, Knox greets each person warmly, as if he knows them. If he doesn't know them, he at least shows that he cares they exist.

I trail behind him, hands in my pockets like a lost puppy, and I'd give just about anything to be invisible. The place looks like a children's Sunday school class, complete with a deluge of Fisher-Price play sets. I wonder, if like the toy I had as a kid, that barn door would moo if I opened it.

Knox eventually takes a seat, pats the one beside him and I begrudgingly take it. A mix of men and women claim the remaining seats and I count them out—there's ten of them and the two of us. Except for Knox, everyone is staring at me, all wondering who I am and I don't know that answer.

I cross my arms and pull my feet underneath my folding chair. A woman with shoulder-length gray hair—the type that makes her look wise versus ancient—starts the meeting. She's in a black, tight turtleneck I would feel strangled in.

Like other meetings Knox and I have attended, we begin by reciting the twelve steps, but when they say something about alcohol, I silently add jumping off cliffs.

"Hi, everyone, I'm Denise," the lady with the black turtleneck says.

"Hi, Denise," we all reply in unison.

"My husband has been an alcoholic for ten years, and I've been attending these meetings and working on being an enabler for the past five years."

My head snaps up so fast I'm surprised it doesn't fall off. We're at the wrong meeting. This is an Al-Anon meeting. Not an AA meeting. My heart pumps nervously, and I start to sweat. Like I'm expecting lightning to strike me in response to our mistake.

As my butt starts to lift from the chair, Knox reaches over and shoves me back down. A quick glare over at him and he gives me a nonchalant shake of his head. With how easygoing this guy is, I can never imagine him as an alcoholic, but he says he was and I can only wish to have a fraction of the peace this guy carries in his little finger.

"We have three visitors today," Denise continues. "One is Dr. Martin." She gestures toward the aging black man in a gray suit. "As most of you know, he is a family therapist who specializes in addiction. He joins us every so often to help us work through some issues. I believe most of us know Knox."

"Hi, I'm Knox," he says regardless of her introduction. "I'm an alcoholic, and I've been sober for five years."

They welcome him, most of them clapping as if his sobriety is a celebration for them. He gives a little wave of appreciation and they smile in return.

Denise lays her happy gaze on me, and I shift uncomfortably. "Hi, I'm Sawyer." Because that's as far as I've gotten in any meeting we've gone to. The people in my main meeting, the one where I first met Knox, know my problems through private conversations I've had with them, and they have welcomed me with open arms, but I've yet to stand up and talk. No one forces me to. They're all patient, but with each meeting that passes, I feel the pressure to stand up and say something.

Like now.

"And I've never been to an Al-Anon meeting before."

Knox gives me a side-eye and I hate how everyone in the circle is staying silent, giving me space to talk . . . or not talk. If I stay quiet, they'll let me, and move the meeting along, but considering these are people who have to deal with people like me who have an addiction, I feel like I need to give them something. "I have an addiction issue, and I'm trying to overcome it."

"Welcome, Sawyer," Denise says, and everyone else greets me warmly as well. "Knox called and asked if the two of you could come visit with us this week, and this is something we occasionally allow—giving an addict the opportunity to listen to those of us who love someone with an addiction issue."

I nod my appreciation while sinking in my seat. I'm guessing that this meeting is made to make people like me feel like crap—and I probably deserve it. I settle in and do what I've been doing best at these meetings for weeks—I listen.

I listen to stories of loved ones losing jobs, losing friends, losing family, losing their lives. I hurt for them as they talk about years of silence, of arguments, loneliness and isolation. Of money issues, broken homes, and how alcohol becomes a demon that possesses.

"It's hard for me to stop being an enabler," Jennifer says. She's midtwenties-young, and her father has been an alcoholic since she started to walk. From her perspective, he's a perpetual first-time AA attender. It's the second meeting where he falls off. "If I don't take care of him, who else will?"

"But maybe that's what he needs," Dr. Martin says in this calm, soft way. "Maybe you need to stop taking care of him."

"And then what?" Her eyes widen as she challenges him. "At least now he's somewhat functioning. I get him up, he goes to work, and I bring him his lunch to check in on him to confirm he's not drinking. He finishes his shift, he comes home and it's a good day if I can get dinner in him before he opens a beer. It's an even better day if I can get him showered and shaved before he passes out. If I stop taking care of him, he'd never go to work, he'd never eat and he'd end up on the street alone. I can't do that." She hits a hand to her chest. "I love him and I can't let him be like that."

"What type of life is that for you?" Dr. Martin asks.

She looks away, wiping at her eyes. "I don't know how to stop taking care of him. It's my responsibility. Always my responsibility. Who am I if I stop?"

"The better question," Dr. Martin says, "is who will you become when you stop living his life and start living yours? The last time I was here you talked about applying for college. Have you done that?"

Jennifer hurriedly brushes at her tears again. "I love him." She doesn't answer his question directly, but it's an answer nonetheless.

"We know you do," Dr. Martin says. "But remember, we've talked about how alcoholism, addiction, is a disease. Unless he experiences the fallout of his actions, unless he hits rock bottom, he might not want to get help. It's like having cancer and being told you need to have an operation and chemo treatments. Would you go through surgery and chemo unless you knew for a fact you had cancer?"

Jennifer shakes her head.

"Your dad doesn't honestly realize he has this disease. He has to understand this disease inside him before he understands the path to save his life."

"I've told him!" Jennifer shouts.

"Yes." Sitting beside her, Denise reaches out and takes Jennifer's hand. "Just like I told my husband, but some people don't see the disease until they themselves are forced to stare at the MRI results. I know you feel like you're helping him, but you're hurting yourself."

Jennifer weaves her fingers with Denise's and with easily thirty years' difference between them, they're united, like sisters. There's silence then, and I'm not sure what's supposed to fill it. Jennifer has Denise, Denise has Jennifer, and everyone else has taken their turn speaking. But there's this collective holding of a breath, as if waiting for the fall, and that silence seems to be directed at me.

Maybe it's not. Maybe I'm tired of being silent. Maybe Knox is right, maybe I need to find my voice. But what do I say? This isn't my meeting. I'm not the one dealing with someone I love having an addiction. I am the addict. I have no right to talk, no right to share, but it feels like a compulsion, a need for me to speak.

"I remember once, the first wedding anniversary after my mom and dad divorced, my mom went out with friends. It was supposed to be a 'screw him, the bastard' party." My arms are already folded over my chest, but somehow I hug myself tighter. "My mom brought Lucy and me to her friend's house, and we stayed the night there so my friend's dad could watch us while the moms went out."

Knox is watching me, they all are, and I stare at the ground, pretending they aren't. "I remember that the air mattress I slept on had a hole and had deflated to the carpet within an hour. The floor was hard, I was uncomfortable, and in the middle of the night, I remember my mom and my friend's mom had returned."

A muscle in my jaw tics, and it's like the memory and the words have become lodged in my throat. I clear it and force myself forward. "They made a ton of noise. Laughing, yelling, running into things. I remember hearing stuff fall on the floor and glass breaking. A few minutes later, my friend's dad walked into the bedroom I was in, and my mom was hanging over his shoulder and he laid her on the bed. I remember how embarrassed I was that my mom was such a drunk mess that when she needed to use the bathroom, she couldn't figure out how to take off her own pants. I saw how uncomfortable my friend's dad was so I volunteered to help her."

I stop talking then because the anger and shame I felt in that moment that she couldn't care for herself, especially in front of strangers, still tears me up. I rake a hand through my hair to help shake some of the bad memories away. "After that, Mom had me stay home and babysit Lucy when she went out with her friends."

It's serious. Everything is way too serious. The mood needs to lighten. A joke. A story. Something everyone will think is funny and laugh. Something my mom and her friends cackle over every time they get together. I don't get it. Never have, but I've learned there's many things I don't get. "Ever since that night, my mom and her friends like to go out on the weekends, and as a joke, one year, they bought each other breathalyzers so no one would get a DUI."

I smile to try to take the sting away, like what I said was hysterical, but no one is laughing. Not even me. The fake smile fades and it's sadly satisfying that I'm not the only one who doesn't get the joke.

"How old were you?" Dr. Martin asks.

"When they gave each other breathalyzers for Christmas?"

"No, when you first started taking care of your mom."

"Eleven." Just like Veronica when she found out her entire life was going to change. The itch I've been fighting off for weeks overtakes me, becomes a driving need that makes my vision hazy. I'd love to jump. To find a cliff, to run toward the edge, to fling my body over and fly.

I close my eyes, then flinch as I desperately try to shake the urge. My skin prickles, the itch too much for me to bear. Having nothing more to offer anyone, I glance up at Denise. She nods like she understands me and ends the meeting.

I'm up and out of my seat the moment it's socially acceptable.

Knowing Knox, he has a half hour of good-byes to give. He can do them, and I'll wait by the car.

I open the heavy wooden door, slip through it and before I can reach the exit door, the door to the class opens. "Sawyer."

My forehead furrows at the sound of Knox's voice. I glance over my shoulder. "Take your time in there. I need air."

Knox closes the classroom door behind him and stares at me as if confused. "Why didn't you tell me your mom is an alcoholic?"

I slowly assess him, wondering if he pounded a shot back in the Sunday school room. Maybe they keep the stuff hidden behind the Little People airport. "My mom's not an alcoholic."

Knox's easygoing manner is replaced with intentional hesitancy. "Okay. I hear you, brother. But to humor me, do you mind answering a few questions?"

Yes, actually, but I slouch against the wall and give a single nod. Knox leans his back against the opposing wall, right next to a child's drawing of a man sitting inside a whale. "Your mom drinks?"

"Yeah. Like everyone else does. She doesn't touch alcohol at all during the week, but on the weekends, she'll have a few."

A few bottles . . . a night.

Knox stares at me, through me, like he can smell the lie. My spine tingles and the need to defend feels a lot like anger. "She's a single mom with two kids and a stressful job. She does a ton for me and my sister. She's a good person." I think of how she's slaved to take care of us over the years without much help from my dad. "She's a great person."

"I never said she wasn't," Knox says slowly.

"She can't be an alcoholic. She only drinks on the weekends."

Knox rests his head against the wall, his eyes still pinned on me. "When she drinks . . . can she stop at one drink? Or does that first drink always lead to drunk?"

Always to drunk, and the muscles in my neck tighten and my shoulders roll back as I push off the wall. As if his questions are fighting words. "My mom isn't an alcoholic."

Knox tosses his hands in the air. "My bad, my brother. What do you say we go get some food? My treat."

I shove my hands hard into my jeans pockets. I don't want to go get food. In fact, I'd tear off my left arm if that meant he'd drive to a quarry so I could jump. The longer it takes to answer him, the more I'm aware that he can read my mind and knows what I long to do—which is why he's offering food.

"I'm thirsty," I say, my attempt to speak in terms he'd understand.

"So am I," he says. "Sometimes we don't get hamburgers to help you. Sometimes we do it to help me."

Yeah. I guess that's the point. Not saying anything else, we both leave feeling parched.

VERONICA

t's Saturday, nine in the evening, and I'm on the hunt for more EVPs by slowing down and speeding up the frequency of the audio we took at the cemetery. Sawyer was here earlier, but he left at five as he had a meeting at work and then has to help clean the pool areas of the Y.

Mom has moved from the piano to the window seat and she's intently watching me work. Dad's lounging on the couch, the remote is on his chest, football is on the television, and he's sound asleep.

My cell vibrates with a text. Glory: Please be careful. An angel has warned me that something is moving downstairs.

I raise an eyebrow: What does moving mean?

Glory: It means be careful. Did you visit someplace new in your search for spirits? If so, where? I'm scared you've brought something dangerous home.

I tap my fingers against the desk, weighing how I should answer. We went to the cemetery on Mitchell Hill.

She takes longer than I like to reply. Have you been avoiding the downstairs?

My lips squish to the side, as I've been spending time there with Sawyer . . . making out.

Glory: V?

Me: I haven't spent a lot of time there.

I can practically feel her sigh even though she's miles away. I can only imagine the reprimand playing out in her head—I'm a magnet, I make things worse, the zombie apocalypse is going to happen if I'm downstairs.

Glory: I'm out of town for a festival, otherwise I'd be there. I'm worried, V. You're in danger. You should stay with Jesse or Nazareth until I return.

I glance over at Dad again. I can't. Dad just returned from a trip. It's the first time I've seen him in five days.

Glory knows Dad doesn't believe in anything supernatural so she understands why I can't leave. Please be careful.

Me: I will be and I think you're overreacting. I'm fine.

I put down my phone, and while I'm used to Glory's constant concern about me and this house, this particular warning unsettles me. I tap my fingers against the desk again then stand and move to the window. I flip on the outside light and the backyard is illuminated. Sawyer's car is gone and so is his mom's, which means the downstairs is currently empty.

Empty and dark. Neither is good, and the combination for spirits is inviting. If we really did bring something new home, it's probably moving around the downstairs, curious about its new surroundings. Growing in strength.

Movement in the back of the yard causes me to flinch—the hammock. It swings. My heart stalls. A moment of frozen fear. A ghost? But then as it moves again, I make out a figure. A tiny shadow with a mermaid doll. This is all wrong.

I'm out our door, down the stairs, out the front, then call her name as I go around the back. "Lucy!"

She sits up on the hammock, holding her mermaid doll tightly to her chest. I slow my stride as I approach and force a smile on my face. "Hey."

"Hi." Her eyes are puffy, like she's been crying, and my lips turn down.

"What's wrong?"

She shakes her head, the way small children do when they are mad or in fear. I steady the hammock and sit, keeping my feet grounded so we don't swing. "Whatever it is, you can tell me. We keep each other's secrets, remember?"

Lucy combs her fingers through her doll's hair then glances at the wide-open back door of the house. "I don't like being alone in there."

I remember feeling like that at her age. All the lights are on in her apartment and the back door hangs open. It's my home, and while the second and third floors have a welcoming glow, I'll admit there's something sinister about how the dim light reflects from her part of the house. "Is your mom gone?"

She barely nods then holds her doll over her nose, eyes peeking through, as if hiding.

"Why didn't you come upstairs? You know you can hang with me."

Lucy raises the mermaid doll higher so I can no longer see her eyes. As if doing so has made her disappear. Bereft that I have no idea how to get through to her, I lean back in the hammock and watch the fading evening sky above. I suddenly have a ton of respect for Sawyer as I had no idea how much patience it must take to care for a six-year-old.

Movement, and Lucy snuggles next to me. Her head on my shoulder, her mermaid doll she still clutches now lying on my stomach. The evening is cold, her skin colder and I wonder how long she's been out here alone.

I wrap an arm around her and try to rub some warmth back into her freezing body. Above us, dark clouds float past stars and I must be tired as I usually find joy in the night sky, but all I can think about is how warm it is upstairs.

"I saw you and Sawyer kiss," Lucy finally says in a quiet voice.

"Does that bother you?" I ask.

She shakes her head against my arm. "He says you're his girlfriend."

"I am."

"Mommy left."

I go still, scared to even breathe. How her little voice shaking indicates this wasn't a mom trusting her six-year-old to watch cartoons as she ran to the corner store for a few minutes. "Did she say anything to you when she left?"

"I think she forgot me."

My throat thickens at her deep sorrow. "Maybe she didn't," I lie. "Sawyer texted me and told me to find you. Maybe she contacted him."

Lucy lifts her head and there's confusion there. "She said not to tell Sawyer, to stay in the apartment and she wouldn't be gone long. But she's been gone long so she must have forgot."

"When did she leave?"

"After Sawyer left."

Lucy shivers, and I'm done being patient. She needs to be under two pounds of blankets and have a gallon of hot cocoa in her stomach. "Well, Sawyer will be home soon, and in the meantime, I need help decorating my Christmas tree. So let's go to my place."

She shrinks against me. "I don't want to get in trouble. I don't like it when Mommy yells."

Well, I don't want Lucy to die of exposure. "Everything will be okay."

I stand from the hammock, and Lucy takes my offered hand. As I walk toward the first-floor apartment to shut the back door, there's a sudden yank on my hand. I glance down and Lucy has dug her feet into the ground and she's pulling hard on me. "Don't go in there."

"I'm just going to shut the back door so no bugs get in." Or wandering robbers.

"Don't!" Lucy snaps. "The monster is in there. He's making Mommy worse."

I convulse with her words and feel ice hardening my veins. "What monster?"

"The one that changes, the one that comes in the middle of the night."

I don't know a monster like this. "When exactly do you see this monster? How is he making your mom worse?"

She yanks so hard on my hand that she loses her grip and falls flat on her bottom. The cruel ground causing the air to rush out of her body. I crouch to help her, but she smacks my arm and the feverish look on her face causes me to flinch.

"The ghost there is bad!" she shouts. "So bad! He watches me! He *watches* me!"

My heart beats so furiously that it pounds in my ears. I glance at the first floor and the way the blinds are uneven in the window makes it appear as if the apartment is sneering at me, mocking my growing fear.

No, this is my home. I will not be scared of it. I step toward it, and Lucy scrambles to her feet and rushes me. "Don't! Don't go!"

"I'm just going to shut the back door."

"Don't leave me!" she yells. Tears fill her eyes, escape down her cheeks, and her fear, her grief, tugs at my heart. "Please don't leave me alone."

"Okay," I say, "I won't go."

She allows me to swing her up onto my hip, and Lucy buries her head in my neck. I gently hug her close as I walk her away from her back door, to the front of the house and the safety of the second floor.

Lucy can barely function in Sawyer's sweatshirt yet she's doing her best to set out my Peanuts nativity scene near the Christmas tree. The sweatshirt is the one he had loaned me the night we first kissed and I have yet to give back as it smells like him and I love the reminder of our night together. When I offered it to her as a blanket, she hungrily pulled it over her head and wears it like a hug.

I stand by the window, watching for Dad. My anxiety level is higher than it should be. When I came up with Lucy, he went down the stairs. He wasn't happy that a six-year-old was left home alone, especially for so long. Nor was he happy when I told him the back door to the first floor was wide open. Then there was the pièce de résistance—Lucy's sob-filled rant about stalking monsters. There's been no sign of Dad since he disappeared into their kitchen.

My cell is in my hand, and I look again at the message Sawyer sent me minutes ago: On my way.

Guilt niggles at me as Sawyer told me how important it was for him to be at work as he's had to take off too many days due to his mother's schedule, his swim schedule and AA meetings, but what else was I supposed to do? Lucy needs her brother.

A knock on my door, and I'm relieved when I see Sawyer on the security monitor. I cross the room, open the door, and I ache with how haggard he appears.

"Hey," I say. "I'm sorry to have texted you. I know you needed to work."

"Don't be." He walks in and pulls me in for hug. "I'm glad you did."

A brush of a kiss along my temple causes my heart to flutter, but then he lets me go and heads for his sister. "Hey, Luce."

Lucy brightens and abandons Snoopy as the Little Drummer Boy and runs into him. He lifts her and she winds her arms that have been swallowed by his sweatshirt around his neck.

He hugs her tight and after about a minute of her strangling him, he takes her to the couch. Sawyer has to pry and gently coax Lucy from being buried into this chest. He does it yet keeps her on his lap.

"Where's Mom?" Even though it's apparent Sawyer is attempting to sound lighthearted, the strain is clear.

"She left."

"Did she say where she was going?"

Lucy shakes her head.

"She told Lucy not to tell you," I say. Lucy's head swivels toward me, her expression clear that she believes I'm a traitor, but I soften the blow. "But I told her that your mom reached out to you so she didn't mean it."

Lucy exhales while Sawyer's face hardens. He knows the first part is the truth, the second part a lie.

"It's late and we have to go visit Dad tomorrow." Sawyer tries again for light. "How about a quick bath and then I'll let you watch cartoons on my phone with me in my room?"

Lucy edges away from Sawyer. "I want to stay here. The ghost here isn't mean. The ghost here is nice." She looks to me then. "Right, V?"

"You told my sister that there are ghosts in this house?" Sawyer's voice is low-pitched, and eerily steady. Storm clouds rage in his eyes.

I fiddle with my bracelet. For the first time in my life, I'm unsure of my thoughts . . . of my actions. "Lucy told me that first night that she was scared of ghosts."

"And you told her that they aren't real, right?" he presses.

I stare at him, he stares at me, and a sickening sensation fills my stomach. "I told her that there was nothing to be scared of."

His jaw twitches as he hears what I didn't admit—that I didn't deny the existence of ghosts and that her nightmares and her fears might have something to do with that. He stands and walks away from me toward the window seat where Mom sits. He stands next to her with his arms crossed and stares past the glass as if that can help his anger.

Mom looks up at him and then at me. "He's angry with you."

I nod because he is, and I understand why. Lucy shifts on the couch and studies me.

"I saw you nod," Lucy whispers. "Are you talking to your mom now?"

Sawyer turns his head and looks at us. "I didn't hear you, Lucy. You'll need to speak up."

"Because I wasn't talking to you," she answers.

He goes back to staring out the window and while he looks incredibly tall and strong, he also appears very lost. I ache for him. He's seventeen, and he's a dad to his sister and a parent to his mom. I'm not sure anyone would know how to fix this, and I'm certainly not helping.

I crouch in front of Lucy and she reaches out and touches one of my curls.

"Can you see my mom?" I whisper.

She shakes her head. "Can you see the monster downstairs?"

Lucy appears crestfallen as I shake my head as well.

"That doesn't mean they aren't real," she whispers, and her words, for some odd reason, break my heart. Lucy says there's a monster living downstairs, Glory has said the same thing, and a sickening sensation causes me to flush hot.

There's something in this house, something evil, and it's threatening Lucy. My eyes stray to the two shells and rolls of sage still on the kitchen counter.

"If you use that sage, it will drive me out." Mom appears in front of me and her eyes are angry. This fury baffles me, causes a pit of sadness that I've disappointed her, but I'm confused as to what to do.

"Lucy's scared," I whisper.

"And you'll be alone. Is that what you want?"

Alone. Anguish rolls through me, painful shards of glass tearing through my soul. "No."

"No to what?" Sawyer asks from across the room and my head whips in his direction. Crazy. It's there, just a hint of it in his expression. He senses something's not right—not right with me. My heart pounds that I've been caught—by him.

The door opens and Dad plows in. He's a focused steamroller and the whole world stops when he sees me, sees Sawyer, and then his eyes fall on Lucy. Worry. Dad wears it like a second skin. He worried for years about Mom, has worried incessantly about me, and now he has taken on the heavy burden of worrying about Sawyer and Lucy.

"I hope you don't mind," Dad says to Sawyer, "but I walked through your apartment. Everything looks in place."

Lucy wraps the long arms of the sweatshirt around herself. "No monsters?"

Sawyer glares at me and I wish I could disappear.

Dad softens. "No. There's no such things as monsters."

Sawyer crosses the room, and Lucy goes willingly into his arms. "Thank you for taking care of Lucy and checking the apartment. There must have been a misunderstanding between me and Mom about our schedules involving Lucy. I promise it won't happen again."

I will Sawyer to look at me as he leaves, but he doesn't, causing my heart to hurt. Unable to stand this, I walk after him and he stomps down the stairs. Each loud thud on the stairs a dismissal to me. He reaches the first floor, rounds for his apartment and I call out to him from over the banister. "Sawyer."

I expect him to keep walking, but he pivots quickly on his heels. "She's important to me. More important than your need to prove something that doesn't exist."

He means Lucy, he means my need to prove to my dad ghosts are real. As if she knows she's part of the reason and is embarrassed about it, Lucy hides her head in the crook of his neck.

"I know," I say.

Sawyer shakes his head in disappointment, as if I could never understand. "Tell Lucy that none of what you said is real. Tell her ghosts are just stories. Tell her you lied."

Lucy lifts her head. She wants me to tell her that I was wrong, but I'm not wrong. Ghosts are real. They are. They have to be.

"I like you," Sawyer says. "More than like, but when I'm pushed against a wall, I'll choose my sister every time."

Just like I'll choose my mom.

His expression falls, as if my silence has crushed him, and that causes a slicing pain in my chest. Sawyer leaves, shutting the door of his apartment behind him, and I sink onto the stairs, resting my head against the spindles on the banister. The problem is I under-stand. More than he knows. Because how he loves Lucy, I love my mom, and how he doesn't want Lucy to hurt, I don't want to lose my mom again and that's what I'm facing.

With my heart bleeding, I close my eyes and silently weep.

SAWYER

Monday September 23: Cured a lot today. Was in my chair all morning after the mail was delivered, and all afternoon in bed. Had a nice nap.

Poor Morris! Gee, I feel sorry for him. He was in bed all day and then came down to movies. His temp was 101.2. I told him to go up—but might as well talk to the wind.

My fault. That's what Mom said. I was supposed to be home. She said I had agreed to be home by seven so I could watch Lucy, but I never said that. We never had that conversation. Mom was so damn insistent that my brain began to separate as I wondered if she was right and I was wrong.

Lucy was alone and was it my fault?

"Lucy, how about you go and help Tory make chocolate-chip cookies in the kitchen?" Dad enters the living room of the condo he shares with his newest and very pregnant girlfriend.

It's a three-bedroom deal and the place is decorated like an advertisement for Pottery Barn. Never thought of Dad as the multiple-throw-pillow type. He tosses two of the pillows on the floor before sitting on the light blue couch so I guess he isn't. Makes me wonder how long he'll stick around with this woman and this baby.

My gut twists. This baby is going to be my half brother. Does that mean when Dad splits I'll be responsible for him, too?

"What do you think?" Tory rubs her swollen belly and smiles kindly down at Lucy. Tory, oddly enough, is not in her twenties. She's not as old as Dad, but she has the type of job that includes a 401(k) and health benefits. She's going to need that when Dad decides he's done playing round two of family man. "We'll have a great time, and that will give your dad and Sawyer some time to catch up."

That's what I've been avoiding all day. I drove Lucy to Louisville this morning. Since then, we've been out to breakfast, to the movies, out to lunch, to the zoo and now back here for a home-cooked dinner. Until now, it's been easy to sidestep any conversation that goes deeper than "How's school?" from Dad and "Ew, that giraffe pooped," from Lucy. Especially when Lucy has stayed stuck to me, but now Tory and Dad are seeking to conquer and divide, and I can't think of a good reason fast enough as to why Lucy should stay.

But maybe I can go with her . . . "I can help," I say, and Lucy looks like I gave her a puppy.

She slides off my lap, and as I go to stand, Tory places a hand in the air. "Sorry, this is a girls-only thing."

Lucy's shoulders roll forward with disappointment as she walks into the kitchen, and I slam my butt back to the chair. But I take out my cell, pop in an earbud and start swiping through my cell like I know exactly what I'm searching for, but I don't. Other than I need a distraction.

After a few minutes of scrolling through YouTube videos, Dad does what I don't want and breaks into my world. "Sawyer."

I release a frustrated breath. I brought Lucy. Can't that be enough? I glance up at Dad and find him staring at me. He looks older than I remember, though I saw him this past spring. Lines have formed around his eyes and gray peppers his black hair.

Dad leans forward and folds his hands. "How are you?"

"Good."

"School's going okay?" It's the hundredth time he's asked variations of both of those questions.

"Yeah." I drop my eyes back to my cell, but Dad doesn't take the hint.

"How's swim?"

"Fine." Eyes still locked on my cell.

"Are you dating anyone?"

"Nothing you need to know about." There's a twinge of guilt that I haven't reached out to Veronica since I left her place last night.

Dad falls silent, and I hope he'll do what he did when I was a kid: lose interest in me and turn on the TV.

"Look . . ." he says.

I briefly close my eyes to keep myself from rolling them.

"There's something you mentioned a few weeks ago that's been bothering me."

His leaving me responsible for Lucy and Mom when I was eleven bothers me, yet I can keep my mouth shut.

"I pay child support."

He's a liar. Mom told me before we left to expect this from him. She said to ignore it and let her and her lawyers handle everything. Lucy and I just have to make it through dinner. From the scents wafting from the kitchen, that shouldn't be long. We'll suck down our food, keep our mouths shut and then we run for home. "Okay."

"Why would you mention that I wasn't?"

Silence from me.

"Is that what your mom is saying?"

More silence from me.

"I know I haven't always been the most hands-on dad, but it's not all my fault. Your mom hasn't made it easy for—"

"Easy?" My head snaps up. "You think we've had it easy?"

"That's not what I'm saying."

"I think it is. You divorce Mom, and leave her," leave me, "and force her to take care of us while you go and do whatever you want."

"Is that what this is about?" Dad asks like he's confused. "You're still mad at me for the divorce?"

I glance over at the kitchen. How long does it take to warm up a ham?

"I don't know what lies your mom has been feeding you, but your mom and I were both miserable in the marriage."

"So you get a divorce and now you get to be happy. I guess that's the point, huh? We struggle to take care of each other and you get a hall pass. Showing up whenever it suits you. I forgot that the only thing that matters is how you feel. As long as you're happy, then it doesn't matter that the rest of us suffer due to your choices."

Dad's jaw hardens. "What was I supposed to do, Sawyer? Stay in a marriage that was strangling me?"

"As I said, as long as you're happy, right?"

"That's not fair." Dad lowers his voice.

"Fair? I had to switch shifts to drive up here today. Mom takes care of us full time and works a full-time job while you take every other holiday, and when I was a younger, every other weekend. Like we're the class pet to bring home. Is that fair? Then you complain about seeing us, but you never once make an effort to come to where we live."

He unlaces his fingers. "I have a job, and when your mom moved she said she'd bring the two of you to see me."

I don't want to listen to this anymore. I stand and pull my keys out of my jeans pockets. Dad shoots up from the couch. "What are you doing? Tory's making dinner."

"I'm taking Lucy and heading home. You wanted a visit. You got it. If you want to see Lucy again, you're going to have to come see her yourself."

I start for the kitchen and Dad places a hand on my arm as if he can stop me. "I know I haven't been the picture-perfect father, but there's more to this story than you know. Things I promised not to tell you. But regardless of any of that, I'm trying now."

He's trying now because regret sucks. "Lucy, let's go." His guilt, his regret isn't my problem.

> *Tuesday October 1: Well, Diary, mother is in bed. She got up this morning and tried to work, but nothing doing.*
>
> *I stayed in bed because my throat isn't any better, but when I heard about mother's being in bed, I got up and went over to see her. She looks badly. I do hope she'll be better soon.*

Evelyn's mother also had TB and was in the same hospital as her. They fought, they talked and Evelyn worried. I get that—more than I want. In the backseat of my car, Lucy sings as she braids her doll's hair. My sister has a pretty voice. It's a sweet sound and she can naturally hold a note.

I turn off the state highway and onto Main Street. It's seven in the evening, the fall night dark, and autumn leaves drift past the beams of my headlights. We're almost home, and my skin itches for a jump. Dad's been texting since I left. Mom's been texting wanting to know what happened and why Dad's upset. Sylvia's been texting to find out what's next on the project, and Veronica hasn't texted at all.

I guess she's giving me space. Space I don't know if I want or need. I left her apartment pissed last night and I'm still pissed. My little sister wakes up in the middle of the night screaming because she believes there's a ghost, and Veronica won't do anything to help stop it. How can she be okay with that?

But I miss her.

I watch movies, TV, and see shows where teenagers date, go to movies, have fun. What I wouldn't give right now for that to be my life. To not be responsible for anything other than homework due Monday and choosing which movie to see on a Friday night.

I'd love to pick Veronica up with flowers in hand, go grab a sandwich, and see a movie where we hold hands. Then when we arrive home for the night, I kiss her a little too much, for a little too long. To the point she's happily breathless and my head is spinning.

My blood runs warm just with the idea of holding Veronica in my arms again. Peace settles in my soul at the idea of sitting next to her. It's weird how quickly she's become a part of my life—a part I don't want to go without.

"We're almost home, Luce," I say, and Lucy looks up at me impassively and continues to play with her doll's hair. "You know ghosts aren't real, right?"

I glance at her in the rearview mirror, but she doesn't react.

"There's nothing to be scared of in the house. It's your imagination. Once you accept ghosts are just stories, your nightmares will stop."

In the mirror, I spot that Lucy lifts her gaze to me. "V said ghosts are real."

"She's wrong." I pull up along the curb in front of the house, and Veronica's on the front porch steps. She's sexy in her red plaid skirt, knee-high striped socks and short denim jacket. She looks up, our eyes meet and I want to hold her, be with her, but at the same time . . . Lucy's scared.

Lucy undoes the seat belt of her booster seat, hops out of the car and runs up the front walk to V. They hug and I take my time getting out of the car. Lucy's a million words a minute as she tells Veronica about the movie, the zoo, and her soon-to-be baby brother. Veronica glances at me then, sympathy in her eyes.

I move one shoulder to let her know I'm fine, that I don't care, yet I hurt all the same.

"What's that?" Lucy points at something behind Veronica on the porch. She reaches for the items and in her hands is a large seashell and two huge sticks of something.

"This is sage," Veronica says to Lucy, "and do you know what it does when we burn it?"

Lucy shakes her head, and I'll admit I'm curious, too.

"It gets rid of unwanted negative energies. Like your monster."

Lucy lights up. "So if we burn this, my monster will go away."

Veronica nods, but then Lucy's face falls. "If we burn this, does that mean your mo—"

"Everything will be okay." She cuts off my sister and gives her a curt tip of her head. "Do you want to help me? That is if it's okay with your brother." Veronica glances up at me, hope and hesitancy mixed in her expression. She's asking for me to forgive her.

"Will it work?" I ask, each word dripping with skepticism.

"Yes." Veronica sounds sad with the answer. "Sage will drive away anything in the house we come in contact with."

"Lucy, can you wait for me in the foyer?" I ask.

My sister looks at me then at Veronica then complies. She doesn't close the door all the way, but instead leaves it open a crack.

"What happened with your mom last night?" Veronica asks.

I work my jaw as Mom's explanation still bites at me. "It was a misunderstanding. She thought I was coming home earlier than I was."

"So you knew you were supposed to be watching Lucy?"

No. Mom swears we had the conversation, but I wouldn't forget something like that. Not when it comes to Lucy. I move my arms as the itch to jump becomes stronger. What if there's something wrong with me? What if I'm the one losing my mind? "As I said, it was a misunderstanding. I appreciate you helping. Your dad, too. I promise I'll do better next time."

I promise. The phrase feels like a sledgehammer to the chest as I don't feel like I should be promising anything to anybody anymore when I can't even promise to myself that I won't do what I'm dying to do right now—jump.

"Why do you cover for your mom?" Veronica asks, and the world takes on a red haze.

"I don't."

"You do," she says carefully.

"She's a single mom who works hard and who has two kids. She shouldn't have to juggle everything, and it's not her fault I mess up."

"It's not on you to be perfect."

"I'm not perfect," I shout. "I'm so messed up in the head that I jump off cliffs, remember? I'm the weirdo of my friends who can't read right or get his crap together in order to have qualified academically for the state meet last year. I'm the one with the no-show dad. I'm not even close to perfect. I'm not good enough for that."

Veronica and I stare at each other, her strong-willed eyes never breaking away from mine. But there's something else there, physical pain, emotional pain, and that causes the anger in me to crack as my own words come back to haunt me. "I didn't mean weird was a bad thing—"

"Will you allow me to sage your apartment or not?" She cuts me off with a touch of attitude, reminding me of our first interactions back in August. Tonight, I came home angry with her, and now, she seems angry with me. The punches keep on coming.

She's waiting on an answer and I give her an honest one. "If this doesn't help Lucy's nightmares, you have to tell her ghosts aren't real."

"This'll work," Veronica says. "I care about Lucy, and I don't want her to be scared."

I hear what she's not saying—she's not willing to make the admission, but she is willing to somehow voodoo Lucy's nightmares away. A placebo on the illness. "This is a deal breaker for me. If this doesn't help with Lucy's nightmares, you have to tell her the truth. And you can't talk about ghosts with Lucy anymore. Me and you— we're able to play around with the make-believe, but Lucy can't tell the difference."

I hate that Veronica breaks eye contact with me. "I hear you."

I want Veronica and me to work, but I need Lucy's nightmares to go away. "I'll give your idea a try."

VERONICA

"What are you doing, V?" Mom had whispered in my ear when I had picked up the shells and the sage sticks earlier today. "If you do this, it will drive me out. Is that what you want? For me to leave?"

No, it's not what I want. It's the last thing I want, but I have to help Lucy.

"I'm only cleansing the first floor," I responded. "Go to the third floor and you'll be safe."

Mom did what I asked, and now I'm terrified she's right and I'm wrong. With each second that passes, I shake more from head to toe. From fear, from grief, from physical pain.

This morning, I woke up with a splitting headache. The type that was tough to roll out of bed with, the type that makes my head feel fifty pounds heavier than normal. My spine aches from having to find the strength to stay upright. The migraine has become worse and worse. My vision doubling at times, my stomach sloshing with the promise of future vomiting.

I didn't want to leave my bed or my room, but this is important. Lucy is important. Sawyer is important. And there's a bit of selfishness in this, too. If I don't do this and do it right, Glory will come and sage the entire house and then my mom will be gone for good. I can't risk that. Her being here is a lifeline, and if it's cut off, I think I might die.

Glory told me that in order to sage a house, I have to want the spirits to leave or they'll stay. If I sage every part of the first floor, if I will every spirit away from this house except for Mom, then she should be okay.

My boots are heavy on my feet as I walk through Lucy's room, the last place in the downstairs apartment I haven't cleansed. My makeup is heavy, uncomfortable, but otherwise there's no doubt Sawyer would have picked up on my translucent skin, the dark circles under my eyes—he'd see the pain.

I just need to get this done, drive off Lucy's monster then make it upstairs before my migraine makes it to the point of no return—before Sawyer sees me at my rawest.

The windows of the first floor are all open and the cool autumn wind rushes in. I shiver and the smoke of the sage stick blows into my face. My eyes burn and I wonder if that is the spirits I'm tossing out fighting back.

I raise my hand and it shakes as I move the smoke from inside of Lucy's room toward the window. "I wish you well someplace other than here. You are not welcome here anymore. It's time for you to move on, and I am ordering you to leave."

Doing what I ask, Sawyer follows up behind me with a burning sage stick in hand. He mimics me, doing what I do, saying what I say, but his words are weighted with disbelief. I'm betting on sage being sage and my belief being enough to cast everything but my mom out.

Lucy watches us from the doorway, a mixture of perplexed and curious. I hold the bundle of smoking sage to her. "This is your room, Lucy. You have more power over it than I do. Can you help drive the ghosts away?"

She holds her hands behind her back as she walks in, but then takes the sage and does exactly what I tell her to do, saying exactly what I tell her to say and with each step she becomes emboldened, as if taking control of her world and circumstances.

"Are the ghosts gone yet?" Lucy asks me.

They should be. "Yes." I leave the room and head to the kitchen to find the shell so I can put out the burning sage.

Lucy follows behind me. "Where will the ghosts go?"

"I believe they go to heaven," I say. "If that's where they decide to go."

"Why wouldn't they want to go there?"

"I don't know, but God gave us free will. He's not going to force us to go anywhere we don't want. It's up to us to make the choice."

"If the ghosts choose to go to heaven and can go to heaven, why don't they go to heaven when they die instead of staying here?"

In the kitchen, I grind the sage stick out into the shell. "I don't know."

Lucy glances over her shoulder then does a conspiratorial lean into me. "Why did your mom stay?"

I put the shell on the table and crouch in front of her. "I think my mom knew how badly my dad and I missed her so she stayed to make sure we are okay."

"Don't you want her to go to heaven?" she whispers, and guilt rushes me. Shouldn't I?

Lucy angles in so close I can feel her body heat. "By doing this are we sending your mom away?"

"She should be fine. I told her to hide on the third floor."

"But doesn't smoke travel up? Isn't that why we have to stay low to the floor if there's a fire?"

My heart skips several uncomfortable beats.

The front door of the apartment opens and my forehead furrows, causing a slicing ache through my skull. I force myself to my feet and spot Sawyer walking through the foyer, waving the sage, muttering words. Then he turns up the stairs. The world tilts.

"No," I whisper as my heart pounds in my ears. "Mom."

I race for him, but I feel slow, like I'm stuck in wet sand and being pummeled by waves. Sweat beads along my forehead, along my chest, and my breathing becomes labored.

"Sawyer!" I meant it as a yell, but it comes out just above a whisper and I grasp the railing as he starts waving the burning sage at my door. "Sawyer, stop!"

A loud pop in the middle of the staircase. Loud enough that I jump. Loud enough that Sawyer spins, almost causing him to lose his balance.

A glint of white blinds me, and I blink to find Mom sitting on the middle of the stairs. She inclines her head as she looks at me then at Sawyer. My mouth dries out as a combination of panic and hope spreads through me. Will he see her?

He's staring in that direction, so intently, but his eyes are moving, roaming, scanning and I deflate. I'd give close to anything if anyone else could see her because then I'd know for sure that I'm not dying.

"The sage is hurting me." Mom winces like she's in pain. She flickers in front of me and my heart tears in two.

"Put out the sage," I say.

"What?" Sawyer asks.

"Put out the sage!" I yell. "Put it out! Put it out now!"

Sawyer fumbles with the shell in his hand, but does what I ask. Mom continues to flicker and the blood drains from my face.

"If you won't tell your father . . ." Mom holds her head like she did when she was in pain with her tumor. Back then, it was fate's fault she hurt, and now her pain is on me. "Will you tell Sawyer that your tumor is growing?"

I shake my head and Sawyer's eyes narrow in my direction as he must have caught the movement. "You okay?"

"I raised you better than this, V," Mom says. "I raised you better than to play with people's hearts. Leo knew the truth and he made his choice."

"He knows," I whisper, and my palms grow cold and clammy as Sawyer had to have heard me, regardless of how low I talked.

Sawyer's eyebrows pull together. "Veronica, what's wrong?"

"He knows you have a small tumor that causes migraines," Mom pushes. There's anger in her tone. Anger I don't understand. "You're not being honest with him, V. Tell him the truth or walk away from him now."

Sawyer's eyes dart between me and Mom, but he doesn't see her. He only sees me staring at her and I can't force myself to look away.

"Veronica." Sawyer starts down the stairs slowly. One step at a time, as if he's terrified of scaring me off. "Are you okay?"

I grow hot all over, heat flashes in my blood and sweat rolls down my back. I'm roasting alive and my knees become weak as I start to feel dizzy.

"Tell him, V!" Mom yells, and the entire world narrows as my vision becomes dim.

"He'll leave me if I do," I mumble, but the words feel wrong coming out of my mouth. As if my tongue is too thick, as if my lips have gotten too big. Sawyer reaches Mom and smoke still rises into the air.

I throw out my hand and scream, "Mom!"

The smoke hits her and she flickers, her hand reaching out to me. I stumble up the stairs, try to grasp her, to pull her away, but as my hand is about to make contact with hers, she disappears and a sob tears through my body. "No! Mom!"

A quickening, sinking sensation. The world beneath my feet bottoms out and I'm sucked into a blackness. My arms flail, searching for something to hold on to, and I smack something solid.

"Veronica!" Sawyer shouts, and I grab on to him, not just his body, but his voice. I'm drowning. But somehow, like back in the river, if I cling to him I'll be able to float. "Veronica, talk to me."

"Mom," I whisper, and I'm somehow moving through the air. "We hurt Mom."

"I got you," he says. "It's okay, I have you."

I suck in a clean breath as if I'm breaking through to the surface of the water and when I open my eyes I can see again. I'm drenched in sweat, and I'm on cold sheets of a mattress close to the floor. It's Sawyer's bed. His room.

He hovers over me, smoothing my hair back as if I'm a broken doll. His face is so white that I'm concerned he no longer has any blood.

"Veronica?" he says again, and the fear in his voice breaks my heart.

I have to clear my throat twice before I can talk, and even when I do, it's barely a whisper. "I'm okay."

"You're not okay. You zoned out on me, said all sorts of weird crap—words that didn't even go together—and then collapsed to the ground. None of that is okay."

Blinding pain crashes through my skull. What is this? What's happening? My migraines, even the worst ones, are never like this. My lower lip trembles as tears burn my eyes. Oh my God. Oh my God. Nausea causes my stomach to roil, and I roll away from Sawyer as I'm terrified I'm going to vomit on him.

"Veronica, what is it?" Fear oozes from Sawyer's voice. "Tell me what's wrong."

Another sharp pain rips through my brain and I double over on the bed. I can't talk, I can't think, I can only hold my stomach as I dry heave. My head throbs so intensely, so loudly that it's as if my heart is beating in my ears.

"Veronica!" he shouts.

"C-call . . . N-N-Nazareth." The air rushes out of me with another punch of agony. "M-m-m-migraine." My cell. He needs my cell. I reach for my pocket, attempt to take it out and it disappears from my hand. "Please, c-c-call."

"I will," Sawyer says, close to me. "I'm calling now."

SAWYER

Thursday October 3: Weight 116 ½ lb.

Sat with Morris tonight, and I'm so ashamed of myself, Diary. I had the blues, or rather I <u>have</u> the blues and I let it all out on him, but he's a peach. Was great to me.

I shove Lucy's choice of dolls and doll clothes into her backpack. My cell is pressed to my ear, and like it has time and time again, it rings. When I go into Mom's voice mail again, I end the call with a mumbled curse. Sylvia said her mom is home tonight and she didn't hear that anyone had any plans. Where the hell is my mom?

"Mommy says not to use that word." Lucy sits on her bed with her doll in her lap.

"She's right. I'm wrong. It's not a word anyone should use. What else do you want to take?" I told Sylvia I needed help with Lucy, and she's on her way to retrieve my sister until Mom returns home from wherever it is she ran off to without telling me.

"Is V okay?" Lucy asks.

I try to imagine what this all must look like in her eyes. Monsters, ghosts, burning sage, cleansing, Veronica crumbling in pain, me carrying her to my bed, Nazareth—the tattooed and black-framed-glasses giant—showing up and carrying Veronica to her apartment while telling me to keep Lucy away, and now me in this frantic pace to get Lucy taken care of so I can check on Veronica. It must feel like a bad dream.

"She gets really bad headaches sometimes and they make her feel sick. She won't feel good for a bit, but I'm sure she'll feel better soon." I hope that's true. Veronica told me her headaches could be bad, but I never imagined anything could be like that. "It would probably cheer Veronica up if you made her a card."

"I can do that. We're celebrating Christmas soon so I'll put a tree on it." Lucy twirls her fingers in her doll's hair. "I think getting rid of the ghosts is what hurt V."

"It's not." Not sure how long Mom will be gone or what's happening with Veronica, I shove PJs into the bag along with clothes for school tomorrow.

"V liked her ghosts and they never hurt her. She loved them." Her lower lips trembles. "It's my fault she's sick."

It's not and I don't want her to carry that burden. I drop the backpack to the floor and sit on Lucy's bed. I hold out my arms and she clambers across the sheets and onto my lap. I hug her tight and kiss the top of her head. "It's not your fault."

"If we hadn't tried to get rid of the monster, V would be fine."

My heart rips open as I'm sure that's how it appears to her. Consequence of an action. A plus B equals C. "Veronica has this thing in her brain that shouldn't be there." I search for the words to try to explain a tumor to a six-year-old.

"But you don't understand how much V loves her ghost." Lucy's voice becomes higher in pitch—frantic with tears and she pushes her head into my shoulder. "They talk all the time. V talks to her and she talks back. V said that having her there made her feel better."

"Veronica isn't really talking to ghosts. They aren't real."

"Maybe V isn't sick. Maybe we broke her heart," she continues like she didn't hear me. My T-shirt starts to become wet with her tears. "V needs her ghost. That way she knows that she wasn't truly gone."

Dammit, Veronica. She must have told Lucy about the EVPs. "The sounds Veronica had on the recorder aren't real."

Lucy adamantly shakes her head. "No, they talk. V whispers to her when people are around so they don't know she's talking to her

288 ❧ KATIE McGARRY

mom. She said no one would understand, and she's right, no one understands when you see something no one else does. Just like they don't understand my monster."

My entire body jolts and I gently push Lucy back so I can look her in the eye. "Did you say Veronica talks to her mom?"

She convulses as sobs rack her body. "I promised I wouldn't tell! I promised I wouldn't tell!"

I pull her close again, rubbing her back, shushing her, telling her it's okay, but my mouth and my actions are disconnected from my brain. Her mom. Does Veronica actually think she sees her mom?

"We shouldn't have done it." Lucy sobs. "Because the monster is my monster. It's not V's monster. I wanted to get rid of the monster, but I don't think it will go away because it followed us here. I should have told her that the monster only follows me."

Another jolt, but this one angry . . . deadly. "What do you mean the monster followed you?"

"At our old house. The monster was there, too. Right before we moved. It followed us."

"Sawyer?" Sylvia says from the doorway. "Your front door was open so I let myself in. Is everything okay?"

Sunday October 6: I'm pretty mad tonight, Diary. I got the lecture of my young life from my esteemed friend Morris. Jiminy, I was surprised tho. Of course, I deserved it but then we do not always like to hear the truth.

He made me feel about as big as . that. Listen, Diary, I don't think he gives a snap about me. But gee, I'm not going to worry. If he doesn't, he needn't. I don't see why he keeps coming over if he doesn't like me. Temp 99.4. Got medicine.

It's like I'm walking in a dream. No, not a dream. A nightmare. The house.

It feels wrong. Like the walls aren't drywall and support beams, but instead flesh and blood. That I'm somehow not in a building, but a body that inhales, exhales and consumes. I feel swallowed up and digested, and I was more than willing to send my sister out the door with the prayer that she stay out.

Ghosts.

Monsters.

Veronica collapsing in pain.

My lungs twist as I climb the stairs. The door to Veronica's part of the house is ajar. Her father isn't home. She had said he had a load he had to take to Indiana, and he left early this morning. Even if I called him, there's nothing he could do besides drive back. Even if he was here, what would he do?

I consider walking in, but don't. What did Veronica say about why she knocks? Because one should always be concerned about who they are letting into the house—it could be death.

My brain niggles at me. She's the one who wants to be invited in. My head falls back with the pain of realization. She believes she's death.

I knock. A gentle sound, but it echoes along the empty foyer. Kravitz opens the door a few more inches and he takes up that small space. Multicolored Mohawk and stone-cold eyes behind thick, black-rimmed glasses. A fighter's build with a bored stance. "What?"

"I'm here to see Veronica."

"She's sleeping."

Good. "I still want to see her."

"She doesn't need you."

He's probably right. "I need to see her." What do I say to him to help him understand I don't mean her any harm? What do I say as I don't understand a damn thing happening with Veronica at all? "How bad is her tumor?"

His posture changes, like he took on some of the burden and pain weighing me down.

"I care about her," I continue in a low voice, "but what I saw today scared the hell out of me, and I need to understand what's going on."

He glances away then rolls his neck like he's frustrated. "If you're worried about your project, she'll be fine. Just give her a few days and she'll be back to doing your work for you."

"I don't care about the project. I care about her. I either get answers from you or I get answers from her dad."

"He's on the road."

"He has a phone, and I have the number."

Nazareth opens the door the rest of the way and I enter. The room is bright with every possible light on, but it feels strained. As if it's fighting against the darkness assaulting the windows and it's on the losing end.

Kravitz leaves the door open and sizes me up. "V's not a joke."

"I agree. She's not."

He doesn't look like he believes me. "She's my best friend. There's nothing I wouldn't do for her. That includes kicking your ass."

My shoulders roll back—to brace for a punch, to throw the punch. I'm wound so tight that my fist hitting flesh might be the adrenaline release I need. "Rumor around school is that you're some sort of pacifist."

"Thanks to my mom, most days I am, but I'll flip on a dime if you mess with V."

"Right about now, I'm feeling the same way about you."

He almost smirks.

"Where is she?"

"In her room."

I step toward the stairs and he slides in front of me. "I don't trust you."

"She does."

He doesn't move, and I consider taking the swing. "Why do you assume the worst of me?"

Kravitz pins me with a glare. "Do you know how many times

V sat in front of you in school and listened as your friends talked about her?"

"I never said anything."

"You're right. You didn't add anything, but you didn't stop it, either. You laughed along. Just because you decide to not have a voice doesn't make you innocent. She was in front of you all those years and she was invisible to you. At least her feelings were. You and your stupid friends assumed because V sees life differently and lives in her own way that she didn't feel. But she was there and she does feel and your words tore her down. I know you two got something going on now, which means she's forgiven you, but I haven't. She's got too big of a heart, and I'll be damned if you tear it apart."

My chest aches. I never start gossip—that's not who I am. But I don't finish it, either. I go with the flow with my friends, listening and then following along. Just like Knox said—the person who blends in, who has no voice other than to make people happy. Only adding a comment here or there to enter the conversation. Guilt thickens my throat. Alphabetical order. Isn't that what Veronica said when we started working together?

Screw me, she's always been right there. "I didn't mean anything."

"Most people never do, but that doesn't make it right," he continues. "Jesse thinks you're a rebound. I think she's lonely. Either way, you'll end up hurting her, even if you don't mean to, and she doesn't have time for that."

"If you don't like me, why'd you let me in?"

"I didn't let you in to help you," he says. "This nonsense has already gotten out of hand with the two of you. You know more than you should, and she said you two are casual. Maybe you were. Maybe that's how it started out, but you're on the verge of hurting her. When she feels better you need to break this off before you hurt her in ways you can't take back."

"I'm not ending anything."

Kravitz steps into my space and looks at me with vacant eyes. "You think you're strong enough to be with her?"

"I am."

"You're not. Loving V requires sacrifice. It means you don't get to be selfish, and you don't get to call the shots." He shoves a finger into my chest and emotion shakes his voice. "It means having your heart ripped out again and again, but you stay by her side, supporting her, because she's one of the best damn people you will ever meet. You don't have that in you. Not the boy who doesn't have the guts to stop his friends from talking crap about a girl he says he cares about. Because that's what's happening at school. Since she's been with you, the rumors are getting worse, and she hears each and every single word. She doesn't have time for that crap, and she deserves a hell of a lot better."

The raw pain rolling off him cracks something in my chest. The type of pain I've only seen a few times from people in my life at funerals. Something I only felt once and that was when my mother and father told me to choose between them. I see grief.

She won't walk in without permission.

Death.

Ghosts are in the house.

Her mom.

She wants to believe.

It's real.

The world tunnels in then tunnels out.

"The tumor's worse than what she's let on."

He doesn't deny it, just stares at me like he's a horseman of the apocalypse and I'm on his list. I move to go around him, he slides with me. My hands come up, I push him back, his arms come up and when I'm ready to block and throw a blow a voice comes from behind me.

"Let him through." Jesse Lachlin. An unlikely ally enters the apartment. "She'd want to see him."

"He's bad news." Kravitz fumes.

"Yeah, but that's not our choice. It's never been our choice."

With a final glare at Kravitz, I let my shoulder hit his as I sprint across the room and up the stairs. I glance right and see what must be her father's bedroom, then left. Veronica's laid out on the bed, a crocheted blanket over her sleeping form. A soft light on her dresser keeps her from being eaten alive by the shadows stalking the room.

I enter and a sweet herbal scent hits my nose. Pot. On the bed-side table is a smashed-out joint on a ceramic plate. I rub my eyes as exhaustion sets in. Kravitz, Lachlin and Veronica were never ston-ers. They were helping her deal with her pain. Damn. Just damn. No one at school has anything on them right.

Veronica is pure beauty—her blond ringlets rest against the pil-low and the soft light glistens off the strands. She's incredibly still. So much so that it aches, and it's like she feels my pain as her eyelids crack open.

"Hey," she whispers.

"Hey," I say back.

She opens the palm of her hand, her fingers weakly beckoning to me. "Lie with me."

Anything. I would do anything for her.

Doing as I'm told, I slip off my shoes, slip into bed and close my eyes as she rolls into me and I hold her tight.

VERONICA

"You're dying." Mom and I sit on the beach watching the waves roll in and roll out. This is where she takes me when I dream. To the beach. Blue skies. A slight breeze. The taste of salt in the air, but today, on the horizon, there are gray storm clouds.

"I know."

Mom turns her head toward me. "No, V. I need you to understand. This is real. This isn't a decision you can take back. You need to tell your father. I know you think you're okay with dying, but you aren't. You're afraid."

"I'm not. I know what I'm doing."

Warmth along my other side and it's not from the sun. My skin tickles. The pleasing kind. A caress. I look and there's Sawyer. He's holding me, in my room, in my bed. His fingers run through my hair and I love the gentle pull. "What do you know?"

"That I'm dying."

"Who are you talking to?"

"My mom." I glance back at her and she's watching me as if she's curious. The wind blows through the palm trees and through her hair. "She never left me."

"I promised I wouldn't," she says. I smile as the fuzzy feeling associated with Mom overwhelms me, but Mom frowns. "I wish you had more time. I wish you could have what I had."

"What did you have?" I ask, confused, as I have everything I need.

There's a gentle tug on her lips. "College. Oh, V, you'd love college. I know your father has given you a ton of freedom, but it's a different taste of freedom there. You get to learn about all the things that fascinate you while trying to pin down who you are without anyone else in your way. And then the feeling of working your first real job—the one you know you were born to do. I want you to laugh. The type of laugh that only comes with experience. The one that is drawn through years of understanding that life is so precious and that laughter is the best medicine for the soul."

"I laugh now."

Mom tilts her head as if I don't understand. "And then I want you to love."

"I do," I whisper.

"Not just family or friend love, but soul-mate love. The love your father and I had."

Have. She's still here. Their love hasn't died. "I do love."

"Who do you love?" Sawyer draws my attention back to him, and I brush my fingers along his strong jaw. I enjoy how he moves closer, as if my touch is water on parched land.

"You."

"Me?" His blue eyes dance yet there is pain in them. Pain I wish I could take away.

"Yes, you."

He rests his forehead against mine as his hands tenderly slide along my back. "I love you, too. So much it consumes me at times. Scares me, too."

"Why does it scare you?" I ask.

"Because I'm broken."

I shake my head. "You're not. You're just a little lost, but that's not broken. But you're finding your path. You just have to learn how to be the you I see with everyone else."

"I'm not you," he whispers. "I don't have your courage."

"Sure you do. You just misunderstand courage."

"How?"

"You think you have to take care of everyone else," I say. "You think that's courage. You have to learn there's a difference between loving someone and taking care of them. They aren't one and the same."

"He'll take care of you, V," Mom warns, and I flip my head back in her direction. I blink repeatedly as the wind has picked up on the beach and the thunderheads grow in sizes and roll toward us. "If you get sick, he'll stay by your side until the very end, and that will break him. It's what his problem is—he loves everyone else so deeply that he loses himself. He enables them to the point that he breaks. That's the reason he jumps and the next time he jumps, it will be because of you."

Lightning strikes the beach and the explosion causes me to jump. Arms tighten around me as my heart picks up speed. Mom starts to fade and I reach out to her. "Mom? Don't go!"

"It's okay," Sawyer whispers in my ear. "Everything is going to be okay."

SAWYER

Wednesday October 23: It was a beautiful day today. I just cured all day long. I loved it out. Hated to come in.

Went over to see Bray today about my throat. He told me to keep sort of quiet. Guess it must be worse. Gee, I can't help it. I can't be keeping quiet forever.

I've been silent a long time, but I don't think I can keep quiet forever, either.

Veronica didn't come to school on Monday. I don't know why I was disappointed when it was to be expected. When I left her apartment around two, she was in a deep sleep. No longer talking to me, no longer talking to the air, no longer restless as if she was being tormented in her dreams, just sleep.

I didn't want to leave. I wanted to stay, but Jesse told me he'd seen my mom's car pull in. I expected to walk into the living room and be berated for not being home, for her to be frantic that Lucy wasn't asleep in her room, but she wasn't waiting for me.

Instead she had gone straight to her room. Her bedroom door was closed and light seeped from underneath the crack. She was ignoring me. Ignoring Lucy. We had seen Dad, and even though that was because she pushed us, for the next forty-eight hours, we were traitors.

That crap got old a month after the divorce.

Twenty minutes into first period, my mind had checked out. Ten minutes later, I watched the clock tick on the wall and did a countdown to the bell. My grades were still teetering, I had a swim meet this coming weekend and skipping was the last thing I should do, but staying was no longer an option. I had to see her. I had to see Veronica.

She said she's dying.

She said she loves me.

The bell rang, I left and didn't find her at her house. I texted. No response. Feeling like a caged animal, I tried the only other place I could think she would be. About a twenty-minute ride out of town, I parked in front of Jesse Lachlin's trailer. No answer at the door, but then I followed the sound of an engine.

The walk wasn't far, the fall morning brisk. Dew lay like a blanket in the valleys of the land. In the distance is a tractor with a hay baler attached and every so often a huge, rolled-up bale of hay plops out.

I stop walking when I spot Nazareth Kravitz leaning against a tree trunk. He looks at me with that same impassive boredom, but I learned a lot about this kid—there's more to him lurking underneath. Maybe he and I aren't so different after all.

As the tractor comes closer, I notice that the door to the tractor is open and that Jesse Lachlin is standing half in the cab of the tractor, half out as he's laughing and talking with whoever is doing the driving. I'm sure that's against OSHA regulations.

When the tractor is an acceptable distance from us, Jesse leans into the tractor pointing at things and the tractor comes to a stop and the engine dies. The world becomes oddly quiet as Jesse grimly glances at me, at Nazareth, and then back at me. He hops off and Veronica emerges from the cab of the tractor. She has a breathtaking smile on her face as she mumbles something to Jesse. In a blink of an eye, his glum expression is gone and he lights up as he laughs with her.

She and Jesse talk and then he tips his head in my direction. Veronica looks over at me and her posture falls. That's a nice kick in the gut. Jesse jumps off the tractor and Veronica follows. He doesn't join her as she heads in my direction.

"Nazareth," he calls, "can you help me move a limb that fell from a tree? It's heavy and I don't feel like chopping it up. I figure we can move it out of the way."

Nazareth heads his way, and the two of them disappear into the tree line.

Veronica's a sight in a short, black, pleated skirt, an off-the-shoulder knitted blue sweater with a tank underneath and Wicked Witch of the West green-and-black-striped tights. On her feet are black combat boots. The boots are like her father's, just the right type for kicking ass. Her short blond curls are pulled up into a ponytail on top yet several strands have declared rebellion and bounce near her face.

"Did you and Nazareth have a nice conversation while waiting on me?" she asks, and I wonder if she knows about our conversation last night.

"He didn't say anything. Not today, at least."

"Don't feel bad. He doesn't talk to many people. That's what happens when you're a walking, talking, residual haunting." She watches as he disappears into the trees.

I find that interesting, but Nazareth isn't why I'm here. "How are you feeling?"

"Better. Shouldn't you be at school?"

"Shouldn't you?" I counter.

"I'm co-opting. You know, learning a career hands-on? I should probably inform the counselor, but she probably would tell me no. Anyhow, I'm a farmer this month. I only have until October to learn it all and then I've decided to be a vet."

I can't tell if she's testing me or teasing. Maybe a little of both. "So no more school for you?"

"I wish. I'll be back, but as I've said before—rules are optional for me." She winks then, a bit of a smile, but it quickly fades.

Veronica's cool as the morning as she walks past toward a tire swing hanging off the branch of the tree I'm standing under. She sits on it and lightly swings. Indifferent to me, to the world, to what happened between us. This is the literal definition of night and day. Friday night, she was in my arms and each touch was as hot as an August night. Last night, we whispered words of love. This morning, she's impassive. "I'm worried about you."

"You shouldn't be," she says. "We aren't supposed to get all emotional, remember?"

I do. That was the deal, but . . . "Things changed."

She becomes crestfallen. "Look, I like you, I really do, but—"

"You told me you loved me last night."

"I was high."

"I told you that I loved you back."

She closes her eyes as if that causes her pain.

"Look." She reopens her eyes. "We had a great time together, and you're a great kisser, but I told you I wasn't looking for anything serious. After you getting upset with me about Lucy and ghosts and now it appears that you're overreacting with the headache last night, I think it might be best if we return to just being project partners."

"Project partners?" I challenge. After what we've gone through together? After what she's become to me? After I allowed her in?

"We had fun," she says like that should be the end of the conversation. "Maybe when we get past this awkwardness and this strange breakup, we can kiss again sometime."

My jaw twitches at the idea of a casual hookup. I get that's what society tells me is every man's dream, but that's not what I want. Not from anyone. Especially not her. "I want more."

"More kissing?" Veronica gives me a drop-dead smile as she stands from the tire swing. "I didn't realize I was that good at it."

"I want more than kissing."

Her flirtatious smile fades. "And we should have never put a label on things. We should have just stayed casual. That would have been better for both of us."

"I love you." I drop it out there, leaving me naked and raw and her holding my heart. "It's done, Veronica. It happened. You trying to take three steps back doesn't change that."

Veronica nibbles on her lower lip. A move that means deep thought and conflict for her, one that makes me think incredibly too much of how I'd love to kiss her lips again and how I hate it when she looks sad. I reach over and with my thumb, smooth out her mouth, and her eyes snap to mine. The sadness is gone, replaced by a spark.

I cup her cheek and caress her soft skin. Veronica swallows then her tongue darts out to lick her lips. She breathes in deeply as if she, too, is having a hard time keeping her heart rate calm. Energy builds in the air around us, so potent that it practically crackles.

"That's all this is," she whispers. "We're attracted to each other. That's it. And that attraction works and works well. You're confusing it for emotion."

"I'm not," I say softly. "I love you."

"You shouldn't."

"But I do."

"But you shouldn't." Veronica steps back, rejecting my touch.

"Why?" I run a frustrated hand through my hair. "You're smart and you're funny and I'm fascinated by all of your quirks. You love life, you don't judge and you're so damn beautiful that it hurts to look at you. I think about you all the time—when I wake up, before I go to bed. I dream of you. I look forward to seeing you so I don't understand why I shouldn't care."

"Because I'm dying!" she shouts.

"You don't know that. You said the tumor was small, but you're fine!"

"I lied! The tumor's growing. My headaches are worse, my symptoms are worse, I know that you know I see my mom! That's not normal. Not even for me. I want her to be real. I need her to be real, but I'm not stupid. I know what it might mean. I know that I'm dying."

Her words echo through the field and through my soul. She said it last night, but I knew it before her whispers. Yet I still had tried to talk myself out of it, but there's no rationalizing it away. The admission is a crushing weight, it's a rope tied to my ankle that's stuck to the bottom of the quarry pond. The moisture lining the rim of her eyes tells me she just delivered the gospel truth.

I can't breathe, and I flinch as I fight the need to double over. It's like someone has punched me in the throat then in the gut.

"My decision about how to handle the tumor—that's why this project is so important to me. I want to show my dad that when it's time, when the tumor progresses like Mom's did, that we don't have to go through all the terrible treatments. That he can just let me live my life and permit me to enjoy whatever time I have and then it's okay to let me go because I won't be leaving him alone. Not really. If I prove ghosts are real, he'll know that I'll still be with him—just in a different way."

My lungs burn as my heart beats wildly. It was there—the truth, the whole time.

"We're project partners," Veronica whispers to me as if she's angry, and I'm the reason why. "We stay on track, we do our project, and because you can't handle keeping emotions out of it, we aren't together and we won't kiss again."

"Why?"

"Why what?"

"Why can't I be with you?"

Her face contorts. "Because you'll stay with me, that's why."

My eyes widen as if she doesn't get that's the point. "That's what people do when they love someone."

"It's not what I want you to do—not with me."

"Why?"

"Because this isn't how it was supposed to go. You were never supposed to know I was dying. We were never supposed to fall in love. We were supposed to have fun and enjoy our senior year and make a million memories. And then we were supposed to graduate. You were supposed to go to college and I . . ."

"Was supposed to die?" I finish for her. "And I was supposed to leave and forget you?"

She nudges the grass with her foot. "It's what happens when people leave this town."

"I could never forget you!" I roar.

"I know that now, and I don't want this for you! I want you to live!"

"Don't you get it? The only time I live is when I'm with you."

"Because maybe I'm just another adrenaline high," she pushes. "Have you thought of that? You don't want to jump anymore so you hang out with the weird girl who does weird things to get the high so you don't have to face the fact that your mom is an alcoholic and that you enable her every step of the way."

My entire head moves as if I was slapped in face. "What did you say?"

Veronica looks down like she's ashamed, as if she's sad. "Your mom is sick, and it's killing you."

"She's fine," I say, but the words feel empty, and I don't understand the growing anger inside me. "You don't know what you're talking about."

"You're right, I probably don't, but it seems obvious."

"She's not a drunk!" I shout. "Alcoholics drink all the time and my mom is sober during the week. Yeah, she drinks a lot, but she's not a drunk! She's not!"

Veronica places her hands in the air in a show of retreat. I curse aloud then run a hand through my hair. This isn't what I wanted—a yelling match with the girl I love.

"You and me," she whispers. "We've run our course."

My chest feels as if it's splitting in half. "Please don't do this."

"I'm not doing anything. We're project partners. Friends. That's more than we were last year."

"But I love you," I say doggedly.

She lifts her head and meets my gaze. "And I'm doing this because I love you back. I was selfish to let this start. I was selfish to let it continue. I can't be selfish anymore. I'm not going to fight the

304 % KATIE McGARRY

tumor. I'm going to die, and I can't let you tear yourself apart—not for me."

"*This* is tearing me apart."

"Not like it would if you stay."

I step toward her, invading her space, and she lowers her head again.

"Please," I whisper. It's a prayer; it's a plea. "Don't do this."

She shakes her head, and when she looks up at me with tears in her eyes, my heart shatters. I wrap my arms around her and she falls into me. We hold each other, cling. Desperate to make the most of the last few minutes.

"I love you." My voice breaks, and I squeeze her tighter.

"I love you, too," she whispers against my chest.

Veronica lifts her head and allows her fingers to brush along my neck. She edges up, I lean down, and we kiss. She tastes sweet, her tears salty, and I pour myself into her. Begging her to change her mind, letting her know how much I care.

She pulls away, and it kills me to let her go. Veronica stares at me for a heartbeat, as if she might run back into my arms, but then she pivots on her toes and leaves. Into the tree line, away from me and toward where Lachlin and Kravitz have disappeared.

Loving V requires sacrifice. That's what Kravitz said.

Veronica's dying. Her tumor is growing and she's dying. The knife of that truth cuts me so deep that the pain is blinding. It doesn't feel right. The world is only bright because of Veronica. Without her, it will be as black as midnight.

Joy. Veronica is life and joy.

The world has a hazy sensation, and my stunned brain takes a moment to readjust. I blink to help clear the confusion, to bring back focus. To force the sky to be above me, for the ground to be below me, for everything to become right again. I blink a second time, my vision does clear, but the world doesn't return to its previous state. Not in the way that it should.

The sky is still blue. My sneakered feet touch solid ground. The grass and trees are still rooted in spot, but it's all different. Veronica is living, but at any moment could be dying . . . and she won't prevent it from happening.

A weird tingling in my veins as there is this driving need to yank her off the railroad tracks as a speeding train approaches, but then my lungs seize. That's the problem. What she's been trying to tell me—there's no way off the track, only a way to slow down the speeding train. Death is inevitable, it's only a question of how long and painful the collision will be.

A cool fall breeze wafts over my skin. It feels good after standing in the warm sun for so long. I stare down at the hairs on my arm, watch as they rise and fall with the light gust. Funny how I've never noticed how those hairs move before or how I never took a moment to realize how the wind feels against my skin . . . or the sun . . . or how this moment is specific to fall.

I glance around and the trees are no longer green. A mixture of yellow, reds and oranges are starting to invade the green, and then I spot the dried leaves. The ones that didn't make it through the brutal heat of summer. The ones that didn't outlast the others. A withered brown leaf falls from a branch and drifts to the ground. It won't be green again or have the opportunity to be yellow, orange or red.

There's rustling to the left and Kravitz leans his shoulder against a tree, watching me.

"That's why she speeds up holidays," I say, and my own voice sounds foreign. "She's trying to live as many of them as she can before she dies."

He nods then looks away. I rub the back of my head and doing so doesn't help undo my new sight, but I'm not sure that I'd want it to.

Loving V requires sacrifice.

Those words are a ghost whispering in my brain. Nazareth was right in that I didn't understand before, but now, with these new eyes, I do.

VERONICA

Sawyer: I'm not letting you push me away.

Me: I'm not pushing you away. We're staying friends. It's better that way.

Sawyer: Not for me. I'm not scared.

Standing on my front porch, my spine straightens. He's not scared. Saying it as if I am. Me: Neither am I.

I expect a rapid-fire response, but there's nothing. Silence. As if he said all that there is to be said. That his statement was the final word in an argument I was just gearing up to fight.

He's not scared.

Like he even understands what there is to be scared of.

Me: I'm not scared.

It needed to be definitively declared, but somehow the second text causes some of my confidence in myself to drift away. Doubt whispers in my mind—am I scared? . . . But of what? Losing him? Losing Mom? Of death? Of dying?

Not wanting to think too much more about it, I walk through the front door to the foyer and find Glory sitting on the steps, blocking my way. Just the sight of her exhausts me, and I lean back against the door as I shut it. "I am seriously not in the mood."

"Hello, V. I smell sage."

"That would be because I burned it. Are all the evil things lurking in the house gone?"

"No," she answers, and I feel like banging my head against the wall. "They're muted, but not gone, which is why I've been able to sit here. They're still talking, attacking, but it only feels like a tickle on the inside of my skull."

I don't know if I should feel bothered or relieved. I push off the door and Glory stands. I climb the stairs, let us into my apartment and Glory chooses to sit in the middle of the couch. She pats the space next to her. I join her and wish for the thousandth time that it was my mom I was sitting next to and I could physically feel her. I broke up with Sawyer and every part of me aches. I want my mom's hug. I want her touch. I want her caring words.

I glance around the living room, specifically at the window seat, and my stomach churns that she's missing.

"How do you feel the cleansing went?" Glory asks.

"I had a massive headache and then I broke up with my boyfriend. So I guess it depends on where you fall on your feelings for Sawyer and me together." Mine were the good feelings and now I feel empty.

Glory slowly assesses me. "Why did you break up with Sawyer?"

I shrug.

"Is it because of your tumor?"

I meet her eyes yet shrug again.

"You have a bad habit of this," Glory says.

That catches my attention. "Of what?"

"Pushing people away."

"I think you have that wrong. People push me away."

"What about Leo?"

"He's the one who left."

Like my mom used to, Glory tucks a curl behind my ear. Missing Mom's affection, I lean into the touch. It's not Mom, it's not the same, but it's more than what I have now.

"I'm curious," Glory says. "When are you going to stop making decisions based on your mother's death?"

I flinch away from her. "I don't do that."

"I believe you just implied that you broke up with Sawyer because of your tumor."

"You don't understand Sawyer, and you don't understand what it's like to watch someone die like Mom did. I don't want that for him."

"So to save the people you love from heartache, you're choosing what you think is a fast death?"

"Yes," I say then feel confused. "I'm not choosing to die."

"God knows what's in your heart, V. There's no point of hiding what He's already seen. He's been sending angels to talk to me about you." Glory looks me over in that way she does with clients when she claims to be reading their auras. "What do you believe your mom chose?"

"A slow death," I say.

Glory surveys the living room, and my skin prickles with how her gaze lingers over the window seat. Mom's not there. At least I don't see her, yet guilt rushes through me.

"Why are you letting your mother haunt you?"

My mouth dries out and my head swivels as I desperately try to find Mom in the room, but she's nowhere to be found. Oh, God, what if by burning the sage I have muted the other spirits enough that Glory now senses my mother? If she does, she'll force Mom to move on. I know this to the depths of my soul.

Glory places both of her hands on my cheeks and forces me to focus. "You have to learn to let go of the dead or they will drag you to death with them. You know this. You cannot permit death to have a foothold in your life."

This is why I refuse to go into a house without gaining anyone's permission. A story I heard once, as a child, and it stuck with me. Vampires have to be given permission or they can't enter the house. Vampires are death and death can't enter unless you allow it. For years I wondered, had my mother too easily welcomed death in? Or maybe somehow I had without knowing. It made me wary of how I let people into my life—what effect they could have on me without my being aware. It also made me wary of letting myself be cared for by others.

I shake my head with the thought. It's stupid, I know, but it's a childhood fear that manifested and grew as my mother's condition worsened.

"As long as you continue to let your mother linger she'll haunt your every move, your every decision, your every action."

Wetness burns my eyes. "But I love her."

"I know you do, but keeping her this close is stopping you from living."

I jerk and Glory drops her hands. There are heavy footsteps on the stairs and the sound of Dad whistling one of his favorite songs. As soon as Dad opens the door, Glory and I will pretend we were never having this conversation, which equal parts thrills me and terrifies me. "I'm living."

"Whether you understand it or not—you have made the same decisions your mother has—you're choosing a slow death. All I've seen for years is a girl preparing to die. That's not living, V. That's dying. I don't see a girl who's living. I see a girl terrified of her future."

SAWYER

✒

Friday November 8: Same old everything. Cure and cure and then some more cure.

Ida, Tillie and I took a walk this afternoon. That is, we took a <u>ride</u> to the Ray Brook house. We went in to see Harry Brown. Jiminy, Diary, he looks simply dreadful.

How many people did Evelyn know at the hospital who died? And how did she handle it?

A thump, the sound of something heavy in the living room. My eyes flash open and I jerk up with the sight of a figure in front of me.

"Sawyer," comes a small voice with a light tremble and a light tap on my arm. A much-needed adrenaline rush courses through me and the high is almost as good as jumping. "Sawyer, wake up. You need to find Mommy."

My sister holds her mermaid doll to her chest and she's stroking it so quickly I'm afraid she'll make it bald. I take the earbud out of my right ear as the left one must have fallen out at some point, then place my hand over hers to stop the frantic petting. In a swift motion, I pick Lucy up to have her sit beside me on the mattress I still haven't placed in a frame.

"I told you, Mom's hanging out with friends." Truth is, I don't know where Mom is. She hid away from us in her room last night, and she hadn't bothered coming home when it was time for Lucy to go to bed or when I finally gave in to sleep.

She never answered my texts, never answered my call, and didn't seem to give a damn I skipped school today. Between my grief over Veronica and my worry and anger involving my mom, I'm a bottle rocket ready to explode, but I've been able to stay home and away from jumping because of my sister. She needs me and I'm holding on to that for dear life.

"Did you have another nightmare?" My voice is cracked, groggy. I don't need to check my cell for the time. Lucy's become a clock herself and she strikes me awake right at midnight. At least she's not screaming like a maniac. She might not be stage-five uncontrollable, but I don't like how she's shaking like a damn bunny facing a wolf.

"The monster's back and he was huge." Her lower lip trembles, and she wipes at her eyes as they fill. "He hovered near the door of my room. He walked in, and he was like a shadow. Then he left, checked your room and then went down the hallway toward Mommy's room. You need to go check on her. He knocked over the lamp."

The monster. In the house. I push off the mattress. Lucy has nightmares, but I don't like hearing about shadows and I sure as hell don't want to hear about shadows knocking over lamps. I grab my baseball bat. "Stay here."

I flick on the light to my room so I don't leave her quaking in the dark and toss her my cell. "If I yell, you run upstairs to Veronica, okay? Her daddy is there, and he'll take care of you. You tell them to call the police. You tell him to stay there and protect you and Veronica. Do you understand?"

Lucy strangles her doll and nods too quickly.

The bat hangs from my fingertips as I walk into the dark living room. I flip the switch, but there's no light. I flip it down then back up. Nothing. The hair on the back of my neck rises and my eyes narrow. Something's wrong.

If there's someone in this house, I'm going to beat the hell out of them and then drag them upstairs to Ulysses. With the way that guy threatened me with his eyes for just the possibility of hurting his daughter, I'm sure he'll happily take care of any bastard that's stupid enough to break into this house. Bet the man owns swamp-land where he dumps the bodies of people who look at his daughter the wrong way.

Remembering our first night here, I raise the bat to my ear and slowly maneuver through the living room. As I place my foot on the floor, stinging pain. I lurch back and spot pieces of the broken lamp. My heart thuds in my ears. I didn't hear it break and that causes my blood to course faster. My headphones were in. Music was playing. How much haven't I heard while living here?

"Lucy," I say in a low tone, a steady tone, as I'm trying real hard not to show emotion. "I changed my mind. Call Veronica now. While you're on the phone with her, circle behind me and go up the stairs to Veronica's."

"What about Mommy?" Her voice trembles.

"I'll get her, but I want you safe first."

Lucy does what I ask, my cell to her ear, Veronica's face on the screen as it rings. Her feet pad across the room at a run, the front door flings open, so hard that it bounces against the wall, and I maneuver along with her to spot her sprinting along the foyer and then up the stairs.

I'm slow as I make my way toward the kitchen, eye the empty room, and then creep along the hallway for Mom. Music plays from behind her closed door. It's a slow song with a mixed-up beat and a creepy deep voice. I lean forward, place my hand on the knob and it vibrates under my skin from the bass. "Mom."

I listen for a few beats and I hear something. Her voice—a grunt like she's in pain—then a man speaks. It's rough, it's demanding and something dangerous pops in my chest. I barrel though the door, bat by my ear, ready to swing. A man has her pinned on the bed, his hands holding her down. "Get off her!"

"Sawyer!" Mom gasps as the man rolls away from her. Her blond hair falls wildly over her bare shoulders. She grabs a sheet and pulls it over her body. Her naked body. A man with a hairy chest snatches a pillow and puts it over a place I shouldn't be seeing.

My brain convulses, like a DVD stuck in the player. "What the—"

"What are you doing?" Mom bites out and her anger feeds mine.

"Me? What am I doing? Who is this?"

Mom pulls the sheet up higher as she sloppily reaches for the speaker on the bedside table. She hits it once, twice, and finally gets it right on the third try. I grow eerily cold as I let the bat drop from my ear. "Are you drunk?"

"I had a drink," she said.

A drink? "It's Monday night. A school night. In fact, where were you today? Did that drink take you all damn night? Is this who you were with while I took care of your daughter?"

"Get out of here, Sawyer." Mom slurs my name.

"Where'd you get the drink?" I demand. "Because you haven't been shopping. You drank all that was in the house on Friday."

Mom leans up on her knees, sheet still wrapped around her, and spit flies from her mouth as she shouts, "Get out!"

Shifting on the bed, the hairy-ass bastard that was just up on my mom is reaching for his pants. He stops moving as my pissed-off attention switches to him. "How do you know her?"

"Don't answer." Mom wipes at her nose, an indication she's about to ugly cry.

I raise the bat to my ear again, and there's no doubt he reads in my expression that I'd have no problem swinging it and pounding him into next week. "How do you know her?"

His hands shake as he tries to put his pants on, but he's trashed as well. Some sweaty, middle-aged guy with a beer gut was just on my mom, and I'm kicked in the gut when I spot the gold ring on his left hand. "How do you know her?!" I yell.

"At the bar. We met at the bar."

"When?"

He glances at my mom for an answer, for affirmation, but I'm running this show. Not her. I step toward him, and he scrambles back on the bed until he hits the wall. "Tonight. We met tonight."

"How many nights does she go to a bar and pick up men like you?"

"I . . . I don't know." He looks at Mom again, and as I start to swing he throws up his arms for protection. "A lot. She's there a lot, but this is my first time going home with her."

First time—for him. How many nights after Lucy fell sleep, after I fell asleep with earbuds in did this happen? Monsters. My mom was bringing home the monsters. I point the bat at the door. "Get out."

"You can't tell him to leave. I'm your mother!"

"Yeah, and you suck at it!"

The man grabs his shirt, his shoes, and leaves his socks behind. There must be one brain cell working because the man bolts.

"I'm a grown woman!" she screams at me. "I have the right!"

"To leave in the middle of the night? To not even tell us where you're going? How often do you do this, Mom? How many nights have you brought strangers into our house in the middle of the night with you drunk as hell to screw some guy while Lucy slept down the hall? What type of mother brings that type of danger into our home?"

Everything I had explained away for months comes crashing down on me. "The money, Mom? Was it really just an error or have you been drinking it away? Is Dad the liar or are you? He's been sending the child support checks and you've been lying to me about it, haven't you?"

Mom picks up the speaker, throws it at me, but I duck and it breaks into pieces when it hits the wall. "Get out of here!"

Gladly. I throw the bat at the wall and it leaves a hole in the drywall.

VERONICA

L ucy's wrapped tight in one of my blankets and is sitting on my lap. Unable to sleep after my conversation with Glory, I answered my cell on the first ring. My heart had skipped a beat. I sent Sawyer away and that one ring caused me to want to take it all back. But then I heard Lucy's terrified voice, followed quickly by the sound of her banging on the door.

Dad didn't listen to Lucy's pleas that he stay with us. He was down the stairs before I could gather Lucy in my arms. Besides shouting up at me to stay here and that things were under control, I haven't heard again from either him or Sawyer. Each second that passes is marked by a heart palpitation.

The door to our apartment opens, and we whip our heads in that direction. Dad enters first. His weary eyes meet mine and I say a silent prayer of thanks that he's okay. He steps to the side and Sawyer walks in. It's Sawyer, but not Sawyer. There's no joy in his eyes, no smile full of life. He's grim and looks as if he's aged. On his shoulder is an overstuffed backpack and in his hands is an equally overstuffed duffel bag.

Lucy slides off of my lap as I stand. Another heart palpitation, but this one so painful, I grip my chest. "What happened? Why are you packed?"

316   KATIE McGARRY

Sawyer drops to his knees and holds out his arms as Lucy runs into them. They hug like two people who have gone to war and seen terrible atrocities. They hug as if it's the one reason the two of them still breathe. They hug like a brother loving a sister and a sister loving a brother.

He kisses her cheek and releases her, and she wraps both of her hands around one of his as he stands. "Thank you," he says to my dad.

Dad nods. In a way I've seen him do only with people he deeply respects. "I meant what I said, you and Lucy are welcome here."

"I know, but I need space. I . . ." Sawyer appears small then, and lost. "I need time to figure things out."

"It's a standing offer."

It's Sawyer's turn to nod and then he tugs on Lucy's hand for them to leave. I lose the ability to breathe. He's leaving, to God knows where, for a reason I don't understand, all without even looking at me.

The shock is so overwhelming that it takes me longer than it should for me to thaw, for my body to move. He's gone. Sawyer's gone. I sprint across the room, ignoring my father's calls to give him space, and I'm down the stairs and out the door.

Sawyer's bent over the backseat of his car parked near the curb, strapping Lucy into her car seat. He stands and shuts the door, and I finally find my voice. "Sawyer!"

He spins and looks at me as if startled, as if I'm the spirit in the night he can't believe he sees. We stare at each other. His blond hair appears silver in the moonlight and he's the one who is a ghost—lost in a world he doesn't seem to understand.

"What happened?" I ask.

He shakes his head and glances away. My entire chests aches with the sadness radiating from him.

"Where are you going?" I ask.

"I don't know." His voice cracks. "A hotel tonight. I think. Maybe Sylvia's tomorrow. I . . . I don't know yet."

"Sawyer," I whisper as I don't know what else to say.

"You broke up with me," he says, and there's a harshness to his tone. "You broke up with me because I love you. You're pushing me away, and I don't understand why."

I bite my lower lip to keep the pain of his truth away, but it doesn't help. "I know." And I want so badly to tell him I was wrong. That I am wrong. That his text messages made me question my decisions and that Glory's words have shaken me. I want to be selfish and take it all back, but I can't. Not now. Not when something has happened that has torn him to shreds. I can't add an additional burden to his already heavy weight.

"I want to jump." Sawyer scrubs his hands over his face. "I want to jump so bad."

Unable to stand his agony anymore, I stumble forward and I silently thank God when he holds on to me. I hug him tight, as if I could squeeze out all the hurt. "I love you, Sawyer. I swear to you, I love you."

I look up at him, he cradles my head with his hands and he kisses me. His lips warm, the movement as soft as a whisper, his emotions as strong as a prayer. As fast as it starts, it ends and then Sawyer's gone. Away from me, walking around the front of his car, and without another glance at me, he climbs into the passenger seat, starts his car and leaves.

I stand there, my arms crossed over my chest, holding myself together as I realize that Glory is possibly right. I am dying, not from my tumor, but from a slow, crushing bleed in my heart . . . and I'm terrified.

SAWYER

Sunday November 10: Nothing extra doing today. Didn't go on the cure all day.

Stayed inside all afternoon. It wasn't nice out anyway.

Morris was over tonight. Nothing specially important discussed, but had a nice time anyway. Gee, Diary dear, I'm just crazy 'bout Morris. I think he's splendid. He sure is great to me.

Veronica loves me. I believe her, and I'm holding on to her words to keep myself upright.

It's two in the morning, and Lucy's sound asleep in the double bed in our small town's only decent hotel. The stuffed animals I was able to shove into the bag stand guard as sentries near her pillow.

My cell's in my hand and I keep waiting for it to vibrate, but Mom hasn't tried to contact me. Not a call, not a text, nothing. She was drunk tonight, which means she's probably passed out, maybe in her own puke since I wasn't there to clean her up. Why I feel guilty about that, I don't know, and that only pisses me off more.

I sit on the patio, and the sliding glass door to the room is ajar about two inches so I can hear Lucy if she wakes, and the drapes are open so I can keep an eye on her as well. Beyond me is the in-ground pool that's closed for the season. If there was water still in it, I would already be doing laps, but it's empty. A lot like me.

"What's doing, brother?" Knox is a black shadow at first, but turns into flesh and blood as he steps into the dim porch light. He offers his hand, I take it, and then he drops into the aging plastic chair next to mine.

The surfer boy looks as if I woke him in January during a deep hibernation. I guess I did. "I'm sorry for calling."

"Don't be. Being here is part of the job. Someday, you'll pay it forward, become someone's sponsor, and you'll be the one hustling in the middle of the night."

I snort. "For when I meet the other person addicted to jumping."

He's good enough that he chuckles, then sobers up. "That person is out there, brother, and the universe will cause your paths to meet. I just hope you'll say yes to helping instead of no."

Me, too.

"Only reason I'm not at a quarry jumping right now is because I'm responsible for Lucy." I rub my hands together as I lean forward. "To be honest, I thought about leaving her with Mom so I could jump." I pause. "And I've been trying to convince myself she'll be fine by herself here for an hour. I won't do it. I won't leave, but I hate that I have the thoughts."

"Focus on the positive. You didn't leave her at home or here. Instead you called me and we're going to hang out until you're strong enough to be on your own."

"I don't know if I'll ever be strong enough."

"You already are. Everyone else can see it in you and you're just the last to know."

I rub my hands again then lock my fingers tight enough together that there's a shot of pain. "I think Mom has a drinking problem." The words feel foreign, and there's a part of me that's already trying to dissuade myself from this truth. "She can go days without drinking, though."

"Yeah, but when she does drink, can she stop?"

She thinks she can, but . . . "No."

"Alcoholism comes in many different forms. Everyone thinks of the stereotype—the guy in the wife-beater, unshaven, a belligerent drunk who beats anyone in his way. Alcoholism affects all sorts of people, from all different walks of life, and it affects people in all different types of ways. The one thing we alcoholics have in common is that alcohol rules us. We never rule it. Even when we don't drink—it still has the power to knock us on our asses. I tell myself daily that there's no safe place for me and alcohol together. There never will be."

I hear his words, understand them almost, but it doesn't help this dark anger festering inside me. "Mom has been bringing men into our house in the middle of the night. She's drunk. God knows if the men are drunk. What I do know is that some of them have looked in on my sister and scared the crap out of her."

The mere thought that those men watched my sister as she slept causes my hands to close into fists.

"How are you feeling, brother?" Knox asks.

I'm exhausted. "Angry."

"And you're going to be, but I will say this: there's one benefit to being an addict."

Doubt it. "What's that?"

"You understand what it's like to have a problem—a disease— you have a hard time controlling, and you know what it's like to be desperate to find someone who understands and will forgive you when you mess up. You know how to hate the illness, but not the person."

My eyes shut tight as the back of my head hits the wall behind me. Anger pushes back at him so hard that I'm surprised he's still upright in his seat. "No offense, but I really don't want to hear this."

"If I remember my stories correctly . . ." Knox continues like he has no fear to tread where I wish he wouldn't. "Someone in your life has already shown you that grace."

Veronica.

She didn't bat an eye when I told her my secret, and she called me out on the fact I'd want to jump again, too.

"Maybe," Knox says. "Just maybe, God put that person in your life knowing there'd come a time when you might need to show that grace to someone else."

I crack my neck to the side as fury races through me. "Did you not hear me when I told you that Mom's been bringing strange men home in the middle of the night? That some of those men crept into my sister's bedroom? That her screaming is the only thing that may have protected her? Or did you miss how Mom's been lying to me about money?"

"You angry?" Knox asks.

"Angry? I'm a nuclear bomb."

"Good. Then maybe you'll stop enabling her and she'll get some help."

My forehead furrows. "I don't pour the alcohol down her throat."

"You step in and clean up after her, then you play her role when she can't."

"She's my mom," I spit out. "And that's my sister in there. What am I supposed to do? Abandon them?"

"No," Knox says slowly. "But you need to start looking at how you handle your relationships. Like I had to evaluate my relationship with my parents. Am I doing the thing that will make them happy or am I doing the thing that will help put them on a path to get better? We want the people we love to be happy, but there's a difference between instant-gratification happy and long-term happy. Long-term happy—it often means you do things in the present that don't feel good."

I stare at the empty pool and try to imagine what it would look like with the water shimmering. "I've been taking care of her for so long, I don't know how to stop."

"You need to find your voice."

I shake my head, not understanding.

"What's the first step in Al-Anon and AA?"

"Admit that we are powerless over alcohol and that our lives have become unmanageable."

"Key word for you right now is 'admit.'"

Frustration shimmies down my spine. "I am admitting it."

"Not to me, but to the world. One of alcoholism's greatest weapons is silence. How many people have you told about your mom besides me?"

No one.

Telling people.

My mother is an alcoholic.

Will they believe me?

Maybe.

Maybe not.

But I need to start living for me.

VERONICA

Sawyer: I didn't jump. I thought you'd be worried.

Me: I was. I'm glad you texted and I'm glad you didn't jump. How are you?

Sawyer: My mom's an alcoholic.

Me: I'm sorry.

Sawyer: I know.

Me: I love you.

Sawyer: I love you.

Me: I don't want to push you away.

Sawyer: Then don't. I've got to go. I'll text when I can.

The text messages were from earlier this morning. Since then, I went to school without him. Sylvia braved leaving her friends at lunch to sit with me. Everyone at school stared. Lots of people talked. I decided we were friends when she acted like she didn't give a damn what people thought because she sat with me.

"Do you know what's going on with Sawyer?" she had asked. "He's not at school and he's not answering his texts. Besides that, he's been off. Since before last spring and he's been getting worse. Sawyer and I don't always see eye to eye, but he's my friend and I care."

"I know some things, but not all."

"Will you tell me what you do know?"

I wish I could, but I'm loyal to him. "It's his business to tell."

She pursed her lips, unhappy, but replied, "I can respect that. Can you at least tell me he's okay?"

The urge is to say he's fine because that's what people do, but I'm tired of lying. "He's not. He'll need his friends."

"Then it's a good thing he has us." Holding a tray full of food, Miguel had dropped down next to Sylvia.

"He's really going to need you two," I agreed.

Miguel's face contorted as he shook his chocolate milk. "I said 'us,' *amiga*. Not unless you plan on checking out."

Sylvia and Miguel watched me for an answer. I thought I was checking out, but I don't want to anymore. "I'm in."

In.

Not pushing away.

It's an odd feeling. A bit frightening. A bit exhilarating. A bit sad that Sawyer wasn't there to experience it with me.

"How was your day?" Dad drags me back to the here and now as he places the hamburgers and French fries he made for dinner on the table.

"Okay."

Dad sits and doesn't bat an eye when I position my cell next to my plate, but does glare at the laptop I only slightly push away. He knows I'm hoping for a call or a text from Sawyer, but he's not okay with me doing schoolwork during dinner.

"Have you heard from Sawyer?" he asks.

"Not since this morning." I pour ketchup onto my plate even though I'm not hungry. "Do you think I should text him or should I wait for him to reach out to me?"

Dad takes a huge bite from his burger and takes his time chewing. "As a guy, I'd say give him space."

"But what if he's stuck in his own head and needs encouragement?"

Dad sets his burger down. "Your mom was good at that. She'd know when I needed space and when I didn't."

"How do I know when to give space and when not to?"

"I've never been good at emotional stuff, peanut. I only knew how to love your mom."

"And me," I add. "You love me."

Dad doesn't say anything, just stares at his plate. "It's moments like this that I wish she were here. She'd guide you better through life."

Is she? Guiding me to a better life?

Mom haunts me.

Mom chose a slow death.

Glory says I'm choosing the same.

A slicing pain through my skull, and I convulse but force myself to stay upright in the chair. Dad cuts his gaze away from the plate to give me the eagle eye. "You okay? I thought I saw you shake."

"I think you're seeing things. When was the last time you had your eyes checked?" I hate that the lying has gotten easier. Dad stares at me for too long, then starts eating again.

Mom sits on the window seat, and since Glory left yesterday, she hasn't moved from there. Hasn't talked to me. But then again, I haven't talked to her, either.

I'm not choosing a slow death. I'm choosing a full life. Glory's wrong. I know she is. Mom tilts her head then, as if she's a puppet on a string. Absolutely no emotion passes over her face and I shiver then glance quickly away. My cheeks warm, ashamed that my mother has frightened me.

I comb a hand through my curls and pull slightly at the strands as I stare at the words on the computer screen. Most of the words are spelled wrong. Red wiggly lines underneath. But I can't seem to understand what I've done wrong.

What is wrong with my brain today?

"Are you cold?" Dad asks as he puts down his burger again and

326 🦂 KATIE McGARRY

slips to the edge of his seat. My mouth dries out as I know that expression—he smells blood.

My cell pings, and I breathe out with the distraction. I check it, hoping it's Sawyer, but instead it's Sylvia. I wanted to let you know Sawyer just pulled up and it's my mom's girls' night at my house. Say some prayers. I think things are about to get tense.

SAWYER

Saturday November 9: Took a half day today. Cured until 11 o'clock and then came in and went to services.

My throat is just as sore as ever. I don't know what I'll do if it keeps on like this.

don't know what I'll do if my life keeps on like this, either.

Sylvia opens her front door before I knock or ring the doorbell. "Hey."

I shove my hands into my khakis. They aren't pressed like normal. Wrinkled to hell and back, but life has been complicated. "Hey."

She steps out onto her stone patio, leaving the door slightly ajar. "What's going on with you? Your mom is in the kitchen going off with how moody you've been—and the weird part? She doesn't even seem to know you didn't go to school today. Are you okay? And where's Lucy?"

"Lucy's with a friend, and I need to talk to my mom."

"Okay. I'll get her."

She doesn't understand. "No. I need to talk to my mom in front of everyone."

Sylvia holds out her hand to me. "Do you need a friend to stand by you?"

Those are the same words I said to her when she decided to come out. Sylvia's news that she shared with her family years ago was good news. The scary part was everyone else's reaction. "My news isn't good." I'm hoping it will eventually be freeing, but there won't be any joy found in my words. "You don't know what I'm going to say. At the end of this, you could chose her side."

"I like your mom," Sylvia says. "But you're my friend. I've been your friend. Just like you've been mine. Whatever it is you'll say, I'm not going anywhere."

"What if I tell you I've been jumping off quarry edges into water for an adrenaline rush? And that it's a problem for me?" I'm so damn raw that a part of me might run if she rejects me.

Sylvia studies me, longer than I like. "I'd say that's so much more of a better explanation of how you broke your arm than that weak excuse of the pool deck."

True. "When things calm down for me, you, me and Miguel need to talk."

"And I can't wait to listen." She pauses. "Miguel's here. We were hanging out in my room. Besides the moms, there isn't anyone else. Is the cliff thing why you're here? Why you skipped school and why your mom is so upset?"

I shake my head. "I could use a friend, but I get it if you choose my mom at the end of this."

She extends her hand toward me. "I told you, I'm here. And maybe, at the end of all of this, I'll get to choose you both."

"I'm going to tell everyone Mom's an alcoholic. I've been covering for her for years, and I'm not doing it anymore."

The shock that registers on Sylvia's face had to be near a 10.0, but she quickly recovers. "Okay." She nods like she's agreeing to something in her head. "Wow. That's big, and we're going to get through this—together."

Sylvia takes my hand, and my gut twists as I hear all the women laugh from the kitchen. "How much have they had to drink?" Maybe this wasn't the best idea.

"Not much." Sylvia leads me down the hallway. "They just got here twenty minutes ago. But . . . your mom's been here longer."

Which means she's had more than a few. When I walk into the kitchen, Mom stops laughing and her expression completely drops. Her eyes are feverish, a sign she's a good bottle in, and her cheeks and nose are ruddy from alcohol in her blood.

She's the life of the party, everyone's best friend, and I'm tired of wondering if she'll be coherent enough to get herself home at night or into bed. I'm exhausted from staying up to make sure she doesn't puke in her sleep. She's spent money we need. Has brought strange men into our house. She's put a huge burden on me. My mom terrified my sister, her daughter.

My mother put us both in danger.

Raw fury enters my veins, causes the muscles in my jaw to tic, and then I notice how Mom's hand flinches toward the bottle of wine. The way my body reacts at the edge of a cliff.

Mom's sick.   *I am, too.*
But I believe I'm going to get better.
                          Does that mean she can, too?

The room goes silent as they notice me standing there with Sylvia by my side. Footsteps from behind and then Miguel's on my other side. Friends. I have friends who have my back.

"Do you want to tell them," I say to Mom, "or do you want me to? Either way. One of us is talking."

Mom starts to rise. "I'm sorry, everyone. This is what I've been talking about with Sawyer being moody. He and I need to go home and talk this out privately."

"Where's Lucy, Mom?" I ask, and she goes completely still.

"You were supposed to pick her up from ballet today and you didn't. And don't tell me it was my day, because it wasn't."

Mom blinks. "Did you get her?"

"Where did she spend the night last night?"

"In her bed."

"Try again. Actually don't. She and I slept in a hotel last night, but you didn't notice that, did you? Because you're used to scheduling your work appointments late because you're sleeping off the bottles of wine you had the night before and letting me take care of Lucy in the morning."

"Sawyer." Mom trips over the back of Hannah's chair, but catches herself against the wall. "Not here. We're not doing this here."

"I'm not staying silent anymore. If you don't want to talk about Lucy, let's talk about the multiple bottles of wine that you drink by yourself on the weekends."

Mom goes ghost white. "You need to stop."

"Or we can talk about the child support payments you've lied about."

"Sawyer!" Mom shouts.

"Or we can talk about what happened last night, or do you even remember it?"

Mom falters, Hannah stands and wraps an arm around her. Sylvia squeezes my hand and the encouragement is needed, but it's also a reminder. My mom was the first adult in this room to stand and hug Sylvia, offering her acceptance in one of the toughest moments of her life.

"You have a problem, Mom." I do my best to keep a gentle voice even though I'm angry. So incredibly angry. "You're sick. I get it. But you have to be the one who wants to get better."

"He's lying," Mom says quietly, but the second time around, she's louder. "He's lying." Then to me. "I know you've been off because of things with your father, and I know it's been tough for you falling for a girl who's dying from a brain tumor, but that does not give you a reason to come in here and make up things about situations you understand nothing about."

My eyes shut tight as Sylvia places her arm around me and Miguel lays a hand on my shoulder. Both as a reminder to swallow the anger I want to spew at her for hurting me and for continuing to spill Veronica's secret, and to show me that they, too, hate what she just did.

"You have a problem with drinking." My voice is pitched low, full of fury, but at least I'm not yelling.

"I drink! Everyone drinks! That's what happens when you're an adult!"

"Not when you can't control it!" I finally shout. "Not when it's my job to take care of you. Not when you bring strange men into the house in the middle of the night and put us at risk."

"I don't have a problem!" she yells.

"You do and until you admit it and get some help, Lucy and I won't be living with you."

Mom goes pale and she dips like her knees give out. She stays up thanks to her grip on the chair and Hannah's help. "What did you say?"

"We're leaving. Now."

Demons race from her eyes. "You can't leave and you sure as hell can't take Lucy."

My throat swells as I know the following words are going to be a knife through her soul, a betrayal she might never forgive, but I can't let Lucy live like I have and I can't let myself live like this anymore, either. "I'll text you when we get to Dad's."

Mom throws herself forward, hits the chair, and I wince as her hands slam on the tabletop to stop herself from falling. "Is that what this is about? Is your father feeding you these lies? Are you so desperate for him to love you that you're making me the bad guy?"

It's hard to breathe and my eyes burn as everyone turns to stare at me. I'm seventeen and I don't want to do this. I don't want to be the adult in the room. I don't want to be the one begging my mom to realize she has a problem. I don't want to break her heart.

"I love you, Mom. Lucy does, too. I'll be in contact soon." I look at Hannah, begging her to understand. "She has a problem, and we need your help."

I turn, half expecting Sylvia and Miguel to stop me, but they don't. Sylvia grabs my hand, Miguel turns with me, hot on my heels, his hand still on my shoulder for support.

And my mom . . . she cries, she yells, and I do my best to block it all out.

VERONICA

"You were correct," Sylvia says when I open the door to our apartment. "Sawyer definitely needs his friends, and right now, he really needs you."

If anyone had told me last August that Sylvia Ricci would be at my house at eight in the evening, asking for me, I would have recommended they be checked for a brain tumor. But it's funny how life changes and how her being at my door is more normal than I could have expected.

One look at her troubled eyes and I grab my father's overly-large-for-me leather jacket off the hook on the wall.

"V," Dad calls out. "I want you home by ten."

I circle on my toes, surprised by the curfew. Dad's at the sink, finishing the dishes I was helping him dry and put away. His back is toward me, but I can tell by the way he holds his shoulders that he's on full alert. He'll be watching me closely now. Closer than I prefer. "No problem."

Dad glances over his shoulder at me and my stomach dips. It's there—the deep worry.

"I'm okay, Dad," I say.

He absently nods and returns to the dishes. Time. Dad and I need to spend more time together. That will make him feel better.

But with Sylvia standing near the door and with Sawyer needing me, time together will need to happen later.

Not able to leave him so upset though, I go to him and hug him. Dad hugs me back, a tight squeeze, and then mumbles something about me getting going.

Sylvia and I leave, and once we're on the front porch, I pause to let her take the lead. She goes around back and heads for the tree line. She takes out her cell and turns on her flashlight. I do the same.

"Sawyer and Miguel already hiked to the TB hospital. Sawyer wanted to go up first to be alone for a few minutes, but Miguel and I didn't feel like that was a good idea. I stayed back and packed more stuff for him and Lucy. Sawyer didn't want to linger here in case his mom came back. I promised him I'd find you when I was finished and bring you up. He wants to see you before he goes."

"Goes?"

Sylvia offers me a sympathetic tilt of her head. "He wants to be the one to tell you."

I nod and we begin the steep ascent up the knoll. We start huffing and puffing halfway up and beneath Dad's leather jacket I start to sweat. I don't want to take it off though as the cruel fall air is biting at my exposed skin.

We finally reach the stone steps of the abandoned hospital, and eager to see Sawyer, I take two at a time. Sylvia hesitates at the bottom.

"Are you okay?" I ask.

"This place seriously scares the crap out of me."

I glance around the old place that glows silver beneath the moonlight. She's scared. I'm scared, too, but not of ghosts behind closed doors. I'm more scared of how much further Sawyer can be pushed before he'll completely break.

"Go on ahead," Sylvia says as she wraps her arms around herself. "I'll stay here. Miguel said that they were on the east side of the building's porch."

No, that won't do. I extend my hand to her. "I don't think any of us need to be alone." Not anymore.

Sylvia scans the area, the darkness and the shadows. She braves the stairs and laces her fingers with mine. We're slow as we walk along the stone porch. Sylvia's head turns at each little sound, her wide eyes roaming the inside as if she's preparing for an impending attack.

Deep in my soul, I know no attack is coming.

"How are you so relaxed?" Sylvia asks. "Growing up in this town, all I've heard about are the terrible things that have happened here. All the deaths, the sketchy medical practices, the satanic rituals once the place was abandoned. This place is nothing but evil."

"Is it?" Sawyer asks when we turn the corner, and my heart leaps at the sight of him leaning against one of the stone pillars.

"I don't think this place is evil," I say.

"Neither do I." Sawyer takes out a folded bunch of papers from his back pocket and if he didn't look so incredibly sad, I might have smiled. It's Evelyn's diary.

"How can you say that?" Sylvia asks as she lets go of me.

Sawyer looks at me, extends the papers in his hands in Sylvia's direction, and I nod my head in affirmation. He pushes off the pillar and hands the diary to Sylvia. "When you're done, give it back to Veronica. It belongs to her."

Sylvia reverently takes the papers and Miguel drops an arm around her shoulder. "Let's give them some space." Miguel stares straight into my eyes. "When you two are done, he doesn't go anywhere without me."

"Okay," I say. They leave, and I give Sawyer my undivided attention. "You told them."

"I'm not keeping quiet about my mom anymore."

"I figured that, but that's not what I mean. You told them that you jump."

Unsure of himself, Sawyer shoves his hands into his pockets. "Seemed like the right thing to do. If I'm ratting out Mom, I should probably rat out myself."

I reach out, slip my fingers over his wrists and coax his hands out

336 ✻ KATIE McGARRY

of his pockets. He complies and pulls me in for a hug. The moment I rest my head on his chest and feel his strong arms around me, I close my eyes. All the stress, the tension, the fear bottled up inside me drains away, and I wish we could stay like this forever.

Sawyer kisses my head then rests his cheek against me. The strong release from his lungs tells me he's also been searching for peace, and for these brief few minutes at least, he's found it. He sighs again, but this time, it's with heaviness. I reluctantly pull away, and he takes my hands in his.

"What happened?" I ask.

"I confronted Mom in front of all of her friends at Sylvia's house."

My eyebrows rise. "Wow."

"Go big or go home, right?" He tries to smile, but it fails.

"How did that go?"

"Bad. Bad enough that I'm not sure she'll forgive me."

"She will," I say, but I don't know if it's true. I hope it will be true. I hope that this will be the catalyst for her to get some help, but I also know that the sucky part of free will is that we don't always choose wisely. "What happens now?"

Sawyer shrugs one shoulder. "I called my dad and told him that Lucy and I were coming sometime tonight and that there were problems with Mom."

"How did he take that?"

"I'm not giving him much of a choice, but he seemed okay. Concerned. He has a lot of questions, but I told him I'm not telling him anything until I get there."

My lips turn down as I stare at the floor. It's like a hole has opened up below me and I'm falling. Sawyer's doing what he needs to do, and I hate the ramifications for me. He's leaving, there's no way for him to know for how long, and for all I know, he's leaving forever.

It's what people do when they leave this town—they don't look back.

I inhale deeply and force my head up. "You're doing the right thing."

"I hope so. None of it feels good so maybe that means I'm on the right path. God knows I've been doing too many things that feel good for too long and it hasn't gotten me anywhere worth going."

I lean forward and nudge his shoulder. "What about me?"

Sawyer smiles, a real one, the type that touches his eyes. "You have been one of the most difficult situations in my life. I expect you to turn right and instead you walk on your hands going backward. Under your yearbook photo, your senior quote needs to be 'unpredictable.'"

I laugh, so does he, and then he lets go of one of my hands to cup my face. "I am so in love with you."

"Same," I whisper as my heart is breaking. He's leaving, and once he's gone, he'll let go.

Sawyer leans forward, brushes his lips against mine and my heart flutters into overtime. So much so that I'm dizzy and feel like I'm floating on air. I'm in the happiest of places that I will ever be.

He rests his forehead against mine. "I finished Evelyn's diary."

"What did you think?"

"When I started, I thought it was going to be nothing but gloom and doom. She was given a life-threatening diagnosis, but then she still had this energy bursting off the pages. She got down, she was homesick, and she got sad. But overall, she was happy."

Surprised by his answer, I edge back a little and meet his eyes. "She was."

"It makes me look at this place differently." Sawyer scans the walls.

"It does." For me, the old TB hospital has been a mystery, but not the type of mystery that most people believe. "Makes you wonder how many people who stayed here to cure also had their first kiss, met the loves of their lives, made best friends and had moments of laughter. All people focus on is the bad things that happened. Yes, people died, but there are people who tried to live a full life while they were here. There are people who got well enough to leave and live their lives away from here. We've talked so much about residual hauntings and that they're all bad. Makes you wonder if there are residual hauntings that are good. Surely the good ones would be more powerful than the bad."

Sawyer lets go of me and walks toward the large window opening and peers inside. "I've been thinking a lot lately—about me, Mom, Lucy and Dad, about what everyone wants from me and about myself as an addict and how I need to change. Until recently, I never thought of myself as an enabler, but I am. I've spent years bending and twisting myself to make people happy. First my dad after the divorce, then Mom, then Lucy and then teachers, friends and coaches. There's only been one time in my life when I've ever felt like me and not a shadow of the person I thought people needed me to be and that is with you."

Sawyer looks at me then, the love and sadness on his face so powerful that it's a battle to not weep.

"I love how you live," Sawyer says, but there's something in how he says it that makes me feel like he's about to drop something heavy. Something not good.

I blink because Glory said I wasn't living. She said I was dying slowly.

"Being around you is exactly what I needed," he says. "To see how you live life your way even though the world tells you it's wrong has given me courage. It's helped me in seeing that I'm an enabler to the people in my life because all of my decisions are based upon making everyone else happy in that moment, and not doing what's best for me or best for them."

I feel like Sawyer and I are standing near the edge of a cliff, but instead of both of us walking away from the edge, it's like we're teetering and one of us may fall. The sick sloshing in my stomach warns that it might be me.

"You asked me once if I believe ghosts are real, if residual hauntings are real."

"I did," I whisper.

"I didn't, but now I do."

I hold my breath, waiting for the fall.

"I've been making the same damn decisions based upon the same damn moment for years. Dad's request that I live with Mom, the burden of responsibility on my shoulders, and Mom's tears at night. I was eleven and those ghosts have haunted me every second of every day. Who knows, maybe the sage did work and it exorcised my ghosts. I'm not enabling anymore. No ghost, no residual haunting is going to make my decisions anymore. I'm going to be thinking about my best interests and the best interests of those I care for—even if those decisions aren't what makes them happy."

I swallow. "That's good."

He nods, then turns to fully face me. "I love you, Veronica, and I love how you love life."

The "but" hangs precariously in the air. The cold wind blowing through the trees and the empty hospital make me shake. I pull Dad's jacket tighter around myself.

"How did you get Evelyn's diary?" he asks.

"My mother found it and gave it to me."

Sawyer nudges the loose stone of the window with his shoe. "Why do you think she gave it to you?"

"So I wouldn't feel alone in my diagnosis." Even though Evelyn and I don't have the same thing, we both faced the same fate at a young age. "You read the diary. Evelyn was in a TB hospital and lived life to the fullest."

"Yes," Sawyer agrees. "But she also was fighting her disease. My question to you, Veronica, is why can't you live life and fight the tumor at the same time?"

"Because it's a fight I can't win," I snap.

"So Evelyn thought she could win hers? Over 110,000 people died every year in the US from TB in the 1900s. In 1918 there was an influenza pandemic that killed 675,000 Americans. You read her diary entries. Evelyn talked about the flu spreading through the hospital.

How many people did she say good-bye to? How many were sent home?"

"They could have gotten better."

"You've researched this hospital, same as I have. They tried to send people who were beyond hope to die at home. And think of the friend Evelyn would go and visit at a different part of the hospital, how terrible she said he looked. Evelyn was surrounded by death, a fight she had to know she probably wouldn't win and still she fought. She doesn't die at the end of the diary. She was living. Why won't you do the same?"

I'm stunned silent.

"Why?" Sawyer pushes. "You say you admire her, you say you read her diary so you wouldn't feel alone, you say your mom gave it to you for a purpose and I'm asking why you're giving up."

"I told you, I won't die like my mom."

"Fine, but maybe you should try living like her first before you decide on dying. I didn't know your mom, but I know you and I've met your dad and I'm betting your mom lived a life that was like no other."

I tremble. Not from the cold, but from how his truth strikes me deeply.

"Does your dad know you think the tumor is growing?" Sawyer asks quietly.

"Don't you dare tell him. That's my decision. Not yours. You told me your deepest secret and I would have never betrayed you like that."

Sawyer sadly shrugs his shoulders. "Maybe not, but maybe it should have never been a secret to begin with. Keeping Mom's secret didn't help anyone. Keeping mine hasn't helped, either."

"But how does telling anyone help if that person doesn't want help?" I challenge and immediately regret my words. "It'll be different with your mom."

Sawyer winces like he's in pain. "It could be different with you."

My soul literally shatters.

"I love you, Veronica, and I'm not enabling anyone anymore."

"You have never enabled me."

"I haven't," he admits. "But if you ask me to keep your secret when it's best that I don't, I am enabling you."

I straighten, my chin held high, like I'm a wounded animal being threatened. "Are you going to tell my dad?"

"I've got my own bad news I have to share with my own father," Sawyer says.

It's not a yes or a no, and my stomach twists. For him. For me. "Where does this leave us? With you leaving? With my dad in the dark about my tumor growing?"

"You should tell your dad. Even if you still decide not to fight the tumor, I'm telling you that secrets only hurt, not help."

"My situation isn't the same as yours."

"A secret is a secret."

Nausea races through me. "What's going to happen between us? Are we done?"

Sawyer walks toward me. My heart beating with each of his steps. He doesn't stop until he's close, very close. So close that his heat envelops me.

In the moonlight, Sawyer is beautiful. Heartbreakingly so. He looks down at me. Eyes filled with love and sorrow. My heart skips when his fingers brush along my cheek. "I remember the night I saw you up here. Standing on the window ledge, staring down at me with no fear. A blond halo of curls. A stare that could strike down the strongest of men. Beauty given by a god. Like some sort of apparition there to tell me that my world would never be the same."

"In a bad way?" I whisper as he places a hand on the curve of my waist. His touch makes it hard to think, to breathe.

"In the best way."

I turn my head toward his touch, kiss his hand, and he pulls my body into his. We melt together. As if out of the billions of people in the world, and stars in sky, the two of us were made perfectly for one another.

"Can we just stay this way?" I whisper. "Just like this? Forever?"

"I wish we could. If we did, I'd be the happiest man." Sawyer combs his fingers through my hair. The pull gentle and comforting.

"As far as I'm concerned," Sawyer says in a hushed tone, as if a lullaby, "we're not done, but the decision's more yours than mine. I'm not going to enable you on this. You tell your dad about your tumor growing and I'm yours. I'm not saying you have to change your mind on how you handle your tumor, but I'm not doing secrets. Someone once told me loving you requires sacrifice. They're right. I want to be with you, you want to be with me, but giving in now to be happy just for a few months isn't enough. I want more, and I want you to want more, too."

Sawyer's fingers slip to my chin, he lifts my head and brushes his lips to mine.

And then as if he didn't just absolutely crush me, hadn't become such a needed fixture in my life, Sawyer lets me go and leaves. Feeling weak, I lean my back against the cold stone wall for support. I shake from head to toe, not from the dropping air temperature, but due to the cold welling up inside me.

"Veronica?" Miguel asks from the corner and flashes the light of his cell in my direction. "Are you okay?"

I swallow then try to nod, but fail.

"Tell me when you're ready to head back," he says. "I'm with you, and Sylvia's with Sawyer now. We don't want anyone to be alone."

Alone. Faint footsteps from inside the hospital and I immediately turn my head to the sound. There's a shadow and I squint as it comes closer. With every centimeter forward, the shadow solidifies and my pulse picks up speed. I know that white dress, I know that blond hair, and I jump at how Mom's face is now that of an expressionless porcelain doll.

She shouldn't look like that. She shouldn't be here. She is tethered to the house. She shouldn't be anywhere but there.

"Veronica?" Miguel steps closer. "What's wrong?"

Miguel said he didn't want me to be alone. For years, I haven't been alone. Not really. Not when so many ghosts have haunted me, but now, I know nothing for sure other than I need to go home and I need to go home now.

SAWYER

Thursday November 7: PEACE. Weight 119 lb.

Great day today, alright, Diary. About dinner time, when we were all in the dining room, Benny Nabel announced that the Armistice with Germany had been signed. Then what a celebration we did have! We marched way over to the Pryor singing and cheering and then the boys came back behind us. At supper we had another parade. The West Wing fellows being the Kaiser.

After supper we had our entertainment in the MacDonald Solarium.

November 7, 1918—Armistice Day—the end of World War I. Evelyn was battling tuberculosis, the Spanish flu was devastating the US and the world, and this all happened while a war was being waged.

Then there was peace.

Is peace possible?

Lucy's sound asleep as I pull into a spot in front of Dad's condo. I place the car into park and glance in the rearview mirror at my sister. I hear all the time on TV and in the movies that kids are resilient. Question is: why should they have to be?

Maybe this is what should happen before anyone becomes a parent—*I (insert name) agree that when I become a parent, I therefore understand that my children's needs come first. That for at least eighteen years, it's not about me. It's about them.*

Doesn't seem that complicated, right? Not when you look at eighteen years in the grand scheme of a hundred. But adults don't do that. They like to play dress-up with their kid for a year or two, maybe be excited when they play a sport or land the role in the school play, but then after the hour is up and the pictures are taken for the sake of "making a memory," they declare that they need to find themselves when they figure out kids are hard.

Adults see children as toys or a solution to a problem, instead of a hard commitment. I don't think carrying a sack of flour at school is going to impress upon anyone what it's like to listen to my sister scream night after night in fear.

Maybe I'm bitter. No, I know I am, and I guess that's one of the many things I'll need to work on. Right after I tell my dad he's stuck with us for possibly a lot longer than he would have ever intended.

My cell pings for maybe the hundredth time in the past hour—all from Mom. All an indication she's drunk.

Mom: Please come home. This is all a misunderstanding.

Mom: Please. I don't want to be alone.

Mom: Sawyer, I need you here.

Mom: Please respond to me, Sawyer.

Mom: I love you. Do you not love me anymore?

That's the problem—I do. I don't know how to reply, and guilt settles in. Is it my job to help her see she's an alcoholic?

Lucy shifts in her seat and her eyelids flutter open. She looks at me. I watch her. My job, right now, is to take care of her.

Light flashes from the porch as Dad opens his front door. He steps out and his very pregnant girlfriend stands at the door, holding it open. I think of Veronica unwilling to enter a house without permission, feeling that she was death, she was hurt, and that people should think twice before allowing her into their lives.

Maybe Dad should be scared of me and Lucy. Trouble seems to follow us. I exit the car and my father stops in front of me. Concern oozes from him. "What's going on? Your mom has been calling me nonstop."

Great. "Have you answered?"

"I did. Once. But she didn't make any sense."

I rub my eyes then start for the backseat, but Dad gets there first. "I'll get her."

I feel helpless as Dad extracts Lucy. She doesn't automatically wrap her arms around him, instead looks at me for approval. Should she trust him? I don't know, but right now he's our safest bet. I nod and she apprehensively leans into him, her exhaustion winning out.

Dad carries her into the house while I bring in our bags. I try to say a warm, "Hi," to Tory as she lets me in. I then follow Dad up the stairs. What was once the baby's room now has two twin beds complete with pillows and comforters.

I stop short as my brain stops working. "Where's the crib?"

"Our room," Dad says as he pulls back the covers then lays Lucy on the bed.

"The baby will be fine with us in there when he's born," Tory says from the hallway.

Dad tucks Lucy in and mumbles some comforting words. She's so tired that she automatically rolls into a ball and closes her eyes. I wish anything was that easy for me. I back out of the room, Dad does the same, leaving the door halfway open. We return to the living room, and he and I stare at each other like we're strangers who pass by each other on the way to class. Someone we know, but don't.

"Would you like something to drink?" Tory asks.

I don't, but she wants to do something so I accept. She leaves, and Dad sighs heavily before dropping into a chair. I sit on the couch and decide to be honest. "I've been mad at you for a while."

"I know."

"I wouldn't be here if I had anywhere else to go."

"I know that, too." He meets my eyes, and I want to look away but don't. "But you're welcome here, and we want you here. I know I've messed up in the past, but I'm ready to be the dad you need now. Whatever it is, you're my son, and we'll figure it out."

I don't believe him. There are too many years of missed visits between us. Too much heartache of me choosing Mom's side. But he has welcomed me and Lucy in. Odds are, he has paid his child support on the fifteenth and thirtieth every month. "I'm sorry for showing up like this. You aren't going to like what I have to say."

Dad rolls his neck. "What's your mom done, Sawyer?"

"When I tell you, I'm not going to play this game anymore. The game where I tell you something about Mom, you blame her for everything and I'm stuck in the middle. I don't like it when she does it with you. I've always hated the game, and I'm the one who's been on the losing end of it. I tell you what's happening, and you work with me, not against me."

"I hear you, and I appreciate the honesty. Maybe that's what you and I need, to say what's on our minds instead of holding back."

To use my voice . . . the voice I'm finding. "Lucy and I need your help. I've got problems, and I'm learning how to deal with them. But the biggest issue at the moment is Mom's in trouble and I don't know how to help . . ."

VERONICA

One A.M.: Lightning-sharp pains through my skull. I toss and turn in my bed, hands on my head, crying into my pillow so Dad won't hear.

Two A.M.: My entire head pounds, a constant jackhammering. I do my best to stumble down the stairs as quietly as I can without waking Dad. Hard to do when the agony is so intense I can barely crawl.

Two-thirty A.M.: I drag myself into the downstairs bathroom, shut the door, and vomit into the toilet.

Three A.M.: I lay in the fetal position on the cold tile floor, the pain so overwhelming that I'm terrified that this time, I really am going to die.

Die.

My eyes burn and I shiver. This is not how I want to die. I don't want my father to find me on the bathroom floor. I don't want to be alone.

Alone.

Mom promised I'd never be alone. "Mom?" My voice is a crack, a broken whisper. "Mom, where are you?"

The window seat. That's where she was last. I try to push off the floor, but the heavy pain in my skull makes it impossible to stand.

Crawl. My only option is to crawl. On my knees, on my stomach, I inch along the floor then thank God that I hadn't closed the door all the way. I push it open and then claw my way across the room. Near the stairs, a fresh wave of torment starts and I collapse to the ground.

I roll with the dry heave, and I'm so hot that sweat rolls down my face. Yet I'm also cold and clammy. When I open my eyes, I spot Mom's bare feet near the window seat. "Mom?"

Her feet move, and I sob with relief when she comes my way. Then I want to cry again when she's not the emotionless porcelain doll, but my mom. Flushed cheeks, concerned eyes, radiating love. She crouches next to me. "You're sick, peanut."

"I know." A slicing pain registers at the back of my head and then strikes down my spine. I cry out with it and then do my best to muffle the sound. "Is it scary? Is it scary to die?"

For the first time, Mom touches my face. Her hands are cold, but I welcome the caress. So much that hot tears well up in my eyes and fall down my cheeks.

"You're very sick, V. You need help."

"Is it scary?" I push. "I need to know if death is scary."

She pushes the hair away from my face. "I can't let you do this to yourself. I can't. I love you too much." Mom turns her head toward the stairs. "Ulysses! Ulysses, I need you!"

Dad. She's calling Dad. "I don't want him upset." I double over as the pain seems to come from everywhere at once. "I love him, and I don't want him to hurt."

"This is what you don't understand about love, V." Mom touches my cheek again. "He loves you and you can't stop him from loving you. You don't get to decide when he hurts and when he doesn't hurt. All you get to do when someone loves you is either push them away or accept the love they are willing to give. If you push them away, you're knowingly hurting them. If you let them love you, there will still be hurt, but at least then you'll both have moments of happiness."

Mom turns her head again towards the stairs. "Ulysses! Come down here, now!"

I sob, the tears flow down my face and drip onto the floor. "He can't hear you. He can't hear me. Please tell me this is not how I'm going to die."

"Ulysses!" Mom shouts so loud I flinch.

"V!" Dad's feet pound against the stairs. "V! Where are yo—" Dad goes stark white then bolts for me and falls to his knees. "What's happened, V?"

"It hurts." The world has a funny feeling to it as I convulse with a dry heave.

"Your head?" Dad asks. "Is it your head?"

"She's dying, Ulysses!" Mom screams next to him, right in his ear. "Save her! You save our baby!" She flickers, and then yells again, "You save her! You promised me you'd save her!"

"I'm scared, Mom. Please don't leave me! Please!"

Mom grabs my hand, and I grab it back. "I'm here, peanut. I'm not leaving."

"Tell me it's not scary to die, Mom! Please tell me it's not scary to die!"

Dad grabs my face and forces me to look at him. "Who are you talking to, V? Tell me who you're talking to."

My throat swells and I shake my head, not wanting to answer, but then I think of Sawyer. I think of lies. I think of pain and I think of how I don't understand why Mom won't answer if death is painful, if death is scary. "I don't want to die. I'm scared, Daddy. I'm scared. I don't want to die."

Dad leaves me and I writhe as sharp pains hit my skull again. Hands again on my face, warm ones, not cold. Dad's deep voice, "I need an ambulance."

He gives his name, our address, all while wiping tears from my face, shushing me. "It's okay, V. It's okay."

It's not okay. Not at all. "I'm scared, I'm scared, I'm scared." Mom flickers again and that causes my heart to break in two. "No! You can't go! You can't go, Mom! I'm scared!"

"Who do you see?" Dad grabs my face again. His cell no longer to his ear. "Who are you talking to?"

"Tell him," Mom's voice is weak. "Tell him."

"Then you'll leave!" I cry.

Mom crouches in front of me, kisses my forehead and whispers, "I was never here. I've only been in your mind."

Then she's gone and I can't breathe. The pain through my entire body is too much for me to bear. I thrash, my body whipping in ways I can't control, and the sound I make is inhuman.

"V!" Dad shouts. Then I'm in his arms, and he's holding me tight. "I'm here, baby. I'm here. Don't you die on me! Don't you dare die on me!"

I grab on to the front of his shirt as the convulsions end. Darkness tunnels my vision and my mind has a fuzzy haze. "Don't let me go, Daddy. Please don't let me go."

"I won't, baby." His voice breaks as I struggle to stay awake. "I swear to God, I won't."

My mind is aware before my body. The first thought—there's no pain. None. In fact, it's a strange feeling, a floating feeling, like I'm not connected to anything at all.

My heart skips a beat and my chest constricts. Oh, God, I died.

Sawyer

Dad

Nazareth

Jesse

Scarlett

Leo

Oh, God, I didn't do any of it right.

"V?" Dad says, and there's pressure on my hand like someone is holding it.

My chest. My heart. The pressure on my hand. I felt it all. I'm not dead. Not yet. I swallow and turn my head. It takes a lot of effort to open my eyes and when I do everything is blurry. Blinking doesn't help. Just makes Dad a blob of a blur and I'm unable to make out anything else.

"Dad?" For as much effort as that took, I should have been a lot louder.

"I'm here, peanut."

"I can't see right." Panic sets in. "It's too blurry. I can't make anything out."

I can hear footsteps farther away, the squeak of a chair next to me and the pressure of Dad's hold on my hand tightening. "We'll figure it out. It's okay, baby. I promise it will be okay."

My mind runs at a million miles an hour, and I grab his hand back to make sure he won't go away. "The tumor's growing. I see Mom and I know I shouldn't see Mom. I don't want to die. I thought I did, but I don't. I don't want to die. Please help me not die."

"Shh," he says, and my hair is pushed away from my face. "We don't know if the tumor has grown yet."

"I've known. I've hidden it, it's grown. I should have told you. I'm sorry. I'm so sorry."

"It's okay. Everything's okay. We're in the ER. We think you had a seizure. We're waiting on the nurses to take you to the MRI scan. We'll know more then."

"I'm sorry," I say again, and tears burn my eyes. I lied to him. I disappointed him. I've lied to myself. "I'm scared." I've been scared, and I've been trying to tell myself that I'm not.

"I know, peanut." His voice breaks, and he clears it. A hand on my face and my tears are brushed away. "I'm not going to let anything happen to you. I promise."

My eyes close again, against my will, and my mind starts to drift. But then I snap my eyes back open. "Tell Sawyer I told you."

"I will."

"I mean it."

"I will. I called Jesse. He and Scarlett are in the waiting room.

They're texting Sawyer and Leo with updates. Nazareth has been here in the room with me. He just left to get the nurse to tell them about your sight, but he'll be back. Go back to sleep, V," Dad says in a soft voice. "You've got a big fight in front of you, and you're going to need your strength."

VERONICA

Living.

           I am alive.

But my brain . . .

     isn't quite working right.
     It happened fast.

         Maybe life happened slow.

My memories don't work so good.
Not even when life is happening in the moment
     I still can't remember.

"When's the surgery?" I ask.

"You already had the surgery," Jesse says next to me. He's in the chair next to my bed. His legs are stretched out, his baseball cap covers his red hair. He was watching TV, but now he glances over at me. The hospital room is dark except for the dim light over my bed. On the other side of the room, my dad is asleep on a plastic couch.

"When?" I ask.

"A few days ago."

My forehead furrows. "Why didn't anyone tell me?"

"We did."

I shake my head and stop as it feels weird. I go to touch, but Jesse reaches out and gently puts my hand down. There's an IV in my arm, and I don't remember that, either. "I only remember the ER."

"That happened two weeks ago."

I blink. "I don't remember."

"I know, and it's okay."

It seems like I should feel emotion, but I don't. With how dark it is outside and how quiet it is in the hospital, it seems like I should be asleep, but I feel wide awake. A twinkling light catches my attention, and there's a moment of cloudy awe in my hazy brain.

There are Christmas lights strung across the room. On the dresser across from the bed is a tiny prelit Christmas tree and a menorah along with wrapped presents. The menorah means Nazareth has been here. He's Jewish, and I celebrate the holiday with his family.

"Is it December?"

"No. I wish I could take credit for it, but Sawyer and his friends did this for you. I have to admit, it's brilliant. Nazareth brought the menorah in, and he's been a show-off, bringing a present in every day." Jesse tilts his head toward Nazareth who sits in the chair next to him. There are two chairs next to my bed, and it's odd how I didn't notice that before.

"Hanukkah is better," Nazareth says, "More days of presents."

It's a memory of a joke between us, and I want to smile as I try to remember it, but it bothers me that I can't remember the joke nor do I remember how to smile. "Does Sawyer know I had surgery?"

"Yes, he comes every day around five," Jesse says. "He stays until ten. You tell him he smells like a pool. Sawyer would stay longer if he could, probably all night, but his dad is strict on curfew. Plus Sawyer wants to be there at night for his sister. He brought you flowers today."

I frown as I look at the red roses on the table next to me. I don't think Sawyer lives with his mom. He said something about living with his dad, but all that information is right there behind a glass wall in my brain and I can't quite grasp it. "That's a long drive for him."

"It's a long drive for me. We're in Louisville. Scarlett comes on the weekends. She's the one who braids your hair and you tell her not to let us touch your hair again. I'll admit, when I did your hair, it was scary."

I don't understand at all. "Then why are you here if this is Louisville?"

"Because you're our best friend," Nazareth says.

I glance between them as I'm starting to feel small. "Did I know about the surgery?"

Nazareth nods. "We tell you. You forget. We've been betting on which questions you'll re-ask the most."

"You're a night owl," Jesse says. "Your dad needs to be awake during the day to talk to doctors so we volunteered for the night shift. Your dad won't leave this room, but he does manage to sleep while we talk. To be honest with you, I'm glad we got the night shift. You're more fun then."

"You sleep too damn much during the day," Nazareth agrees.

I'm curious which question I ask the most, but then decide it's not important. "Am I broken?"

"No," says a new voice and I watch as Leo walks into the room. He closes the door behind him, hands Nazareth a water then Jesse a Sprite. "You've never been broken."

It's Leo. Is that possible? "I'm dreaming."

"You're not," Leo says. "I can't be here as much as everyone else, but I come when I can."

"Are we friends again?"

Leo glances at Nazareth and Jesse, then back at me. "It hurts every time she asks," he mumbles. At least it's what I think he mumbles.

"I know," Jesse says to him. "But at least she's giving you the same answer every time."

"True." Then Leo stands at the end of the bed. "I want to be friends again. You've always been my best friend. But it's up to you, V. I'll be here as long as you want me."

He has always been one of my best friends, too. "I want to be friends again, but I still have a tumor." Wasn't that the problem?

"They took out as much as they could during the surgery," Leo says. "Your dad says they feel positive that the chemo and radiation will get everything else. But even if it's still there, I still want to be your friend."

That sounds like a good thing. I think. A ghost of a memory worries my forehead. "I think I was pushing people away. Is that what I did? Is that why we stopped being friends?"

"It wasn't just you." Leo drops his head, and then when he lifts it, he seems overwhelmed, yet happy, and my brain doesn't understand. "But it's okay. I'm sorry I messed up. It won't happen again."

Confused, I look over at Jesse. "This is real?"

"Yes."

I study Leo. "You're okay that we're friends again? Because I'm dating Sawyer, so it's just friends." An image of Sawyer leaning into me, the sweet pressure of his lips on mine and then him showing me red flowers pushes through. Did that happen today? "I'm in love with him."

Leo gives me a crooked grin. "It's good, V. He and I had dinner together last night."

Now that is weird. I look back at Jesse again. "Are you sure this is real?"

"It's real, and you're not broken." Jesse points at his head. "The confusion and memory losses are from swelling in the brain. The doctor says it's normal, and you'll get better."

I cock an eyebrow and the action feels weird against my head. "So I'm normal now."

Nazareth, Jesse and Leo laugh. Harder than they should, as if it's the funniest, most joyous thing they've ever heard. They calm down, then share a glance, not one of tension, but as if relieved.

"Naw, V." Nazareth winks at me. "You'll never be normal."

I think that's good, but then I don't remember why that's good and then I don't remember why I should be happy. I have a brain tumor.

I glance over at Jesse, and I'm surprised to see him sitting there. "When's the surgery?"

VERONICA

She's dead.

I wake with a start and my hands shake.

Mom, I was dreaming of Mom. Her beautiful laugh, her beaming smile, the way she always made me feel better on my worst days. I glance around the room and she's not here. If she was really a ghost, she'd be here. Period. Which means she wasn't real. She was never real.

And she's gone.

I try to sit up, but the IV in my arm yanks. Pain, and I flinch.

"Are you okay?" Dad jumps from his spot next to me in the chair. His finger on the red emergency button next to the hospital bed.

Tears burn my eyes, my chest aches and I can't seem to catch my breath. I place a hand over my heart as it hurts. Hurts so bad. Pins and needles, it's ripping apart.

Dad presses the button over and over again as he watches me. "Tell me what hurts. Is it your chest? Can you breathe?" He pushes and keeps pushing and the sliding glass door of my ICU room opens so quickly that it startles me.

Two nurses walk in, one immediately taking her stethoscope from around her neck. "What's going on, V? Are you in pain?"

"Yes." I can barely make out the words, choking with the lack of air.

"Where does it hurt? Your head?"

"My . . ." I can't suck in air. "My chest."

"Her chest?" Dad's worry causes my heart to jump. "Is it a clot?"

Calm and emotionless, the nurse pushes another red button on the wall. One nurse checks my vitals, my blood pressure cuff tightening on my arm as the first nurse leans me forward and listens to my lungs. "Can you take in a breath for me, V?"

I shake my head as my body starts to tremble. I try to breathe in, but it's hard to do. "It hurts."

"I know, honey, and we're trying to figure out why."

Why? I know the why. "She's dead. Mom is dead. She's dead. She's been dead and—" I choke on the next word as hot tears fog my vision. The two nurses glance at each other as Dad seems to sadly be filled with relief.

"Panic attack?" one of the nurses says, and the other nods as she continues to listen to my chest.

She takes the stethoscope out of her ears. "The doctor had some medicine prescribed in case we ran into something like this. We can put it in your IV. How does that sound?"

"Do it," Dad says, and he takes one of the nurses' spots next to my bed. They both leave, and he takes the hand I have pressed against my chest in both of his.

I try to suck in a breath, but it hurts too much. "Mom's dead."

Tears glisten in his eyes. "She's dead."

For days, my thoughts have felt like bubbles blown by a child. My emotions have felt distant, as if I've been separated from them by a glass wall. But now, it's like the wall shattered and I'm being cut open by the shards of glass. The grief—it's overwhelming. Like being blasted by heat after standing in a freezer.

"She was dead, but she came back," I try to say, but the words are sobs. "She came back so I wouldn't be alone. She's the one who called for you that night. You came down because she yelled for you."

"No, peanut, you yelled for me."

"Mom yelled your name!" I shout, feeling like a two-year-old stomping her feet.

"You yelled my name."

I shake my head too fast and Dad drops my hand to capture my face in his hands to keep it still. "You yelled my name, V. You. Not your mom. When I came down you were talking for both you and her. You were carrying the conversation. Sawyer heard you do the same thing a few nights before I took you to the ER. It was the tumor. A hallucination. Your mom's gone, V. I'm sorry, she's gone."

My throat constricts, my entire body trembles and I can't see through the blurriness in my eyes. "I don't want her to be gone."

Dad's voice breaks. "I know, baby. I don't want her to be gone, either."

The sound that leaves me is my heart breaking. My shoulders shake and my father wraps an arm around me, then another arm weaves under my legs. I'm lifted and then he's holding me. My arms twine around his neck like I'm a child and I cry. I cry hard, I cry long, and my shoulder is wet as Dad weeps with me.

A nurse walks in, we ignore her, and something cold enters my veins. My mouth tastes weird and a few minutes later, the tears are less, my breathing eases and my father holds me as he hums an old Aerosmith song—my mom's favorite.

I wake and I'm in bed. Sawyer's beside me. My head is on his chest, his arm is wrapped tightly around me. The light in the hospital room is wrong. Plus, I can hear rain hitting the roof. I pop my head up and then remember that we're home.

I'm home. It's Sunday, I've been home since Friday and Sawyer's spending the weekend with me. I sigh heavily. Chemo starts tomorrow, but I'll worry about that then as there's nothing I can do about it now.

There are purple and pink lights strung around my room. A basket full of chocolates and jelly beans is on my bedside table. Very colorful construction-paper bunnies and eggs are taped all over my room thanks to Lucy. There are stuffed rabbits of varying size thanks to Sylvia and Miguel—and I try to ignore the fact that everyone at school now knows that I had brain tumor surgery and that Sylvia and Miguel have been running holiday drives for me so I can have as many holidays as I want for as long as I want. Yes, the sentiment is nice.

Greer told me last night that once I was done with chemo and radiation that we would do a Passover dinner together—even if it's not officially Passover. A celebration, like that of the Israelites, of death passing me by.

Because Dad is awesome, he's allowing Sawyer to sleep in my bed with me. I think he wanted to say no, but then saw how I smiled at the idea of Sawyer next to me. Anyhow, all I do is sleep, and Sawyer's a trooper for spending hours watching reruns on cable while waiting on the brief few minutes that I'm actually awake.

The only time Sawyer leaves me on the weekends is to go to his AA meetings with his friend Knox. He doesn't see his mom. She's in denial of her problem, and his father filed for emergency sole custody and won. Now, his dad is going for permanent full custody.

Sawyer and his father easily fall into fights, but Sawyer mentioned that since his brother has been born, they fight less. At least that's what I think he said. It all could have been a dream.

"Hey, sleepyhead." Sawyer gives me a hesitant smile.

"You smell like a pool," I say, but I've grown to love the scent. It makes me think of him and the nights we used to kiss for hours.

"You say that a lot."

"Because it's true." I rest my chin on his chest and hate that even though all I've done is sleep, I want to sleep more. "I'm sorry I'm not good company."

"It doesn't bother me. Remember—we had a deal. You told your dad the truth, and I'm yours."

I scoot up the bed and rest my head on my pillow so that I'm on the same level as him. "Will you kiss me?"

Sawyer's smile grows and his eyes twinkle. "Your dad's going to kick my ass if he finds out."

"I won't tell. I mean, I'd have to at least be awake to do that."

Sawyer chuckles. "True." His eyes darken as he looks at my lips, an indication he's been thinking about this as much as I've been dreaming about it—all the time.

He leans forward, and the electricity of that moment right before the kissing sizzles in the air. My skin prickles with excitement, and when his lips meet mine, I can barely breathe.

His lips move, my lips move, and when I place my hand on his chest because I want so much more, Sawyer pulls away. "Your dad's coming."

"No, he's not." But then my door opens and I can't help but laugh. Dad looks at me, looks at Sawyer, and then scowls. He leaves, but doesn't close the door.

"My dad has a camera in here, doesn't he?" I ask.

"Yeah." Sawyer's body shakes as he laughs. "In case you should need him while he's downstairs."

First thing I'm going to do when I'm not so damned tired is take an ax to the security system in the kitchen.

D ad is chatting nonstop, which means he's nervous. He's moving around the first floor of our apartment gathering things into a duffel bag. Picking up anything and everything he thinks we might or could ever need for my first chemo treatment.

I sit in the window seat, my knees drawn to my chest. Gentle rain pats against the windows. The house feels weird. It's home, but not home, and I'm a bit empty. Mom's not here. I miss her. Desperately.

My cell pings and I glance down at it to find a text from Sawyer:

Where's the first place you want to go when you're done with your treatments?

I frown as it feels like I should know that answer. I frown deeper as I realize I don't have any type of answer. I never really thought about life past graduation. It has always been right here, right now. The beach?

Sawyer: Why the question mark?

Me: Because everything feels like a question mark.

Dad jogs up the stairs, and thankfully, stops talking for at least two beats. My cell pings again. I expect Sawyer, but tilt my head in surprise. Glory: I'm here if you need someone.

I stare at her words then scroll through my cell. One ring and she answers, "Hi, V."

"Hey."

"How are you?"

I could lie, but don't feel like it. "Scared."

"Understandable."

"Have you searched my future?" *Am I going to live?*

"Do you want me to?"

I squish my lips to the side. "If it's good news then yes."

"Your future is based off your decisions, you know this. Nothing is ever defined."

While I do know this, it's not why I called. "Was my mom ever here?" I don't pretend that my lying about Mom for months hasn't been a topic of conversation for people in my life.

There's silence on her end. "Is she there now?"

"No. I haven't seen her since the night Dad took me to the ER. But does that mean she wasn't real? I mean, I spent months researching ghosts and hauntings and I saw things and experienced things that proves there's something more, something beyond."

"There is something more. There is something beyond."

"But was she real?"

Glory sighs heavily into the phone. "Your dad would like me to tell you no. In fact, he's told me point-blank to tell you no. I never felt

364 ஜ KATIE McGARRY

her, V. She never appeared to me, she never talked to me, but that doesn't mean she wasn't real. As far as I'm concerned, I'm grateful for whatever happened that night. That conversation you had with your mom, yelling out for your father—that saved your life."

She's right. It had. Things had happened in my brain. Things the doctors were able to stop. Otherwise, Dad would have found me dead in the morning. I let Glory go and stand from the window seat.

I'm slow as I touch the different pieces of furniture in my house, my home. The couch where Mom and I would curl up together after her treatments. The table where Dad and I have shared many meals. The desk where I spent hours poring over Dad's finances for his business, and then my eyes fall on the piano. The one that my mother played when she was a child. The one she taught me how to play before I could sing my ABCs. The one I spent hours playing for her when she was sick and she said it was the only thing that brought her joy.

Then she died and I stopped. Maybe Glory was right. Maybe it was in that moment that I decided to die, too.

Dust covers the aging, upright piano and I rub my hand along the wood. Dust bunnies float in the air and fall to the ground. I push back the wooden cover and my heart thumps at the sight of the white resin keys. It's been so many years there's no doubt that the piano is out of tune, yet I'm drawn to hear the chord.

I try the C first, then my fingers spread out for the chord. The pitch is off, but the sound is sweet. I close my eyes as the music vibrates along my skin and in my blood.

The piano bench scratches against the floor as I pull it out and sit. My left hand touches the keys, pushes down, and I breathe out as the automatic movement of my hands makes me feel as at home as the scent of waffles on Saturdays.

I'm rusty, definitely off, the piano is way out of tune, but the music feels . . . good.

In the silence after the last note finishes ringing, I turn and find Dad staring at me. Tears in his eyes, and it hits me, he's missed this. "That was beautiful, V."

It wasn't. It was full of flaws. I know it, he knows it, but what was beautiful was that I finally found the courage to play.

barely make it to the toilet, my hands catching the rim as I fall forward with the dry heave. There shouldn't be anything left in my stomach, but somehow I still throw up bile.

I'm sick. So sick, and I don't want to be sick anymore. Chemo sucks. Radiation sucks. My life sucks. Each time, I think my reaction to the treatment will be better, but it's not.

I lay my head against the cold porcelain rim of the toilet and Sawyer's on the floor next to me. Lifting my head, placing a newly washed and dried towel under my cheek, he wipes a cool washcloth around my mouth and neck.

He doesn't have to lift my hair—there's no hair left. Tears prick my eyes, and my nose runs as I start to ugly cry. I don't want to do this anymore.

Sawyer rubs my back and says soft, comforting words, but he doesn't understand. I don't want to be sick anymore. I hurt. My stomach hurts. My head hurts. My skin hurts. I hurt.

"I'm sorry you're doing this," I can barely say before a rush of nausea hits me hard and fast. I turn my head back into the toilet, again.

Sawyer goes to the sink. The water turns on and when he returns, the washcloth is cold against my neck.

"Oddly enough, I've had years of experience. This time, though, it's my choice. With Mom, I felt like I had to. Now, there's no other place I'd rather be."

I shake my head. "I don't want you to have to do this with me."

"Maybe you need to learn it's not about you. It's all about me."

I glance at him like he's crazy. Did he just say this moment is about him? He winks, cracks a grin and I somehow laugh. Which is appreciated, yet also causes me to dry heave, again.

A part of me wants to die as the nausea overpowers me, but my will to live is stronger.

So much so.

Nazareth is reclining at the window seat when Sawyer carries me out of the bathroom. He lays me on the freshly made bed—something Nazareth or Dad must have done while I was in the bathroom. My best friend holds up a joint.

"A special plant from your mom?" I whisper-ask as my throat is raw from all the vomiting.

He shakes his head. "Medical grade. Mom's curious what the legal competition is like. Your dad had me go with him to pick this stuff up. Felt weird to walk into a store with a prescription for pot."

"Medical marijuana," Sawyer corrects. One of my specialists is in Ohio, and Dad and Nazareth were able to get the prescription filled there.

I smile. Sawyer kisses me on my shaved head, and while the action makes me feel loved, it also makes me feel self-conscious. I look up at him, and when he smiles down at me, it's as if I'm beautiful and that just makes me love him more.

"Text me when you get home," I whisper.

"I will. Get some sleep."

We say "I love you," he shares some odd boy handshake with Nazareth, and he's back on the road to Louisville for the week.

SAWYER

Ulysses makes dinner every night I'm here, and has Nazareth, Jesse, Scarlett or Leo spend an hour or two with V to give me a break to eat, catch up with Lucy and relax. He even makes it on Sunday nights and insists that I eat before I hit the road for Louisville.

At first, I felt awkward, but then quickly figured out we both needed the time. Time to sit. Time to talk about our worries with Veronica. Time to talk about our own exhaustion. Time to talk about the other areas in our lives. Plus, the man is a damn good cook.

Tonight, we had steak. We hug before I leave and he promises to text updates on Veronica's appointments tomorrow.

With my backpack slung over my shoulder, I text Dad to let him know I'm on my way. Things aren't always easy between us, but we're both trying. I cut him slack because he went from having no kids to three. He cuts me some slack because he feels guilty for dropping the ball on the whole parenting thing.

Lucy likes Tory, and she likes Lucy back. The biggest bonus— Lucy's in therapy and only wakes two times a week crying. Each night without tears is a win in my book.

I trot down the stairs, go out the front door, and my stomach sinks when I spot Mom on the steps. Dad didn't just win emergency custody of me and Lucy, he was also granted a temporary restraining order for us. One that's close to ending, but one that's still in effect. One that has kept Mom from talking to me while I've visited Veronica.

She turns on the step and looks at me. It's Mom, but not Mom. There's no makeup on her face, her hair isn't perfectly done. In fact, she's imperfection. She's in sweats and an oversized sweatshirt to help against the cold, wet, winter evening.

A jolt of recognition causes a pain in my chest. The sweatshirt is one of mine.

Was the restraining order too much? In my opinion, yes, but at the same time, I appreciated the space.

"I saw your car, and I've been waiting on you," she says. "Hoping you'd come down soon."

Hurt. It bleeds from me. And in this moment, I realize how much I miss her.

I take the two steps and sit down beside her. Not close. Her on one side of the stairs, me on the other. Ulysses asked me if I wanted him to kick her out of the apartment, and I told him unless she wasn't paying rent, no. I don't want the worst for my mom—I just want her to want to get better.

Mom's nervous. I haven't seen her like that very often. She unfastens and refastens her Fitbit over and over again.

I stare out into the dark evening. The rain is steady, the air temperature, cold. I pull up the zipper on my jacket and watch as my breath comes out in a billow of smoke.

"How's Veronica?" Mom breaks the silence.

"Okay. The chemo and radiation are making her sick and we're having a tough time finding medications that can help with the nausea. But I think Ulysses found something today that may work. The doctors are being aggressive with her treatment and are hopeful. I won't lie. It's going to be a long road, but the doctors think everything's going to work."

I hope it does. I need it, too.

"That's good," Mom says. "I've been praying for her."

I've been praying for Veronica and Mom. In fact, all I feel like I do anymore is pray. It's a constant conversation in the back of my head between me and God. One that never shuts off.

"Sylvia and Miguel keep me updated on her condition and treatments."

"That's good." I steal her response. I talk and text with Sylvia and Miguel often. See them occasionally when I'm in town to see V. They've both been by to visit her. Not nearly as much as Nazareth, Jesse, Scarlett and Leo, but they consider her a friend now and V feels the same.

"They keep me updated on you as well."

Same.

"They said you're still swimming?"

"Yeah. As long as Veronica keeps doing well, I plan on swimming in some club meets starting in February. I met with the swim coach from the University of Louisville. He's interested in me. A few other colleges have shown interest, too."

She brightens. "That's good."

It is. Swimming keeps me focused and away from jumping off cliffs. Gives me an outlet. Something Knox has encouraged, Veronica has encouraged, and Dad has encouraged. But it was Ulysses that convinced me—explaining his experiences with Veronica's mom and the importance of taking care of myself so I can better take care of the woman I love.

"Sylvia said you're homeschooling?"

Sort of. "I'm still enrolled at the high school here. Because I'm so close to graduating, my teachers are working with me so I can do my classes online." And because I know she's hungry for information: "Lucy's in school in Louisville. It's a good one."

A fancy one that Tory's friends and family rave about. Some sort of Latin school that only goes so many days a week. I was wary at first, but Lucy loves it, and I like the extra time with her during the day. "They've been patient with Lucy. Understanding, too. Something she needs."

A flash of hurt and guilt strikes Mom's face and that hurts me. Why did I have to say the last part? I let out a frustrated breath as I realize I might have said it on purpose—to hurt her. Because I am still angry and forgiveness is a fickle beast.

"Have Sylvia and Miguel told you that I've stopped drinking?" she asks.

I nod. They told me that she hasn't touched alcohol with any of her friends. Sylvia said Mom's story about her drinking varies with whom she's talking to, but she's shot straighter with Hannah than with anyone else. Any inconsistency in her stories bothers me. Also, not knowing what she's doing in her free time is a hot-button topic.

"Can I be honest with you on something?" she asks.

I nod again, not really sure if she's capable of such a thing.

"Not drinking hasn't been nearly as easy as I thought it would be. Because that's what I thought for a long time—that if I wanted to, I could stop. I just didn't want to. But not drinking, especially with you and Lucy gone . . . it's been hard."

"Are you still drinking?"

"No," she says too quickly.

Anger tightens my muscles and I glare at her.

Mom immediately glances away and her face draws down. "It's not easy. I try . . . but it's not easy."

"I get it."

"I don't think you do," she says with bite. "You don't understand how I just feel so . . . so . . ."

"Thirsty," I finish for her. I look over at her and when she finally meets my eyes, I say, "I get it."

Her eyebrows draw together. "How?"

I look down at the text I wrote to Dad about heading back to Louisville, then figure I'll just send him another telling him I'll be an hour or two later, that I decided to head to a meeting before hitting the road. "Want to go somewhere with me?"

"Where?"

"A meeting I like to go to. There's this guy there, Knox. He has a way of explaining things to me about how I feel in ways I can't do yet."

Mom wraps her arms around herself, making herself smaller. "What type of meeting?"

She still doesn't quite see it—herself as an alcoholic—as someone who needs help. I get that, too. "The type of meeting where they're okay if you come a hundred times and call each one your first visit because they understand that you belong there way before you do. A place that gives you the space you need or the support you need if that's what you choose. It's a place that doesn't judge. I like it there. I think you might, too."

Mom's eyes flit around me. "I don't understand how you know about these things."

"If you come with me, I'll tell you."

Mom glances down at the oversized sweatshirt and sweats, and I shake my head. "Just come as you are, Mom. In fact, it's the best way to go."

She stands and pulls down the sweatshirt, a sign she's unsure again, but she does take the step that I want in the right direction. "Okay. I'll go."

VERONICA

It's late summer. Above me, there are a million stars in the sky. Below my bare feet is cool sand. Beyond is the dark ocean. The waves roll along and then crash on the beach. A constant, repetitive noise that's music to my ears.

There's a breeze tonight. Not enough to whip the sand into a frenzy and sting my sensitive skin. Just the perfect type that when I hold out my arms, turn my face up to the wind and close my eyes, I feel like I'm flying.

There's hair on my head now. Not a lot. Just enough that I can feel the breeze lift the baby-fine tendrils. My hair doesn't seem to be growing back the same as before and the doctor said that's normal. It's not my typical blond, but a tad bit darker, more golden, and so far, my hair is flatiron straight. It's not long enough to determine whether or not it will curl, but there's something deep within me that says it won't.

I'm changed, and somehow it feels appropriate for my outside appearance to reflect what has happened on the inside. I started my cancer treatment one person and I'm leaving it another. Some parts better, a few worse. But that's change—finding beauty in the imperfections.

On my last scan, there was no sign of the tumor and my port was removed. No one is ready to say *remission* yet, but when the doctors smile at me now, it's with light in their eyes. As if they really weren't sure that what they had hoped for before could really happen, but now it seems possible.

Water laps at my feet and the bubbles tickle my toes. The air tastes of salt and sand. I breathe in deeply and do my best to take it all in.

My immune system is slowly repairing itself, but to appease Dad and my doctors, we're avoiding large crowds on this trip. During the day, we hang out at the condo Sylvia's parents own then venture to the beach at night. The condo is fancy, is on one of the highest floors of the building and has a balcony overlooking the sea.

Sylvia and Miguel allowed Sawyer and me to have the corner bedroom with the view of the ocean. We spend a lot of time with the door to the balcony open, lying tangled up with each other, kissing then watching the deep blue water. He'll whisper to me that he loves me, I whisper that I love him back. Both of us are more than ready to move on from doctor appointments, treatments and test results.

Sawyer talks about his plans to swim in college and how he's not sure yet if he'll live on campus or live with his dad who will soon be moving into a house with more bedrooms. I stay quiet as I'm a bit baffled by the idea of a future. I never allowed myself the possibility of one, and standing on the edge of the ocean, I feel very small.

My future is now as huge and wide as this sea—who will I be in the midst of it?

In the water, Miguel, Sawyer and Sylvia laugh, and thanks to the moonlight, I watch them. Shadows in the moving water. They're all accomplished swimmers and didn't blink twice at entering the ocean without the light of day.

A tall shadow moves from the water, and Sawyer has a contagious and fantastic grin. He's dripping from head to toe and half naked, water cascading over his pronounced muscles, and I can feel the heat of the blush on my cheeks. He's beautiful and he belongs to me.

"Swim with me."

If I had eyebrows, they both would have raised. They haven't grown in yet, but I'm hoping they will soon. "I didn't just go through countless rounds of chemo to drown in the ocean. I sink like a rock, remember?"

Sawyer places a hand on the curve of my waist and draws me into him. I'm in a bikini, he's wearing a Speedo. My entire body grows very warm with so much skin-to-skin contact.

"I remember you floating just fine." Sawyer rubs a hand up and down my back, and I curl further into him. "Besides, I promised then and I promise now that I'll get you back to dry land."

I purse my lips, still unsure.

He reaches up and smooths out my mouth, causing my heart to beat faster.

"Once you get through the breakers, the water is smooth, like glass, and it's warm. Just a few feet out there's a sandbar where the water will only reach your knees." Sawyer leans down and brushes his lips along my neck. Pleasing goose bumps form on my arms. "Trust me to take you out. I'll even carry you if you want."

Carry me. He's carried me for months. To and from the bathroom, up and down the stairs. To and from the car for appointments. I'm tired of being carried. I'm ready to live.

A rush of energy courses through me and when Sawyer takes in my expression, his wicked smile matches mine.

"I remember that smile," he says with a spark in his eyes like he's reliving a good memory. "It either meant I was about to get schooled by you or that I might need bail money. What trouble am I about to get into?"

I laugh and I love how his body vibrates against mine as he chuckles with me.

"Teach me to swim," I say.

Sawyer tilts his head like he thinks that's a terrible idea. "Now?"

"Why not? You teach kids who can barely walk to swim four out of seven days a week." Sawyer teaches at his swim club and local Y in Louisville. "Surely you can teach me."

"Yeah, but in the ocean? In the dark?" He squeezes me closer, but being smaller and because he's slick from the ocean, I'm able to twist and duck out of his arms.

I walk backward into the surf. Adrenaline pumps quickly in my veins from excitement and fear. "I'm alive, Sawyer, and I'm ready to live again."

His eyes wander up and then down, a seductive slide of his gaze, as if he's also very interested in living. "There are rules for learning to swim."

"Rules don't apply to me, remember?"

"Oh, I remember." His smile leaves me nearly breathless, then the wave that crashes into my back steals the rest of the air from my lungs.

I squeal, Sawyer's immediately by my side, his hand holding mine, but he doesn't sweep me up, instead he is talking me through what to do. I laugh, Sawyer laughs, I swim, almost sink, then swim again. I fail, I try again, I fail, I sort of succeed.

The waves roll up then down, always one right after the other, but I don't give up. I never give up. And neither does Sawyer. He's right beside me. Patient, kind, and doesn't once try to do it for me. He encourages, but he lets me fight on my own.

And then we reach the sandbar, laughing. I fall into his arms and we kiss, kiss some more, and we enjoy every second of living.

SAWYER

⟨ℒ⟩

Monday November 18: It started out to be pretty nice today and then it rained. Helen and I took a little walk this morning. We had rehearsal this afternoon from 4 to 5 and another tonight from 6:30 to 7:30. It went fine tonight. Better than it ever has before.

We had services tonight. Rev. Lubin came. Saw Morris and talked to him for awhile.

Found part of MacD's sketch for Thanksgiving. Haha.

I often reread the last entry of Evelyn's diary. I don't know if I'm searching for some sort of clue of what she was really thinking in the moment or searching for context of what happened next.

The only solace is that the entry was . . . simple, peaceful. The living of the day-to-day with the idea that tomorrow will definitely come.

Veronica plays the piano. I thought her voice was the most beautiful sound in the world. It still is, but listening to her play is a close second.

She's taking lessons now, and she's considering applying to a conservatory. Not for this coming year, as she's missed all the deadlines, but next. She's focusing on finishing her senior year online this summer and then on honing her musical skills. Veronica was able to keep up with some of her classes this past year, but there were some that were too much.

One step at a time, that's what Ulysses told her. She and I took that to heart.

I sit on the couch in her apartment, a computer on my lap. Sylvia, Miguel and I finished the senior thesis paper without Veronica—but it was a scaled-down version because the leader of our team wasn't there to help us properly. We did great on it, but it wasn't what any of us truly thought it could be.

Now with Veronica back to work on graduating, we asked if we could redo the paper with her, even though the three of us already have our diplomas. Veronica and our English teacher agreed.

Veronica's senior thesis paper is due this week. She has finished her part, Sylvia and Miguel, too. Ninety-nine percent of my part is done, I just have to add my final reflection.

Ghosts.

Hauntings.

I start to speak softly into the mic for the computer to type . . .

Last August I started this paper as a skeptic; ghosts weren't real, so therefore neither were hauntings. But I know now that's all wrong.

Ghosts are real and so are hauntings. I know because I've been haunted for years by the ghosts of my past. To clarify, using the terminology from earlier in this paper, a residual haunting. An emotional circumstance that was so powerful it became imprinted in my soul—playing over and over again in a loop, thereby affecting my every decision.

But here's the thing about coming to terms with hauntings and ghosts being real—you can eradicate them. Get rid of those things that follow you around, affecting every aspect of your life. A cleansing like the one performed in the house as discussed above.

At the start of this paper, I didn't believe in much—love included. But by digging deep into myself, by confronting those things that scare me the most, I found love. Love for my friends, for my family, for the woman I love and more importantly, for myself.

The music from the piano ceases, and I glance up to find Veronica looking thoughtfully at me. An angel with a devil's grin. "Are you done yet?"

"Just one sentence away."

"Good. I was texting with Sylvia and Miguel and they said there's this haunted schoolhouse that's doing tours this evening and I so want to go. Jesse, Scarlett, Leo and Nazareth are thinking about going, too. And then I was thinking we should get ice cream."

"Has anyone else caught on that the paper's over?"

"Yes, but you have to admit the research was fun."

The best. Life altering. I turn back to the computer and speak the last line: *Now, I am definitely a believer.*

AUTHOR'S NOTE

Evelyn Bellak was sixteen years old and had tuberculosis.

She was a real person. Her words, dreams, hopes, and fears became immortalized in a diary that exists today in the safekeeping of the Adirondack Research Room at the Saranac Lake Free Library.

While the quotes used from the diary are from Evelyn Bellak, everything else about this story is fictionalized. It is my great hope that through Veronica and Sawyer's story, the hope and love reflected in Evelyn's diary will live on.

A special thank-you to Michele A. Tucker, the curator of the Adirondack Research Room at the Saranac Lake Free Library, for keeping Evelyn's diary safe and for allowing the world to read her precious words. Also thank you for allowing me permission to use quotes from Evelyn's diary in this novel.

Bellak, Evelyn, *Fond Memories of Ray Brook: A Diary*, Jan. 1, 1918–Nov. 18, 1918, courtesy of the Adirondack Research Room, Saranac Lake Free Library.

Also, thank you to Shirley Morgan for writing *Well Diary . . . I Have Tuberculosis*, a research of Evelyn's life and the tuberculosis outbreak in the United States. I love that you fleshed out who Evelyn was beyond the pages of her diary.

If you think you or someone you know might be affected by alcoholism and/or depression, here are some resources that might be able to help.

AA https://www.aa.org/

Al-Anon https://al-anon.org/

Crisis text line for depression: https://www.crisistextline.org/depression

Suicide hotline: https://suicidepreventionlifeline.org/talk-to-someone-now/

PLAYLIST

THEME:

"King of My Heart" by Bethel Music, Steffany Gretzinger and Jeremy Riddle

"What Ifs" by Kane Brown (featuring Lauren Alaina)

"Plush" by Stone Temple Pilots

"Broken Halos" by Chris Stapleton

"Shallow" by Lady Gaga and Bradley Cooper

"Meant to Be" by Bebe Rexha and Florida Georgia Line

VERONICA:

". . . Ready for It?" by Taylor Swift

"Delicate" by Taylor Swift

"This Is What You Came For" by Calvin Harris (featuring Rihanna)

"Mary Jane's Last Dance" by Tom Petty and The Heartbreakers

SAWYER:

"Believer" by Imagine Dragons

"Interstate Love Song" by Stone Temple Pilots

"Whatever It Takes" by Imagine Dragons

"Thunder" by Imagine Dragons

VERONICA AND SAWYER'S FUTURE:

"Heaven" by Kane Brown

"Simple" by Florida Georgia Line

"Setting the World on Fire" by Kenny Chesney (with P!nk)

ACKNOWLEDGMENTS

To God: *Psalm 136:1* and *Isaiah 41:10*
—Thank You for always being by my side.

As always, for Dave.
—Because my heart still melts when you look over at me from the driver's side of the car and you sing a lyric of a song to me that fits exactly how we love each other.

For A, N, and P.
—Thank you for continually teaching me.

A huge thank-you to Suzie Townsend, Cassandra Baim, KP Simmon, Amy Stapp, Diana Gill, Saraciea Fennell, and Tor Teen for believing in Veronica and Sawyer's story.

To my wonderful group of friends, family, critique partners, and beta readers who have helped and loved me along the way: Colette Ballard, Kelly Creagh, Bethany Griffin, Kurt Hampe, Bill Wolfe, Wendy Higgins, Kristen Simmons, and Angela Annalaro-Murphy.

And to my readers.
—I am forever grateful for your love and support!